The Battle at the Moons of Hell

HELFORT'S WAR:
Book I

Graham Sharp Paul

BALLANTINE BOOKS • NEW YORK

A Del Rey Books Mass Market Original

Copyright © 2007 by Graham Sharp Paul

Excerpt of *Helfort's War* Book Two © 2007 by Graham Sharp Paul

All rights reserved.

Published in the United States by Del Rey Books, an imprint of The Random House Publishing Group, a division of Random House, Inc., New York.

DEL REY is a registered trademark and the Del Rey colophon is a trademark of Random House, Inc.

This book contains an excerpt from the forthcoming mass market edition of *Helfort's War* Book Two by Graham Sharp Paul. This excerpt has been set for this edition only and may not reflect the final content of the forthcoming edition.

ISBN 978-0-345-49571-6

Printed in the United States of America

www.delreybooks.com

OPM   9   8   7   6   5   4   3   2

A DROP INTO HELL

With a deep breath, Michael Helfort started *Moaning Minnie* on her way dirtside, firing the planetary heavy lander's main engines at full power to wipe out enough of her orbital velocity to put her into a rapidly steepening parabolic fall to the ground. As *Minnie* fell, the rest of the assault lander stream fell around her, the landers cocooned in a huge cloud of active decoys, the attack blossoming out in all directions into a huge cloud that was too confused, too complex, and too fast moving for ground-based radar to distinguish high-value targets from decoys.

With *Minnie*'s height unwinding rapidly, Michael shut down the main engines and spun *Minnie* back, nose first, ready for reentry. He could see for himself the threat blossoming in front of them as long-range search radars appeared on the display.

But that didn't matter too much.

An assault lander could do very little against long-range weapons systems except stay as far away from them as possible. It was up to the planetary assault vessel supporting the attack from orbit—in this case the *Shrivaratnam*—to provide volume defense for the entire assault lander stream.

"Command, Tac. Threat Red. Multiple battle management radar emitters. Stand by . . . *Shrivaratnam* reports multiple ABM missile launches."

ABMs! Shit, Michael thought. Antiballistic missile systems were designed to take out missiles before atmospheric reentry, a role that made them extremely good at hacking big, fat, and relatively slow assault landers out of the sky. But there was nothing much Michael could do about them except worry and leave them to *Shrivaratnam*. ABMs were too big, too fast, and, with tacnuke warheads, much more than any lander's thin skin of ceramsteel armor could withstand. As he commed his neuronics to display the overall command plot, he was happy to see that the ABMs, for which an undefended stream of assault landers was the easiest of easy meat, were having a hard time of it.

But a handful did slip through . . .

For Vicki

Acknowledgments

To my wife Vicki, Tony and Barbara Horgan, Nick Horgan, Tara Wynne, Russ Galen, and Jim Minz and the team at Random House. My thanks to all of you for your encouragement, critical advice, and support.

Rear Admiral Jan Fielding, the flag officer commanding, Federated Worlds Space Fleet College, sat back in her chair and sighed heavily as she turned to the large picture window behind her desk.

"I don't like this one little bit, Joseph," she said, staring out at the broad expanse of parade ground across which squads of first-year cadets moved like small black robots, harassed and harangued every step of the way by other small black robots. But Fielding saw none of them, her face troubled and drawn.

The tall, solidly built man standing slightly to one side nodded as Fielding turned back to her desk. "Not many of us do, sir. But now that Admiral al-Rawahy has endorsed the official report of the board of inquiry, there's nothing more to be done. But at least the matter was dealt with administratively rather than under military justice."

"I know, I know. But Admiral al-Rawahy's as concerned about this whole matter as we are."

"I wouldn't know, sir." Bukenya's voice was so deliberately diplomatic, the sharp-edged planes that made up his face so carefully arranged into an expressionless blue-black mask, that Fielding couldn't help smiling.

"Yes, yes. Quite right, Joseph." Fielding accepted the unspoken criticism. What admirals might or might not have said to each other was not something she should be talking about. "Okay, let's get on with it."

"Sir." Turning, Bukenya moved to the door and pulled it open a little too sharply, Fielding thought. Let's not make it any worse than it already is, she told herself.

"Senior Cadet Helfort? The admiral will see you now."

"Sir!"

The young man, immaculate in razor-creased dress blacks, marched into the room and came rigidly to attention in front of the battered oak desk, a relic from Old Earth, it was said. Only a slight trembling of the fingertips and a thin sheen of sweat across the forehead betrayed his feelings. The admiral watched as Michael Helfort fought to slow his breathing before looking her square in the eye.

"Senior Cadet Helfort, sir."

"At ease, Helfort."

"Sir."

For a moment Fielding found herself dragged back more years than she cared to think about. It had been a long time since she had last seen Helfort's father, but the boy could have been he. Relatively short by Fed standards, Michael Helfort had his father's well-muscled, thickset build, the shoulders broad, the same untidy hair. A fraction too long, though, even for a senior cadet about to graduate, she noted. The eyes were his father's, too, hazel in color and deeply set in a faced tanned to a dark brown. But most noticeable was the way he looked at her; he might have his father's eyes, but he had his mother's penetratingly direct gaze. She'd been a very fine officer, as Fielding recalled, and a loss to Space Fleet; some even said that Kerri Helfort had been the finest rear admiral Space Fleet had never had.

The admiral shook herself. This was no time for reminiscing, no time for worrying, though she didn't like to think about what Helfort's parents would say when they got the news. She turned her eyes back to the old-fashioned paper document that sat dead center on the otherwise empty desk. The single page of thick cream-colored paper, signed by Vice Admiral al-Rawahy and sealed with his massive red wax seal, heavy with the power and might of the Federated Worlds, mocked her concerns. Leaning forward slightly, she started to read, her voice flat and colorless.

"To Senior Cadet Michael Wallace Helfort, serial number FC021688J.

"From Vice Admiral Abdulla bin Issa al-Rawahy, director of Fleet training, Federated Worlds Space Fleet."

Fielding paused. This was not right. Michael just stood there motionless, the sweat threatening to bead across his forehead.

Fielding forced herself to continue.

"Whereas the board of inquiry convened by my authority on Monday 15 June 2398 Universal Date, having reviewed all relevant evidence and having heard all persons with knowledge of the matter under inquiry, namely, the unsafe operation of Planetary Heavy Lander (Assault) Registration Number PHLA-789465 while under your command on Thursday 14 May 2398, Universal Date contrary to OPS-MAN-PHLA-2245, has completed its report.

"And, whereas the conclusion of the board of inquiry that you, Senior Cadet Michael W. Helfort, did act in a manner risking injury or death to crew, passengers, and ground-based civilians has been endorsed by me following my full and detailed review of the report of the board of inquiry, I hereby delegate the matter for administrative action by your military commander, Rear Admiral Jan Carlotta Fielding, Flag Officer commanding, Space Fleet College of the Federated Worlds.

"Signed and sealed this day, Friday 3 July 2398 Universal Date, by me, Abdulla bin Issa al-Rawahy, vice admiral, director of Fleet training, Federated Worlds Space Fleet."

Fielding placed the document back on the desk, taking a moment to position it dead center before looking up directly into the eyes of the young man in front of her, eyes that, she was pleased to see, looked straight back at her unblinkingly.

"Senior Cadet Helfort. Do you understand what I have just said?"

"Yes, sir."

"Are there any questions that you would like to ask at this stage?"

"No, sir." Helfort stood unmoving, the sweat beading on his forehead threatening to run down into his eyes.

Fielding nodded. "Very well. In that case, I am required by Article 2349.7 of the Federated Worlds Code of Military Justice to ask you whether or not you accept the findings of the board of inquiry. If you do not, and it is your right not to, the report of the board of inquiry together with any comments by Vice Admiral al-Rawahy will be forwarded to the commander in chief, Federated Worlds Space Fleet, for further review. If you do accept the findings, it rests with me to determine the administrative action to be taken as a consequence of the report. Do you understand?"

"Yes, sir."

"Do you require further time to consider your answer or to consult any natural person or any licensed AI-generated persona?"

"No, sir. I do not."

"Very well. What is your decision?"

"Sir, I accept the findings of the board," Helfort said stiffly.

Thank God, thought the admiral. She had watched Helfort through half-closed eyes as he'd struggled to make the right decision. You are your parents' son, she thought, and you've made the right decision even if that painful fact may not be clear to you right now.

"Very well. Lieutenant Commander Bukenya will attest to your decision, a copy of which will be commed to you and to your personnel file.

"It now falls to me to prescribe what administrative action shall be taken as a consequence of the report of the board of inquiry." She paused while Bukenya handed her a second thick cream-colored document, this one marked with her own red seal, smaller than al-Rawahy's but still impressive. As it always did, it struck her how archaic a lump of red wax stamped onto a bit of paper really was even if it was DNA-coded and time-stamped to make the document unarguably genuine. But still, that was the way things were done in the Federated Worlds Space Fleet, as they always had been. Who was she to argue?

The admiral started to read in the same flat voice she had used before, utterly devoid of emotion. As she watched, Helfort stood ramrod straight with an impassive look on his face. He didn't blink even when a bead of sweat rolled down his forehead and into his left eye. "First, the conclusion of the board of inquiry shall be noted in your personnel file for a period of five years unless extended by the administrative decision of a duly qualified authority.

"Second, you shall requalify as command pilot on the planetary heavy lander subject to your achieving an overall qualification score of not less than 98 percent.

"Third, all additional seniority due to you by virtue of your academic and professional performance while a cadet is void. Therefore, upon graduation, your seniority date as a junior lieutenant shall be 1 September 2398."

For the first time Michael visibly flinched. Twelve months' seniority, the product of three hard years of effort, gone. Just like that.

Fielding placed the document on the desk. "An attested digital copy of Admiral al-Rawahy's endorsement and my administrative actions will be commed to your file. These hard copies are for your own personal records." Fielding pushed the two papers to the front of the desk.

Michael just stared at them. "Sir."

"Well, pick them up, Helfort; they won't bite."

"Sir."

With all the reluctance of a man about to pick up a red-hot poker, Helfort reached forward to take the documents from the desk. Somehow Fielding knew that Helfort would never look at them again.

"Unless there is anything else in relation to this matter that you wish to raise at this time, you are dismissed."

"No, sir. Nothing." Helfort came to attention, turned, and was gone almost before Fielding and Bukenya realized it.

As the door closed, Bukenya looked at the admiral. "He will see that as very harsh, especially the loss of seniority. That'll put him behind some real, uh"—Bukenya paused—"some real underachievers."

The admiral smiled briefly at Bukenya's understatement. He should have said "jerks" because that was what some of her students were despite the best efforts of the college staff to turn them into half-decent Fleet officers. "He will. And that's why I want you to talk to him. His new skipper is a good man. And I just happen to know they are in for some interesting work. So tell him to hang in and let him know that I will be talking to Ribot on his behalf. Despite what the board of inquiry says, he's a very good officer, an outstanding officer, in fact, and we do not want to lose him. But for God's sake tell him to say nothing about what you talk about."

Bukenya half smiled. "Deniability, sir?"

"Damn right. Now go to it; I've got things to do. One of which is putting a vidmail together telling his parents what I've had to do to their son."

As Bukenya left, the admiral leaned back in her chair as she commed her flag lieutenant.

"John, can you contact Admiral al-Rawahy's secretary and tell him that I would like to speak to the admiral, please."

Michael's stomach churned with the absolute, total wrongness of it all. He half walked, half ran down the stairs from the admiral's office. Two first-year cadets were firmly shoved aside as he pounded down to the ground floor and out into the hot Terranovan sun. His neuronics chimed softly to tell him that the team was waiting for him in the senior cadets' mess. Bugger them; they could all wait. Head down, he charged on, unseeing.

"Well, well, well. If it isn't Senior Cadet Helfort, or should I say Mister Helfort, late of the Federated Worlds Space Fleet."

Michael stopped dead in his tracks. He didn't need to turn around to see who had spoken. The anger roared in his head. Uncaring, he turned to face the small group that stood casually against the wall of the admin building. Bastards, he thought. They've been waiting for me to come out. Without thinking, his fists balled and he closed in. "You fucking bastard, d'Castreaux. I'm going to kill you for this."

D'Castreaux paused for a few long moments and smiled. "I think Mister Helfort is upset. What do you think, Jasmina?"

Senior Cadet Jasmina Karayan smiled back. "I think his dad's going to kill him. Don't you?"

At that point Michael snapped, starting toward d'Castreaux, hands coming up to wring the life out of the sneering scumbag who stood in front of him.

"Helfort!" Bukenya's voice was like a steel wire whipped across the back of Michael's neck. He stopped, hands only centimeters from d'Castreaux's throat. Instantly, the anger was gone, replaced by an ice-cold certainty.

"Another day, d'Castreaux," Michael hissed. "Depend on it." Michael turned to face Bukenya, coming rigidly to attention.

"Sir."

Bukenya pointedly ignored him. "You four. Do you have business in administration?"

"No, sir," the four chorused like four submissive but still triumphant sheep.

"Right. Present in an inappropriate area without reasonable grounds. Fifty demerits each. Now get out of my sight."

The four snapped to attention, saluted, turned, and marched smartly away. But every step told Bukenya that they thought fifty demerits was a very cheap price to pay for the pleasure of seeing Helfort fresh from his place of execution.

Pausing only to comm the demerits into the cadet's files, Bukenya stood in front of Michael. "You are a bloody young fool, Helfort. My office, now."

"Sir."

"Close the door and sit down, Michael."

Michael did as he was told and perched uncomfortably on the edge of a battered armchair. He had heard Bukenya swear it came from the wardroom of the old *Adventure*. Michael had looked it up: The *Adventure* had been scrapped after receiving severe damage at the First Battle of Jackson's World back in '37, so it was possible. But how a serving spacer could lug around a large, lumpy, and extremely unattractive sixty-year-old armchair was something he thought could be open to question. But not now. He jerked his mind away from the subject of Bukenya's armchair—funny how you could think of something so totally irrelevant at a time like this—and focused his gaze in the approved college style directly onto Bukenya's face.

Bukenya's tone was harsh. "This conversation never occurred; if asked, all we discussed were your future prospects and how you could best put the matters of the last few months behind you. Call it psychological and career counseling. Do I make myself clear?"

"Clear, sir," Michael said, wondering what on earth this had to do with the unsafe operation of Federated Worlds Planetary Heavy Lander (Assault) Registration Number PHLA-789465 while under his command contrary to blah blah blah.

Bukenya sat back in his chair, another battered and lumpy example of the species. His voice softened. "Goddammit, Michael. Why did you let those fools provoke you? They're not worth it."

Bukenya paused as he struggled back out of his armchair to go to a small cupboard behind his desk, from which he produced a bottle of twelve-year-old Gabrielli whiskey. Well depleted, Michael noted in passing.

"Who would have thought that a planet largely settled by Italian migrants would have such a way with malted barley?" Bukenya poured two generous measures and passed a glass across to Michael, who still sat perched uncomfortably on the edge of his chair, totally confused by Bukenya's behavior. The fact that he still had a future in the Space Fleet was just starting to sink in—d'Castreaux hadn't been the only one expecting Michael's career to be cut short—and with it the dim beginnings of hope, but he was still reeling from the impact of the admiral's words. The loss of seniority, the fact that his precious leave would be cut short by having to requalify as command pilot on one of the college's long-suffering and very battered heavy landers—and with a minimum 98 percent rating no less!—and not least what his father, Captain A. G. Helfort FWSF (retired), and mother, Commodore K. D. A. Helfort FWSF (retired), would have to say, hurt and hurt badly. He drank deeply from the glass and felt the burn as the alcohol slipped smoothly down his throat.

"Ready to talk?" Bukenya was back in the depths of his armchair. Michael nodded.

"The admiral wanted me to talk to you off the record, as it were. You need to understand that there are . . . well, there are a number of people who . . . Let's just say there are people who are not very happy at what just occurred. You have one of the best records of any cadet, not just in your year but also for as long as people can remember. So the idea that you risked the lives of your crew and of innocent civilians on the ground by deliberately resetting the terrain avoidance system to manual just to impress people like d'Castreaux and Narayan is frankly incredible.

"If I know anything at all, Helfort," Bukenya said intently, leaning forward, "I know that you understand your limitations. You don't yet have the skill or experience to pilot a lander at low level without the terrain avoidance system engaged, and you know it."

Bukenya sat back in his chair before continuing. "So if you did not reset terrain avoidance, then who else did it but one of your two fellow crew members, most likely d'Castreaux? As your tactical officer, he was the only one who had the authority apart from you, though how he did it without leaving a proper execute record in the log is something the lander design authority is looking into." Even if, Bukenya thought bitterly, that same design authority hadn't been able to bring itself to admit to the board of inquiry that there might have been deficiencies in the lander's datalogging system, that there might in fact be a way around the access security protocols.

"Is that what you think, sir? Is that what the admiral thinks?" The forlorn hope in Michael's voice tore at Bukenya.

"For what it's worth, and I'm sorry to say it's not much, it is what we think. It's what a lot of people think. Your parents are well remembered in the Fleet and still command great respect and affection, which helps. But the sworn evidence of two Federation officers under oath backing up the datalogs showing that you or, rather, someone in the command pilot's seat did in fact set the system to manual just to show off is all it takes to prove you a liar, I'm afraid. Even the Fleet legal service couldn't shake them, and you know how tough they are."

"But sir—"

Bukenya's hand went up to stop Michael cold. "And regardless, you were the command pilot. So even if d'Castreaux and Narayan did what you say they did, you should have picked it up. Without terrain avoidance, a lander is a lethally dangerous lump of metal at low level, and you were in command, Michael. You should have spotted it. No excuses. Just a pity that nobody had their neuronics set to full recording to catch d'Castreaux in the act.

"But the admiral does want you to know that she believes in you, that many in the Space Fleet believe in you. More important, she wants you to believe in you. But you have to put this behind you and move on. As for the d'Castreauxs and Narayans of this world, let their futures take care of themselves. I think you'll find that . . . well, let's just say that history has a way of repeating itself."

Michael thought about that for a few seconds, and then it clicked. "You mean d'Castreaux's father, sir? I heard about that. Discharged in '81 or something." Michael paused as the implications of Bukenya's words sank in. "But I thought that he—"

Again Bukenya's hand stopped Michael dead.

"Forget I even mentioned it. It really doesn't matter what happened. Eighty-one was a long time ago. What matters is what happens now, next month, next year. And speaking of next month, the admiral will be speaking to Lieutenant Ribot, your new captain. I know Ribot, and so does the admiral: We served together in the *Ulugh Beg*. He's a good man and a fair one, so make the most of the opportunities he will give you."

"Sir." There was nothing more that Michael could say.

"And Michael."

"Sir?"

"Ignore d'Castreaux and his crew. Thanks to some serious work behind the scenes, you are still in the Fleet. So when you see them, by all means make the most of that small victory. But physically assaulting d'Castreaux or Narayan is one surefire way of making all that hard work a waste of time. And that, young man, would seriously upset some people you shouldn't upset."

Michael sat for two long quiet minutes, head hanging, as he struggled with the enormity of the defeat that d'Castreaux and Narayan had inflicted on him. Finally, his head came up.

"Okay. It still hurts like hell, but Space Fleet is the only thing I've ever wanted to do with my life, so no, I won't throw it all away."

"Good. And remember, say nothing to anyone. Not even your parents."

"I won't, sir."

"Oh, and once again, irrespective of who sets the terrain avoidance system, remember that it's always your responsibility as command pilot. And put your neuronics to full recording when you're around people you don't trust. Now, finish your whiskey and go. I've got work to do."

"Sir."

The team looked at Michael in stunned disbelief.

The tightly knit group who were Michael's closest friends had crammed into his tiny cabin to hear the outcome of the board action and were having as much trouble as Michael coming to terms with the enormity of the injustice. Ramesh Gupta, perched awkwardly on the corner of Michael's dresser—even he, strong and sinewy as he was, could not displace Karen Sutler's massive hundred-kilo frame from its commanding position in the middle of the battered relic that probably had seen generations of cadets pass through— actually had his mouth wide open in shock. Nicco Guzevic was twisting his beret to the point where it was beginning to come apart; David ben-Gurion, Karen Jacowitz, and Charles Mbeki stared wide-eyed in disbelief, and Bronwyn Kriketos had tears in her eyes.

"The slimeball pigs."

As ever, Anna Cheung was the first to speak. And then, all at once, the entire group was in full flow. If words were deeds, d'Castreaux and Narayan were dead meat.

"Guys, guys, guys." Michael held up his hands until the rush of swear words, abuse, and threats of grievous bodily harm slowed to a stop with a final "Bastards" from Michael Takahashi and an "I'll tear d'Castreaux's fucking head off" from Jemma Alhamid. Slight as Jemma was, Michael knew she could and would if she got half a chance.

"Look. They could have thrown me out, but they didn't. And at the moment that's all I care about. As for d'Castreaux and Narayan, well, let me just say that their time will come. But it'll be when I'm ready and not before. Understand?"

"But Michael, how can you be so, well, so rational about this? I don't understand." Anna's green eyes bored into Michael, and his heart kicked, as it always did when she looked right into him like that.

"Because I know what I really want, and I'm not going to let a pack of low-life creeps put me off track. Besides, as Bukenya said, irrespective of who touches a lander's controls, it was my responsibility as command pilot."

This time Michael did not try to stop the torrent of words; he figured that it was not a bad thing to have the team think that Bukenya was being a smart-ass even though in their hearts they all knew Bukenya was right. Michael sat back, jammed into the corner, and enjoyed the residual warmth from Bukenya's whiskey until the flood subsided. He let the silence stretch until he had the team's full attention.

"So this is what we are going to do. Fuck them all, I say. The Dog and Duck at 20:00 to celebrate my survival. Be there on pain of death. And for God's sake, one of you make sure I get home okay. I don't want another session in front of the admiral ever again."

Anna stared at him as if he were mad. They all did. And then she flung herself at him, wrapping her arms around his neck so tightly that for a moment Michael thought he might choke.

* * *

The provost marshal's neuronics chimed softly, interrupting a deep and meaningful, if slightly one-sided, conversation with two first-year cadets guilty of the unspeakable crime of not moving from A to B with sufficient speed. "Go. Don't do it again," he said to the two cadets, who left in a hurry, astonished not to have picked up an unwelcome load of demerits.

The admiral's avatar bloomed in his neuronics as he accepted the comm, her AI-generated image absolutely faithful right down to the steely look in her eyes. It was a look that marked Rear Admiral Jan Fielding as a woman not to be trifled with.

"Admiral, sir. What can I do for you?"

"Vasili. You've heard the news about Helfort?"

"I have, sir. And I'm pleased to hear that the Fleet won't lose him, after all. He's a good lad."

"I agree. But Vasili, I am concerned that tempers are running high and that there may be trouble. I think it would be better if . . . well, if certain people were on duty tonight."

"Would those be the people I have just detailed off for spaceport patrol tonight, sir?"

"If the patrol includes d'Castreaux and Narayan, then yes." What a pleasure it was, the admiral thought for a moment, to work with people who were ahead of her.

"Done, sir. And my spies tell me that the Dog and Duck is the focus of tonight's activities, so I'll have Petty Officer Nu'lini and the shore patrol close at hand just in case. And I'll keep an eye out to make sure things stay under control."

"You are a good man, Vasili." The admiral chuckled. "Just make sure Petty Officer Nu'lini understands that there are to be no defaulters at the commander's table tomorrow. None. Well, not from the vicinity of the Dog and Duck, that is."

"Understood, sir. None it will be."

"Good night, Vasili."

As the landlord of the Dog and Duck shoveled a disheveled and very drunk Michael and the rest the team out the front door and into the early hours of a cool clear Terranovan night, the singing started.

"Oh, back of Casmirati, where the waters runs deep . . ."

But it was sad and mournful, all anger gone, for the moment at least.

The provost marshal grinned as he commed Petty Officer Nu'lini before gunning his jeep down the side road back to his house and his sleeping wife.

"Make sure they get home okay, Jack."

"Will do, sir."

Thursday, July 16, 2398, UD
Offices of the Supreme Council for the Preservation of the Faith, City of McNair, Commitment Planet

"Chief Councillor?"

The old-fashioned intercom on the massive paper-strewn desk interrupted Jesse Merrick's concentrated study of the substantial document in front of him. Not for him the convenience of face-mounted microvid screens. Like most Hammers, he preferred to read paper and always had.

"Kraa-damn it, Jackson, I said no interruptions." Merrick's face was dark with irritation; he had hoped to sign off the half-yearly review of the budget for the Hammer of Kraa Worlds that afternoon. It was a job he hated not least because every year it was the same old story: a hopelessly optimistic budget to start off with, approved by a compliant and craven People's Assembly without so much as a single critical question, economic shortfalls almost from the first day of the new fiscal year in January, a crisis by March (a bad year) or May (a good year), and an emergency budget review in June before a whole new mess of cobbled-together emergency measures went back to the assembly for approval. And always against a background of simmering civil unrest.

If the business of running the Hammer Worlds wasn't so serious, it would be a farce.

The only problem was that each year the farce got blacker as the Hammer Worlds stumbled farther and farther into an economic quagmire. No matter where he looked or how hard he tried, no matter how much he put the fear of Kraa into the bureaucrats, no matter how much he lashed Jeremiah Polk, councillor for the economy and finance, he could not see any way to change the situation. Unless the prohibitions on geneering and artificial intelligence (AI) were lifted, a proposition that would have him condemned to death by the Supreme Tribunal for the Preservation of the Faith if he ever spoke it aloud, the Hammer economy would stay stuck in second gear.

No. Geneering was absolutely proscribed by the Hammer's founding charter, and the ban on AI was the product of five bloody years of civil war. It didn't matter that the chief councillor privately thought that there had to be some way to reconcile the two with the demands of doctrine. Neither ban would change—ever. Removing those two pillars of the faith was as likely as Bodger, his faithful if rather dim-witted dog, becoming chief councillor.

And talking of contenders for his job, he wished he could say that Jeremiah Polk's chances were as bad as Bodger's, but increasingly the bloody man was looking like a real threat, he thought wearily. There had been a time when one of his favorite pastimes had been to encourage Polk to think that one day he would sit at the chief councillor's desk. It had pleased him to see the pompous son of a bitch take his sarcastic goading seriously, although in retrospect maybe all he'd done was encourage the Kraa-damned bastard.

Maybe you're not as smart as you think you are, Merrick, he told himself.

"Yes, Jackson. What do you want?"

"I thought you might like to know that Brigadier General Digby has arrived, sir." The confidential secretary's voice was flat and without emotion.

"Have him wait." Merrick's voice showed no trace of apology even though he belatedly remembered that he had specifically asked the long-suffering Jackson to tell him when Digby arrived.

After taking care to mark his place in the massive budget document and making a fruitless attempt to bring some order to his desk, Jesse sat back in his chair and wearily rubbed his eyes. By Kraa, he was tired, and he shouldn't have been. He was only fifty-three years old and in the prime of his life, yet he felt an enormous weight of responsibility on his shoulders, a burden that only death would allow him to put down. There had never been such a thing as a happily retired chief councillor, and given the blood-soaked nature of Hammer politics, there probably never would be. Well, he consoled himself, at least I won't have to live as long as all those heathen bastards out there. They were welcome to survive for 150 years; he'd be more than content with his Kraa-allotted 100.

Merrick keyed the intercom. "I'll see Brigadier General Digby now."

Seconds later, the door opened and the squat, heavily muscled figure of Brigadier General Julius Digby entered, thinning gray hair cut to a short stubble. Like a small dark tank and as energetic as ever, Merrick thought sourly. Does the man never slow down? He quickly put the thought aside as unworthy. Kraa's work demanded energy as well as skill, experience, and an unshakable belief in doctrine, he reminded himself, and Digby had them all. And Kraa knew how important the task Digby was charged with was. Not for the first time, Merrick asked himself whether he should have sought the approval of his fellow councillors for what he and Digby had planned. As always, he concluded that there was no way he could trust such a bunch of garrulous, lily-livered fools. No, the risks were great enough without adding the possibility of early disclosure. The Federated Worlds' response if they discovered what he and Digby were up to was not something he enjoyed thinking about. No, keep it compartmentalized, get the task done, and no one will be the wiser. The rewards were what mattered, and they were so enormous both for him and for the hard-pressed peoples of the Hammer Worlds that the risks had to be entertained.

There was no real choice. The future economic and social well-being of all the Hammer Worlds depended on it.

Merrick waved Digby into a chair.

"Brigadier General Digby, welcome back. How was Hell?" Merrick asked. It was his usual little joke and about as jolly as the chief councillor ever got. Not for nothing did his enemies, and they were legion, call him the Grim Reaper.

"Hell, sir." That was Digby's habitual response. "By Kraa, that place is well named. A more damned collection of lost souls is hard to imagine. But Prison Governor Costigan has things as well under control as ever."

"He wasn't curious?"

"He was very curious but took great care not to ask any questions. I think he knows when to keep his mouth shut, and I suspect he also knows how quickly he would join his charges if he didn't."

Digby's face made it clear how much he enjoyed the thought of Prison Governor Costigan, a miserable and bitter man at the best of times and a man never easy to deal with, becoming one of the tens of thousands of unfortunates condemned to labor in the mass driver plants on the moons of Revelation-II, the second planet of the Revelation system.

The planet was unofficially but widely referred to as what it was—Hell. A living Hell. Unfortunately for its inmates, Hell and its moons were an important part of Commitment's economy in a system devoid of other sources of mass for fusion-powered mass driver engines. Without ultracheap mass for starship engines, no space economy could work and the Hammer would be doomed. And without AI-based management, geneering, self-replicating robotics, and all the other things held by the Path of Doctrine to be absolute abominations, prison labor was the only economical—if marginal—way to operate the mines spread across seventeen of Hell's twenty-two moons. It also solved the problem of what to do with the countless unfortunates who fell afoul every year of Doctrinal Security, trapped like flies in the endless webs of half-truth, deceit, treachery, and revenge spun by DocSec's enormous secret army of informers.

Oh, yes, it was a good place to put those Hammers who strayed too far from the Path, Merrick thought. It was also a good place to consign any out-system travelers stupid enough to wander uninvited into Hammer-controlled space without a good excuse for being there, and there was no such thing as a good excuse. If they were lucky, Hammer prisoners would eventually return to civilized Kraa society. But offworlders would labor in the mass driver plants until old age, overwork, or a brutal beating from a bored prison supervisor finished them off.

"Digby, that was a very uncharitable thought. I'm sure Governor Costigan is—and I hope will remain—a valued member of the Faith."

The chief councillor's faint, almost imperceptible smile, more a sneer than a smile, betrayed him. He watched as a tremor ran barely visible through Digby's squat frame. Just as well, Merrick thought, pleased with himself. It never hurts to remind your subordinates they should fear you, and Digby clearly had gotten the message that he was no less expendable than Prison Governor Costigan.

"It was uncharitable, sir," Digby agreed. "But I'm sure Costigan will not let us down. He'll treat the arrival of a shipment of off-worlders the same as any other shipment of transgressors. With ruthless efficiency, as usual and without question."

"Good, let's hope so. We have enough to worry about as it is." Merrick's words were an order, not a wish, and Digby nodded his acceptance. "So, General. Your report?"

"Well, sir, I have completed the review of the various options open to us, and I'm happy to report that it confirms Frontier as our best choice. It is a matter of public record that the Frontier Worlds Development Corporation successfully completed its planned fund-raising in August last year and placed contracts for an integrated phase one terraforming package with Planetary Dynamics Corporation two months later."

"And the name of their new planet?"

"Ganesh, sir. The second planet of the Acadia System."

Merrick's face soured, his mouth a bitter line across his creased and pallid face. This problem had frustrated him longer than he could remember. The Hammer had neither the resources nor the technology to terraform planets quickly. That meant there was no chance of settling the fourth habitable planet of the Hammer Worlds, Eternity, in any useful time scale, never mind H-5, H-6, H-7, and all the rest of the unnamed candidates for terraforming over which the Hammer had planetary development rights in perpetuity. In fact, even the simple act of choosing the name Eternity summed up the inability of the Hammer to get things done.

The Supreme Council for the Preservation of Doctrine had taken months to approve the new name in the face of strenuous opposition from the Teacher of the Worlds John Calverson. An affront to doctrine, he had said over and over until Merrick had had great trouble not reaching down the council table and strangling the fucker. Calverson should spend more time caring for the souls of Kraa's people—which was his job as the Hammer's supreme spiritual head, after all—and less on endless nit-picking doctrinal arguments, Merrick thought sourly. And always egged on by Polk, which didn't help.

So the Hammer would continue to be hamstrung for as long as doctrine required it. To add further pressure, the trade and technology embargo against it remained in place. Merrick snorted derisively. Why should the Hammer sign the Planetary Use of Nuclear Weapons Treaty? If Kraa's purposes required the use of nuclear weapons against planetary targets, Kraa's people would use them and the rest of humankind be damned.

Meanwhile, not only was Frontier developing Ganesh, the Federated Worlds were about to settle the first wave of colonists on Roper-III, the Sylvanians had started on Guardian-I, and the Earth Alliance had plans not only for 40 Eridani A, B, and C but for Pi 3 Orionis as well, not to mention a whole clutch of orbital habitats and other worlds targeted for mineral extraction, low-g manufacturing, space tourism, and so on.

Not for the first time, Merrick cursed the Hammers' fate, a fate that condemned them to seemingly endless stagnation without the hope of growth. Kraa's blood! It wasn't just the

major polities in humanspace—the Old Earth Alliance, the
Federated Worlds, the Sylvanians, the Javitz and Delfin
Federations—that were terraforming new planets as fast as
capital and skill allowed. Even the smaller systems were ex-
panding: Frontier, the Buranans—by Kraa, the list was endless. Everywhere it was expand, expand, expand. Even that
rabble on Scobie's World had plans for terraforming in an
adjacent star system, and they were practically a Hammer
vassal state. And the Hammer? Nothing. It couldn't even de-
velop a new orbital habitat.

Merrick stopped himself dead. This was getting him
nowhere.

All those things might be true, but, he thought viciously,
they were going to change. And the Feds were going to help
them get started. After that, it would be up to the Hammer,
but the time saved would be measured in decades; the exten-
sive use of the latest geneered bacteria and organisms would
see to that. That was another reason Merrick couldn't talk to
his fellow councillors about the matter, he thought. But
meeting the growing demands for more living space could
not be deferred in favor of long-winded sermons from
narrow-minded, stiff-necked priests like John Calverson.
The stresses imposed by the growing population of the Hammer Worlds, made all the worse by a seriously underper-
forming economy, were beginning to open up the social fault
lines in a way that had the Supreme Council increasingly
concerned. Not that they had any answers other than more
propaganda, more repression, more violence.

Well, let's try more hope, Merrick thought as he turned his
attention back to the man waiting patiently in front of him.

"Continue, General."

"Sir. I was about to say that my contacts on Terranova tell
me that the prime contractor, Planetary Dynamics Corporation, has begun final assembly of the terraforming package.
Package elements have started to come from the subcontrac-
tors' plants on Anjaxx, New Paradise, Suleiman, and Planetary Dynamics's plant on Nuristan. As things stand, they are
due to ship out to Frontier in early September. And best of

all, the last-ditch Frontier Supreme Court challenge mounted by the Deep Ecology Coalition with the support of the Naess-Rolston Foundation has been thrown out on its ear, so the last legal barriers are now gone."

Merrick grunted. He would have liked to see a bunch of cosmic preservationists try to tell him what he could and could not do. "Who's the carrier?"

"Prince Interstellar Shipping Lines. The ship is the *Mumtaz*." Digby smiled.

"Ah, Prince Interstellar. Now I see where this is going. I know I shouldn't ask, but indulge me. That man we implicated in the *Protector* incident, what was his name?"

"Jean-Luc d'Castreaux, sir. A very, very nasty piece of work but more than happy to cooperate when General Cassidy's agents presented him with the autopsy reports on the bodies he stupidly left behind."

Merrick watched Digby grimace at the memory. Even Merrick blanched a little. The Hammer could be a brutal and merciless place, but mostly out of necessity. Its reputation for single-minded cruelty in the pursuit and punishment of anyone who strayed from the Path of Doctrine, even if only slightly, was well deserved and widely feared.

But for sheer cold-blooded sadism, what d'Castreaux had done was worse than anything the Hammer had ever committed in the name of Kraa. It was just d'Castreaux's bad luck that a Hammer light cruiser dropping out of pinchspace short of the planet Fortitude with a serious systems malfunction had literally stumbled on the three bodies, still roped together and heading for interstellar oblivion. And it had been d'Castreaux's even worse luck that the cruiser had had a captain smart enough to recognize foul play when he saw it and to work the vectors back to see where the bodies had come from. After that, it had been just a matter of patient investigation to track down who'd been responsible. It had taken more than five years to sift d'Castreaux's name out of the thousands of Feds involved in the bitter fight for Space Battle Station *Protector,* but in the end there had been no doubt.

"Yes, d'Castreaux. Pity he was kicked out of the Fleet by

the Feds. He would have been much more useful as a serving officer, especially if he'd made it to flag rank. But of course his wife is the real force behind Prince Interstellar." Merrick smiled. He enjoyed blackmail, which was why he forced an unwilling intelligence department to feed him the juicier cases, source protection be damned. He was chief councillor, for fuck's sake. Who was he going to tell?

"She is. But every dog has his day, and d'Castreaux has done what we needed him to do." Digby's satisfaction at successfully completing the hardest part of the project was evident.

"Yes, well, don't look so bloody smug, Digby. We have a long way to go yet."

"Yes, sir, you're right. We do."

Digby paused as he collected his thoughts.

"As I was saying, thanks to d'Castreaux and, I have to say, even more thanks to his wife's complete lack of concern over computer security, we were able to set up the access tunnel into the *Mumtaz*'s AI from a maintenance terminal she had at home. Once the tunnel was in, a contract team from Scobie's World did the rest. With the AI onboard the *Mumtaz* successfully subverted, our people onboard can take control any time they want. It takes only a single codephrase spoken into any comms port, and the AI is ours and so's the ship." Digby's hand reinforced the point with a sharp chop.

"Scobie's World? Outsiders! I don't much like the sound of that, General, let me tell you."

Digby had to struggle not to let his frustration at Merrick's hyperactive sense of paranoia upset his report, though to a degree Merrick had a point. Scobie's World, the closest system to the Hammer, was notoriously corrupt and freewheeling, a place where everything was for sale. And, for those willing to pay the price, that included even the most secret of Hammer secrets.

"A two-man team, sir. They had to come to Commitment to be briefed before starting, so it was logical that they work from here as well. They weren't too happy, but then, money talks. They knew they were working on an off-world mership master AI but not which one, and in any case, the minute the job was done, I had them picked up and neurowiped. They're safely tucked away on Hell now, and there they'll stay."

For once, Merrick had the good grace to look faintly apologetic.

"Fine. So *Mumtaz* leaves when?"

"Six September. She will drop out of pinchspace to avoid the Brooks Reef gravitational anomaly 200 light-years out of Terranova. My team will take control as soon as *Mumtaz* has sent her pinchspace drop report. They'll broadcast a fake jump report followed immediately by a coded message to let us know the hijack team has control and then microjump her clear of the Brooks Reef's network of surveillance drones before altering vector to jump direct to Hell, where she'll down-shuttle the original crew. There will also be a replacement crew at Hell—the hijackers don't know that, of course. I'll meet the *Mumtaz* there, and we will jump to Eternity to be safely in orbit before she's reported overdue at Frontier. No one will be any the wiser. Just another unexplained casualty of pinchspace like all the others."

"And getting your people onto Terranova in the first place?" Merrick knew how difficult it was to circumvent Terranova's security AIs.

"Already done, sir, thanks to careful adjustment of personal identity records with the help of a certain avaricious person inside the Ministry of Planetary Security. The Feds would have a fit if they knew how cheaply some of their people can be bought." That was the Federated World's Achilles' heel, Digby thought. There was always someone for whom money was everything.

"Weapons?"

"Not needed. A properly coordinated and timed attack on the officers and crew using a high level of violence and intimidation will achieve the results we want. Off-world commercial spacers rely too much on their AIs for security, but we've dealt with that. Once we have control, the weapons we need are in the armory, and my information is that they are not DNA security coded, so using them won't be a problem."

The rest of it is detail, Merrick thought, nodding. Digby has things well under control. But there was one final question.

"Deniability, Digby." Merrick's voice was harsh, his eyes stabbing. "You recall my instructions, I trust."

"Believe me, sir, I do." How could he forget Merrick's promise that he would die a slow and painful death at the hands of DocSec if the Hammer's links to the hijacking of the *Mumtaz* ever leaked back to the Feds.

Digby ticked the points off on his fingers.

"I've used multiple cutouts between us and all field operatives. Even d'Castreaux has no idea that he's actually working for the Hammer. I've double-checked with General Cassidy: The agents did not know who was behind the blackmail, and none of them will live to know why they had to force d'Castreaux's cooperation. The mership AI hackers I've covered. The hijack team thinks it's just an act of piracy funded by faceless interests out of one of the Rogue Planets, and only the team leader will know *Mumtaz*'s final destination, and he'll be told only when the ship is in pinchspace four days out of Terranova. And he and the rest of his crew will be spending the rest of their lives on Hell. The sensors on Eternity have been bypassed, so all the duty operators in deepspace ops are seeing is prerecorded data, and I doubt anyone will pick up on the fact that it's the same data looping over and over on an annual cycle. And no survey or other activity is planned around Eternity or in the Judgment System, for that matter, for at least thirty-six months."

Digby paused to catch his breath. He knew he had to get this bit right if he wanted to live to enjoy a long and happy retirement.

Thoughts marshaled, he continued. "As for the passengers of the *Mumtaz,* all of the men who aren't part of the terraforming technical support team, as well as anyone who looks like a potential troublemaker and obviously anyone from the military, will go to Hell. The rest, including women and children, will be landed on Eternity to be part of the terraforming ground teams, and there they will stay. Those who don't cooperate . . ." Digby did not need to say it again.

"As for *Mumtaz,* it will have an unfortunate accident in pinchspace when it finally jumps out of Eternity nearspace: The AI has a self-destruct subroutine already loaded that will blow every hatch wide open and disable the pinchspace drive. But best of all, the Feds will not suspect anything in the first place, and so they won't be looking. Losing ships in pinchspace doesn't happen often, but it does happen.

"And finally, the terraforming management team will all be Kraa citizens currently serving out their time on Hell. Believe me when I say, sir, that they will be model citizens.

"So I believe our operational security is good. The keys will be keeping the lid on Eternity and Hell to make sure nothing leaks out. But we are very good at that sort of thing." Digby smiled a bleak and wintry smile.

"Good," Merrick said, looking pleased. "I don't think we need to talk again. I want a personal report back from you when the terraforming process is safely under way. And when the time is right, I'm going to ask you to brief the Council in person. I think they should know who made it all happen."

"Thank you, sir," Digby said to the top of Merrick's head as he turned to leave.

Once outside the handsomely imposing pink granite building that housed Chief Councillor Merrick and the Supreme Council's secretariat, one of the very few Hammer government buildings worth looking at, Digby stopped in the predawn gloom of another of Commitment's forty-nine-hour days to catch his breath, a deep unhappiness pulling his spirits down.

Digby had never gotten used to the long drawn-out days, and he positively hated waking up in the middle of the night one day and in broad daylight the next and so on ad nauseam. His native planet of Fortitude had twenty-six-hour days and was a much more pleasant place to live. Fortitude also had seasons, unlike Commitment, where each forty-nine-hour day blurred into the next, the weather was average all the time, and one never had any idea where one was in the year unless one checked with the net.

But it wasn't just being stuck on Commitment. The problem was that he was tired, a sick tiredness that came from years of doing things that he knew were wrong. Outwardly, he had been a loyal, energetic, and motivated servant of the Hammer for over thirty years, but that was just a matter of survival, something he liked to think of as behavioral camouflage. The real problem was that underneath his carefully contrived air of controlled competence, he knew, he really knew, without any illusions at all, the Hammer for what it truly was—a brutal totalitarian regime, as vicious and self-serving as any in human history and one whose leaders paid lip service to Kraa while concentrating all their efforts on staying in power while accumulating as much wealth as possible, with every cent ripped from the pockets of ordinary Hammers.

Not that he really had anything against the Path of Doctrine except that he just didn't believe in any of it. The idea that the collection of oddly shaped rocks discovered on Mars by one Peter McNair were the only surviving relics of an ancient civilization dedicated to the universe's supreme being, an entity called Kraa, was complete and utter nonsense. McNair had been an indentured colonist with a particularly vivid imagination, vivid, in fact, to the point, in the opinion of any reasonable person, of being barking mad. But an absolute lack of any credible evidence hadn't bothered the Kraa fundamentalists any more than it had stopped people on Old Earth still, even now, from believing that aliens in flying saucers had landed way back in 1950 something.

Digby shook his head in disbelief. Aliens in flying saucers! Humanspace was full of gullible fools, and the Hammer Worlds had their share, that was for sure.

For his part, from the day when he had begun to think for himself, Digby had known that the whole Kraa myth was just so much bullshit even if, in the interests of staying alive, he had never said as much, even to his wife. Over the years that had followed, his interaction with the most powerful and monolithic religion in human history had been confined to as few temple attendances as he could get away with and a steadfast refusal to debate even the smallest point of Path theology.

It was still one of the enduring mysteries of the universe how, in the space of a few short years, McNair had been able to strike a chord deep inside ordinary people to create the largest fundamentalist movement in Earth's history. The movement—the Path of Kraa, they called themselves—had gathered pace rapidly, funded by probably the most ill-advised donation of all time: the entire estate of the software multibillionaire Vasco Fargas. With that sort of financial backing and McNair's virulent blend of idealistic hope and extreme intolerance, conflict was inevitable. A vicious civil war that wracked five continents, killing innocent people in the tens of millions, soon had erupted, quickly threatening to spread to the other planets of the Old Earth Alliance.

Finally and at huge cost, a frustrated Alliance had exported the problem onto what now were called the Hammer of Kraa Worlds. The only drawback was that where once there had been at its peak perhaps millions of hard-core disciples of Kraa, there were now billions of them, many as bigoted and unforgiving as any person could be.

Digby sighed. There was sure to be a day of reckoning with the rest of humankind. He just didn't want to be around when it arrived.

As for the Path of the Doctrine of Kraa, what a joke! How the fuck did McNair know that the supreme being's name was Kraa? The so-called artifacts had no writing of any sort on them. But the Path had supported the Digby family. In a vast and unknowable universe, that had been enough to keep him going, with the Hammer's mess of unresolvable contradictions and stupidities pushed to the back of his mind. But the price had always been high.

But now, after a lifetime of shedding blood, almost none of it from the true enemies of Kraa, Merrick wanted Digby to sacrifice another—what?—two or three hundred innocent lives, and once again in the name of Kraa. In the name of Kraa! To keep Merrick in power, more like it. For a few seconds Digby couldn't breathe, weighed down, almost crushed, by the remorse and the accumulated guilt of years of unquestioning service. He stood rigidly still as he struggled to get his rebellious body under control, to get his breath back, to calm his racing heart. Kraa's blood, he thought savagely, he'd almost lost control of himself. When did that ever happen to a brigadier general of marines? But then the stark realization hit him. This simply could not go on, he could not go on, he had to do something because if he didn't, he would destroy himself.

The problem was that he didn't have the faintest idea what to do, but he was nothing if not a determined and focused man. Buoyed by a sudden overwhelming urge to make some amends, however small, for a lifetime of wrongs, an urge he could not, would not deny, he waved his car over and climbed in. "Corporal. Take me to the office."

"Sir."

As the car accelerated away, Digby sat back, his face impassive but his mind racing. The more he thought things through, the more certainly he knew exactly where this insane plan of Merrick's would end up. He cursed himself for his willful refusal to look beyond the project itself, to see the full and awful consequences of a project of which he had been the chief architect. His project. His responsibility.

If the shit hit the fan before they finished, not only would Merrick be gone but his own life would be forfeit, too. He had seen too many changes of chief councillor to have any illusions about what happened to the loser's people. And if they actually completed the project, Merrick would dispose of everyone involved—from Prison Governor Costigan and himself down to every last man, woman, and child who helped build Eternity—before revealing it to the Council and the rest of the Hammer Worlds.

He laughed out loud. You've done a great job, Digby, he thought. So busy looking at the details that you failed to see that win or lose, your life is over. And worse, this insignificant little affair in all probability would be the trigger for the next war between the Kraa Worlds and the rest of humankind.

If you stood back, it was obvious what would happen. Yes,

Merrick would be hailed as the savior of the Hammer Worlds. Yes, the man in the street would buy the divine providence claptrap that Merrick would feed him to explain the miracle on Eternity. Yes, the apparatchiks would go along with the deception. Yes, the clans that controlled the Hammer economy would fall into line; why wouldn't they? A new planet meant growth, and growth meant money. And yes, Merrick's position as chief councillor would be unassailable.

But none of that counted for a pinch of shit. Sooner or later the Feds would work it out.

Knowing what he did about the Feds and their awesome technological capabilities, his plan for terraforming Eternity would be a success. But that success would tell the Feds, if they hadn't already found out, that technologies well beyond the capabilities of the Hammer Worlds had been applied to terraform Eternity.

And when they worked that out . . . Well, all the Feds would have to do would be to connect the dots and then the shit would really hit the fan. In very large bucketloads.

And that meant only one thing—another war. But this time Digby didn't think the Feds would settle for anything less than the unconditional surrender of the Hamnmer.

As if the previous three hadn't been destructive enough. Kraa's blood. It was only twenty years since the last fracas, and Kraa only knew how many had died that time around!

He reflected on the matter for a few more minutes, and then all of a sudden his mind was made up, all doubts gone so quickly that it took his breath away. A quiet commitment settled over him. For all its military power, the Hammer Worlds could not afford another war, and he would do, must do, anything in his power to try to make sure that the *Mumtaz* did not become a casus belli. The chances weren't good, but he would do, must do, his absolute best.

All of which was fine, he mused as his car pulled up in front of the low gray fortresslike building that housed the supreme headquarters of the Hammer Defense Forces. But how the hell was he going to derail the *Mumtaz* project without being killed either by Merrick if the bloody man survived or by the rest of the Council if Merrick did not? There was a nasty little problem, but it would just have to wait for another day.

"Thank you, Corporal. That's all for today. I'll walk home tonight."

"Sir."

Friday, July 24, 2398, UD
Federated Worlds Space Fleet College, Terranova Planet

The serried ranks of graduating cadets, resplendent in dress blacks and the gold of their newfound rank of junior lieutenant, broke apart as friends and parents dressed in every color imaginable rushed the parade ground to seal the moment. In an instant, the tightly choreographed performance of military discipline that had brought three years of cadet training to an end had been replaced by a milling mass of people, the air bright with laughter, excitement, and relief.

Michael hung back.

This should have been his day: Right up to the end he had been a strong contender for the Sword of Honor. But at least, he reflected, it had gone to one of the team. He consoled himself with the thought that Jemma Alhamid might have beaten him anyway, they were so close in the rankings; she had shaded him in the final tactical exercise of the year, after all. Michael stood alone. In a difficult and long conversation with his father, he had been emphatic that nobody from the family was to attend, a hard thing to ask of a retired Space Fleet commodore mother, not to mention a Space Fleet captain father, he had to admit. But as he had pointed out, the time for the family to be present was when he had achieved something he was proud of and could celebrate in the eyes of the world.

As it was, it wasn't easy. The sideways glances, the hurried looks, the whispered exchanges—isn't that the cadet who . . . —were almost more than he could bear. All Michael wanted to do was to be away from this place and alone. Well, give it another hour and he would be alone, alone, that is, except for Lieutenant Hadley, his assault lander command qualification instructor. Michael wasn't sure how happy Hadley would be at being kept back; not so unhappy, he hoped, that getting the required 98 percent he needed to requalify would be mission impossible.

Gradually the mob thinned, leaving Michael alone at the bottom of the imposing steps leading up to the main entrance of the college. Time to go, he thought as he turned to make his way back across the huge college parade ground. He might as well put in a solid couple of hours on the assault lander simulator to get ready for Hadley the next day.

"Michael, wait!"

Michael turned back to see Anna, followed by every member of the team, hammering down the steps two at a time—well, in Karen Sutler's case, three at a time. Or was it four? God knew, she had the legs to do it. The group came to a shuddering halt in front of Michael.

"Oh, hi, guys. Thought you'd all be gone by now."

"You didn't think we would all piss off without saying goodbye, did you?" Charlie Mbeki's tone was indignant, as if, Michael thought with a smile, he had just suggested that Charlie had been sleeping with the provost marshal's incredibly ugly offsider, Chief Petty Officer Ramona Diaz. Come to think of it, he had seen Charlie trying to kiss Chief Diaz once, but it had been very late at night and very, very dark, and Charlie had been more than a bit drunk. That little lapse in judgment had cost Charlie seventy-five demerits. Even the officer of the day appeared to have great difficulty accepting the idea that any cadet in his or her right mind would want to kiss Chief Diaz; the team suspected that only that thought had stopped him whacking Charlie with a hundred demerits.

"No, no, no," Michael protested, relieved that they hadn't gone. "I knew you'd track me down. A lot easier than the other way around. I've seen better-behaved sheep, I have to say."

"Smart-ass. If you'd met my mother, you'd understand why I move around in random jerks. If she kisses me one more time and tells me how wonderful I am . . ." Nicco Guzevic grimaced at the thought.

"Bull, Nicco. You love it when your mom tries to cheer you up. You don't fool us," said Bronwyn Kriketos, planting a huge wet kiss on his cheek. "I'd be depressed, too, if I only graduated in the third quartile."

"Heartless bastard," Nicco responded amiably. "Michael, I've got to go. The up-shuttle won't wait, and neither will Carlsson Space Lines. It's been an honor. Stay in touch. You know where to find me." With a firm shake of the hand and a pat on the cheek, he was gone.

Two minutes later and with a bruised hand courtesy of one of Karen Sutler's power grips—Michael swore she practiced for maximum effect—everyone was gone except Anna. The mélange of Chinese, Asian, African, and European blood that ran in her veins together with generations of very expensive cosmetic geneering combined to produce a face so striking that it nearly stopped Michael's heart when he looked at it.

"Michael, what can I say?" Tears sprang into the corners of Anna's eyes as she put her arms around his neck. "You know what you mean to me, so don't lose me somewhere in your life."

"Anna, no chance. We've had too many good times for that to happen." A memorable weekend high in the New Tatra Mountains behind the college sprang unbidden to mind; Michael shoved the thought away firmly. "Comm me when you get to the *Damishqui;* I hear she's a good ship, and my dad says Captain Chandra is a very good operator."

"Yeah, I hear she is." Anna paused. "I don't know if we should prolong this; it's going to be really hard not having you around after three years."

"I know. I'll miss you," Michael said, still unsure of Anna and what she really meant to him and what he meant to her. Despite the time they had spent together, there had been other people in their lives during their college time, and both knew how many friendships struck early in a Space Fleet career, whether casual or intimate, failed to survive the pressure that distance and separation created. Space Fleet had no respect for personal relationships, Michael thought moodily. Never had and never would.

Abruptly, Anna tilted her head up, kissed him full, long, and hard on the mouth, then spun on her heel and was gone without another word. Michael stood there feeling empty and flat.

After a few moments, he turned and set off for the assault lander simulator building.

Thursday, July 30, 2398, UD
Space Marines Headquarters, City of McNair,
Commitment Planet

The walls of Digby's small office seemed to close in on him as he stared at the e-mail on his workstation screen.

It couldn't be, he thought, it couldn't be. But there it was, in plain Standard English. The Sylvanian National Day reception had been canceled.

Digby cursed quietly but fluently and at great length.

Canceled. As simple as that. Not that the cancellation came as a surprise. The Sylvanians had been very rough on the captain and crew of the Hammer tramp spacer *Geronimo's Spear* when they had discovered that its cargo was not medical supplies, which were allowed into the Hammer Worlds under the Allied Declaration of Embargo of 2282, but rather rail-gun power management systems, which most definitely were not. The diplomats had been wrangling for months, with the Hammers as usual knowing nothing and conceding less. Digby wondered whether the foreign relations people actually had done the canceling; he thought it more likely the other way around. Those Sylvanians were a precious lot.

But none of that helped him.

The Sylvanian National Day reception had offered Digby

his only opportunity to meet Ashok Kumar without drawing the attention of Doctrinal Security and thereby risking his own death warrant. And now the opportunity had gone. Captain Ashok Kumar, the Sylvanian embassy's military attaché and its one and only senior military member of staff, was the one man on Commitment whom Digby was prepared to trust to do something quickly. He and Kumar went back a long way, nineteen years to be precise, to the bloody shambles that had followed the Battle of Delta Chimensis in the closing days of the Third Worlds War. Captured along with the shattered remnants of MARFOR-13, his interrogator had been none other than a very young Lieutenant Commander Kumar, a man Digby got to know quite well in the long days that followed. A hard man, a tough and persistent interrogator, not a man you could ever like but decent despite that.

And Kraa knew the Sylvanians had plenty of reasons not to be decent to any Hammer—the use of tactical nuclear weapons for one thing, small ones, thank Kraa, but still nukes, slipped past defenses badly stretched by the chaos of a full-scale Hammer planetary assault to fall on the cities of Vencatia and Jesmond. The only thing that had saved the Hammer was the fact that the nukes had been launched by renegade elements outside the chain of command. But it had been a close thing: Digby remembered as if it were yesterday the crippling fear that had gripped him at the thought of his family disappearing in the blinding flash of a fusion air burst. With that sort of history, even with the passage of almost twenty years, Digby knew that the fight would be to the death the next time around.

Struggling to work out how he was going to live up to his newfound resolve, he put his head in his hands, a small, solid, and in many ways quite unremarkable man seated behind a small cluttered desk in a windowless office deep below the ground.

After a long pause, Digby slipped on his lightweight comms headset and fired up his workstation. If Kumar wasn't going to come to him, he'd have to go to Kumar. Thanks to DocSec's obsessive interest in the minutiae of people's lives, a quick walk through the Section 4 knowledge base should tell him more than enough about Kumar's daily routine to allow him to set up an "accidental" meeting.

It was his only chance.

As he started work, Digby said a quiet word of thanks to Chief Councillor Merrick. The bloody man was obsessive about the operational security of the Eternity project, the blackest of all his many black projects. Understandably, of course. Chief councillor or not, any leak would see Merrick in front of a DocSec firing squad in no time flat. Thus, he'd given Digby unrestricted access to every knowledge base in the Hammer Worlds to make sure the Eternity project stayed black.

Much more important, he had an account allocated to him by the chief councillor personally, an account DocSec's normally relentless investigators wouldn't go near. Even they had more sense than to ask what the chief councillor was up to.

Wonderful place, the Hammer, he thought as he bent to the task of finding what he needed to know about Captain Ashok Kumar. If you worked for the chief councillor, you could pretty much get away with anything, go anywhere, do anything, know everything about everybody.

Until the next chief councillor took over.

Then you were dead.

Thursday, August 6, 2398, UD
Planetary Heavy Lander (Assault) 005338 Berthed on
Space Battle Station 1, in Orbit around Terranova

Michael realized that not once in the two weeks of his lander command requalification had Lieutenant Michael Hadley said one word more than was absolutely necessary.

The silent, moodily uncommunicative Hadley had not cut him one inch of slack or encouraged the slightest hope that he might get the 98 percent he needed if he was to have the career

path he wanted. As a member of the warfare branch of the
Federated Worlds Space Fleet, that meant only one thing as far
as he was concerned: assault lander pilot. The alternatives—
most likely a career as a navigator or an intel spook, or, even
worse, a transfer to the engineering or logistics branches of the
Fleet—just didn't bear thinking about. Still, Hadley hadn't
failed him yet, so maybe he still had a chance.

So far the atmosphere had been heavy and formal, and
Michael hated it. Maybe Hadley was pissed off at having to
change his leave plans; Michael had no idea. Seeing
Hadley's glowering, almost sullen face the day after graduation had been more than enough to kill off any idea Michael
might have had of talking about Hadley's private affairs.

He sighed and settled deeper into the battered and scarred
command pilot's chair of *Moaning Minnie,* more properly
known as Planetary Heavy Lander (Assault) Number
PHLA-005338, his combat space suit stiff and uncomfortable as he waited for Hadley to complete briefing the directing staff who'd be controlling the opposition forces Michael
was up against for the final live exercise of his requalification.

Michael looked around the flight deck with affection. As
landers went, *Moaning Minnie* wasn't a bad ship. Michael
had flown it many times before. Everything worked, and its
AI was reasonably stable and had no bad habits that he knew
of. For the tenth time, he had his neuronics call up the mission and, eyes shut, methodically worked through the mission plan and the supporting threat summary step-by-step,
item by item. He knew the THREATSUM (Threat Summary) forward and backward by now, but at least it was
something to do while he waited.

Mother, the lander's AI, broke his fierce concentration to
tell him that Hadley had come aboard. Finally, Michael
thought as he closed the mission file and stood up to await
Hadley's arrival.

He didn't have long to wait.

"Right," Hadley said as he settled himself into the tactical
officer's chair alongside Michael, ignoring the rest of
Michael's team ranged to the left and right of him. His voice

became very formal. "Junior Lieutenant Helfort. You have command."

"Roger, sir. I have command. Stand by." Michael activated the lander's CombatNet; it would stay open until the mission had been completed. With a deep breath to steady himself, he started in on the checklists, the slow and tedious process of confirming that *Moaning Minnie* was ready for the torture he was going to put her through. One by one, his crew signed off, and finally the ship was ready to go.

"All stations, ship is go for launch. Stand by for drop in"— Michael checked the master mission timer—"ten minutes. Helmets on, suit integrity checks to Mother. Command out."

Michael commed BaseNet. "Space Battle Station 1, this is PHLA-005338, mission call sign Golf Charlie. Ready to launch at designated drop time. Golf Charlie over."

"Roger, Golf Charlie. Stand by, out."

Settling his helmet onto its neck ring, Michael quickly ran through his own suit checks and, visor down, confirmed suit integrity. He uplinked the results to Mother and confirmed for himself that Mother had fifteen good suits onboard: fourteen crew and one pax. Hang on. A passenger? Who the hell could that be? he wondered, but he had too much to think about to bother checking. Flipping his armored plasglass visor back up, Michael turned slightly to look at Hadley out of the corner of one eye. The man who carried his fate in his hands was sitting unmoving in the tactical officer's seat, staring out at the vast gray bulk of Space Battle Station 1's hull as it curved away from them.

Michael turned back and sat motionless. There was nothing to do but sit and wait in silence. Michael felt the pressure bear down on him. An open-mike circuit, CombatNet was quiet except for the breathing of the loadmaster, Chief Petty Officer Sara Gemmell. For some reason, before launch she breathed as hard as if she'd just run a race, a long one and uphill at that. Nerves, Michael supposed. He didn't have the gossip, insults, and facetious comments that normally characterized the minutes immediately before a launch to take his mind off what was at stake.

"Michael." Hadley's voice came up on CommandNet and cut across his thoughts.

"Sir?"

"Good luck." Hadley turned away and resumed his sphinx-like study of SBS-1's hull.

"Tha—" Michael's surprised acknowledgment of the first words from Hadley not specifically called for by a checklist or standard operating procedure was cut short as BaseNet came up. "Golf Charlie, this is SBS-1. You are clear to drop under SBS control. Departure pipe is Violet-34. Acknowledge, over."

"SBS-1, Golf Charlie. Roger, clear to drop, departure pipe Violet-34, over."

"Golf Charlie, SBS-1. Roger. Good hunting. On dropping, immediate chop TACON to assault mission command. Over."

"SBS-1, Golf Charlie. Roger. Out."

With a sigh, Michael sat back. If anything, he felt even more nervous. Seven minutes thirty seconds to go. Damn it, this couldn't go on. Michael commed CombatNet again.

"Okay, folks. The BUFF outside the windows has given us launch clearance, and we will drop as scheduled in . . . seven minutes and twenty seconds. At which point you will be relieved to know that our esteemed loadmaster will cease heavy breathing."

"I am not a heavy breather," came Gemmell's indignant and entirely predictable reply. It was what she always said.

"That's not what I hear," chipped in Petty Officer Taksin, Michael's weapons supervisor for the day.

"You cheeky young pup, Taki. I'll have you know . . ."

CombatNet caught the chuckles of *Minnie*'s crew, and Michael felt the pressure ease. These were good people, well trained and experienced. He'd done missions like this successfully before, and he'd do them again. Having started the traditional prelaunch banter, he sat back and let it wash over him, the chatter wandering through the social lives and idiosyncrasies of the crew with careless abandon.

At one minute to go, it was down to business.

"Okay, folks, one minute. Visors down and stand by. Final checks. Call them in."

In a matter of seconds the final checks were in. It was time to go.

"All stations, this is command. *Moaning Minnie* is go for launch. May God watch over us this day," Michael said, offering up the traditional spacer's prayer before any launch. Notwithstanding the fact that the human race had been dropping down gravity wells for hundreds of years, the process was a violent one that stressed the best-designed and best-built spacecraft to their limits and occasionally past them. Over the centuries, descent from orbit had taken the lives of far too many good spacers and was not ever to be taken for granted no matter how good Fed technology might have become.

The seconds ticked away. BaseNet came to life. "Golf Charlie, forty-five seconds to drop. Automatic drop sequence commenced. Over."

"Roger. Golf Charlie out." Michael shrugged himself down in his straps and commed CombatNet. "Stand by, everybody." And finally, with a firm shove, hydraulic rams pushed *Moaning Minnie* away from the massive hull of Space Battle Station 1, out of any residual effect of its artificial gravity, and started the assault lander on its way planetward.

The assault landing process was as rough as people and machine could tolerate and as quick as the lander's command pilot could make it. That way, the trip was short and sharp, a decidedly attractive tactical advantage. Loitering at high altitudes in hostile airspace was not a life-extending strategy and one that the assault lander pilots did all in their power to avoid, short of actually breaking the lander into pieces.

Barely a minute after *Minnie* had dropped clear, the assault commander gave the order.

"Bravo Mike, this is Alfa. Authenticate Kilo Oscar. Immediate execute Ops Plan 41 Bravo. I say again, immediate execute Ops Plan 41 Oscar. Stand by, execute!"

With a deep breath, Michael started *Moaning Minnie,* which already was positioned tail first in anticipation, on her way dirtside, firing her main engines at full military power to wipe out enough of her orbital velocity to put her almost instantly into a rapidly steepening parabolic fall to the ground. As she fell, the rest of the assault lander stream fell around her, the landers cocooned in a huge cloud of active decoys, the attack blossoming out in all directions into a huge sphere that was too confused, too complex, and too fast-moving for ground-based radar to distinguish high-value targets from decoys.

With *Minnie*'s height unwinding rapidly, Michael shut down the main engines and spun Minnie back nose first, ready for reentry. He could see for himself the threat blossoming in front of them as long-range search radars appeared on the threat display. It was becoming increasingly clear that whoever had set up the exercise, the enemy had a threat profile that, as always, looked exactly like the Hammer of Kraa's and was determined to kick *Minnie* hard.

But that didn't matter too much.

An assault lander could do very little against long-range weapons systems except stay as far away from them as possible. The combination of poor maneuverability at very high speed and a limited self-defense capability made landers easy meat. It was up to the planetary assault force supporting the attack from orbit—in this case, lead by the hypothetical FWWS (Federated Worlds Warship) *Shrivaratnam* from which *Moaning Minnie* supposedly had dropped along with 139 other hypothetical assault and ground attack landers—to provide volume defense for the assault lander stream, and Michael was pleased to see that the *Shrivaratnam* had made a good start in suppressing ground radar sites and launching the follow-up waves of decoys needed to confuse the enemy's tactical picture further. The radar sites were bound to be dummy emitters, though, he thought, and God only knew which ones were the "real" missile radar and launch sites.

"Command, Tac. Threat Red. Multiple battle management

radar emitters. Stand by . . . *Shrivaratnam* reports multiple
ABM missile launches."

ABMs! Shit, Michael thought. Antiballistic missile systems were designed to take out missiles before atmospheric
reentry, a role that made them extremely good at hacking
big, fat, and relatively slow assault landers out of the sky. But
there was nothing much Michael could do about them except
worry and leave them to *Shrivaratnam*. ABMs were too big
and too fast and, with tacnuke warheads, much more than
any lander's thin skin of ceramsteel armor could withstand.
As he commed his neuronics to display the overall command
plot, he was happy to see that the ABMs, for which an undefended stream of assault landers was the easiest of easy
meat, were having a hard time of it.

But a handful did slip through.

Michael watched as the ABMs closed in relentlessly, the
more heavily armored ground attack landers leading the assault stream filling the space between them with short-range
missiles and sheets of chain-gun fire, with reddish-yellow
flares marking their successes. But two landers lost their battle to fend off the massive missiles, Michael wincing as mi-
croyield tacnuke warheads exploded in searing balls of
blue-white energy, turning the landers into useless lumps of
metal slag tumbling end over end to burn up in the atmosphere below. But then there were no more ABMs, and
Michael watched in relief as Mother downgraded the ABM
threat from red to orange. He wasn't allowed to stay relieved
for long.

"Command, Tac. Threat Red. Expect antilander missile
launch at twenty-seven minutes on current track."

"Roger, Tac." No surprises there. He'd seen the missile
control radars come online, and there were a lot of them,
which wasn't good. Michael risked a glance across at
Hadley. His face was tight with concentration, with the
screwed-up eyes that came with looking at neuronics
dataflows.

As *Moaning Minnie* began to tear into the first thin tendrils
of Terranova's atmosphere, the lander's thrusters started

banging away to hold the finless, wingless machine at the right angle for reentry. Then Michael felt the vibration slowly begin to build as deceleration started in earnest. The lander's artificial gravity rippled as it absorbed the growing influence of Terranova's gravitational field.

As he studied the command plot, his relief evaporated. Shit, he thought. The missiles would be on them quickly, and the threat wasn't quite what the THREATSUM had predicted. For a start, there were many more medium-range missile control radars than predicted, and with them went hypersonic antilander missiles, truly nasty pieces of Hammer engineering. Big by Federated Worlds standards, they were very fast and agile enough to stay locked on to even the most desperately flown heavy lander. That and a conventional chemex warhead big enough to punch a hole through lander ceramsteel armor with no difficulty made them a real lander killer.

But there was only one way down, and Michael turned his focus to the job at hand: getting *Minnie* and her crew home safely, threading her way through the layers of defense standing between him and his objective.

Plummeting almost vertically nose first past 90,000 meters, Mother pulled *Moaning Minnie* up into a steady 40-degree angle of attack as the lander punched into the atmosphere in earnest. In seconds, *Minnie* had disappeared into the heart of an incandescently hot fireball as her still-massive residual kinetic energy bled off into the air ripping past the hull. For the moment they were safe; no weapon system yet invented could get even a half-decent targeting solution out of the enormous ball of ionized gas that had wrapped itself around *Moaning Minnie,* and even the Hammer didn't like popping off tacnukes inside their own atmosphere. Not that Michael was completely happy. This element of the reentry would have been familiar to the pioneers of space flight centuries earlier, and he hated every painful second of it as the lander's speed bled off. One day, he said to himself, one day maybe the designers would work out how to get a lander through ionization ass first, with the main engines firing all the way to get her dirtside as quickly as possible. But good though lander technology was, that happy day was a long way off.

Any minute now, Michael thought.

"Ionization finish in ten seconds. Speed now 12,200 kph, altitude 51,500 meters. Standing by to maneuver." Mother's calm tones belied the storm still raging outside.

And then they were out; it was time to screw up the opposition's missile firing solutions. "Standby max g aerobrake, stand by, stand by. Now!"

Mother didn't hang around. She rammed *Moaning Minnie* back almost onto its tail, holding the lander at an 85-degree angle of attack to present the lander's flat underbelly nearly at right angles to the airflow. For an instant *Minnie*'s artgrav, as always slow to react, allowed the gravity to push Michael into his seat as the lander shed speed. *Minnie*'s airframe was twanging and twitching as it absorbed the enormous stresses being imposed on it by turbulent air ripping past, the lander's kinetic energy dumped into the freshly reenergized plume of intensely hot gas coming off its underbelly.

"Weapons, Tac. Decoys now."

"Decoys away." Taksin sounded bored, not at all like somebody sitting inside a 750-ton lump of armored ceramsteel plunging groundward with all the finesse of a huge boulder.

With decoys safely away, Mother powered up the main engines to stab *Moaning Minnie*'s blunt nose straight down at Terranova's surface, now only 48,000 meters below them. As the lander settled into a nearly vertical dive, Mother slowly extended its variable-geometry wings to mark the beginnings of the lander's transition from a brick to something more like a proper aircraft and then cut the main engines to let *Moaning Minnie* drop into free fall, pushing Michael's stomach up into his mouth before the artgrav could respond. The height unwound at a dramatic rate before Mother extended the wings and started the slow and careful process of pulling the lander out of its headlong plunge to earth. Michael's neuronics were plugged into the lander's neural system to make doubly sure that the huge stresses on the lander's wings stayed within acceptable limits. Even so, the synthpain was uncomfortably intense. Michael's concern was well

justified. The lander's foamalloy wings were incredibly strong,
but even they would have trouble taking the load imposed by
a 750-ton lander trying to pull too sharp a recovery.

At last, the lander leveled off at 5,000 meters, and Mother
allowed it to slow before bringing the main engines back up
to power, turning the lander slowly back toward the landing
site.

"Tac. How do we look going in?" Michael asked.

"Well, we are in the first wave, so in theory the opposition
has only a hazy idea of where we will land, at least to start
with."

"Other than the college spaceport, you mean?" said
Michael, at which Hadley actually laughed. Good, Michael
thought. Things were looking up if the man could take a joke
and not bite his head off.

"Play the game, Helfort. As I was saying, the only advantage we have is where we will hit the ground. Ah, good.
Mother thinks this is the optimum final approach track." The
track bloomed in Michael's neuronics. Pretty simple: two
doglegs, both over water, which was always nice, a sharp
turn onto a short final approach, which would be fun, and
then onto the ground. But no terrain to hide behind for the
final approach, which was a pity. They had twenty-three minutes to run, and Michael offered up a small prayer that there
wouldn't be too many surprises.

His hopes of a quiet run in were dashed fourteen minutes
later. With no warning, Fusion A tripped offline, immediately depriving Michael of his starboard mass driver–
powered main engine. Seconds later, the cross-feeds that
would have allowed the starboard main engine to draw power
from Fusion B on the port side went down as well. Fucking
terrific, Michael thought.

As Michael cursed silently under his breath, *Moaning
Minnie* first sagged and then wallowed back to height, adopt-
ing the characteristic skewed posture of a lander running on
one engine as Mother quickly ran Fusion B up to full power
to cover for the loss of Fusion A.

"Command, propulsion. Software lockout of Fusion A and

cross-feed to starboard mass driver. No chance of recovery without command emergency override." It was Petty Officer Aguilar, about as excited as a lump of rock as usual.

Software lockout, Michael thought. Thank you, directing staff, you bastard offspring of flea-ridden camel herders.

"Roger, propulsion. Mother. Maintain track."

"Command, Tac. *Shrivaratnam* reports six Kingfisher fliers at 100 k's inbound bearing 280."

"Shit, shit, shit," Michael muttered. Hostile fliers. Just what they didn't need as they slowed for landing. "Roger that, Tac. Confirm *Shrivaratnam* engaging?"

"Negative. All assets assigned to higher-priority tasks." Hadley's face reflected what he thought of that piece of twisted logic.

"Command, roger. GAs?" Michael asked, more in hope than in expectation. While they had a good air defense capability, the heavily armored ground attack planetary landers were tasked primarily with protecting the marines as they deployed and then with breaking up enemy counterattacks in the hours after the landing, when the marines were at their most vulnerable. Their weapons were designed with close ground support in mind, not atmospheric dogfights, and so, per planetary assault standard operating procedures, responsibility for protecting the assault stream as it funneled in to land rested with the *Shrivaratnam*, her massive infrared planetary attack lasers more than capable of breaking up even the largest flier attack.

"Negative. Ground attack landers are fully committed."

Oh, well, thought Michael. Doesn't hurt to ask. But they were well and truly on their own.

"Stand by hard turn left," Mother announced.

"Weapons, Tac. On my mark, full spread decoy deployment—we've got less than 65 k's to run, so we'll throw everything at the hostiles to try to break radar lock." As Hadley spoke, Mother yanked *Moaning Minnie* around onto the first of the final doglegs, the max-g turn making *Minnie*'s fabric groan in protest. The lander's synthpain levels fed through to Michael's neuronics, rising uncomfortably

as the wings, now fully deployed, flexed alarmingly under
the huge load of the tightest turn Mother could get away
with.

"Roger, Tac."

"Sixty k's to run. Stand by hard turn right." Mother was at
her soothing best. But her reassuring tones belied the desperate situation *Moaning Minnie* was in. Hostile fliers and
landers did not mix well, especially when the top cover normally provided to landers by the ships orbiting overhead apparently had been tasked to higher-priority targets.

"Weaps, Tac. Decoy release on the turn."

"Weaps, roger."

This time Mother outdid herself. Tipping the lander on its
ear, the foamalloy wings flexing sharply upward under the
load, the synthpain almost unbearable, Mother powered up
Fusion B to overcome the loss of Fusion A. That drove
Moaning Minnie around in an impossibly tight turn, the g
forces ramming her crew deep into their seats despite the
best efforts of the lander's artgrav. Even at the best of times,
Minnie and her clan were not known for their agility even
with wings fully deployed, but raw vectored power from the
lander's remaining main engine and lots of it was a wonderful thing.

"Thirty k's to run," Mother announced calmly as the lander settled onto the final dogleg.

Hadley and Taksin timed it beautifully. As the lander
turned, decoys streaked out from *Minnie*'s sides. Almost instantly, the swarm of decoys came online, and all of a sudden
there were *Moaning Minnies* everywhere—some running
with the ship along its new course, some on the old course,
and others on every track in between. Two were even running
away. Perfect timing, Michael thought, absolutely perfect.

"Command, Tac. Estimate eight seconds to hostile missile
release."

"Command, roger."

"Command, Tac. Hostiles have gone to restricted search
mode. I'd bet my pension we've been selected."

"Command, roger. No takers."

"You do surprise me," Michael muttered under his breath. Who else would the staff controlling the exercise select for a missile attack?

"Command, Tac. Hostile missile launch. Time to target sixty-four seconds."

"Command, Mother. Stand by turn hard right."

"Abort, abort." Michael's voice cut across Mother. "Turn left under the decoys and cut the corner onto the next turn. Put us back on the final track with 1 k to run."

Even if what she had wanted to do was standard operating procedure, Michael could see that no matter how hard Mother turned, *Moaning Minnie* would be uncomfortably close to the debris of missiles closing in on them at 5,000 kph. Even if they cooked off on the decoys, the warhead debris would spread out in a high-velocity cone to envelop the fleeing *Minnie*. And if they survived, they would still have to get *Minnie* back where she belonged—back on track heading for the landing zone to dump her hypothetical load of heavily armed marines and their mounds of equipment precisely where they wanted to get off. Sure, the risk was small, but it was a risk. But by turning left, *Minnie* could duck under the decoys and give the incoming missiles no time to decide that she was a better target.

"New track up, *Shrivaratnam* approved. Stand by, forty seconds to turn, fifty seconds to missile impact."

"Roger. Command approved."

"Stand by turn left." This turn would be uncomfortably sluggish with no starboard engine to overcome the port engine's opposition. Hopefully, it won't matter, Michael prayed.

And around they went, smooth as silk this time, Mother winding the power back as *Minnie* settled down for the final approach.

"Command, Tac. Stand by missile impact in ten . . . Stand by. Multiple warhead explosions behind and above us; no hits, no collateral damage. *Shrivaratnam* reports hostiles breaking off. Ground attack commander reports landing zone sanitized and secure, clear to land."

Michael heaved a sigh of relief.

"Roger that, Tac. Mother, command approved to au-
toland." Michael itched to take manual control and do it himself, but he told himself not to be stupid. Although he knew
he could hand fly the lander down, it would be a big mistake.
Poor situational awareness, less than sixty seconds to run,
and another sharp turn to port with the starboard engine out
to boot. No, let Mother do it, he decided.

And a lovely job Mother did.

As a subdued rumble told everyone that the gear was
going down, Mother extended the lander's massive triple-
slotted flaps, the fourteen-meter-wide strips of plasteel
rammed out to bite hard into the air still ripping fast past the
lander's hull. Michael's hands clenched unconsciously as
Mother began the countdown to the pitch-up maneuver that
so impressed the hearts, minds, and stomachs of new re-
cruits. It wasn't surprising that landers always had to be
hosed out after recruit flights, Michael thought. There were
few experiences like it. He knew that even experienced lander pilots like Hadley never enjoyed something that felt all
wrong, and with one engine out, it was going to feel a whole
lot worse.

With less than one kilometer to run and with *Minnie*'s
speed decaying slowly, Mother pulled the lander sharply
back onto her tail. The belly-mounted mass drivers, which
were capable of holding a lightly loaded lander in the hover
if need be, went to full power to fire mass directly ahead to
kill the lander's still-enormous residual kinetic energy. Walking the blowtorch, the maneuver was called, and for good
reason, as Mother powered up Fusion B, with plumes of incandescently hot hypersonic water vapor ripping and blasting the earth as the lander slowed for landing, its nose angled
up nearly vertically into the sky. Losing speed rapidly,
Moaning Minnie came low across the threshold as Mother,
neatly rotating the lander forward and down hard onto her
gear, cut the power and popped the chute. The lander's crew
members were thrown hard up against their safety straps as
Mother brought *Minnie* to a shuddering halt, titanium ce-
ramic brakes nearly white-hot and howling in protest.

Minutes later, with the hypothetical marines safely delivered and on their way to wherever marines went when they finally got dirtside, the exercise was over and *Minnie* was taxiing slowly off Runway 28 Left. As the lander made its way to the stand, Michael rapidly completed the shutdown checklist with Mother. Finally, with a small screech of protest from heavily punished brakes, Mother brought *Moaning Minnie* to a stop, the lander bobbing its nose down for a moment as the nose gear absorbed the last remnants of her kinetic energy. The final shutdown items, and that was it. Exercise over. Survived. Thank God.

Michael commed CombatNet for the last time. "Thank you, team—helmets off. Free to disembark. A memorable trip, I think. See you all in the Dog and Duck at 20:00 tonight. First round is on me."

"And the rest," came a poorly disguised voice to general laughter. Aguilar, Michael thought.

"Command, Pax 1."

Michael started as he realized that Bukenya had been with him all the time. Well, no better way to show who you believed in, he supposed.

"Sorry, sir, didn't realize you were aboard." Michael tried without success to hide his surprise.

"Wouldn't have missed it for the world"—Bukenya laughed—"and well done. That looked very good from where I was sitting. And I'd forgotten how much I really enjoy assault landings with one engine out."

"Thank you, sir. Pleased you had fun. I'll catch up with you later." Seconds later, Mother had popped *Minnie*'s accesses open and deployed the stairs. Michael unbuckled and climbed stiffly out of the command pilot's chair. Then it struck him. Had he passed?

He turned to Hadley, already asking the question, but Hadley stopped him dead.

"Don't ask. Somebody much more senior than me wants to tell you the good news, so don't drop me in it by letting on that I've already told you. But you should know that if you had taken manual control from Mother for the final approach, I would have failed you. But you didn't, and I know you won't believe me, but that was the best decision you

made all mission. Wait here till I call you down." And with
that Hadley was gone, space-suit boots clattering down the
vertical ladder that led from the lander's bridge down to the
upper pax deck.

Ten long minutes later, Michael finally got the call, emerging from the long-suffering *Moaning Minnie* to give her hull
an affectionate pat of thanks as she sat patiently clicking and
clinking in the late evening sun, the residual heat of her reentry radiating off a blackened fuselage. As Michael came
down the stairs, he could see Admiral Fielding standing patiently at the foot of the stairs, Hadley to one side and
Bukenya to the other. Michael hurried down and came to attention as smartly as his combat space suit would allow.

"Junior Lieutenant Helfort reporting, sir," he said, saluting
stiffly. The admiral returned the salute and then took his hand
and shook it until Michael thought it would fall off.

Finally releasing her grip, the admiral smiled. "Lieutenant
Hadley has briefed me, and I have to say I agree with him.
That was one of the best-flown assault landing missions by a
junior pilot I have ever seen, Helfort, so my congratulations.
Get some experience under your belt and you'll be a certainty for combat flight school. Sorry about the loss of Fusion A and the cross-feed. You can blame me for that and not
directing staff. Oh, and I also agree with Lieutenant Hadley
on one other thing. If you had taken manual control for landing, he would have been right to fail you.

"But you didn't, and that's why you are going to be a good
pilot. So well done, Helfort. You are back on track. Make
damn sure you stay there."

"Yes, sir. Thank you, sir."

"Well, that's it. Good evening to you all. Where's my damn
car?" Fielding muttered as she turned and walked away
across the apron.

Hadley looked at Michael for a moment. "You know why
I was so pissed off at the beginning?" he asked.

"No, sir," Michael replied.

"Because if I passed you and then you went and messed
up, I would be remembered throughout the Fleet as the man

who let Helfort off the hook. But then, I hadn't ever flown with you, so how was I to know any better?"

There was nothing Michael could say.

"So you've passed. Full mission debrief at 08:00 tomorrow, and we'll see what you didn't do right. In the meantime, a long shower and change and then down to the Dog and Duck, I think."

For his part, Michael could think of nothing he would like to do more.

Sunday, August 9, 2398, UD
Arcadia Spaceport, Ashakiran Planet

At long last, Michael thought as the down-shuttle thumped emphatically onto the Arcadia spaceport's Runway 09 Left.

Since leaving the college Saturday morning, he had been traveling continuously without sleep, though traveling wasn't the best way to describe what he'd been doing. Hanging around waiting would have been more like it. Michael had concluded long ago that it was one of the immutable laws of the cosmos that up-shuttles never connected with merships, which in turn never connected with down-shuttles.

The tension of the previous months had slowly begun to seep away, but he was more tired than he had ever been. But it was not just physical exhaustion; three years as a cadet had taught Michael how to cope with lack of sleep. No, it was more than that. It was almost as though he were just emerging from a prolonged coma and his body just didn't want to play, all energy spent. Michael would have been happy to stay where he was and let the world move on without him. He closed his eyes and waited for the OK to disembark.

Five minutes later, the aerobridge was connected and the sparse complement of passengers began to disembark. Michael waited until almost everyone was off before he forced himself to his feet, grabbed his bag, and walked off the shuttle. His brief words of thanks to the cabin crew were the most he had spoken for days. Quickly through the retinal scan and DNA identity check, he collected his case and headed to check-in for the red-eye to Calvert, the enormous bulk of the spaceport echoing and empty as Sunday night wound its way to its usual dull conclusion.

Much to Michael's surprise, he had passed out into an exhausted sleep the minute Mitrakis Emirates Flight ME 0255 had lifted off from Arcadia, heading for Calvert, 4,400 kilometers away.

He was only woken by the thump of the landing gear locking down as the big Boeing maneuvered on its final approach, the two wing-mounted water-fed mass drivers barely audible as they powered up for landing. Through the window, Michael could see the early dawn flushing a mauve-black eastern sky a golden pink, but the ground below was still dark, with only pools of light thrown by the carefully shaded streetlights of Calvert to give him any sense of terrain. For some reason and even though he had slept only a bit under six hours and that in seats whose design, he swore, dated from the dark ages of air travel, Michael felt different. He was still very tired but no longer felt half-drugged.

Twenty minutes later, Michael was outside breathing the fresh air of his home world for the first time in almost twelve months. He struggled for a moment to remember whether it was autumn or spring; autumn, he thought after considering it for a while, not that Ashakiran's seasons were much different from one another: The planet had only a four-month year and a 19.5-degree axial tilt, after all. He stood there, heedless of the steady trickle of early-morning passengers coming and going. It was easy to let the southeast trade winds wash over him and enjoy the sounds of the breeze as it moved through the trees, palms, and bushes—a disorganized unruly riot of whites, blues, reds, golds, yellow, lilacs, and purples, all with the luscious, heady aromas of geneered plants and set against a leafy backdrop of every conceivable shade of green with the odd purple or red for variety—that framed the approach to Calvert airport.

With renewed energy, Michael headed for the Avis office.

With his identity checked with the usual excruciating care, his credit established, and pilot's license painstakingly verified to give him the privilege of hand flying the machine, Michael took temporary loan of a two-seat Honda flier. It was a new model he hadn't seen before, and very neat-looking it was. A single piece of molded plasglass screen flowed back and over the passenger compartment before turning down to blend seamlessly into stubby variable-profile plasfiber wings. A FusionIndustries commercial microfusion plant driving a single-vectored water-fed mass driver, a noise reduction shroud, a retractable tricycle undercarriage, eight reaction control nozzles, and a simple tail assembly completed the machine. Inside the cabin, there were two big brightscreen multifunction displays, both rendered totally redundant by neuronics, thought Michael. Why did Honda and every other flier manufacturer insist on installing them? A two-axis sidestick controller, yaw pedals, throttle lever, and radio selector completed the pilot's station.

With the flight plan completed and uploaded to Calvert Control, Calvert airport's airspace and traffic management AI, Michael took care to establish good relations with the flier's AI, called Mother, naturally, and blessed with an engagingly firm tone of voice as if to say she had seen quite enough hire flier pilots in her time, hadn't been impressed by any of them, and would Michael please behave himself. That done, Michael rapidly completed the prelaunch checks, got the OK for his flight plan from Calvert Control, and uploaded the approved flight pipe to Mother.

Calvert airport's house rules allowed noncommercial flier operations only under the joint control of Mother and Calvert Control until clear of restricted airspace around the airport. So it was Mother and not Michael who taxied the flier out to the small satellite strip south of the main runway complex. She held the flier on the brakes while the mass driver ran up to full power, the jet efflux ripping and howling, the steam plume driving down the runway behind them before Mother let the brakes go, slamming Michael back into his seat before lifting the flier sharply up off the ground and into a steep climb.

Michael was happy to sit back and gaze out at the Coral Bight as it slowly came into view below the plasglass nose of the flier, the deep blue ocean stunningly pretty under the blush pink of an early-morning sky. His daydream was interrupted by Mother's no-nonsense tones.

"Mr. Helfort. We shall shortly be levelling off at 10,250 meters. Calvert Control authorizes you to take control at that time. Any departure outside approved flight pipe Purple 24 Alfa will result in my taking control for the remainder of the flight. Please acknowledge."

"Roger, Mother," Michael sighed resignedly. "Acknowledged."

"Thank you, Mr. Helfort." Mother's voice was firm.

As he took control, the flier was alive under Michael's hands as he reveled in the crisp responsiveness of the Honda machine, turning off the machine's AI-controlled ride-smoothing system so that he could fly through the occasional bump as the flier hit small patches of low-grade clear air turbulence.

All of a sudden the weight of the last few months dropped off his shoulders as he enjoyed the simple pleasure of flying.

Above him, the sky, broken only by a light scattering of high altocumulus clouds, and the occasional contrails of a high-flying jet, had turned a deep blue as they cleared the salt haze pulled off the Equatorial Sea by the nearly constant southeast trades. Out to the left, the early-morning sun had cleared the horizon and was beginning to make its presence felt; Michael had to have Mother darken the plasglass to compensate.

Three hundred kilometers south of Calvert, the flier crossed the southern coast of the Calvert Peninsula. Ahead of him, Michael could see nothing but the endless blue of the Coral Bight, broken by atolls of fast-growing geneered coral; immense irregular patches of white shaded down through every tint of blue imaginable until blending into the cobalt of the deep ocean, their windward edges fringed with brilliant white necklaces of broken surf. Beyond the bight lay the Atalantan Mountains, with six peaks over 15,000 meters, but they were more than 1,000 kilometers ahead of him; Michael doubted he would see them before the turn to the southwest.

The minutes passed as Michael flew onward, happy and content for the first time in months, the journey interrupted only by a steady stream of traffic information as the flier wove its way through the mass of flight pipes funneling early-morning traffic into Calvert from Manaar, York, and the Petrov spaceport to the east.

Five hundred kilometers southeast of Calvert, Michael banked the flier onto a course that would see him across the Tien Shan Mountains and on his final approach to the Palisades, the mountain retreat of the Helfort family and the perfect place, he thought, to recover both physically and spiritually.

The flier whispered on; Michael was immersed in the simple routines of flying until finally the peaks of the Tien Shan began to take shape in front of him. They were emerging slowly from the surface haze, as awe-inspiring and spectacular as the first time he remembered seeing them as a little boy.

From the broad, mangrove-fringed coastal plain that ran across the foot of the Coral Bight from New Beijing in the north to Harbin in the south, thickly wooded slopes of geneered hardwoods rose up into the foothills before giving way to conifers and then scrubby bushes, mosses, and lichens. Finally, at almost 7,000 meters, even the geneered vegetation introduced to Ashakiran centuries earlier had to admit defeat. Above that point, only broken rock and snow covered the steep slopes running up to the awesome granite cliffs of Mount Izbecki to the left—all 15,690 meters of it and to this day conquered only by cliffbot-assisted climbers—and its equally imposing sisters to the right. As Michael flew across the coast and into the foothills, steadily lifting the flier to the 12,500 meters needed to cross the Tien Shan, Mount Izbecki and its companions came into sight,

Mount Clarke and Mount Christof at 14,990 and 14,450 meters, respectively, the jet stream ripping long tails of cloud thick with ice and snow off their rocky summits.

And then, finally, between mountain peaks to the left and right and framed by sheer granite cliffs rising impossibly sheer for more than 2,000 meters, the High Pass appeared, visible at first as little more than a thin dark streak down the face of the huge cliffs between the Izbecki and the Clarke-Christof massifs. Slowly the streak opened up as the flier closed in to reveal a narrow gorge. Not for the first time Michael wondered at the arrogance of pushing a tiny flier into a narrow pass more than 12,000 meters above sea level with no place to go but straight ahead.

"Mother, positive nav check, please." Michael wanted to make absolutely sure that the 800-meter-wide gap he was heading for at 1,000 kph was the right 800-meter-wide gap and not some dead end.

"Confirmed. In pipe Purple 24 Alfa for transit of the High Pass en route to the Palisades," Mother responded confidently.

Good, Michael thought as he eased the flier back to a more sedate 500 kph. He would hate to have to do a screaming high-g turn in front of a cliff that the flier couldn't climb over.

And then Michael was into the High Pass itself, the walls suddenly closing in on him at a truly frightening rate. The granite cliffs rushed past, an impossible blur, and all of a sudden he was seized with an outrageous sense of joy. Thumping and crashing through the turbulence of jet stream winds howling through the gash in the Tien Shan, the Honda was firm and true under his hands as Michael followed the twists and turns of the High Pass, the huge canyon weaving its way between the two giants of the Tien Shan. At times less than 300 meters above the snow and massive jagged rocks of the pass, the Honda slamming and bucking in the turbulent air thrown up from the broken ground, Michael could see the flier's shadow racing ahead of him like some demented thing careless of what lay ahead as the rising sun squeezed its way down to ground between high rock walls.

Mother brought him back to reality.

"Caution. Approaching lower limit of flight pipe. Minimum permissible altitude on this pipe segment is 12,400 meters. Maintain altitude or return control to Mother." If Mother's voice could have sounded cranky, it would have. Michael sighed as he pulled the flier clear of the flight pipe's lower limit, the moment gone. But still, what a moment it had been.

Minutes later, Michael reefed the flier around in a last tight turn to the left, the High Pass rushing past his window, seemingly so close that he could touch the snow. Then the sheer cliffs of Mount Izbecki dropped away in a heart-stopping fall down to the jumbled, cracked, and fissured surface of the Radski Glacier, the vast white expanse of its broken surface streaked gray and brown, long lines of rock ground off the valley walls scarring the pristine white surface of the ice below.

What a sight it was. Drawing ice from four smaller feeder glaciers high above it, the glacier cascaded in frozen disarray almost 7,000 meters down steep-walled valleys cut knife-edged into the sheer face of Mount Izbecki before melting into the pale waters of Radski's Lake, a blue-green gem opalescent even in the morning shadows and framed by a tangled white, black, and gray confusion of snow, rock, and debris. Away from the wall of broken ice feeding into the lake, the Bachou River flowed across a broad rock lip before dropping in a plume of broken water and spray toward the valley floor a good 1,000 meters below. The plume of water shredded into a fine white spray long before it reached the bottom, tendrils of mist eddying and curling across and down the rock face as they fell.

Taking care to stay well within the approved flight pipe, Michael put the flier into a circle to lose height. The massive bulk of the glacier below the lander wheeled past the plasglass as the flier orbited slowly downward.

And then, finally, 500 meters above Radski's Lake and with the lonely granite pillar marking the grave of Samuel Radski plainly visible on the shattered and chaotic slopes below the glacier, Michael turned the flier homeward down and across the Bachou River as it rushed from the Radski down to join the Clearwater. Ahead of and below him, plainly visible in the clear air, lay the thickly wooded hilltop on which the Palisades had been built.

Michael was almost home. He cut the power to idle, disengaged noise reduction, and, angling the flyer sharply downward, began the final approach.

The Palisades was an unremarkable house in all ways but one.

Quite small and rectangular in shape, it was made of the local fine-grained red hardwood for which the valley of the Clearwater River, cutting its way for thousands of kilometers across the heart of Van Manaan's Land, was famous. The house was blessed with a large west-facing deck that ran across the entire front from one end to the other and from which the huge prairie that filled the basin of the upper Clearwater Valley ran away into the distance, backdropped by massive banks of clouds coming off the Karolev Ranges hundreds of kilometers to the southwest. Another southerly buster coming, he thought. Behind the house, the enormous bulk of Mount Izbecki rose impossibly tall and sheer above him, looking for all the world as if it were about to topple forward onto the house below. Just an illusion, Michael had to remind himself, so powerful was the feeling of imminent destruction.

It was an overwhelming, awesomely beautiful place and one that firmly reminded him how insignificant he and his affairs were.

A bottle of Lethbridge pilsner close at hand, Michael sat waiting for his father to clean up after coming up-valley from the little town of Bachou where his post-Fleet business—geneering and growing the glorious red-flowered, deep purple- and green-leafed Flame tree—was based.

A bang of the screen door announced his father's arrival, his own beer securely in hand. Seconds later, Michael was engulfed in his father's characteristic no-holds-barred hug. Finally, they broke apart. His father was the first to speak.

"I have been so worried about you. It's good to have you home. Mom had some stuff to do. She'll be up later, and with a bit of luck Samantha will have caught the shuttle from Manindi." Always "Samantha" and never "Sam," Michael noted in passing.

A long pause followed as the two looked at each other. Michael broke the silence.

"Dad . . ." Michael's voice cracked; he couldn't go on.

Andrew Helfort's hand went up. "Michael, my boy. I've spoken to Admiral al-Rawahy and to Admiral Fielding, so I know all about what really happened. Let's not talk about it anymore. The sooner you put it behind you, the better."

Michael's voice was thick with emotion. "I know, Dad. Fielding was great, and so was Bukenya. I know what I have to do, and I will do it. But why, Dad, why?"

"Who knows, Michael, who knows? They are a bad bunch, the men in the d'Castreaux family. As long as anyone can remember, they always have been, and it looks like they always will be. It's a pity. Gaby d'Castreaux's okay, though why she'd marry a pig like Jean-Luc is beyond me." Andrew Helfort frowned. "But the one thing you have to remember is that it's not personal. If d'Castreaux Junior is anything like his father, and I am sure he is, then you were just in the wrong place at the wrong time. Just another easy target of opportunity."

Andrew Helfort took another long sip of his beer. "So tell me. How did you come from Terranova?"

"Cheng Space Lines, on their new ship, *Reliant*. Very nice, if interstellar travel can ever be nice. Crap connections, though. As usual."

Andrew Helfort laughed. Some things never changed. "Cheng Lines are a good bunch. I know Anson Cheng; he's a Flame tree collector, and he seems to like what we do. Though they are all good these days, even Prince Interstellar. Gaby d'Castreaux is a pretty straight shooter; her people seem to like and respect her, which is more than I've ever heard anyone say about Jean-Luc. Imagine being saddled with someone like him," his father said.

Andrew Helfort took a deep breath before continuing. "You know that d'Castreaux Senior was medically discharged?"

"I did know. It was common knowledge at the college, mostly because there was a feeling that it had nothing to do with medicine at all—hard to pin down; nobody really knew anything definite. But asking questions was always a good way to upset d'Castreaux Junior, so it was just rumors. You know what Space Fleet is like."

"I do. Suffice it to say that all I know, and God knows it's enough, is that d'Castreaux Senior is a psychopathic killer with a taste for torture." His father's face was taut with distaste, eyes narrowed and mouth a thin tight line. "But a coward with it, never willing to take much risk, which slowed him up a bit, thank God."

Michael's shock was complete, not just at the news but at his father's very matter-of-fact delivery. "So how was he caught?"

"That's the problem; he never was. Well, not officially. And it was only Admiral Fielding's persistence that got rid of the bastard. Fielding was skipper of the *Cheng Ho* at the back end of the Third Hammer War, back in . . . oh, '79 it would have been. Youngest planetary assault vessel captain ever, as I recall. Anyway, Fielding's ops officer blew the whistle on d'Castreaux; at the end of the war, d'Castreaux had been detached from *Cheng Ho* to clear out one of the Hammer's space battle stations, and he was unable to resist the temptation to deal with some Hammer prisoners his way rather than in accordance with the Geneva Convention. Fifteen of them there were, and while I wouldn't piss on a Hammer if he was on fire, I couldn't do what d'Castreaux did."

As he took another sip of his beer, Andrew Helfort's face was hard. For all that the Third Hammer War had ended almost twenty years earlier, Michael knew how bitter the fight had been and how many good friends his parents had lost.

"So how come no one dropped d'Castreaux in it? Surely someone would have spoken up." Michael's face betrayed his puzzlement.

"Well, d'Castreaux might be a psychopathic killer, but nobody has ever said he's stupid. Far from it, actually. That bastard is as smart as they come. He made sure that his internal security team was involved as much as he was, God knows how. But people were very bitter at the end of the war. The massacre of the crews of the *Ardent* and the *Clementine*—almost two thousand men and most of them wounded—by those godless Hammer bastards had tempers running very high. So I suppose they rationalized it away somehow. Prisoner mutiny, they said. There was some forensic evidence to contradict the story but not enough to stand up in court. Not even enough to get a balance of probabilities finding, never mind a beyond-all-reasonable-doubt verdict."

Andrew Helfort took a long slow drink.

"No bodies to autopsy, you see; blowing the hull made sure of that. And by the time anyone suspected anything, the bodies were well away. God knows where they ended up." A long pause followed as Michael's father squinted into his beer. Another sigh.

"Anyway, no one would talk openly, and Jack Wilson, Fielding's ops officer, found out about it only when two of d'Castreaux's security team members got drunk and said too much one night. Boasting, they were, to one of Jack's petty officers. Said much too much. Bad mistake. A week later, one died in a backstreet brawl on Pasquale-V. A month after that, the other was left brain-dead by a suit malfunction, and that was what made up Fielding's mind. One could have been an accident, but two? Never. Fleet legal turned up some earlier incidents involving d'Castreaux that looked suspicious during the antipiracy campaigns around Kelly's Deep and Damnation's Gate in the early '70s, and he was implicated in the disappearance of a young couple on Jascaria when he was there on Admiral Leahy's staff as a lieutenant. That was back in the early '60s, I think. But the court AI's proof of guilt probability never got better than 58 percent, so no conviction was recorded. Pity. Only a few percent off a balance of probabilities finding, which would have been nice.

"So that's where things ended up, formally at least. Fielding finally got Space Fleet to pension d'Castreaux off on medical grounds. Even better, she made sure that the Anjaxx police were well briefed on his entertainment preferences. Fielding's cousin was commander of the Anjaxx federal police, and there was enough circumstantial evidence together with the court AI's proof of guilt rating to convince the Anjaxx high court to impose a permanent tracking order on him. So far as I know, he hasn't strayed since. He just sits in that bloody great big house of his outside Cotentin looking out across the Middle Sea, and long may he rot there."

The pain was clearly visible now. Suddenly, Michael realized that he had been told all he needed to know and that making his father relive the bitter years of the Third Hammer War was something he didn't want to do anymore.

Michael's hand went out to rest on his father's shoulder. "Dad, no more. I'll watch out for d'Castreaux Junior, that's for damn sure. And his day will come, depend on it."

Andrew Helfort looked up sharply. "Michael, promise me. Don't think about it anymore. Don't think about him. Concentrate on what's important. You hear me?"

Michael nodded.

"So, talking about what's really important, what's happened to the lovely Anna? Will we see her this time? Will—" Andrew Helfort's well-intentioned if unwelcome foray into Michael's love life was, much to Michael's relief, cut off in midquestion by the arrival of his mother's flier as it climbed steeply out of the valley below before turning with characteristic flair to land on the pad behind the trees, the mass driver briefly shattering the peace as she killed the flier's forward speed. Anna was not someone he found it easy to talk about even to himself and certainly not to his father.

"Come on, Dad. Mom's home. And I think I saw Sam." And with that, Michael was out of his seat and running through the house and out into the trees.

Dinner that night was quiet but relaxed and close with just the four of them. In the hearth, a fire blazed to fill the room with a red-gold warmth, while outside the rising wind signaled the outriders of the storm Michael had seen coming off the Karolev Ranges. By morning, it will probably be blowing an absolute bastard, he thought, and pissing with rain into the bargain.

Michael said very little during the meal, content to sit there as the tiredness washed over him in waves, contentment settling deep into his bones like balm. As ever, Sam took up the conversational slack, full of stories of life at the Manindi Center for Oceanic Research, where, at the ripe old age of eighteen going on nineteen, she had secured for herself a prime appointment as chief tank cleaner and general gofer since finishing school. With plans to become a serious marine biologist, Sam was in seventh heaven and made a point of ensuring that everyone knew it. Michael strongly suspected that the fact that Arkady Encevit, Sam's longstanding boyfriend, had managed to find himself a job in Harbin only 750 kilometers from Manindi, a job, what was more, that involved no weekend work, had a lot more to do with Sam's happiness than she was prepared to let on.

Michael awoke with a start. Christ, he had actually dozed off at the table, and so far as he could tell, he had just been told something significant. "Sorry, Mom. Missed that," he said.

"You did." Michael's mother smiled. "I always knew the college was good, but how on earth did they teach you to sleep sitting up and apparently paying full attention to what's going on?"

"Years of sitting through astrogation lectures, Mom. A necessary aid to survival. You should know."

Kerri Helfort smiled indulgently. "Michael, I was just saying that Sam and I have finally fixed a date to go see Aunt Claudia. We're—"

Kerri sighed as Sam cut her off, a bad habit the girl showed no signs of getting over. Sam never even noticed. "You can see Aunt Claudia all you want, Mom, but I'm going to see Jemma. It's been so long," she said firmly.

"Yes, dear, and Jemma's probably the only person in this universe that you would give up Arkady to go see." Game, set, and match to Mom, Michael thought as Sam sat back red-faced and suddenly silent. Michael laughed out loud at the sight and was rewarded by a scowl from Sam.

"Aunt Claudia," Michael said. "I never could work out why she had to up and go all the way out to the Frontier Worlds, but I'm sure she had her reasons. We haven't seen her for what, eight years?"

"Nine, actually, but who's counting? It's all arranged. We go on September sixth and should be back about three months later." His mother's face belied her confident tone of voice and betrayed the struggle going on inside her. Michael knew she badly wanted to see her sister again after so many years but was unhappy at leaving his father for so long, especially when the Flame tree seed harvest was due. Getting the seeds safely into storage was a tricky exercise at the best of times and not one she'd readily trust to Dad and his oafish, unreliable drinking buddy Maxwell Bassini. "Maybe we should wait until after the harvest—"

Andrew Helfort knew his wife well enough to see what was going through her mind. He leaned over and took her hand. "Don't you start again. We've been through this a million times. She's your only sister and you haven't seen her for a very long time, so you must go. You know you must. And it would be good for Samantha to catch up with Jemma. So stop thinking about me. I'll be fine. I've got Maxwell to help out at harvesttime. And despite what you think of him, he's not a complete idiot." Except after too many beers, Michael thought.

Michael broke the awkward silence that followed. "Well, one thing I do know is that Jackson is a long way away. The trip will take how long?"

Sam had it all worked out. "Fourteen days, and that's including the time to get to Terranova first. Of course, I'm going to miss Arkady terribly, but I think it's worth it even if we take ages to get there. Jemma vidmailed me, and there's so much to do and she says the people are really nice and she's dying for her friends to be able to meet me and I think we'll have a great time." Sam finally ran out of breath.

"Arkady, where are you?" Michael whispered teasingly.

Sam ignored him. "As I was saying, fourteen days there and fourteen days back gives us a good two months on Jackson. I bet we won't want to leave, 'specially not to come back to a cruel pig like you, Michael Helfort!"

After a short flight down from the Palisades, Michael got the flier safely back in the hands of Avis. The sheer pleasure of flying the little Honda across the impossibly rugged landscape around the Palisades had been more than enough to make the uncomfortably high cost of hiring it bearable.

The rest of Michael's leave passed in a tornado of furious activity as he attempted unsuccessfully to cram into two and a half weeks all the things he had planned to do in four. A riotous reunion with his friends in Bachou (that was two days gone, of which Michael remembered almost nothing), a four-day trip to surf the Point Barrow break, on a good day, the most perfect left-hander in the entire universe, and then a couple of days to catch up with Charles Mbeki, who was killing time waiting for his ship, the venerable heavy cruiser *Arcturus,* to return from patrol.

But finally his time was up. After the duty visits to family—his mother's instructions had been quite clear that they were not optional—and with less than a week before he had to leave to join his new ship, the less than romantically named deepspace light scout *DLS-387,* he was on his way home to wrap things up, and then he'd be on his way.

Saturday, August 22, 2398, UD
Outside the Diplomatic Compound, City of McNair,
Commitment Planet

The fear gripping Digby felt like a hand plunged deep inside his stomach trying to pull his guts out.

The stress of making his way unseen every second night,

ducking and weaving to avoid the random Doctrinal Security
patrols, was beginning to tell. Worse, time was starting to run
out. This was his last chance. If he couldn't get to Kumar unnoticed this morning, Kumar would not be able to get any
messages up to the fortnightly routine starship courier to
Sylvania—leaving in less than eighteen hours, for Kraa's
sake—for onward transmission to the Feds in time for them
to do something about the *Mumtaz*. And that assumed that
Kumar took him seriously enough to order the mership to
drop out of pinchspace to make the pinchcomm transmission.

Digby could just imagine how a commercial mership skipper, even one under contract to the Sylvanian government,
would respond to that suggestion.

The only thing about Kumar's routine he had managed to
establish was that the bloody man didn't really have one.

Some mornings—Digby laughed bitterly; on this planet,
that could mean anything from broad daylight to, as now,
pitch darkness—Kumar jogged alone. Sometimes, in company. Sometimes, not at all. Sometimes, three days in a row.
Sometimes, not for a week. The only thing definite about
Kumar was that when he did go jogging, he always left the
compound between 06:00 and 06:10. Even better, DocSec
had given up escorting him as it should have; the prospect of
running in the dark early-morning hours clearly was not to
the taste of the average and usually overweight DocSec
trooper.

So it was that Digby stood in the deep blackness of the
trees shading the Avenue of Heroes as it ran up to the one and
only gate giving access to the diplomatic compound and
waited.

Twenty agonizing minutes later and with a heavy heart, he
tasted the bitter fruits of failure. The road from the diplomatic compound had remained empty, the only sign of life
being the bored DocSec guards at the compound gate. Digby
stood in the shadows, lost. He had been sure that, provided
that he was prepared to take the terrible risk, and he was,
there would be a chance to slip a message into Kumar's hand
in time to avert the catastrophe. But Kraa had decided other-

wise. Now he had missed the starship due out that night, and the next one wouldn't go out for another two weeks. Even if he could get a message to Kumar, the man would have one hell of a job getting a seat on any starship at all with the Establishment Day holidays coming up. Digby cursed his fate. It was getting too late.

Digby waited in the shadows, undecided. Did he give up and hope for the best, or did he at least try to lessen the damage by making it clear to the Feds that the entire affair was the unilateral action of a chief councillor gone mad? Would they even believe that? he wondered. He wasn't at all sure that he would. But it was all he could hope for now, to lessen the blow that would surely fall on the Hammer Worlds. He slipped away through the darkness unseen.

He knew he had no choice. He would have to be back in two days to do it all over again. He'd gone too far to turn back now.

Friday, August 28, 2398, UD
Torrance Airport, Ashakiran Planet

Michael turned to walk through security and onto his flight back to the Arcadia spaceport, from where he would catch the up-shuttle to the planetary transfer station.

Behind him stood his mother, teary-eyed, and his father, tight-lipped. It would be months before Michael saw them again, but that was part and parcel of Space Fleet life, as they knew better than he did. Worse, he wouldn't be seeing Anna.

She had commed him to say that *Damishqui*'s program had been changed at short notice to go to Anjaxx and that their two ships would be berthed together on SBS-22 for eighteen glorious hours. But just as Michael's elaborate plans to make the most of the few hours they would have together had begun to take shape, another comm had come in from Anna. It was as unwelcome as it was short and to the point. *Damishqui*'s program had been changed again, and they would miss each other by a day. Sorry, can't be helped. Love and kisses, Anna.

Michael cursed his luck, the Fleet, *Damishqui*, and anything else he could think of.

So slowly that the change had been almost imperceptible, he'd begun to miss Anna, really miss her. That was not surprising, he realized, since he'd spent the best part of three years with her at the college, not really appreciating that graduation meant they would go their separate ways.

"Shit, shit, shit," he muttered aloud as he made his way to the identity station, automatically presenting himself for the routine DNA and retinal checks. No wonder Space Fleet people had trouble keeping a relationship going. They were never together long enough for there to be a relationship.

Michael shut Anna out of his mind and turned his attention to a more immediate concern: the reception that awaited him onboard *DLS-387*. Michael hoped that Fielding's call to his new skipper would at the very least mean that he'd be given a fair chance. Oh, well, he thought as he joined the line to make his way onboard the up-shuttle, only one way to find out. Thirty-five minutes later, as the shuttle blasted its way into orbit en route to the huge transfer station hanging in geostationary orbit, Michael put his seat back. Seconds later, despite the chorus of oohs and aahs of the space travel virgins transfixed by the magical holovid image of Ashakiran as it fell away below the incandescent mass driver plumes of the up-shuttle, he was asleep.

Sunday, August 30, 2398, UD
Deepspace Light Scout 387 Berthed on Space Battle Station 20, in Orbit around Anjaxx Planet

"Welcome aboard, sir. Identity check and orders, please." Even as she saluted, the quartermaster's voice betrayed none of the fun she'd had watching the young officer make a complete mess of crossing the line. She'd known he would do that the second it became obvious that he wasn't going to use the lubber's rail, because crossing the line was not the straightforward exercise it first appeared. As one approached any berthed starship, up was definitely and without doubt up. Down was down. Left was left. Right was right. Easy and, after millions of years of evolution, something the human mind was well able to manage.

But as you crossed the line that marked the change from the space battle station's artificial gravity to ship's artificial gravity, up could be down or sideways or all three mashed together. In this particular case, *387* was berthed so that horizontal became down by way of a sharp, almost 90-degree lean backward coupled with a slight right-hand twist. And Leading Spacer Matthilde Bienefelt had seen everyone from admirals down to the youngest and most inexperienced recruit ignore the lubber's rail and make a mess of a deceptively simple problem: how to cross a red and white striped line, adjust to a new gravity field, and maintain some semblance of balance, control, and dignity in the space of less than a second. But after more than twenty years in Space Fleet, Bienefelt knew full well that the human brain simply could not cope with the instantaneous rearrangement of the forces of gravity through three axes and that Junior Lieutenant Helfort was wasting his time trying. His brain's balance control system would stay shut down until it was ready to cope. That, of course, was why the lubber's rail was provided, though a remarkably large number of spacers let ego override common sense and ignored it.

He would learn, Bienefelt thought, standing patiently as Michael scrambled his way across the threshold and fell rather than climbed down the ladder into the ship's surveillance drone deployment air lock. He arrived at her feet standing up, thanks to a desperate lunge for the ladder handrail.

After a few seconds and conscious that he, like generations of junior officers before him, had just made a complete

ass of himself, Michael's brain came back online and he recovered his balance and composure, if not his dignity. He
presented his thumb for DNA checking and his left eye for
retinal scanning and then commed his orders to Bienefelt,
marking his formal arrival onboard Space Fleet's second
youngest deepspace light scout, the name-challenged *DLS-
387*.

Michael didn't approve of warships not having names, but
Space Fleet policy was unshakable. In its view, there were
simply too many small ships—light scouts like *387,* courier
ships, and a multitude of small auxiliary support ships—to
give each one a name. So numbers it was, something
Michael had always thought depersonalized a ship. That was
a pity. With its master AI, a ship was in a way a living thing
and as such deserved better. Still, that was the way things
were, and he'd never be able to change them.

"Thank you, sir. Welcome aboard. I'm Leading Spacer Bienefelt, and I'm in your division." Bienefelt stuck out a hand
the size of a plate and proceeded to crush Michael's in a grip
like a steel vise. Michael resolved on the spot not to argue
with Bienefelt unless it was absolutely necessary. She was at
least forty centimeters taller than he, maybe more, and probably a good 50 kilos heavier, to the point where she was as
close to being declared a cyborg as any Worlder he'd ever
seen; she'd make Karen Sutler look small. In fact, if she were
any larger, she might be declared an illegal and expelled
from the FedWorlds.

"Sir, the captain asked that you see him as soon as you
came aboard; he's in his cabin."

Michael grimaced. He needed a shower. "What do you
think, Leader? Time to change?"

"I think you'll find that when the skipper says now, he generally means now, sir."

"Oh, okay."

"You have the ship schematics, sir?"

"I do, thanks, Leader. Can someone take my stuff to my
cabin, please." Michael gestured at the battered trunk and a
couple of smaller bags, all of which had been unceremoniously dumped just outside *387*'s open air lock by the bag-

gage bot and containing everything that Space Fleet deemed necessary for the proper conduct of his duties.

"No worries, sir. Leave it with me. Karpov, you fucking worm." Bienefelt turned to the young spacer standing slightly behind and to one side of the quartermaster's desk, "Gear. Junior Lieutenant Helfort's cabin. Now. You've got two minutes."

Bienefelt turned back to Helfort. "I've commed the captain to let him know you are on your way. Anything else I can help you with, sir?"

"No thanks, Leader. It's good to be aboard."

"Good to have you, sir."

Michael hoped she meant it.

And with that, Michael brought up the ship's schematics on his neuronics, nominated the captain's cabin as his destination, and set off through the massive doorway that opened from the drone deployment air lock into the brightly lit drone hangar deck. He paused a moment to catch his breath. Ahead of him, blackly menacing in their stealth coats of radio frequency and light absorbent material, sat two massive Mark 88-K surveillance drones, to the human eye just two bottomless holes. The nothingness was absolute, so completely did they absorb the light thrown at them.

Along the hangar walls, six smaller drones sat in two neat rows on the gray ceramsteel deck, three to a side. My babies, he thought, just the things to keep an assistant warfare officer busy. His neuronics pointed the way down through a small personnel hatch set in the deck to his right.

Michael dropped down the ladder onto 2 Deck, the upper accommodation level, and followed a passageway lined with the usual clutter of pipe work and cabling broken up every so often by damage control lockers, firefighting equipment, and all the other odds and ends that warships used passageways to store. Michael went forward for 10 meters or so before dropping down another hatch in spacer style, boots on the outside of the ladder, hands braking his fall at the very last minute, to thump onto 3 Deck. The ship's main cross-passage, leaving the galley and the wardroom on the left and the combat information center on the right, finally brought him to the captain's cabin at the far end. He hadn't passed another soul. Not surprising, he thought, this early on a Sunday morning. He'd be in bed if he had the choice.

Michael stopped outside the closed door to straighten the rather rumpled clothes he'd been wearing since he had left home. Taking a couple of deep breaths, he knocked on the door.

"Yes, Helfort, come in." The voice was incredibly deep, with rich warm overtones.

Should have been an opera singer, Michael thought irreverently as he stepped into his new captain's cabin.

Twenty minutes later, any irreverence Michael might have felt toward Lieutenant Jean-Pierre Ribot, JP to his friends and captain-in-command of the Federated Worlds warship *DLS-387,* had evaporated in the face of a very detailed statement of what Ribot expected him to do to become a useful member of *387*'s command team. And with the ship due out on patrol in forty-eight hours, the list of things he had to do before it departed seemed to be a million strong. But first things first.

After a badly needed shower, Michael changed into a dark gray one-piece ship suit marked only by his shoulder badges of rank, his name tag, and the deep purple starburst of the Federated Worlds on the left breast. The ship badge that belonged on his upper right arm would have to wait until he could find someone to issue him one from stores.

With the transition from crumpled space traveler to ship's officer complete, he commed Mother. Her avatar was the pleasant face of a middle-aged woman, calm and unflappable and, like most Worlders, the color of milky coffee.

"Welcome aboard *DLS-387,* Junior Lieutenant Helfort." It was a velvet voice, as calm and unflappable as her avatar.

"Thank you, Mother. Please call me Michael."

"Certainly. Welcome aboard *DLS-387*, Michael."

Michael smiled. An AI with a sense of humor?

"Mother, since it's early and most of my division, not to mention my new boss, are away on weekend leave, I would like to get the ship knowledge and safety test out of the way first. Can you set up the guided tour for me? I'll see if I can get it done this morning. I've been through the induction material and done the sims, but this is the first time in years that I've actually been in a light scout."

"Stand by. Ship knowledge and safety induction tour set up. We'll start on 4 Deck aft in propulsion and primary power. Please follow the arrows." As Mother finished, Michael's neuronics pointed the way to the nearest hatch and he set off.

Four hours later, Mother had taken Michael into every compartment, every corner, every recess of *DLS-387*, and there had been a hell of a lot of ship to see. She had taken him through every system onboard end to end, including, and this had been a particular thrill for Michael, the personnel and ship waste recycling system. If he didn't know better, he could have sworn that this particular AI definitely had a sense of humor. She had taken an awfully long time making sure he knew the full intricacies of a system that most were happy to leave to the engineers.

Finally, the induction tour over, Michael sat in his tiny cabin on 2 Deck, eyes half-closed as he successfully navigated his way through the ship knowledge and safety test before finishing up with the two mandatory damage control sims: first a catastrophic loss of hull pressure after a collision with a large meteorite and second a fire. Heart pounding and covered in sweat, Michael and his imaginary team, most of whom had to be directed more firmly than he was used to, finally had extinguished the fire that had threatened to engulf most of 3 Deck from its starting point in the galley.

He sat back to wait for his score.

Mother was not long, and she did not disappoint.

"Thank you for waiting, Michael. I'm happy to tell you that you have achieved a score of 98 percent, thereby passing the mandatory ship knowledge and safety test. I will update your personnel file accordingly and inform the captain, the executive officer, and Lieutenant Hosani."

Michael breathed out with relief. While he had never been in any doubt—Michael was nothing if not good at passing tests after three years of Space College—it was still good to get this hurdle, the first of many, no doubt, out of the way. "Any idea when the XO and Lieutenant Hosani will be back onboard?"

"Yes, I've just gotten an update. They'll both be on the up-shuttle from Anjaxx scheduled to arrive at 20:25 tonight."

"Fine. Can you let them know I've arrived?"

A short pause. "Done, Michael."

"Thanks, Mother."

With that, Michael turned his attention to the next thing on his very long list: space-suit setup. He commed the duty safety equipment operator, one Senior Spacer Carlsson, and arranged to pick up his suit. Setup would take an hour or so, and then lunch would be a damn fine thing.

Michael set off to find Carlsson, who according to Mother was testing one of the lifepods right aft and down on 4 Deck.

Sunday, August 30, 2398, UD
Outside the Diplomatic Compound, City of McNair,
Commitment Planet

Digby stood, as he had done on so many dark mornings, alone on the Avenue of Heroes.

Running away from him all the way down to the Grand Corniche that fronted the eastern shores of the Koenig Channel, carefully shaded streetlights threw sharply distinct pools of orange light, stretching away like a long double string of exotic pearls. Massive trees flanked the road, visible only as ink-black shapes against the star-studded sky; well set back, the anonymous shapes of government buildings loomed gray and forbidding.

As he hung back from the street safe in the deep shadows thrown by the trees, Digby was beginning not to care whether Kumar appeared. He'd seen the bloody man only once in the last ten days, and then in the company of two other men. Thank Kraa, he'd decided to get his wife out-system; confirmation that she'd made it to Scobie's World safely had come as a huge relief. The risks he had been taking had been hard enough to bear; they would have been infinitely harder to take knowing that Jana, too, would suffer if he was arrested loitering close to the diplomatic compound for no good reason.

He did have his running gear on. Even brigadier generals of marines were supposed to stay fit, after all.

Digby comforted himself with the knowledge that for all its fearsome reputation, Doctrinal Security was as slack as most security organizations without an immediate and obvious threat to deal with seemed to be. Its supposedly random patrols were far from random, and Digby would have sworn before Kraa that at least half of them wouldn't have seen an elephant standing at the side of the road unless it was painted bright pink and floodlit with a strobe light nailed to its head. He'd been a marine for far too long not to recognize the signs of low morale, poor discipline, and weak leadership at a glance. He'd even had to dodge the shattered remains of a beer bottle thrown from a jeep as it sped past.

Then, all of a sudden, there was activity at the compound gate. A light came on to reveal a man talking to the gate guards, but it was too far away to tell if he was Kumar. Please, let it be him and nobody else, Digby pleaded, his heart thudding. Please let it be Kumar and let him be alone. Digby waited in impatient agony. They must know him well, he thought, as the faint sounds of laughter came down the avenue. They seemed very chummy; maybe it was not Kumar.

Finally, the man was off and running. Kumar. Please Kraa, let it be Kumar. Nerves jangling, Digby turned and moved down the road to a position 50 meters short of the first cross-street, turning every so often to track the man coming toward him.

And Kumar it was, and thank Kraa, he was alone.

Almost before Digby knew it, Kumar was on him.

"Captain Kumar, it's Julius Digby," he hissed. "Don't slow

down. Keep running and turn right at the cross-street and stay close to the trees. I must talk to you."

And with that, Digby was off through the shadows, hoping like hell that Kumar wouldn't do what common sense would tell him to do: turn around and go straight home.

Moments later, Kumar rounded the corner, jogging steadily up the Avenue of Martyrs toward the sea some 3 kilometers in front of him, hugging the curb, running in and out of the shadows. Suddenly he stopped, bending down as though to adjust an overly tight shoe.

"You've got twenty seconds, Digby, and then I'm gone." Kumar's voice was harsh. No Sylvanian would ever trust a Hammer, and for all Kumar knew, this could be entrapment.

"Ashok, you must trust me. I have a message capsule here for you. It will open only when you say the passphrase 'concurrent,' that's 'concurrent.' Please repeat."

"Concurrent," Kumar replied shortly. "Five seconds."

"Okay. Meet me 100 meters down the road and I'll hand the capsule over. Then I'm gone. You'll know what to do when you read it. If you're stopped, for Kraa's sake, wipe it or I'm a dead man."

The Sylvanian ambassador's normally deep ebony face was gray with anger. He had lost family and friends when Jesmond had been nuked by the Hammer and had little reason to put any faith in them or their works. And now this.

"Ashok, we have to give the Feds time to stop this insanity."

"I wish we could." Kumar's frustration was obvious. "Our next starship courier is, uh, yes, September fifth. The *Dnieper.* If we can get her turned around quickly, there's a chance we can pinchcomm the Feds on Terranova in time to stop the hijacking, but it'll be very tight. Needless to say, asking the Hammer to let us use their pinchcomms system is not an option. I've checked the outbound starships to Scobie's World. All full, thanks to the Establishment Day holidays, with the waiting lists closed as usual. And of course, thanks to Mr. Murphy, the Feds' next courier doesn't arrive until the seventh. So it's got to be the *Dnieper*. Unless, that is, we confront the Hammer now and let them know that we know what they are up to."

Ambassador Kwashomo's hands went up. "We don't even know if this is just an elaborate hoax. And if we do confront them, then what? We have no proof, and everyone involved will be dead by the end of the day. And even if they did believe us, Merrick would go in the usual Hammer bloodbath, to be replaced by God knows which councillor. Probably that devious man Polk. And then the usual Hammer bullshit: We didn't know, it wasn't our fault, blame Merrick, it was his fault, we are so sorry." The ambassador stopped, conscious that he had come close to losing control. "So what do we do?"

Kumar was emphatic. "I think that we have to sit on it at this end. Toppling Merrick, much as we all despise the man, on the basis of a single unsubstantiated report is not our decision to make. I think that it is ultimately up to the Feds to decide what they want to do. The *Mumtaz* is their ship, after all."

"I agree." Kwashomo was equally emphatic. "We cannot stop the project from going ahead, so let's not add any new variables by forcing any changes at this end. Merrick is a madman, but better the madman we know than somebody new. A new madman, dear God! Imagine Polk—the man is such a xenophobe, even for a Hammer. Just what we don't need. The *Dnieper* it is."

"I'll get on it."

Monday, August 31, 2398, UD
DLS-387, *Berthed on Space Battle Station 20, in Orbit around Anjaxx*

Michael fidgeted as he waited for his captain to arrive. Just his luck, he thought, for his first formal task onboard

387 to be acting as accused's friend for the black sheep of his division, one Spacer Angelina Athenascu. Not that Athenascu was a bad spacer, far from it. Her record showed her to be a hardworking, experienced, and competent member of Michael's surveillance drone team, someone to be relied on in a tough situation. But off duty was a different matter, and once again a space battle station's long-suffering provost marshal had delivered Athenascu, left eye a brilliant swollen patch of purple and red, apparently after she'd taken exception to the way a group of marines had talked about Space Fleet in general and light scouts in particular. Unfortunately for Athenascu, her ability to take on the marines had been degraded severely by a very long session in the Fleet club, and she hadn't been smart enough to slap on a detox patch before hurling herself off a table straight into the swinging right fist of the largest marine present.

By the time the patrol had arrived, the marines were long gone, having left Athenascu flat on her back complaining bitterly about marines who wouldn't stand and fight.

387's legal AI had processed all the evidence and, helped by Athenascu's plea of guilty, had duly returned a firm proof of guilt finding. It only remained for Ribot to accept the AI's findings—usually but not always a formality—and pass sentence. Michael's job was to persuade Ribot, against all the evidence, that Athenascu did in fact not make a habit of taking strong exception to marines, that this was a one-time occurrence, and that he should pass only a token sentence, preferably a caution. Michael didn't fancy his chances. With *387* about to deploy, the last thing Ribot would have wanted was to spend his time on was yet another of Athenascu's indiscretions. And it was on record that Ribot had warned her in no uncertain terms the last time around that he didn't want to see her at his table again.

Michael's pessimism was interrupted by the coxswain's stentorian voice as Ribot left his cabin to stand behind the plasfiber lectern that had been set up in the passageway. "Captain's Defaulters! Atten . . . shun."

Returning Chief Petty Officer Kathy Kazumi's snappily

precise salute, Ribot made his tone sternly formal. "Thank you, Coxswain."

"Good morning, sir. One defaulter, sir."

"Well, that's something, I suppose. Okay, let's get on with it."

"Sir. Spacer A. K. Athenascu FR4456778 charged with conduct prejudicial to good order and Fleet discipline in that she did commit common assault on the person of Marine G. J. Waddell MR8919034 in the Fleet club of Space Battle Station 20 at 02:40 Universal Time, Monday 31 August 2398 Universal Date."

Ribot sighed deeply. Michael certainly understood why. Legal protocol prevented Ribot from knowing in advance any more than the fact that he had defaulters to deal with. Who they were, what they had been accused of, how they'd pleaded, and what the legal AI thought all would come as a surprise and, in this case, a doubly unwelcome surprise, Michael had no doubt.

"Bring in the accused."

"Sir. Spacer Athenascu!" Kazumi's voice would have cut steel, and Michael was glad that he wasn't the one having to front Ribot.

"Sir." Athenascu appeared smartly from wherever she had been lurking, coming to a halt in front of Ribot with parade-ground precision, hands tightly tucked into her sides, eyes firmly locked on Ribot's impassive face.

As the coxswain went through the time-honored rituals of captain's table, Michael, now standing slightly behind and to the right of the hapless Athenascu, had little to do but listen as Athenascu confirmed her plea of guilty before the case for the prosecution was presented. Petty Officer Kazumi's experience showed as she simply and concisely summarized the evidence, and in only a matter of minutes the job was done, the legal AI formally confirming that it would be safe for Ribot to accept Athenascu's plea.

For a while, Ribot stood there in silence. He had the option of handing the case over for further consideration, but Michael suspected that Ribot, like most captains, hated hav-

ing disciplinary loose ends hanging around. Thus, it was no
surprise when Ribot announced to an impassive Athenascu
that the charge was proved.

Two minutes later, the theater of captain's table was over,
with Athenascu beating a hasty retreat from a clearly very
unhappy captain. Michael's request that Athenascu's good
professional record be taken into account had been treated
with duly grave consideration by Ribot, but Michael still
winced as Ribot smacked Athenascu with a 500-FedMark
fine and stoppage of fourteen days of leave effective on completion of their current mission. As Michael turned away to
follow Athenascu, Ribot caught his eye and waved him back.

"Sir?"

"Michael. That's the last time I want to see Athenascu at
my table. If I see her on a clear-cut case like this one again,
I'll have no choice but to recommend dishonorable discharge. While I hate to lose a good spacer, she's had all the
chances she's going to get. Space Fleet likes aggression in its
spacers but only when it's accompanied by self-control.
Make that clear to her and make sure she understands that
she has no more chances. None."

"Sir."

As Ribot walked away, radiating extreme unhappiness
with every step, Michael sighed deeply. This was not the
start he'd been hoping for. Oh, well, he mused, things can
only get better. In any case, he couldn't spend any more time
worrying about Athenascu. The final ops conference to review *387*'s upcoming mission was due to start in less than an
hour's time, and Michael intended to be fully prepared for it.

With the ops conference over and only a hurried break for
lunch, the rest of the day involved hard physical work for
Michael and his surveillance drone team, which also doubled as *387*'s cargo handlers.

Of course, Michael thought as he, Athenascu, and Leong
wrestled a recalcitrant cargo container into position outboard
of the mass driver storage bins on 3 Deck, the cargo always
arrives last, and late, and nobody can ever explain why. Despite the mission having been scheduled for more than three

months, the Defense Gravity Project had managed to get the massive gravitronics arrays up to SBS-20 only late that morning, leaving Michael and his team precious little time to get them secured by the XO's deadline of 18:00 that evening and get the ship patrol-ready.

Finally the massive container, painted a light blue to show that it was vented to space and required no external services, was secured and the locking pins were rammed home and checked visually. Mother signaled a secure lock and detached the cargobots, and Leong and Athenascu maneuvered up and out of the brightly lit cargo bay to await the next container.

Michael did the same thing and then paused for a moment.

Above him was the enormous spherical gray-black bulk of SBS-20, to which *387* was securely berthed, its 400-meter diameter dwarfing *387,* her stealthed hull a formless, bottomless, impenetrable black pit punctuated only by the brilliantly lit silvered inner surfaces of the open cargo hatches. Thousands of kilometers below him swam the glorious swirling blues and whites of Anjaxx itself. Beyond and above the planet hung its two moons, both silvery gray in the harsh light coming from Prime, Anjaxx's orange-red main sequence dwarf star only 81 million kilometers away. Providing the background to it all were the billions of diamond-sharp pinpoints of light that made up the rest of the galaxy. It was a sight Michael had never gotten used to and, if his parents were any guide, never would.

"Incoming, sir." Leong's comm interrupted his little reverie, and Michael turned to see the next container, another big one but this time a luridly bright green to show that it was pressure- and temperature-controlled. It swam slowly into view around the sharp curve of the battle station's outer hull, two Day-Glo orange cargobots attached one to each end, their mass driver thrusters firing brief silver-gold plumes of incandescent matter as they moved the container in a slow and carefully coordinated arc around SBS-20's hull.

Moving away from SBS-20, Michael made sure that he and his fellow cargo handlers were clear of the container's approach vector and would not be caught between *387* and the container as it closed; cargobots were very good, but nothing made by humans was infallible. The containers had a lot of mass and, once out of control, tended to stay that way until they either hit something or had been wrestled back under control. Even moving at less than a meter per second, the containers were lethal weapons. And the cargobots' mass driver plumes also had to be watched. The safety sims had some gruesome holovid of spacers who hadn't paid attention, and Michael had no intention of allowing any repeats.

As the container approached, the cargobots began to brake the container. Must be heavy, Michael thought, judging by the prolonged effort it took to bring the huge box to a dead stop 5 meters off the open cargo hatch. "Leong, take the Anjaxx side. Athenascu, the planet side. I'll go behind."

Leong and Athenascu, two bright strobe-marked orange shapes against the black nothingness of *387*, spun on the spot, stopped dead for a second, and then accelerated into position, turning at the last second to drop into place, perfectly set. Show-offs, Michael thought enviously as he maneuvered himself much more carefully and, he would have been the first to admit, clumsily into position. It would be a long time before he was as good as the worst spacer on *387*'s surveillance drone team, but then, they had had hundreds, in some cases thousands, of hours of practice. Michael commed the cargobots, confirmed that they had the correct cargo slot, checked that the team was clear, and then authorized the final approach. As always, despite the impressive finesse with which the cargobots handled the container, the last couple of centimeters required the combined efforts of all three of them to get the damn thing into position so that the locking pins could slide home.

Finally, the container was where it needed to be. Mother signaled a secure lock and detached the cargobots as Leong and Athenascu connected the thick armored power and ventilation umbilicals. Two minutes later, Mother was happy that this was one container that would survive the trip, and Michael and the team turned to await the next; this one, according to Mother, would be the last to go into the starboard 3 Deck cargo space.

* * *

It had been a long hard day by the time the last container had been pinned home and after an exhaustive gear check to make sure nothing had been left behind—captains got pretty upset if they had to stop acceleration to recover lost equipment rattling around loose in the cargo bays—and Michael could dismiss the team. He and Petty Officer Strezlecki did a last fly-past along the containers.

"Looks fine to me," Michael said as he checked out the last of the containers on the port side.

"Me, too, sir," Strezlecki confirmed. "All personnel clear and accounted for. All equipment accounted for. Button her up?"

"Yeah, go ahead."

Michael and Strezlecki pushed back as Mother turned off the cargo bay lights and one by one closed the massively thick armored access doors until all that was left was an absolute and total nothing. Michael knew *387* was there because logic told him it had not moved and he could see her shape as a black cutout against the gray-black hull of SBS-20. But all of a sudden, the sense of form, solidity, and mass, of firm reality that the open cargo doors had provided, was gone. All Michael could see was void, a pit into which he felt for one awful moment he was going to tumble.

Strezlecki also felt it. "That's something, isn't it? Never get used to it even after all these years." Her voice brought Michael back to his senses.

"Christ, thanks for that cheerful thought. I'd rather hoped I would get used to it."

"Never, sir, trust me," Strezlecki said confidently as they turned to make a final inspection of the hull to confirm that every cargo hatch had sealed as flush as Mother said it had, guided only by the ship schematics brought up on their neuronics. Finally, the job was done and they made their way back to the personnel access lock, the ship passing below them unseeable and unseen.

"Any thing else we—I—need to think about?" Michael didn't think there was, but it didn't hurt to ask.

"No, sir, that's it for today. I'm headed for the shower and then to the Fleet senior spacers club—got a birthday bash to attend." Strzlecki's voice made it clear that with a patrol scheduled to last almost two months less than twenty-four hours away, she intended to get in a final round of serious partying before they dropped.

"I wish I had half your luck. Quiet evening for me and then a decent night's sleep would be good." In the frantic scramble to get everything done in time, Michael had managed only about three hours of sleep since he had stepped—sorry, stumbled and fell—aboard *387*.

According to Michael's neuronics, they were only two meters from their destination, and in confirmation Mother opened the outer hatch of the forward personnel access lock. The brilliant white light from inside the ship seemed to come from nowhere.

"Age before beauty," Michael commed, pointing for Petty Officer Strzlecki to go first.

"Remember the rest of that aphorism, sir, and don't tempt me into saying something that should stay belowdecks," Strzlecki retorted as, without fuss or wasted effort, she pushed her boots into the air lock clear of the rungs of the ladder that dropped into the brightly lit space three meters below them. The ship's gravity tugged at her feet and drew her in, gloves braking the fall to drop her neatly to the deck.

Michael laughed. "I didn't want you to see what a screw-up I'm going to make of this," he said as he struggled to emulate Strzlecki's effortless move into the air lock without a great degree of success. First he wasn't dropping fast enough and then he was falling too fast, his boots thumping onto the deck, the weight of his suit almost forcing him to his knees. But finally he stood there as Strzlecki commed the close command to Mother and they waited as the outer hatch closed and the air lock pressure equalized. At last the flashing red light gave way to a steady green, and the inner door opened onto the drone hangar deck.

Ten minutes later, with suit turn-around completed, Michael stood there, his gray one-piece innersuit rumpled and sweat-stained. "That's it," he said to an equally disheveled Petty Officer Strzlecki. "Enjoy the party and I'll see you tomorrow."

"Sir."

As Michael turned to go below, the XO commed him. "Finished?" she asked.

"I have, sir, yes."

"Okay. My cabin, now."

"Sir." Shit. That didn't sound good. What now? Michael thought as he dived for the ladder down to 3 Deck.

Seconds later, Michael was at the XO's cabin. Seeing him at the door, she waved him into the one and only chair in the cramped compartment where Lieutenant Jacqui Armitage both lived and worked. For a couple of seconds, the young woman just stared at him from brown eyes set wide in a ruddy, almost windburned face overshadowed by a shock of barely controlled brown hair, her face a set of flat planes that made it look as if she had been chiseled out of stone. Her mouth had a firm set to it that all of a sudden told Michael that he wasn't there to be told what a good boy he was.

"Pretty good job you and your team did, Michael. You certainly look like you've been working hard."

"Thank you, sir. We have. Though I need a lot more practice before I'm as good as they are."

"That's what I knew you would think, Michael, and that's why I wanted to talk to you. Young officers are always over-impressed by space gymnastics." Armitage paused for a second. And here it comes, Michael thought, at a loss to know what he had missed. "I had Mother analyze the whole operation end to end, and she agrees with me. While acceptable, your oversight of the safety aspects of the operation was close to being compromised on three occasions. Have a look."

Armitage popped Mother's analysis up on Michael's neuronics. "See? Here you got so close in to the container that you missed Leong drifting off-station. A few more meters and he could have been in trouble. Now, he's a good spacer and caught himself in time. But you should have seen it first just in case he didn't. People with their heads down very often don't. And here, Leong again. And here, Athenascu. Too close to that mass driver efflux for comfort. So Michael, the moral of the story is this: You are paid to command, so stand back and command. You are not paid to be just another cargo handler. And nothing will lose you respect faster than a damaged team member. So learn the lesson and do better next time, okay?"

"Sir." There wasn't much Michael could say. Armitage was right.

"Okay. That's all. See you at supper tonight."

Tired but reasonably content even after the moderately severe singeing he had received from the XO, Michael sat quietly in the wardroom on 3 Deck.

Supper over, the wardroom was filled with the give-and-take of team members who knew one another well. Sitting at the mess table, Armitage and Michael's boss, Maria Hosani, were in the middle of a spirited debate on the relative merits of planetary life compared with life on orbital habitats. Michael suspected it was a debate months in the making and with many more to run. Sprawled in the two armchairs at the far end of the compartment in front of an impressive holovid of a large fireplace set into a stone wall, complete with a cheerfully blazing wood fire, were the navigator, Leon Holdorf, and John Kapoor, the proud commander of *387*'s lander, *Jessie's Hope*. Why *Jessie's Hope*? Michael had had to ask. Because, Kapoor had explained patiently, probably for the hundredth time, the rest of the crew wouldn't allow his first choice, *Mom's Hope,* so he'd had to settle for her first name, "Jessie." Yes, and the "Hope" bit, Michael had prompted. That he'd come home safely, Kapoor had said with a faint air of embarrassment and a shrug of the shoulders. Michael had laughed. He'd liked Kapoor from the moment they had met, and as the only other junior lieutenant onboard apart from Michael, he was a natural ally. Though not for long. Kapoor was about to pick up his second stripe.

Sitting next to them on one of the benches that ran down the length of the mess and as officer of the day the only person in uniform was *387*'s chief engineer, Cosmo Reilly. With the aid of a firmly pointed forefinger, Reilly was at that moment making the point very emphatically that warfare branch officers paid too little attention to engineers when it came to the conduct of Space Fleet business. Michael had to smile as he watched Reilly's impassioned diatribe. Long, long ago, Space Fleet had decided in its infinite wisdom that too much engineering was a bad thing for the officers responsible for fighting on the Federation's ships and had split engineering and warfare officers into two specialized streams. The merits of that decision still were hotly argued, a never-ending debate and one that Michael was sure went on in every mess in the Fleet most nights of the week.

Kapoor just couldn't resist. "I remember one time on the old *Zube—*"

"Don't you mean the *Zuben-el-Genubi*?" Reilly interrupted indignantly. "You bloody warfare types can't even get the names of your ships right."

The rest of the officers broke out laughing. Michael just smiled. Clearly, teasing Reilly by shortening ship names was one of those long-running gags that made small ship life bearable. Michael reckoned that Reilly played up to the rest of them by putting on the personality of a cantankerous old space dog.

"Enough of this," Reilly said, waving the debate to a halt as he climbed to his feet. "Time for a walk-around. Can't let the masses think management isn't paying attention." Michael was beginning to suspect that Cosmo Reilly was only half joking; of all the officers onboard, he was the most old-fashioned and almost always had an authoritarian tone to his voice. Be interesting to see what the troops think of him, Michael mused as Reilly left the mess.

Kapoor's voice interrupted his thoughts. "Michael, you're far too quiet. Get your fat ass over here and tell us what you think so far. But before you do, refill these glasses."

As instructed, Michael refilled the two port glasses at the little bar before sitting next to the fireplace, which, if it had been real, would have fried the lot of them long before.

Soon he was deeply involved in a debate about the merits or otherwise of the Honorable Valerie Burkhardt, the Fed

Worlds' current moderator, whether she and the New Liberals had any chance of being reelected to the government in the forthcoming elections, and whether Space Fleet would be better off with a new federal minister of defense given the view commonly held in the Fleet that the present incumbent was a party hack promoted not because she had any talent for the job but because she had a hold over Valerie Burkhardt. Soon the debate sucked in Armitage and Hosani, and by the time Reilly returned from his rounds, the wardroom was well into an appraisal of how the Space Fleet had had to put up with an endless succession of ambitious but not necessarily capable ministers and so on and so on.

Probably, Michael thought as he sat back to let the debate rage around him, if you did a survey, four or five topics would account for 80 percent of all conversation in officers' messes across the Fleet, and this was surely one of them.

Finally, he'd had enough. "If you'll excuse me, people, I am going to make this an early night. Big day tomorrow." He rose to his feet.

"Can't persuade you to step ashore to sample the delights of the Fleet O club? I think everyone else is up for it." Hosani's suggestion was tempting in the extreme, but Michael shook his head.

"Not this time, sir."

"Okay. Get your beauty sleep. God knows you need it."

"Night all, see you in the morning." With that, Michael turned and left. He really must vidmail his parents and reply to Anna's last comm before they left.

As the wardroom door hissed shut behind Michael, the group was quiet for a moment.

"What do you think of our latest recruit, Jacqui?" Holdorf looked at the XO, his face quizzical.

"Too soon to say. But he looks like he'll be okay. He did well enough today for his first time out, and he took the obligatory dressing down without complaint. Remember McPherson's first cargo op?" Armitage laughed as she recalled the three-ring circus that Michael's predecessor had managed to create. "And he turned out okay."

"What do you think, Maria?" Armitage asked.

"Like you said, not too bad for the first day. And he's certainly not hard on the eyes. Pity he's in the chain of command," Hosani said, aiming a playful wink at Armitage, who winced. An improper relationship in the chain of command? Now, that was the best definition of an XO's nightmare Armitage could think of.

Kapoor came to his feet. "Look, you lot! Enough. Time is getting on, and the O club calls. Are we on or not?" His insistent voice made everyone grin.

"I can't see any reason to hurry, can you? Time for a few more drinks?" Holdorf teased, "Unless of course there is a certain someone that John feels the need to get close to."

"Bastard. You know there is. So can we go?" Kapoor said, standing up. "Because if not, I'm off. Night, Cosmo. Keep her safe."

Tuesday, September 1, 2398, UD
DLS-387 Berthed on Space Battle Station 20, in Orbit around Anjaxx

"All stations, this is command. Stand by to drop in fifteen minutes."

The captain's voice jerked Michael back to reality. He and his team, now morphed from cargo handlers into *387*'s emergency extravehicular activity team, were assembled in the surveillance drone hangar, fully suited up with uniforms chromaflaged to Day-Glo orange and personal maneuvering units locked into position on their backs. The wait was beginning to tell on the team. The full EVA outfit added more than 30 kilos to each spacer's body mass. The only thing to do was to hunch forward and let the suit's inherent stiffness take some of the weight. We must look like a bunch of hunchbacked trolls, Michael thought, and big lumpy orange ones at that.

The team had been split into three groups. Two of Michael's team crew members stood by the forward personnel air lock, two waited aft, and the rest—four in all, including Michael, personal call sign Alfa—waited inside the big surveillance drone deployment air lock. Arranged around each group were emergency repair packs and laser cutting equipment. As he stood there, Michael wondered when an EVA team had last been needed in earnest.

He checked his neuronics. Ten minutes to go. "EVA team, this is Alfa. Close up suits, report when nitrogen-free," he commed, to be rewarded by the solid clunks of seven armored plasglass faceplates shutting. His followed quickly as the suit integrity check reports came in from the team.

"Command, this is Alfa. EVA team suit integrity checks complete. Suits nominal."

Helped by an autojected nitrogen-purge chemical cocktail that Michael didn't like to think about and by the suit's 100 percent oxygen atmosphere, the suit AI reported his body nitrogen-free less than a minute later. They were ready to decompress from *387*'s ambient pressure down to a suit pressure of 0.2 atmospheres if required to deploy, something Michael fervently hoped would not be necessary. The minutes dragged past until Michael could have sworn that he now carried not 30 kilos on his back but 300.

"All stations, this is command. *387* is go for launch. May God watch over us this day." And with that, there was a gentle push as SBS-20's hydraulic locking arms pushed *387*'s fully loaded mass away from the space battle station and down its designated departure pipe.

The seconds passed, and Michael began to relax. He had a busy morning ahead of him before standing his first watch in the combat information center at 12:30. By that time they should be clearing the clutter in orbit around Anjaxx and beginning to align *387* for its high-g burn toward its pinch-space jump point.

Two hours or so later and a good ten minutes early for his 12:30 watch, Michael stood at the back of combat information center, ready to understudy Hosani as officer in command.

A bit under 10 meters square, the compartment had as its focus the command chair, which was in the middle of the room in front of a massive high-definition holovid screen 3 meters wide and 2 high that carried the full command plot. Its job was to present the captain and the two warfare officers seated beside him with a complete picture of what was going on. Two command plot operators sat in front of the captain, but below his line of sight so that he had an uninterrupted view of all the bulkhead-mounted screens around him.

Flanking the command plot were two smaller screens, the local or tactical plot to the left and the threat plot—known very unofficially as the "oh shit" plot—to the right. Smaller holovid screens arranged above workstations completed the combat information center's displays.

Moving aft, the workstations on the starboard side managed the *387*'s hugely comprehensive sensor suite: search and fire control radars, high-definition targeting holocams, laser trackers, grav wave sensors, and passive sensors covering the full electromagnetic spectrum.

Bringing up the rear and the last screen to starboard was the surveillance drone control desk. Drones weren't always a lot of use in a shooting war; that was why the desk was tucked away at the back of the combat information center and why the officer responsible for a ship's surveillance drones was always the most junior warfare officer onboard.

The first workstation on the port side managed *387*'s offensive weapons capability. Unlike her bigger sisters, *387* had no rail guns. The stresses imposed and the power needed by the pinchspace rail-gun engines to accelerate a salvo of slugs to 3.6 million kilometers per hour instantaneously were simply too great for a warship as small as *387*. So, for her stand-off offensive capability, she had to manage with twelve Mamba antistarship missiles in two six-round containers supported by twin Lamprey x-ray antistarship lasers, depowered versions of the system fitted to major Fleet units.

The second and third workstations managed *387*'s suite of defensive weapons: hypervelocity armor-piercing discarding sabot chain guns and short-range defensive lasers, both tasked with protecting *387* from incoming missile and rail-gun salvos inside a bubble of space 20,000 kilometers in diameter. But as good as *387*'s point-defense systems were, they could handle only small, low-rate attacks. That was precisely why the captains of deepspace light scouts were so emphatically advised by the Fleet's fighting instructions to stay well clear of anything bigger than themselves.

The last desk on the port side was where active countermeasures—jammers, spoofers, and decoys—were managed.

Finally, in the center, ranged crosswise immediately behind the captain's chair, were the nav, ship control, and damage control desks and, right aft on the port side, a pair of maintenance workstations.

At general quarters, Michael could see that it would be a crowded place with every station manned by spacers in bulky space suits crammed into less than 100 square meters of deck space together with a mess of chairs, workstations, and screens. And the irony was, he thought, that arguably it was all redundant. Neuronics long ago had removed the need for large holovid screens, and it was perfectly possible for the captain and his command team to fight the ship lying flat on their backs in the comfort and security of their bunks.

But there were three fundamental problems with that approach.

The first was good old human nature: Especially when under severe stress, people liked to be able to work close to other people as part of a team.

The second was the objective fact that the big holovid screens, particularly when managed by experienced command plot operators, helped prompt warfare officers to think about things they might have missed in a way that neuronics, with their emphasis on user-controlled data filters, seemed incapable of doing.

But in the end, the real clincher was tradition. Federated

Worlds Space Fleet warships had always had combat information centers, and they probably always would. But he did concede that screen-fitted ships did better than neuronics-only ships, albeit only marginally, and then only in sims. Space Fleet had never dared send a neuronics-only vessel into actual combat, and Michael was pretty sure it never would.

He checked the time. 12:25. Time to go.

"Permission to step across, sir?" he asked the outgoing officer in command, Junior Lieutenant Kapoor.

"Yeah, Michael. Across you come." Kapoor waved his hand vaguely in his direction as Michael stepped across the thick yellow and black line painted on the gray plasteel deck. The goofers line it was called, and to cross it without the officer in command's permission was to ask to have your ass kicked hard.

"Okay. Welcome. Maria is running late—the captain wanted to see her about something—so we'll do the handover and then you brief her while I watch. Okay?"

"Sure. Fine by me."

Within seconds, Kapoor had started to dump everything he thought Michael needed to know about the current state of *387* and its intended plans together with a succinct summary of everything that was going on in Anjaxx nearspace. Finally, the torrent subsided. "Right." Kapoor's tone was firm. "You take Warfare-1, and I'll keep an eye on things from Warfare-2 until Maria turns up. Off you go. You have the ship?"

"I have the ship."

"Good. You have the ship."

Michael settled himself into Warfare-1, the chair to the right of the captain's command chair, and methodically began to review the information Kapoor had given him. Five minutes later, he felt he was on top of things. In the absence of any threat, he had the vid feed from the forward holocams put up onto the command plot, an impressive if not terribly useful view of billions of stars with Anjaxx's second moon in the bottom right-hand corner to provide some context.

Michael set up the local and threat plots the way he wanted them so that he'd be ready to brief Maria Hosani when she appeared.

As ever, when operating in ship state 3—transits in friendly normalspace in peacetime—the combat information center was almost empty. Only Warfare-1, Warfare-2, Sensor-1, and Weaps-1 were occupied. He glanced across at Kapoor, who appeared to be sound asleep. Surely not, Michael thought. It was his first watch. Oh, well, he couldn't worry about it, and if he got into trouble, he could always wake Kapoor.

The watch progressed, with Michael maintaining a cycle of Q&A with the command team as well as keeping regular contact with propulsion control as *387* slowly cleared Anjaxx innerspace at a steady if unspectacular 0.1-g acceleration. Not only was using serious amounts of thrust this close to heavily trafficked space unpopular, pinchspace jumps that deep inside Anjaxx's gravity could produce unpredictable results. During the Second Hammer War back in '14, the old *Adamantine,* hard-pressed by overwhelming Hammer forces, had been forced into a pinchspace jump deep inside Retribution VI's gravity well and had been discovered only by accident by a passing Sylvanian patrol eighteen months later, out of driver mass and drifting in interstellar space 155 light-years from Sylvania. That can't happen today, of course, Michael thought, thanks to the huge improvements made to pinchcomms since, but it was not to be recommended nonetheless.

Slowly, *387* approached the imaginary line marking the edge of Anjaxx innerspace, 150,000 kilometers from the Anjaxx planetary datum. Still wondering where Hosani had gotten to and concerned that Kapoor really looked as though he had gone to sleep, Michael got busy. Damn them, he decided; he would cope. For the umpteenth time, he double-checked the nav plan, taking particular care to ensure that the planned ship's vector was precisely right for the pinchspace jump to Martinson Reef. He made Mother and the nav AI check independently of each other and ran the numbers himself. He was very relieved when all three of them agreed to the required twenty-five significant figures. He took a deep breath. It was time to get the OK from the captain, and with Kapoor still looking for all the world like he was unconscious, he was on his own.

He needn't have worried. Ribot listened in silence and okayed the navplan without any comment. But Michael's feeling of self-satisfaction was short-lived.

"What have you forgotten, Michael?" Kapoor inquired mildly from behind firmly closed eyes.

Shit, Michael thought. What have I forgotten? Think. Think. And it came to him.

"All stations, this is command. We will cross into Anjaxx nearspace in two minutes. As soon as we do, we will initiate a 5-g burn. That'll put us at pinchspace escape velocity in time to jump as planned at 15:32. Command out."

"Good boy. Keep the troops informed, and they'll do the same for you." Kapoor smiled. "And I'll bet you thought I wasn't paying attention."

Michael laughed with embarrassment. "I must say I didn't think you were, so that's one I owe you."

"You're on."

With two minutes to go, Ribot arrived. "Captain in command," Fell announced in her most formal tones.

"Ignore me, Michael. Just do it all as normal." Ribot sank into his seat directly in front of the massive command plot without another word.

"Roger, sir."

The seconds ticked away. One final check with Fell and Asmari to make sure they were clear, and *387* was ready.

All of a sudden, it was as though *387* had been strapped to a massive jackhammer. The ship began to shake as the main propulsion used unimaginable amounts of power to turn tons of driver mass pellets into flaming torches of incandescent gas moving at a significant fraction of the speed of light. Michael felt the artificial gravity twitch and ripple as it struggled to adjust the ship's internal gravity field to compensate.

Almost seven minutes later and with Mother confirming their speed to be the required 150,000 kph, Mother shut down main propulsion. For the first time since unberthing, the ship was quiet, with not a tremor to show for the awesome speed at which they were moving.

"Captain, sir. At pinchspace escape velocity. Vectors are good. We are go to jump at 15:32 as scheduled."

"Okay. Warn the ship's company. And send our pinchspace jump report."

"Sir.

"All stations, this is command. We are go for pinchspace jump in twenty-two minutes. Those of you prone to pinchspace sickness, please take the necessary precautions. Command out."

And then it was just a matter of counting down the minutes. With five to run, Michael gave the order to retract *387*'s massive heat dump panels, and they were ready to go. At 15:32 precisely and with only the characteristic flash of ultraviolet radiation to mark its departure, Federated Worlds Warship *DLS-387* ceased to exist in normalspace.

In what seemed like an endless series of gut-wrenching heaves, Michael celebrated his first operational pinchspace jump. His only consolation was that Ribot, Kapoor, and the rest of the on-watch combat information center crew all joined him in celebrating the jump, though none did it as spectacularly as he did.

Sunday, September 6, 2398, UD
Planetary Transfer Station 1, in Clarke Orbit around
Terranova Planet

Kerri Helfort could hardly wait until they were safely aboard the *Mumtaz.*

Not that she had any particular love of starships, commercial or Fleet. Her years in the Fleet had ground that out of her. No, it was Sam. The bloody girl had become truly impossible. Her excitement at the prospect of the trip to the

Frontier Worlds had reached fever pitch; the prospect of seeing her cousin Jemma had brought on an alarming attack of severe verbal diarrhea.

As Sam chattered on and on, her verbal momentum seemingly unstoppable, Kerri gritted her teeth and prayed that she would shut up, if only for a moment.

Kerri did the only thing she could do: She picked up the pace. With Sam and the cargobot carrying the bags following in her wake, she accelerated down the passageway that led from the up-shuttle to the *Mumtaz,* the walls lined with holovids advertising all the exotic destinations served by Prince Interstellar. Moving at a near gallop, she rounded a corner, and there, 50 meters in front of her, much to her relief, was the welcoming committee from the *Mumtaz.* A short wait, and they were through the DNA and retina identity checks and the valetbot was leading them to their cabin, which was located, it seemed to Kerri, kilometers away.

Eventually they arrived at a small two-berth cabin. Thank God, it had beds and not bunks—bunks were another thing Kerri had had more than enough of in her Fleet time—together with "luxurious en-suite facilities" as the brochure so coyly put it: two small armchairs, a tiny desk, a coffee table, and the usual huge wall-mounted holovid.

Kerri peered into what looked like a cupboard. Aha, she thought acidly. She'd just found the luxurious en-suite facilities. Obviously it was passenger mership code for a very cramped bathroom with just enough space for a toilet, a hand basin, a shower, room to turn around, and nothing else. It would be a long trip, she thought resignedly, and Sam was likely to spend much of it in the luxurious en-suite facilities while she waited her turn. It was a great relief when Sam agreed to her suggestion that she go walkabout and check the place out and they would meet for dinner later. In deference to the passengers, *Mumtaz* would hold to Terranova time for one day before progressively adjusting the clocks to be in sync with Jackson Time—Frontier's only settled planet—for their arrival. A 72.5-hour day would take some getting used to after Ashakiran's 26.8, Kerri thought.

By ten to eight, Kerri had showered and changed and was feeling much better after nearly two hours without Sam's constant rattling on. After a quick duty pinchgram to Andrew to say that they had arrived safely and with her neuronics leading the way, she set off.

The business class lounge and dining room were quite small, smaller than she had expected. *Mumtaz,* which was a mixed cargo-passenger mership, carried only 1,000 passengers, of whom, according to the ever-helpful ship information persona—its AI-generated avatar that of a cheerful-looking and very patient woman—94 were in premium class, 176 in business, and the rest in economy class. The ever-helpful persona told her that the *Mumtaz* was almost full this trip, with 945 passengers in all.

For a moment, Kerri felt guilty about the extra cost of business class, but Andrew had insisted. The trip of a lifetime, and he wanted Kerri to enjoy it. She had eventually given in, and now that she was here, she was glad they had spent the money. Economy class was a good value, but only if almost two weeks of four-berth cabins, shared bathrooms, and cafeteria-style eating was your bag. As she made her way into the plushly furnished lounge, Kerri spotted Sam talking some poor young man to death and, taking a deep breath, made her way over to join them.

Sam was bursting with excitement. "Mom, this is John Carmichael. He's from Ashakiran, too, and guess what? He's going to visit relatives just like we are!"

"John, how are you? Kerri Helfort. I see you've met my daughter." Nice-looking boy and just a bit older, she thought, but old enough to be dangerous. Poor old Arkady had better watch out. She reached out to shake hands.

"Mrs. Helfort." The grip was firm, and the hand warm. "Nice to meet you. Shall we go through and eat?"

And with that the evening slipped into a comfortable haze of small talk interrupted only by a low-key announcement that *Mumtaz* was getting under way and by the obligatory safety briefing. After a while, Kerri just sat back. Sam could be very good company when she put her mind to it, and Kerri enjoyed watching the half-flirting, half-serious way Sam interacted with John. A nice boy. If she was to go off the rails, let it be with someone who would treat her with respect, Kerri thought.

As the meal came to a close, Kerri stood up to leave Sam to John's company, reminding herself as she did not to give Sam any advice on how to manage interpersonal relationships. Previous experience had shown it to be a complete waste of time, and Kerri hated wasting her time. But just as quickly as she had reminded herself, she forgot her own advice.

"I'm off. Not too late, Sam."

"Mom!" Sam was indignant.

"Sorry. John, nice to meet you. I'll see you in the morning, Sam." And with that she was off, leaving them to it. A good night's sleep was what she wanted, even if it was going to be interrupted—she checked her neuronics—in a bit under five hours by the pinchspace jump and the usual dramas that went with it. Prince Interstellar's policy was to have every passenger wide awake when it happened, a policy so strictly enforced that mership captains had been known to delay a jump into pinchspace until the last recalcitrant sleepers were fully awake. Given the alternative, she wasn't complaining.

At 09:00 UT *Mumtaz* sent her pinchspace jump report, and twelve minutes later she vanished into pinchspace.

Kerri Helfort woke with a start, confused for a moment in the half darkness. What warship is this? she wondered. No, she thought, no Space Fleet bunk was ever this comfortable. And then it all came flooding back. She stretched luxuriously. The realization that finally she and Sam were on their way after the frantic buildup she'd had to endure almost made her drop back to sleep.

No, she chided herself. Up and at 'em. Slipping quietly out of bed and taking care not to disturb the lumpy mass that was Sam, she was quickly into her training kit, out of the cabin, and on her way to the *Mumtaz*'s gym, an installation so impressive that it had to be seen, if Prince Interstellar's publicity materials were to be believed.

Kerri Helfort was not disappointed. The gym was impressively large and comprehensively equipped and, even better, didn't smell like someone had been using it to stable horses.

It was also completely empty.

Fine by me, she thought as she stood in the lobby, more an access corridor than a lobby in fact, as the ship's gym's AI ran her through the options. She really was spoiled by the choices. The place had pretty much every form of physical exercise capable of being stuffed into a commercial spaceship, and for those that couldn't, it had the latest in sims. Swimming, running, bikes, horse riding, surfing, walking, resistance work, weights, white water, rock work, zero g, every brand of unarmed combat and ball game known to humankind and more. Much more. If she wanted to, she could climb almost any mountain in humanspace in the middle of a howling blizzard wearing a bikini, sandals, and a beanie. The options were as endless as the imaginations of sim engineers were boundless. No, she decided after a moment. Something simple, something that didn't need a full-function envirosim. A long, hard walk and spectacular scenery—something from Old Earth would be nice—and she'd be well set up for whatever else the *Mumtaz* might have to offer.

Even as she made her decision, the gym began to fill up in a hurry. One by one, a group of men filed past her. For a moment Kerri thought nothing of it, but then she looked closer. It wasn't just any old group of men, she realized. They were all young; they all looked to be in great physical shape and had a disciplined, controlled way of moving. And they said very little, just a few words now and again, but so quietly that she couldn't make out their accents. She watched them as they split up and with no time wasted started on the weight machines, working with a focused intensity that was almost robotic. Military, perhaps? Professional futbol team, maybe? No, military. Had to be. They just had the look.

It was odd, though, she thought. She'd skimmed the manifest looking for any Space Fleet or Marine Corps people she might know and hadn't seen any mention of a group like this. Well, she thought, they have a right to travel, too, whoever they might be. "Come on, Kerri, time to get moving," she said quietly to herself, promptly walking right into another young man as he tried to get past her and into the gym.

"Oh, sorry about that," she said, embarrassed by her carelessness.

"No problem," said the man.

To look at, he was obviously another member of the group now working out in front of her with silent, almost manic determination. Without being too obvious, Kerri moved so that he couldn't easily get past her.

"So," she said casually, waving a hand at the men working out in the gym, "you're part of the team? What do you guys do? Professional futbol, maybe?"

"Please excuse me. I need to get on," the man said quietly, his gray-blue eyes fixed on some distant point over her shoulder.

"Oh, sorry," Kerri said, standing unmoving in the center of the narrow gym lobby, her face sporting her best "I'm a clueless old bat so please indulge me" look. "I don't mean to hold you up, but what do you do? Come on. You're professional futbollers, aren't you? But which team?"

"Madam, please, I . . ."

"Oh, come on," Kerri pleaded, watching with interest as the man struggled to keep control in the face of what he must have thought was a dangerously obsessive woman. "You can tell me. I can keep a secret. Which team?"

The man shrugged his shoulders in defeat. "Not futbol, ma'am," he said resignedly, smiling a thin, forced smile, "We're just a bunch of guys off to Frontier. We're hard-rock miners, and there's an asteroid waiting for us out there. Now really, please may I pass? I must get on." His tone was polite but firm, his accent thick with the flat, stretched vowels of a Damnation's Gate native. Well, that was what her neuronics had decided, anyway.

Kerri had had enough of the young man with the untidy yellow-gold hair and hard gray-blue eyes. Why the man made her so uncomfortable, and he did, she'd probably never know. But if he was a hard-rock miner, she was a cabbage, a very big one. She'd sneaked a look at his hands, and they looked to her like the hands of a man who'd spent a great deal of time practicing unarmed combat. The closest they'd been to rock would have been climbing a cliff.

"Oh, yes, silly me. I do so like to talk," she said gushingly as she stood aside and waved him past. "Please."

"Thank you," he said more curtly than was polite.

Kerri watched him for a moment as he went through. Something wasn't right here. A group of military men, possibly special forces, some of them, pretending to be hard-rock miners? Didn't stack up. But, but, but. All of that might be the case, but it really wasn't any of her business. After all, whatever mischief they might be up to, it would have to wait until they got dirtside on Frontier. There sure as hell wasn't much they could do millions of light-years from anywhere, stuck in the vast nothingness of pinchspace.

Exercise over, aching muscles more than compensated for by a definite sense of virtue at having completed a good, solid workout, Kerri dropped into what was to become her routine for the trip: a brief word with an uncommunicative and sleepy Sam followed by a shower and breakfast and then on to the forward business class lounge. There the holovids presented a truly spectacular three-dimensional simulation of local normalspace as it rushed past them at over 4.3 billion kilometers per second. Even though it was something created by the ship's AI—the actual view outside being only the murky gray-white nothingness of pinchspace—Kerri never tired of it. For a while as *Mumtaz* passed through (around, under, over?) deep interstellar space, there was little to see except the blazing glory of distant stars. But then, in a rush, a star system complete with planets, moons, asteroid belts, and comets would appear before flashing past and disappearing. But what got Kerri was the sense of wonder that the incredible show produced in her, almost a deep oneness with the enormousness of the universe.

It was an effort to get up and go for a walk around the ship before lunch in time for her other passion: contract bridge with a group organized by the ship's entertainment officer. That was followed by a people-watching walk through the small piazza, coffee with Sam at one of the small cafés before happy hour in the business class lounge, followed by dinner, idle conversation, and then bed.

If it hadn't been for the persistent unease she felt about the group of men she had met in the gym that morning, it would have been a perfect day. Stop fussing, she told herself as she drifted off to sleep. They might well be, as she now suspected, a group of mercenaries bound for one of the endless wars that sputtered and flared on some godforsaken world out on the rim of humanspace, but that was somebody else's problem. She'd do what little she could. She would make sure that she had full neuronics recordings of each group member, and once back home, she'd pass them on to one of her contacts in Space Fleet intelligence. They'd follow up if necessary.

Sunday, September 6, 2398, UD
City of Foundation, Terranova Planet

The city of Foundation, Terranova's oldest and, as the name suggested, the first settlement of the Federated Worlds, was quiet in the last few hours before dawn.

Low in the western sky, Castor was setting behind the massive bulk of the New Tatra Mountains. High to the south, the razor-thin crescent of Terranova's second moon, Pollux, cast a faint light across the sleeping city.

The large house on the low hills overlooking the city, and beyond it, the sea, dark and quiet. Inside, the sleeping form of Giovanni Pecora, federal minister of interstellar relations, struggled to resist the increasingly strident demands of his neuronics. But eventually they could not be refused any longer, and Pecora, a bulky man in his early seventies, his dark brown hair laced liberally with streaks of white—unusual for such a heavily geneered society—and red-faced with sleep, swung himself up and out of bed, muttering under his breath.

He accepted the comm.

"Okay, okay, I'm up. Give me two minutes to organize myself and I'll be straight back to you."

Pecora's tone made it clear to the caller, the ministry's duty officer, how he felt about being dragged out of bed that early in the morning. This had better be something worthwhile, something his personal agent couldn't have dealt with, or the duty officer would wish she'd never been born. And why me? Pecora wondered as he fumbled in the dark for his dressing gown and slippers, trying hard not to wake his wife. Suddenly it hit him. The duty officer had called him direct rather than one of his senior ministerial staff, and a cold clammy hand clamped itself around his heart. Jesus, he thought, something has happened, and he was bloody sure he didn't want to know what it was.

Heart pounding, he made his way through to his study and commed on the lights and the housebot to bring a cup of tea. Blinking in the sudden brightness, he sat down at his desk and took out an old-fashioned pad of paper and an antique liquid ink pen, things he always did in moments of stress. According to his grandmother, the pen had come from Old Earth and was over four hundred years old. The fact that it still worked was entirely due to a certain Mr. Fashliki, whose shop in the old quarter was a shrine to long-dead technologies and one of Giovanni Pecora's favorite places.

With a cup of tea safely in hand and the housebot instructed to prepare the next one and leave it outside on the veranda, Pecora finally felt up to the task of facing whatever diplomatic horror the duty officer was sitting on. Taking a deep breath to brace himself—he really was getting far too old for this sort of nonsense, he decided—he put the comm through.

"Ms. Rodriguez. Good morning. What's the problem?"

As the duty officer laid it out for him, reinforcing the key points with clips from Captain Kumar's pinchcomm message, Pecora began to feel physically sick, his stomach starting a slow sour churn. He knew the Hammer all too well from way back, and as he listened, he began to understand not just what the Hammer planned to do but, much more important, what that might lead to.

"Right, I understand all that." Pecora kept his voice level. "And Prince Interstellar was certain that *Mumtaz* had jumped?"

"Sir, I didn't focus on *Mumtaz* in particular. I figured that would get people asking questions we didn't want asked right now, so I had them dump all their jump records for all merships for the last month, and I'm afraid there's no doubt. *Mumtaz* unberthed at 02:43 UT, a bit after 20:30 local, and Prince Interstellar's ops center received her jump report saying that she would jump at 09:12 UT. I've also checked with Terranova nearspace control. *Mumtaz* jumped on schedule."

"Right, then." Shit, shit, shit. Only missed her by two hours, Goddamn it. "Okay, Ms. Rodriguez, thank you for all that. And also let me say that you were right to call me and not the ministry staff, though they won't thank you for it. But don't worry, I'll fix that."

"Thank you, sir." The relief in Rodriguez's voice was palpable, her avatar visibly relaxing, the lines of stress marking her mouth and eyes fading away. Damn good avatar software, Pecora thought in passing. So good that it must have cost somebody a small fortune.

"And well done also for not making it obvious that it was the *Mumtaz* you were interested in. That was smart thinking." And under a lot of pressure, too. Pecora made a mental note: Rodriguez was someone to watch.

Pecora paused for a moment as he thought through the implications before continuing. "But if what we've been told is correct, then someone at Prince Interstellar will connect our inquiry about their ships and wonder just how the hell we knew in advance that *Mumtaz* was going to disappear. So comm the contact details to me, and we'll make sure that we remind them of a few facts of life. Oh, and put a security lock on everything we've talked about, with key access for my and your eyes only for the moment."

"Sir."

"Okay. Leave it all with me, and I know I don't have to tell you to keep this to yourself, but I will. Do not tell another living soul, and that's an order."

"Sir, I've not and I won't."

"Pleased to hear it. Good night."

"Good night, sir."

Pecora leaned back in his chair, cradling a mug of tea in his hand, its warmth a pleasant contrast to the terrible icy fear that gripped him. He felt a million years old all of a sudden. If Rodriguez's report was true, and they needed to be damn sure that it was—the Hammer had been known to leak false intelligence just to make mischief—the chances of this affair not turning into the Fourth Hammer War were very slim indeed. He drank the tea in a series of large gulps and set down the mug before standing up to make his way out onto the veranda. He picked up the next mug—it took a minimum of two to get him going in the morning—and settled into his favorite chair. Giovanni's thinking chair, his wife called it. He had time. The *Mumtaz* was gone, and nothing in God's universe could stop the hijacking now.

After twenty minutes of silent reflection, with the eastern sky beginning to turn pink with the promise of another hot and humid day, its light beginning to pick out the city below him and the bay that stretched out in front of it, Pecora's mood, dark and heavy to start with, was even more depressed. Whatever the Federated Worlds might do, there was one thing they had to do, and that was get the crew and passengers of the *Mumtaz* back. There was simply no way that he or any other member of the federal government would allow their people to remain in the hands of those fanatics.

And that meant confronting the Hammer. And in this case, that would have two inevitable consequences, both guaranteed by the very nature of Hammer's polity, culture, and history.

First, Merrick would go. Even though being chief councillor gave Merrick enormous power, he was not an absolute dictator, and there were certain rules that had to be followed. And Merrick had broken rule number one: Consult your fellow councillors on all matters of significance. He clearly had not, and that put him up against every other member of the

Supreme Council for the Preservation of Doctrine. History showed that when that happened, there could be only one outcome: an orgy of blood as his enemies took the opportunity Merrick's hubris had given them to eliminate both Merrick and as many of his supporters as possible.

The prospect of Merrick and his murderous cronies getting the treatment they had handed out to so many others didn't bother Pecora too much. In fact, justice would be served by what DocSec might do to Merrick. But for a chief councillor, Merrick was somewhat unusual. Surprisingly, the man was quite popular for someone with so much blood on his hands.

Although he could be as brutal as any Hammer chief councillor, he wasn't as dangerously devious and untrustworthy as Jeremiah Polk, the man most likely to succeed Merrick, a man that the analysts on the Hammer desk felt Merrick grossly underestimated. That meant that Merrick's overthrow could lead to civil war. And if there was one thing worse than going to war, it was going to war with worlds whose political leaders depended for their very survival on a credible external threat or, if one did not exist, inventing one.

The second consequence, as inevitable as it was disheartening, came from the nature of Hammer people and their society. As a general rule, Hammers were almost incapable of acting honorably when dealing with outsiders. With some worthy exceptions, they just could not do it. It was not part of their culture to be held accountable by anyone not on the Path of Doctrine; that was precisely why the Hammer Worlds were shunned by most of the rest of humankind. To deal with Hammers at any level was to ask to be ripped off.

And so, any proposition that the *Mumtaz* might be returned with her people and cargo unharmed would be treated with absolute contempt. So, if the Feds wanted *Mumtaz,* they would have to take it back, and the Hammers would not like that one little bit.

All of that was fine up to a point, but Pecora had been around long enough to have learned the most fundamental lesson of interstellar relations. It was a simple lesson best summed up in only one word: *self-interest*. For all the overblown language trotted out by politicians and diplomats, every issue between systems came back to that word: self-interest. Very simple, really.

So yes, the Federated Worlds could act unilaterally to recover the *Mumtaz* together with her unfortunate crew and passengers. If it wanted to. But doing that would be a decision not taken lightly. For all that the rest of humanspace had suffered at the hands of the Hammer, and they had and grievously, the consequences of unilateral action on the interests of the Sylvanians, the Frontier, the Old Earth Alliance, and all the rest would have to be worked through in excruciatingly tedious detail.

Pecora felt the frustration rise. In the end, it all boiled down to only two issues, anyway: the impact on interstellar trade and the impact on system security. Everything else was peripheral. If unilateral action to recover the *Mumtaz* threatened either or, God help the Worlds, both, they were stuffed. A multilateral solution it would have to be, and that meant that weeks, months, even years of negotiation would follow while the Hammers sat back laughing. Meanwhile, the *Mumtaz*'s crew and passengers would be left to rot in some damned Kraa prison camp. Christ, what a depressing thought.

Fuck them all, Pecora thought in a rare flash of unrestrained anger. This time the Hammers had gone too far. If the rest of humanspace couldn't see that, that was their problem. All of a sudden, he knew what had to be done. He'd push for unilateral action, and if the Old Earth Alliance, the Sylvanians, and all the rest were disinclined to go along, then so be it. The Federated Worlds would of course follow due process. Oh, yes. Every tedious step of the way: a formal notice of a state of limited war, properly served, of course, and supported by an affirmed statement of facts and a demand for financial restitution. All strictly in accordance with every word of the New Washington Convention, of course. That should do it, he said to himself, suddenly energized by the thought of taking the fight to the Hammers with or without the support of the rest of civilized humanspace.

Pecora finished his tea—his fourth cup—and got up, legs

and back stiff from inactivity. The eastern sky was now a stunning mélange of mauve shading into blues, golds, and pinks rich with the promise of a hot sunny day. Beyond the city, the ocean was turning from a dark gunmetal gray to an inviting deep blue. It was going to be a beautiful day. Pecora sighed deeply as he strangled at birth any idea he might have had of going down the coast to catch a long lunch at Trinh's and watch the world go by. It was almost six, and the matter at hand couldn't wait any longer.

He put the comm out, tagged with the codephrase "Sampan Two" needed to convene an urgent meeting of the inner cabinet, and went to take a shower.

After some perfunctory small talk, the meeting of the inner cabinet broke up.

The meeting had been a bruising one. Shocked disbelief had shifted to a blend of outrage and frustration before degenerating into interfactional squabbling, with the unspoken question of who was going to be blamed looming large in the minds of most of those present. But as always, Moderator Burkhardt had pulled things together long enough to get the massive if sometimes cumbersome resources of the Federated Worlds moving in the right direction.

It wasn't long before Pecora found himself alone at the table. Throughout the meeting, even if only as an undertone, the mood had been harsh and unforgiving. Over the years, the Federated Worlds and its allies had been dragged into war by deliberate Hammer provocations three times and had hundreds of thousands of deaths to show for it. Although the Sylvanians had stressed that the information was being provided to head off war, that now looked very much like a forlorn hope. If the Federated Worlds moved with speed and precision to recover the *Mumtaz* and its people and minimized the collateral damage to the Hammer, Pecora knew that there was a chance, if only a very faint chance, that the situation would not degenerate into full-scale war.

But he also knew the Hammer. It would take every ounce of diplomatic skill backed by an overwhelming show of military strength to stop them from overreacting. Pecora didn't like the odds. Deep down he knew that if it came to an all-out shooting war, Burkhardt would have great difficulty persuading the public to settle for anything less than the Hammer's unconditional surrender. There were still too many people mourning the deaths of too many loved ones killed at the hands of the Hammer to allow for anything less.

As Pecora left the building, he made up his mind. Planetary security had been tasked with finding out just how in the hell the supposedly inviolate system of personal identity security checks might have been compromised enough to allow a gang of psychopathic hijackers onboard a Fed mership, the intel spooks at Department 24 were going to mobilize their Hammer humint assets to try to find out what the Hammers were up to, and the Data Intercept Agency's massive databanks of electronic intercepts were being trawled to see if anything relevant had been missed.

More relevant to solving the problem if it really was as Captain Kumar had described it, the task of working out how to get the *Mumtaz* back was now in the hands of the people at defense. Even better news was the appointment of Vice Admiral Jaruzelska as commander of an as yet unformed Battle Fleet Delta. Pecora knew Angela Jaruzelska, the Federated Worlds' youngest vice admiral, from the most recent biennial strategic war games and had been impressed with her performance under pressure. The war games simulated full-scale conflict across five star systems and hundreds of planets and were so intense that they had been known to destroy less capable officers.

So, short of declaring war on the Hammer himself, there wasn't much more he could do right now.

He commed his wife. They would take that long lunch at Trinh's, after all, and if asked, he would ascribe this morning's meeting to factional party politics.

387 was now 250 light-years from Terranova, and the drop back into normalspace was imminent.

The trip had been surprisingly busy. Ribot believed in sims, sims, and more sims. Michael and his team had spent hours and hours going through the deployment, setup, calibration, and go-live of DefGrav's remote gravitronics packages. The schedule called for the entire process to take seven days, but Michael was increasingly confident that they could do it in less, not that he would ever admit that to anyone and certainly not to Ribot, who would have immediately moved the goalposts.

For once not on watch—another thing Ribot believed in was giving Michael as much combat information center time as he could bear—a tired Michael stood at the back, well out of the way, as he waited for the pinchspace drop.

"All stations, this is command. Get ready, everybody; we will drop in five minutes." The XO's voice was irritatingly cheerful, and no wonder, Michael thought. Jacqui Armitage was one of the very few people onboard for whom a move into or out of pinchspace caused nothing more than a momentary spasm.

Michael began to steel himself, to try to will his body into behaving itself.

"All stations, dropping now."

With that, Michael's stomach turned itself inside out. But, he consoled himself, perhaps it was not quite as bad as last time. Or so he fervently hoped.

The command crew rapidly got itself back together. With the threat plot reassuringly empty, in quick succession Armitage had confirmed that everyone had survived the drop, deployed the heat dump panels, and begun the process of spinning the ship on its axis, ready to commence its deceleration burn.

"Captain, sir. Command. We are on track, vector correct and aligned ready to commence our deceleration burn, which is due in fifty-five minutes' time. That gives us time to deploy pinchcomms to catch the 22:00 transmission sked and get our drop report away."

"Captain, roger. Let's do it."

Seconds later, Michael watched as the holocams tracked the massive pinchcomms antenna as it deployed. At almost 10 meters across and 3 high, it was an impressively large piece of equipment; it had to be if it was to get the beam accuracy it needed to communicate across pinchspace. To look at, it was just a shallow concave oval shape with the jet-black pinchspace stasis generator mounted dead center. Slowly the antenna emerged, the single massive hydraulic ram lifting it smoothly clear of its armored container behind the surveillance drone hangar. As it cleared the hull, the array began to twitch as its AI hunted out the optimum path to the nearest relay station, in this case a long-range pinchcomms relaysat sitting in interstellar space about halfway between *387* and the Federated Worlds 150 light-years away. It looked like a dog scenting something, Michael thought.

Finally, the twitching stopped as the dull silver array locked on to the pinchcomms carrier wave, ready for the routine 22:00 message broadcast.

"Captain, sir. Command. Pinchcomms are up and locked on, and the jump report has gone. Er, hold on a minute, sir. Something is coming through for us marked flash." Armitage's voice betrayed her shock.

What the fuck is going on? Michael asked himself. Messages with a flash precedence were usually used only to report enemy contacts, and so far as he knew, it was very unlikely that the Feds had gone to war with anybody in the five days since they had left Terranova.

"I'll deal with it in my cabin." From the look on his face, the captain clearly shared Armitage's shock. As Ribot hurried out of the combat information center, Michael was left with a very uneasy feeling in the bottom of his stomach, and it had nothing to do with the residual effects of *387*'s transition back into normalspace. A flash pinchcomm could mean only one thing: bad news, very bad news.

Ten minutes later, Ribot sat alone in his cabin.

The message had finally come through, with the glacially slow data rate of the pinchcomms message broadcast transmission doing nothing for his nerves. The message was short and to the point: *387*'s mission had been aborted, and they were now on their way into Hammer space. Something had gone seriously wrong somewhere, and he had a nasty feeling that *387* was about to get very close to that something, whatever it was.

Taking time only to tell Mother to acknowledge safe receipt of the message from CINCFEDWORLDSFLT, Ribot commed Holdorf.

"Leon. Captain."

The navigator's avatar popped up in a flash.

"Leon. I want a new nav plan for Revelation-II, and I want it yesterday. I've commed you the system identifier."

"Revelation-II?" Leon's voice was heavy with disbelief. "But that's in Ham—"

Ribot cut him off. "I know it's in Hammer space, and no, I don't know why yet. I have to speak to Fleet."

Holdorf's avatar hung there, mouth half-open.

"Leon, for fuck's sake, stop standing there like a pregnant goldfish! Get on with it," Ribot snapped impatiently. "You and Mother get started and get back to me when you've got an 80 percent plan good enough to initiate the burn for the vector change. We'll fine-tune the plan once I have a better idea from Fleet what they want to achieve. Now go. I need to speak to Fleet."

"Sir." With his normally taciturn face working overtime to express a mixture of doubt, anxiety, and fear—Hammer space was absolutely to be avoided at all costs, and the prospect of jumping little *387* direct to Revelation-II was enough to make the bravest person think twice—Holdorf's avatar disappeared.

Ribot commed Mother. "Mother, set up a priority pinch-comm vidlink to Fleet and let me know when you are through to the duty operations officer. I'll take it in the pinch-comms shack. Oh, and warn Cosmo that I'll be using as much ship's power as I need to keep the data rate up. I don't want him finding out only when the lights go out."

"Roger, command."

As Ribot got to his feet to make his way to the pinch-comms shack, Holdorf commed him back.

"Yes, Leon?"

"Sir, I have the first cut of the nav plan, and we are re-aligning the ship, ready to commence the burn. The burn's going to be a right bastard, skipper."

Ribot wasn't surprised. Warships were never intended to do hard left turns at 150,000 kph.

"Okay, do it."

"Sir."

A good twenty minutes later, the protracted pinchcomms conference with Fleet operations finally wound up, and Ribot sat back. He couldn't put off the evil moment any longer. He commed Michael. After the briefest pause, Michael's avatar popped up, the excitement of the urgent changes to *387*'s plans plain to see. At least one of the crew relished the thought of a punch-up with the Hammers, Ribot thought.

"Michael, pinchcomms shack now, please."

You poor bastard, Ribot thought as Michael, face flushed with the excitement of it all, appeared in the doorway. He'd be seeing it all as some sort of huge adventure. "Come in, Michael. Shut the door and sit down." Puzzled, Michael did as he was told, wondering what the hell all of this had to do with him. Ribot took a deep breath before he spoke. "Michael, I have some bad news. You, like everyone else on-board, are wondering what the hell is going on. Well, it appears that the Hammers are going to hijack the *Mumtaz,* and Fleet has confirmed that your mother and sister are onboard. Michael, I'm so sorry."

The blood drained from Michael's face, his skin turning a dirty shade of gray, his mouth working to say words that wouldn't come.

Finally, but only with a huge effort, Michael forced himself to speak. "Are they okay? Have they been hurt? Are they coming back? Why—"

Ribot interrupted what threatened to become a flood of words. "Michael, we have one unconfirmed report that the hijacking is going to take place when *Mumtaz* drops out at the Brooks Reef around midday on the eleventh. But as yet Fleet has no independent verification, none at all. That's why our mission has been scrubbed and why we have been diverted to Hammer space. We need to establish what really has happened.

"Michael, we've got a lot to do, so I need to cut this short, but I wanted you to know first. It'll be difficult for you, but I need you to be at your best. And believe me, I think Fleet means it when they tell me that nothing—and I mean nothing—is going to stop us from getting every soul back. And be thankful that however bad the Hammers are, they do tend to treat women civilians well. So Michael, can you do what I need you to do?"

The anguish in Michael's eyes was replaced by a steady cold-burning anger. "Sir. Of course. Does my father know?"

"No. Fleet's keeping this very tight in case it's just the Hammer trying to make trouble. Let's hope that's all it is. Now, get your team mustered and get Petty Officer Strzlecki checking and double-checking every one of those birds of yours. I want them all 100 percent. We are going to need them. When you've got them started, you can join the think tank in the combat information center."

"Sir."

Ribot finished summarizing the detailed CINCFED-WORLDSFLT briefing he'd received and sat back.

Michael sat unmoving, still white-faced with shock, his mind churning as he struggled not to think about what might be happening to Mom and Sam. Think, Michael, think, he scolded himself. The best thing he could do right now was help *387*'s command team work out a plan that would get things started.

It was a somber, grim-faced group that sat around the combat information center conference table digesting the full import of what they'd just been told, struggling to answer the challenges Ribot had just put to them. They knew what had to be done. Now the question was how, and the profound silence around the conference table more than demonstrated that those answers would not come easily.

With a huge effort, Michael pushed family to the back and duty to the front. Half closing his eyes, he turned his mind inward, comming his neuronics to bring up the standard Fleet mission planning template. Shit, he thought as he took a good hard look at what *387,* the only Fleet unit within hundreds of millions of light-years, was being asked to do.

The mission was clear enough, its objectives spelled out in brutally simple and unemotional language by Ribot.

One, make a covert entry into the Revelation Star System.

Two, deploy surveillance assets around the second planet, Revelation-II, or Hell, as the Hammers called it.

Three, confirm whether the *Mumtaz* had in fact dropped into the Revelation-II/Hell System to off-load *Mumtaz*'s crew.

Four, once *Mumtaz*'s arrival was confirmed, recover surveillance assets, make a covert departure, and jump to the Judgment System for a fly-by of the planet Eternity to see just what the hell the Hammers were up to.

Five, leave Eternity and jump out of Hammer normal-space.

Oh, Michael had almost forgotten. There was a six, a very important six: Under no circumstances get caught.

He breathed out unevenly, his body still hyped by shock and stress. The mission objectives were easy to list. They sounded straightforward, but Michael had done enough combat sims to know that space warfare was never that simple, and the Hammers could never be underestimated.

The easiest part of the new mission—the initial vector

change burn, all thirteen rattling, banging, and shaking minutes of it—had been accomplished. *387,* now many tons of
driver mass lighter than when she had set off from SBS-20,
was aligned for the jump to the Revelation System, a jump
Ribot had said must be the best and most accurate *387* had
ever made.

Michael already had offered up three silent prayers. The
first was to thank the Good Lord that of all the many Fleet
warships, *387* was the one with the Mod 45 navigation AI.
The second was that the Mod 45 would drop *387* into the
Revelation System as precisely as its designers claimed it
would. The third was that they'd get away with it. It had been
a long time since a Fed warship had swanned through Hammer space as brazenly as *387* was going to.

But that left them with the first problem they had to solve.
The huge amount of driver mass used up making the vector
change to line *387* up for the pinchspace jump to Revelation
had ruled out any option for *387* to loiter in the vicinity of
Hell's Moons in the Revelation System and then Eternity
planet in the Judgment System.

Michael sighed in frustration. Any way he cut it, a conventional recon profile meant stranding *387* in hostile Hammer
space out of driver mass, easy pickings for even the most incompetent Hammer captain of the least efficient rail-gun-
fitted Hammer warship. Even Fleet, hard-nosed though they
could be, wouldn't ask that of any of its captains, and
Michael didn't think Ribot was going to volunteer. Anyway,
Fleet hadn't specified the time. No, this would have to be a
quick—very quick—and dirty fly-by of both systems.

There were a few other problems besetting *387* and its
command team.

Dropping in-system was one thing. Just how to do that
without squandering too much driver mass on the one hand
and taking too much time on the other was the first question
Ribot wanted answered. The Hammer's long-range ultraviolet flash detectors were poor; provided that *387* dropped
more than 18 million kilometers from the nearest detector
arrays, it was pretty safe, according to Mother.

So that was okay unless, of course, the Hammer had a warship out deep, in which case it would be all over. But based on the latest THREATSUM, Fleet reckoned that the chances of a Hammer warship being that far out were vanishingly small, an assessment Michael was prepared to agree with. Remote sensors were a risk, but the Hammer usually didn't deploy them deep-field. Actually, nobody did; there was simply too great a volume of space to cover unless, of course, the Hammer knew where and when *387* was coming. But he couldn't worry about that. If they did, they did. He couldn't see how they could know, but it didn't matter.

However, even if *387* was lucky and the Hammers were all safe in orbit somewhere, that still left *387* to make a ten-day, 36-million-kilometer transit at 150,000 kph past Hell's Moons. If they tried to speed things up, that meant a main propulsion burn that even the Hammer couldn't miss. To add to *387*'s woes, to drop accurately out of pinchspace and as close to the 18-million-kilometer detection threshold as possible, *387* would have to do the jump at 150,000 kph. Any faster and *387* risked dropping inside the threshold, and that could make for a bad day all around.

All that was why, Michael thought savagely, the fighting instructions stressed the importance of giving ships undertaking covert operations all the time they needed to slip in and slip out without having to resort to too many main propulsion burns and the like. But time was one thing they did not have.

Then a thought came to him. What if . . . Yes, Michael said to himself. That might do it. After a quick check, it looked okay to him, so with some hesitation he decided to see what the rest of the team thought. To look at them, they weren't having much luck so far.

Michael's hesitant voice broke the awkward silence. "Um, Captain, sir. What if we dropped well short, did a main engine burn to get our speed up, got our alignment spot-on, and then microjumped the last little bit so that the loss of jump accuracy didn't matter so much."

Ribot thought for a moment, then shrugged his shoulders.

"Nice idea, Michael, but a main propulsion burn is something you cannot hide without Krachov shrouds, and those we don't have. The Hammers might not see it immediately, but there is too much risk they would see it, and then they would know we had come visiting."

Ribot sounded troubled. Michael felt for him. There was no obvious way out of this one, time was running out, and nobody, not even Mother (not that AIs were any good at solving problems like this), seemed to have the answers Ribot needed.

Another long moment of silence was interrupted, this time by Hosani. "Actually, sir, Michael's got most of the answer. There might be a way. Look here," she said as she commed the two outermost planets of the Revelation system to come up on the command plot. "We could do what Michael suggested if we dropped behind Revelation-III. God knows, the bloody thing is big enough to hide a burn, and we know the Hammer have no dirtside or orbital surveillance assets there. We could then fire main engines without the Hammer seeing us, slingshot around the planet, get lined up for Hell's Moons, and get the microjump all nicely set up. Might work, and God knows, I think we'd all be a lot happier doing a fly-by of Hell's Moons at 300,000 kph rather than 150,000."

Ribot was silent for a moment, and then he turned to Michael with a smile. "Michael, you might not have had all of the answer, but by God, you had enough of it. And Maria, well done for thinking it through. Leon, that's a beer you owe me for not getting there first!"

"You're a hard man, sir," Leon said, his smile even broader than Ribot's. Michael knew why. They were all happy that there might be a way to do what had to be done without getting themselves killed in the process.

"Okay. So far, so good, but there is one problem left: Will we have enough driver mass to do all this plus the fly-by of Eternity planet or whatever the Hammer call the damn place and still get back to the FedWorlds safely?" Ribot paused, a slight edge of concern in his voice as Holdorf consulted Mother.

Holdorf shook his head emphatically. "In a word, sir, no. The vector change to get lined up for Judgment system and Eternity planet after we have done the fly-by of Hell's Moons is very much in our favor, and Mother can fine-tune it a bit to reduce it to almost nothing, I suspect. So we're okay there. But the vector change when we depart the Judgment system would be extreme." Holdorf paused as Mother crunched the numbers. "Yes, as I thought, roughly Red 150 and Up 20. And we'll be doing 300,000 kph with no large planets to hide behind when we do our burn. There is a fourth planet in the Judgment system, but it's not close enough to be useful."

A heavy silence descended as the group absorbed the latest problem. Armitage broke the quiet this time. "It's staring us in the face. Keep on keeping on. Go straight through to Frontier and mass up at Jackson's World. Mother says the vector change would be . . . yes, Green 30 Up 10, which sounds okay. We can do it once we get well clear of Eternity nearspace."

Ribot thought about it for a moment, then nodded. "Yes, I think that might do it, and we can probably adjust the fly-by of Eternity planet to reduce it some more. But"—Ribot held up his hands—"I think that leaves us dropping into Frontier space at 300,000 kph with not enough mass"—another pause to confirm with Mother—"to drop our speed as we come in-system to match orbits with wherever they send us. The delta-v needed to drop into Clarke orbit is too great. The damn planet's coming toward us instead of away, and we're going to be coming at a very steep angle to Jackson's World's orbital plane."

Ribot paused for a moment.

"That means a mass driver replenishment as soon as we drop into Frontier space just in case we miss badly; otherwise we may never stop, though that's unlikely," he said confidently.

Too confident, Michael thought. Much too confident. Matching vectors to complete driver mass replenishment was difficult enough, but *387* would be arriving in-system after a pinchspace jump made at 300,000 kph. Although the navigation AI's accuracy with the Mod 45 upgrade was much improved, it was optimized for the standard jump velocity of 150,000 kph. At a jump speed of 300,000 kph, the accuracy of the nav AI dropped off dramatically, and that meant *387* could end up missing its planned drop point by millions of kilometers. Ribot would have to talk to Fleet again; Michael could see that.

But, all those were things that could be overcome, and Michael felt a sudden surge of confidence. If Fleet could preposition ships downrange from the planned pinchspace drop point, *387* would have enough driver mass to adjust its vector to make the rendezvous point closest to wherever it was they finally dropped. Yes, as long as they didn't run into any Hammer warships, and Mother's THREATSUM said that was very unlikely, it would work.

Ribot interrupted what threatened to become a very long silence.

"Sorry, folks. Just making sure it all hangs together, and I think it does. Leon, I want you and Maria to work up the final nav plan with Mother based on what we've talked about. Oh, and work in the surveillance drone deployments as well. Michael, you work with Leon and Holdorf on that. As soon as that's firm, we'll pinchcomm the plan through to Fleet and I'll speak to Fleet operations about setting up our safety net at Frontier. Jacqui, you can do the final alignment checks ready to jump once I've okayed the plan.

"I think that the main issues have been addressed. Any more things we need to consider now?" Ribot, receiving a chorus of "no"s in reply, pushed on. "Okay, let's do it." Small tight smiles were all the response he got as the group split up.

Forty-five frantic minutes later, everything had been done to Ribot's satisfaction, and Michael stood at the back of the combat information center watching as Armitage ran the clock down to the pinchspace jump. They were in for an interesting trip, and Michael hoped to God that there weren't any Hammer ships out there that could turn interesting into fatal.

At 22:45, with its jump report sent, *387* pinched out en route to the Revelation System and its fly-by of Hell's Moons in search of the missing *Mumtaz.*

Friday, September 11, 2398, UD
Mumtaz—*Brooks Gravitational Anomaly, Deep Space*

The economy class lounge was a large compartment that normally was studded with comfortable chairs around low tables and filled with the gentle buzz of conversation from passengers making the most of their enforced idleness.

But not now.

The tables and chairs were gone. Packed into the center of the room, wrists held together with plasticuffs, were the survivors of the brutal attack mounted on the *Mumtaz*'s crew by the group of young men who now stood guard in a loose half circle across the front of the room. Light assault carbines looted from the *Mumtaz*'s armory were cradled casually but competently in their arms.

In the front were the bloodied bodies of the seven crew members—three men and four women—who had held out until the last. Their knives and homemade clubs had provided no defense against assault carbines.

The man standing in the door, corn-gold hair falling untidily across his forehead down into hard gray-blue eyes, watched the group as they absorbed the implications of the callous and brutal display of power they had just witnessed, a low murmur of shocked conversation rising and falling like a strange chant. He held up his hand to quiet the assembly.

"My name is Andrew Comonec, and I want you to listen to what I have to say very, very carefully." He paused until he was sure that every living soul was focused on him and what he was about to say.

He nodded casually at the bodies at his feet. "That, my friends, is what happens to those who do not do what we tell them to do. And just in case any of you still do not understand"—Comonec nodded to the guard nearest him and watched impassively as the man walked to the front of the group, pulled out a small pistol, and without visible emotion shot an elderly woman in the head—"what I am saying, then perhaps that little demonstration will make things clear for you."

He paused as a low moaning sound washed over the group, the sheer terror of the moment threatening to turn to hysteria. The passengers nearest the dead woman were screaming in panic.

Comonec lifted his voice, willing his control onto the mob. This was the moment of greatest risk. If a group rushed them, they were dead. Assault carbines or not, they couldn't kill enough people to win. But Comonec was a gambler, and he stretched the moment until he knew he had won, the pure pleasure of the adrenaline rush that came from controlling the minds of hundreds of people flooding through him.

He smiled. "Good. I think you do understand. If you do what you are told, the rest of you have nothing to fear. Nothing at all. You have my word. I will personally see to it that you are all safely reunited with your families and loved ones. But you must do as you are told as soon as you are told. If you do, you will be fine." He smiled again, the smile of someone who cared, a smile completely at odds with his eyes. They weren't smiling. They were dreamy with the pleasure of the kill, of fresh blood.

"Now, what I want you to do is this. We will comm you in alphabetical order so that we can check your details to make sure we know who you are and who we have to contact to let them know you are okay. We'll also remove the plastic ties around your wrists. I know they must be hurting by now, so the sooner we do this, the better. When we've done that, we'll ask you to go to your cabins and stay there for the moment until we get things sorted out. We'll then let you know what happens next with meals and so on. Okay?"

The minute nods of shocked acceptance confirmed Comonec's victory, and his body flushed with the exquisite pleasure of the win. "Right. Let's get on with it, shall we? Andreesen family first. Please come up."

Slowly and reluctantly, a man, his face gray with shock, barely able to control the trembling that shook his body, stood up, closely followed by a woman and two children who seemed catatonic, so slow were they to move.

"Come on. Please hurry. We won't hurt you."

Thirty minutes later it was Sam's turn. No matter where she looked, she couldn't see her mother, and she was almost frantic with worry. Oh, please God, let Mom be okay, she prayed desperately as heart-pounding panic rose in waves, threatening to overwhelm her.

"Helfort, Kerri and Samantha."

Sam rose to her feet, and as she did, she saw her mother, way across the room, rise to her feet also. "Oh, Mom," she sobbed, "thank God you're all right."

They came together at the front of the room. Sam was trembling visibly, tear-filled eyes spilling glistening wet tracks down a face ash-gray with shock and stress as she tried to avoid the blood pooled across the carpet, her head turned away from the shattered bodies of what had once been ordinary people like her. Her mother took Sam's hand and started to embrace her, to tell her everything would be fine and not to worry, but Comonec stepped forward.

"Later, later. There'll be time for that later," he said, pushing them through the door with a brutal roughness completely at odds with his comforting assurances that all would be well.

As Kerri and Sam stumbled through the door and out of sight of the remaining passengers, strong hands grabbed them. Sam started to panic again, and even as that panic spurred her into a last desperate attempt to escape, a gas-powered inoculation gun was jammed into her neck, with only a brief puff of high-pressure air and a short stabbing pain that was gone almost before she could feel it to mark the injection.

"Oh, God," she sobbed. What were they doing to her? Fear turned to terror as the terrible thought that this was the end hit her. With a horrible sense of the inevitable, she realized that it all made ghastly good sense. What good was she to the hijackers? None, none at all. Even as a creeping gray fog started to overwhelm her, she reached out to her mother, who was still struggling desperately to keep a gas gun–wielding hijacker at bay. But to no effect. Even as Kerri Helfort took Sam's outstretched hand, the gas gun hit home.

"Mom," Sam croaked, her voice strangled into an incoherent croak. "Mom, help me."

"Sam, Sam," her mother said, her voice fast being choked off by whatever the hijackers had just pumped into her. "Sam, listen to me. This is just something to keep us quiet, so don't worry. It'll be okay, I promise."

Sam nodded, and then the gray fog overwhelmed her. As her grip on reality began to slip away, the last thing she could hear was her mother muttering to herself: "I knew there was something wrong with those bastards. You should have trusted your instincts, and none of this would have happened. You old fool. You . . ."

And then the fog claimed her.

Three hours later, as the Zanussi family disappeared through the door, Comonec felt the last traces of tension seep out of him.

They had done it. By God, they had done it.

Over a thousand crew members and passengers brought under control by just thirty men. And no casualties. Well, none on his team, anyway. He hoped that the faceless man who'd commissioned the mission didn't get too upset about the *Mumtaz*ers who'd gotten in his way. The man, had been rather insistent, very insistent, in fact, that the job be done without anyone getting hurt.

"Well, screw him, whoever he is," Comonec muttered. The entire exercise had been a work of extreme professionalism, even if he said so himself, and his unknown sponsor was just going to have to see it the same way. What did a few damn Fed lives matter, anyway?

He turned and strode through the door to see the unfortunate Zanussi family moving like zombies back to their cabins. A wonderful drug that Pavulomin-V, he thought, even if being caught with it was a federal offense punishable by ten years in jail. He now had an entire mership's worth of people who would do everything and anything they were told to do without a moment's hesitation or argument.

Leaving instructions to have the bodies disposed of, Comonec commed his section leaders to meet him on the bridge. He had a rendezvous to make, and he intended to be there on schedule. Nothing was going to get in the way of the big fat juicy pile of anonymous cash that was now his by rights.

Saturday, September 12, 2398, UD
DLS-387, Revelation-III Nearspace

For sheer, unremitting pressure, the days since *387* had dropped into Hammer space safely behind the hulking black mass of Revelation-III, a J-Class planet orbiting 7.5 billion kilometers out from its sun, had been like nothing Michael had experienced before.

Apart from doing Ribot's endless sims, the only real work Michael and his team had had to do was to launch the surveillance drone nicknamed *Bonnie* to jump a day ahead of *387* and, they hoped, if there were any nasty surprises, to let *387* know in advance. But apart from an unusually large number of Hammer ships close to Hell's Moons, *Bonnie* hadn't spotted anything out of the ordinary, though as Michael reminded himself, *Bonnie*'s capabilities against stealth warships weren't good—her sensor baselines were too short—so anything could happen. But at least the micro-jump was on.

Now, two and a half days outward bound from Revelation-III, *387* was running in a gentle parabola through the fabric of space-time at over 300,000 kph, and you could cut the tension with a knife. Michael, like everyone else, wanted to get on with it, and he cursed the delays as Holdorf and Mother fine-tuned and fine-tuned 387's alignment and vector to get it ready for the 1.5-billion-kilometer microjump that would drop them safely just over 18 million kilometers from Revelation-II.

For Michael, the pressure was doubled by the knowledge that two of the people he most loved in the world would be so close, if only for a brief few hours. Because he was a rational person, it was easy for him to accept that what he was doing was giving them their best chance of coming through this nightmare alive. But at the emotional level, Michael felt like crawling off into a dark corner and howling out his fear and anxiety.

As the jump approached, the ship was at general quarters, with every system online, every station manned, and every hatch and door firmly shut. Michael and his team stood in the drone hangar fully suited up, helmets on but visors open, ready to cope with the usual aftermath of the upcoming jump. Needless to say, Bienefelt had been her usually chatty self, pointing out in suitably grave tones to Michael how much worse a microjump was than a normal pinchspace jump. It was obvious, she had said, if one thought about it. In the space of a second or so the ship first jumped into and then dropped out of pinchspace, so it was bound to be twice as bad as a normal jump. Michael tried not to think about it and just stood there, hunched over like the rest of his team, in his own private world of despair, waiting for the damn thing to happen. The idea that they might actually meet a Hammer warship almost appealed to him. At least they might get to kill a few of the fuckers.

"All stations, this is command. We are go for pinchspace microjump in one minute. Command out."

Michael took a deep breath and instructed his stomach to stay put. Then the world tipped upside down, and Michael braced himself for his stomach to empty in its usual gut-wrenching way. But the jump never happened. He looked up to see Bienefelt and the rest of his team, including Strezlecki, who was supposed to be on his side, for God's sake, he thought, standing there with smiles on their faces that turned into laughs as they saw the indignant look on Michael's face.

"Bastards," Michael said as he realized he had been taken for a ride. "You unprincipled bastards. So much for mutual respect. Right, I won't forget this. You in particular, Bienefelt. I think additional casualty desuiting drills are what's called for. Petty Officer Strezlecki, you, too." It felt good to laugh, to relieve the tension even for a moment, and with a new resolve that things would turn out all right, Michael held his hand up for silence as Mother finally got a grip on what *387* had dropped herself into.

Closing his eyes, Michael commed into the threat plot and dropped himself into a position in space slightly behind and above *387*. For one horrible moment, as bright red threat symbols blossomed in front of him, he thought they had run right into a Hammer task group. But methodically, Mother processed the passive sensor returns, and one by one the red symbols turned to orange: real enough threats but too far away to pose any immediate risk to *387*.

"All stations, this is command. Secure from general quarters. Revert to defense stations, ship state 2, airtight integrity condition yankee. Port watch has the watch. Command out."

As he opened his eyes, the blackness of deep space gave way to the brilliant brightness of the hangar and the cheerful faces of his team. Michael sighed with relief. They had been at general quarters for an hour, an hour that came off his precious off-watch time. He handed over the watch to Petty Officer Strezlecki as he and half the team desuited.

Michael paused at the ladder down to the accommodation level as the captain came up on main broadcast.

"All stations, this is the captain. Just a quick update on how I see things. I think the best way to sum it up is that I have good news and bad news. The good news, as you may by now have realized, is that we weren't ambushed as we dropped out of pinchspace. We've dropped well outside the detection threshold for their long-range passive sensor arrays, and just as important, there are no Hammer warships inside 15 million kilometers. The nearest hostiles are a couple of Constancy Class light escorts fiddling around conducting what look like basic weapon drills. So it's almost certain we got in undetected. We've also got a good laser tight-beam link with *Bonnie,* and we're getting good data. She's a day ahead of us, say, 7 million kilometers out from Hell's Moons, which is where we hope to find the *Mumtaz,* of course. So hopefully *Bonnie* will pick her up. She's scheduled to arrive sometime on the fourteenth, though we don't know when.

"The bad news is Mother has confirmed and refined *Bonnie*'s earlier report of a large number of Hammer ships around Hell's Moons. Currently, Mother is tracking no less than forty-five warships—three heavy and six light cruisers, twelve escorts of various sizes, eighteen patrol ships, four scouts, and two support ships to round out the group. And that's on top of the space battle station capabilities the Hammer has built into its flotilla base. We're going to watch them closely, but I am pretty well convinced they are not there for our benefit. If they were, it'd be overkill by a factor of about ten, and they wouldn't be in orbit, they'd be deployed in a defensive screen perhaps 5 million kilometers out along our most likely approach vector. Which, by the way, is not the vector we are now coming in on.

"So it could get exciting, though I think that's pretty unlikely. We'll wait and see what they get up to. Captain out."

Michael and all the rest of *387*'s crew breathed out heavily as the captain finished. You didn't have to be an Einstein to work out that forty-five Hammer warships created a bit of a problem for Ribot. As Michael hurried down the ladder, he wondered what Ribot was going to do about it.

That very question was exercising Ribot's mind in no uncertain way.

The last THREATSUM from Fleet had said that there was a 95 percent chance that the number of Hammer warships on station would not exceed twenty, the normal battle strength of the Hell flotilla. To minimize the risks, *387*'s route had been chosen carefully to avoid the vectors used regularly by Hell-based warships, whose commanders, like all humans everywhere, were creatures of routine and habit. But having no less than forty-five warships in-system significantly increased the chance that their behavior would not follow normal patterns.

Ribot's worry, amply shared by Mother, was that Hammer ships would use vectors that intersected *387*'s fly-by vector. Mother's concern was reflected in her revised THREAT-SUM. She now put the overall chance of *387* not surviving the fly-by at one in twenty, which as far as Ribot was concerned was an extremely bad number. Taking on that risk wasn't the problem. Ribot knew that somebody had to find the *Mumtaz* as soon as possible; *387* had gotten the job, and that was the end of it. No, it was waiting for the ax to fall, not knowing if it was going to happen and, if it was, when. Ribot could think of nothing worse.

He commed the combat information center, where Hosani had the watch.

"Maria, I'm going to do a walk-around to see how everyone is. When I've done that, I'm going to put my head down while things are quiet. But call me if you need to."

"Sir."

An hour later, Ribot was satisfied that all was well with his little bubble of civilization as it flew into the heart of Hammer darkness. With no sign that the Hammer ships were going to leave their berths, Ribot slipped into a deep dreamless sleep.

Saturday, September 12, 2398, UD
Planetary Transfer Station, in Clarke Orbit around
Commitment Planet

Ever since the coded pinchcomms message announcing the successful takeover of *Mumtaz* had come through from Comonec, the tension inside Digby had built.

He knew all too well that with every step the project took, the personal risk to him grew. It wasn't just because Merrick needed him less and less. It wasn't just Digby's suspicion that Merrick had no intention of letting him survive. No, it was the Feds. If they showed their hand too early, Merrick would know instantly that he had been betrayed. At that point, as Merrick had explained to him with admirable clarity and force of purpose, Digby's life was forfeit whether or not he'd been responsible for the breach, and he would be handed over to DocSec for disposal.

At least, he thought with some relief as the up-shuttle from McNair finally docked with the planetary transfer station, he was putting himself outside Merrick's immediate reach. If he could delay his return to Commitment for some reason or other and if the Feds took their time mounting their rescue mission, Merrick would begin to believe that he had gotten away with it, and his justifiable lack of trust in Digby might fade to the point where there was no need to dispose of him.

One thing was absolutely clear: If he wanted to survive to see his wife again, he had better not be anywhere near Merrick when the Feds did make their move. The more he thought about it, the more he realized that the best place for him to be, the only safe place for him to be, was dirtside on Eternity, overseeing the terraforming project.

He would have to invent some plausible reasons why a brigadier general of marines who knew less than nothing about terraforming should be heading up the project rather than Professor Cornelius Wang, formerly head of the School of Exobiology at the University of McNair. Wang was now a resident of Hell after some very ill-advised comments on the mental state of the councillor for the preservation of doctrine, one Angus Jessop. Wang's mistake had been to make those comments to his deputy, Marais Landon, a man he'd known almost all his adult life and one of the few people he thought he could trust. Sadly for Professor Wang, his faith in his deputy had been misplaced, and he was on Hell to prove it while Landon enjoyed being the new head of the School of Exobiology.

Though Digby privately agreed wholeheartedly with Wang's statement that Jessop was, and Digby could quote verbatim from the investigating tribunal's records, "a mentally unstable psychopath who was a disgrace to Kraa," he would never be so stupid as to say so publicly. Sadly for Wang, his defense—that he had been very drunk and had meant it only as a joke—had cut no ice with the tribunal. Their unsympathetic view, supported by precedents stretching back to the early years of the Hammer of Kraa, was that alcohol promoted the truth; it did not confuse or obscure it. After a trial lasting all of two and a half minutes and with his character witnesses left outside the tribunal chamber uncalled and unheard—Wang had managed to find two friends not only brave but stupid enough to stand up in public on his behalf—the tribunal did what it was paid to do and found him guilty before passing his case for confirmation of sentence up to the Supreme Tribunal for the Preservation of the Faith.

Two minutes after his sentencing hearing closed, Wang was on his way to a ten-year stay in Hell without the chance to say goodbye to his wife and three children.

But Digby had no doubts, none at all, that Wang would do an outstanding job. By Kraa, he would have plenty of incentives, not the least of which was Digby's firm promise that he would never have to return to Hell again. But it seemed to Digby that he would have to point out to Chief Councillor Merrick that people like that couldn't be trusted, and then it would be obvious that Digby would be best used making sure that Wang and his crew of xenobiologists, xenoecologists, atmospheric scientists, logistics engineers, and the rest—amazing who ended up on Hell, thought Digby—behaved themselves. In the best interests of the project as a whole, of course.

A small security incident would do the trick, Digby decided. Nothing too serious but enough to encourage Merrick to leave him where he was until the Feds came and put an end to the whole lunatic scheme, as they surely would. Of that he had absolutely no doubt.

Five minutes later and much happier in his mind, he was safely onboard the Councillor class light scout *Myosan,* the small starship marked out as one of the chief councillor's personal flotilla by a titanium hull polished to a mirror finish, by gold trim, and by its massive Kraa sunburst symbols, also in gold.

As Digby gave the orders to drop from the transfer station and clear Commitment as soon as possible, he settled back in a comfortable armchair in his private suite, facing the holovid display that was taking feeds from the hull-mounted holocams. *Myosan* was one of the fastest starships in the Hammer order of battle, and if all went well, it would have Digby safely docked at the Hell transfer station in time for breakfast the next day.

The telephone handset embedded in the arm of his chair chimed softly.

"Digby."

"This is Commander Williams. Welcome back, sir."

"Thank you, Commander. Always a pleasure to be back onboard the *Myosan*."

"Thank you, sir. We have received our departure clearance and will be unberthing in ten minutes' time. Allowing thirty minutes to maneuver clear of the transfer station, we will leave Commitment innerspace at 21:43. The microjump is scheduled for 22:20, and it will take just under five seconds to get to Hell."

"How far, Commander?"

"A fraction under 6 billion kilometers, sir. All being well, we'll be docking at 04:00 tomorrow morning."

"Thank you, Commander. For obvious reasons, I'll stay up for the jumps, but then I'll turn in. When we arrive, I'd like you to arrange a shuttle to transfer me to be at Hell Central. I have a meeting with Prison Governor Costigan at 08:30."

"Won't be a problem, sir. Just call the duty steward on 236 to let him know when you'd like to eat or if there's anything else you need. Otherwise, we'll leave you in peace."

"Thank you, Commander."

Late that evening, Michael had the watch. Heart in mouth, he acknowledged Mother's report of a distinctive brilliant ultraviolet flash as yet another starship arrived in-system.

Twenty seconds later, the passive sensors had collected the

data Mother needed to categorize the new arrival as military, possibly a light scout but more likely a courier.

Sick at heart, Michael agreed with Mother that it was not worth waking the captain for. He just wondered how much longer he could keep his last few tattered shreds of hope alive. Where the hell was the *Mumtaz*?

Sunday, September 13, 2398, UD
Hell Planet (Revelation-II) Innerspace

Digby watched the holovid with interest as the little inter-moon transfer shuttle, a modified light utility lander only 20 meters in length with a smooth white plasteel hull punctured only by the obligatory brilliant orange flashing anticollision lights, two mass driver nozzles, maneuvering reaction control jets, and landing gear, pushed away from the planetary transfer station.

Once it was clear, the shuttle changed vector sharply for its run in toward Hell Central, the twelfth and, at 1,570 kilometers in diameter, the largest of Hell's moons and the nerve center from which Prison Governor Costigan managed Hell's only real reason to exist: its network of driver mass plants. Digby had always considered the naming scheme very unoriginal. He had an enduring love of Shakespeare and inevitably would have turned to him for inspiration if faced with the challenge of naming twenty-two moons. But there were no Juliets or Violas, Desdemonas or Cordelias, here. Nothing about Hell was appealing enough for anyone to want to name any bit of it after any person, character, or place he or she loved or cared for.

So Hell-1,-2,-3, all the way up to Hell-22 was all the naming the moons of Revelation-II would get.

As the shuttle pulled away, the bright arc lights of the transfer station quickly coalesced behind them into a single brilliant point of orange-white light, and darkness rapidly took over. The Revelation system's star, an orange-red dwarf, was too small, too dim, and at 5.9 billion kilometers too far away to be of any value as a source of light. Forty-six thousand kilometers below the shuttle, more sensed than seen, discernible only as a black circle cut out of the stars that hung in curtains on all sides, was the massive bulk of Hell—Revelation-II—itself, a U-Class planet with the usual ragingly violent methane, hydrogen, and helium atmosphere and precious little else worth talking about. With gravity of 107 percent of Earth normal, it had been able to host a small scattering of research stations staffed by a handful of brave souls but nothing else.

There had been a short-lived attempt dreamed up by some business expert in the Department of Economic Affairs to operate a tourist center in the vain hope that the cost of supporting the Hell penal system would come down if enough tourists could be persuaded to defray the costs of supporting the hideously expensive Commitment–Hell shuttles.

Needless to say, the scheme had not worked, doomed by the unforgiving economics of getting people into the Hell system in the first place, down to the planet, and then back home again, not to mention the significant fact, ignored by the bureaucrats in their planning, that there was little worth seeing on Hell. Once you had seen one methane storm, you had seen them all, particularly as they all happened in the pitch dark of Hell's permanent night. To cap it all, tourists were not at all keen on sharing their accommodations with criminals even if those criminals were securely held under lock and key.

Finally, when all he could see were stars and faint black lumps that might have been moons, Digby swung the cameras to face the way they were going and keyed the holovid to put up a computer-generated overlay to help him make sense of what he wasn't seeing.

The shuttle covered the 200 kilometers between the transfer station and Hell Central without any fuss, and as they approached, Digby was finally able to make out the dull gray-black shape of the moon and, as they curved in, the blaze of lights that marked Prison Governor Costigan's domain. With 5 kilometers to run, the lander spun on its axis to point its mass drivers at a moon whose 1.7 m/sec^2 gravitational field was able to kill the lander if it dropped from far enough out. With the usual rattling and banging of reaction control thrusters and the occasional thump from the mass drivers, the pilot eased the lander gently down Hell Central's gravity well and onto the brilliantly lit landing pad.

Within minutes the lander had docked and Digby was safely inside the plascrete complex that was Hell Central's raison d'être clearing the usual intense security, and stripping off his survival suit. Leaving his escort scrambling to catch up, he collected his thoughts and set off down the long, brightly lit corridors at a brisk walk toward Costigan's office.

Costigan waved Digby into a seat in front of a large and very ugly desk.

The horrible thing was supposed to look like teak, Digby guessed. It was a pity that it looked like precisely what it really was: a very badly painted assembly of crudely veneered plasfiber panels. And behind the abomination sat Prison Governor Costigan. He was seven or so years older than Digby, and his deeply lined face radiated his trademark unhappiness.

And why not? Digby thought in an unusually sympathetic moment. Hell was hell, and the prison governor's job was probably no fun at all. But enough sympathy, Digby thought as Costigan's personal assistant handed him a cup of coffee. Let's get on with it.

"Governor, first I am happy to confirm that the, uh, target should drop in-system on schedule tomorrow at 12:00 UT, give or take a few minutes. Allowing, say, five hours for the deceleration burn, we should have her standing off a safe distance from Hell-13 ready to do the crew change and for the transfer of personnel for processing."

Costigan nodded. He knew all that. "What about the military? Won't they be curious as to just who this target of yours actually is? Rear Admiral Pritchard runs things pretty tightly around here, and you'll have noticed we've got a lot of ships in-system at the moment."

Digby nodded. "Fair question. For your information, and please do not inquire any further, the target is the Esmereldan mership *Maria J. Velasquez,* here under charter to the chief councillor's squadron. I should also add that she has filed a valid flight plan, has all the necessary clearances from Revelation system command, and Admiral Pritchard's combat data center team has been given strict instructions not to mess with her."

"Oh. Okay. Sounds good. It seems things are going well, whatever those things are." Digby could see that Costigan desperately wanted to know what exactly he was up to.

Digby held up a cautionary hand. "Let's not go there, Governor. Trust me when I say that there are times when you really do not want to know and this is one of those times."

Costigan nodded, but very ungraciously.

"So you have my security team, the replacement crew for the target, and my team of scientists?"

"Yes. Security team in Holding Cage Delta-4, crew in Bravo-1, and your scientists in Kilo-4, all scared shitless, wondering what is going to happen to them. The security team especially. They are all ex-marine personnel with between two and five years to go and good records. A holding cage is not where they would expect or want to be at this stage in their sentences."

"Well, I intend to fix that. I've reviewed the files of everyone you've nominated and can see no problems. I have a few issues with some of the people you've selected but nothing that I can't resolve in the final interviews. Major Nkomo's a very good man, an extremely competent marine. I knew him when he was a company commander in the 3/22nd before his, er, his little falling out with DocSec.

"As soon as we've finished, I want the secure briefing room set up. I'll finalize my security team first. Then the crew and the scientists after that. All the equipment and clothing needed by the crew and scientists is onboard the target. My ship has everything needed by the security team. And the remassing drones for the target?"

"Already on station, standing by."

"Personnel records? I don't want any awkward questions

being asked by the prisons administration people back on McNair."

Costigan waved a hand dismissively. "Fixed. As of today your men are all dead, officially speaking, that is, but the routine notifications to next of kin will, er, how can I put it? Get lost, yes, lost. The families will still expect them when their sentences finish. And I'm classing the new arrivals as Article 41 prisoners delivered by DocSec direct to Hell."

"Article 41?" Digby asked, puzzled. That was something new.

"Prisoners whose files are classified and here to stay until they die. Stops awkward questions. Very popular with Doc-Sec."

"Ah, okay," Digby said thoughtfully. "So, do I need to be concerned about the prisons administration or DocSec stumbling over this?"

Costigan snorted contemptuously. "General, please! You think they care? Prisons administration only cares that the numbers on my books are correct, and they're correct if I say they are. As for DocSec, judging by the number of people they're shipping to me, things on Faith are getting out of hand. Let me tell you, General," Costigan said, finger stabbing the desk emphatically. "DocSec's paperwork is so fucked up, they don't even know what damn day of the week it is. So, no. As far as prisons administration is concerned, they'll just be numbers, and I don't think DocSec will give a shit. They've got their hands full."

Digby smiled. Costigan might be a miserable asshole, but at least he was an efficient miserable asshole. "Good. On top of things as always. I think that's all for now unless there is anything else you can think of, Governor."

Costigan shook his head. "Nothing, General."

Digby started to get up but stopped. "Oh, Governor. One last thing. Get your comsec team to report to me in the conference room as well. I'll need a full sweep and a certificate of clearance from the comsec team leader. I do hope, Governor, that nobody's been tempted to bug the room."

Costigan's face whitened in shock, and Digby realized that he had done just that.

Digby paused for a moment, eyes hard and merciless, before sitting back down in his chair, his thin tight smile completely devoid of good humor.

"Well, Governor. I think you might like to go and make a few calls while I drink my coffee. I think the conference room ought to be ready in, say, ten minutes?"

Costigan could only nod in silent acknowledgment as he got to his feet. If he was at all grateful for the reprieve Digby had just given him, it didn't show.

Digby suppressed a sigh as Costigan hurried out of the office. Nothing would have given him more pleasure than to hand the bloody man over to DocSec, but sadly, he needed Costigan and this was not the time to move against him. But if he survived, he would make sure that Costigan's day would come.

Digby sat back in his chair at the front of the empty conference room.

He flipped his microvid screen up and gave his eyes a long rub. It had been a very long day, and he had the aching muscles to prove it, but finally all was ready for *Mumtaz*'s arrival the next day. The security team had been dispatched to the *Myosan* ready for the next day's final briefings. Digby had never seen men look so relieved. The prospect of arming 120 ex-convicts had caused him and *Myosan*'s commander a brief moment of anxiety, but it had passed just as quickly. The specification called for men with good military records imprisoned for minor infringements of doctrine with young families that they desperately wanted to see again. But the winning card was the offer of migration with their families and a small cash reward to anywhere in humanspace that was willing to take them when it was all over.

No, these men all had too much to lose, and Digby was absolutely confident that he had their trust and loyalty even if he, as an agent of the government that had locked them up in the first place, without any justification, had no right to expect either.

The only risky thing he had to accomplish was the transfer of Comonec and his team off the ship and safely into the hands of Costigan and his thugs. But they knew that the plan called for them to hand over the ship to a relief crew, after which they were supposed to get their second payment and disappear. Well, they'd disappear, all right, but, sadly for them, not one cent richer than when they started.

Digby collected his papers, shut down his digital assistant, unclipped his microvid screen, and called the governor. With some small satisfaction, Digby realized that he had gotten Costigan out of bed.

"Governor. Sorry to disturb you," he said without a trace of regret. "I'm done. Please have my shuttle ready. And no mistakes tomorrow. Anything else you need to tell me? No? All right, then, I'm off. Good night."

Twenty-five minutes later and no more than a blur against the stars, *Bonnie* had crossed the orbit of Revelation-II. Seconds later she slipped unobserved past Hell Central at 15,000 kilometers, missing an unsuspecting shuttle from Hell-9 on final approach by less than 5 kilometers.

The little surveillance drone was one of the triumphs of Federated Worlds engineering. Packed with the best electromagnetic radiation and gravitronics microsensor systems the Worlds' technology could produce, the drone vacuumed data out of Hammer nearspace at a phenomenal rate and, taking extreme care that no Hammer warships or sensors were in the line of sight, fired the data over the tightbeam laser a million kilometers back to *387,* where an increasingly stressed command team looked anxiously for confirmation that *Mumtaz* was in-system.

But *Mumtaz* was nowhere to be seen.

Nine minutes later, *Bonnie* skimmed above the desolate and blasted surface of Hell-11. Then, with Revelation-II's gravity pulling its vector inward, *Bonnie,* nose on to minimize its radar cross section, curved in to pass Hell's Flotilla base and its thick cluster of Hammer warships, the stealth coat absorbing the energy thrown at it by the Hammer's phased-array radar.

For a brief moment a bored sensor operator thought he

might have seen a faint ghostly return, but it didn't last, and in the interests of a quiet watch he didn't bother to do anything about it.

At 00:28, *Bonnie* passed Hell-13 and was on her way out of Revelation-II nearspace.

Wherever the *Mumtaz* was, it wasn't in orbit around Revelation-II or any of its moons.

Tuesday, September 15, 2398, UD
Hell Planet (Revelation-II) Nearspace

Ribot had closed the ship up to general quarters when Hell Central was just over 500,000 kilometers away.

Petty Officer Strezlecki, along with Helfort and the rest of the surveillance drone team, was suited up. But with the ship's artificial gravity shut down to reduce the effectiveness of Hammer grav arrays, the wait was not as unbearable as usual.

What was certain was that after days of anxiety, the strain of not knowing was slowly tearing Helfort apart, to the point where Strezlecki was beginning to get concerned about his mental state. Smart man, the skipper, she thought. He'd known this would happen, had been worried enough to ask her to keep a very close eye on Michael. Squinting sideways past the edge of her helmet, she watched as Michael stood to one side, a light sheen of sweat clearly visible through his open visor underneath the bright orange oxygen mask, eyes unfocused and breathing heavy. She moved a little closer to be by his side.

"Surveillance, command."

Patching her neuronics in, she watched Michael carefully as he took the captain's comm.

"Surveillance."

"Petty Officer Strezlecki? You in on this?" Ribot asked.

"Yes, sir," Strezlecki said, puzzled. Of course she was. As a matter of routine she'd sit in on all comms to and from surveillance. What was the skipper going on about?

"Ah, good. You need to hear this, too, Michael. Even though her registration has been painted out, and she's squawking on Esmereldan ID, Mother has been able to confirm that the UV drop intercept we made earlier is in fact the *Mumtaz*. She's not berthed on Hell's planetary transfer station; she's on vector for Hell-13, where there's a lot of activity—drone remassers, transfer shuttles, and so on. So it seems pretty clear that Fleet's right: She looks to be leaving before very much longer. Not much else to say, Michael, except how sorry I am. But the good news is that *Mumtaz* looks fine, no damage anywhere that we can see, and I'm sure your family is safe." Ribot's voice dried up as he ran out of things to say, and for a moment there was silence.

"Thanks for that, sir," Michael said in a half whisper.

Now Strezlecki understood why Ribot wanted her in on the comm, and she watched as Helfort began to draw himself up straight for the first time in days, his hunched and defeated posture beginning to fade.

But Michael's avatar was still gray-faced. "Michael, are you there? Are you okay?" Ribot sounded concerned. As any good skipper would, Strezlecki thought.

"Oh, sorry, sir. Yes, I'll be fine. Actually, it's a bit of a relief now that we at least know what's going on. And sir, I'm from a Fleet family, and I'm sure that the Fleet will get them all back."

Finally Michael's voice had some of its old strength, some emotion in it, even if his face still didn't, Strezlecki realized.

Ribot couldn't quite conceal the relief in his voice. "Michael, nothing in life is certain except that the Hammers are scum. But I think we can be pretty sure that the Worlds won't take this lying down. There are still plenty of people who haven't forgotten what happened the last time around, so I think it's just a matter of time. That was certainly the impression I got from Fleet operations when I spoke to them, so have faith. I've got no doubts. We will get them back."

"I can't see the Worlds leaving what, a thousand or so people, in the Hammers' hands, sir. So I'm sure you're right." Michael's voice grew in strength and determination with every word, his face beginning to lose its gray pallor.

"Let's hope so, Michael. Now, we've got things to do, so let's leave it at that. I've got to tell the crew what's going on."

"Fine, sir. And thanks."

"No problem," Ribot said. "Command out."

Petty Officer Strzelcki stood for a moment, acutely aware of the fact that everything Ribot had just said applied only if *387* wasn't caught.

"Holy Mary, mother of God!" Holdorf couldn't contain himself, earning a look of savage disapproval from Ribot as the threat plot suddenly blossomed with the bright red lines of a pinchspace gravitronics intercept.

"Command, this is sensors. I have a positive gravitronics intercept. One vessel. Grav wave pattern indicates pinchspace transition imminent. Estimated drop at Green 60 Down 2. Appears to be headed for Hell Central."

Ribot cursed savagely under his breath. *387*'s track had been carefully chosen to keep it well clear of Hammer ships dropping out of pinchspace, which they usually did on the sunward side of Hell planet. Now this bastard was coming in almost at right angles and from God only knew where.

Outwardly unconcerned, Ribot acknowledged the report. "Roger that. Nothing much we can do, folks. Let's hope they are slow to set up after the drop and we'll be past and gone."

Ribot's voice was calm and measured as he offered up a silent prayer of thanks that almost all of the Hammer ships in-system were at the flotilla base on Hell-8, almost 400,000 kilometers away and way outside the radar detection threshold against a stealthed light scout. Even better, they were still showing absolutely no sign of moving.

But this warship was different.

If the Hammer ship was dropping in-system, heading for Hell Central, it would drop when *387* was about 200,000 kilometers away and as a result well inside the radar detection threshold. If the Hammers reset sensors as quickly as they should after a pinchspace drop, if their equipment was working, and if the operators were on top of their jobs, there was a reasonable chance that one of them would pick up *387*. That was a lot of if's, true, but not too much to expect of any half-decent warship crew. Ribot knew all too well how the Hammers always reacted to unidentified warships in Hammer space. Without exception, an immediate rail-gun barrage or missile salvo first and questions, if anything was left to question, second. In that case, there was only one way out: an immediate jump into the safety of pinchspace.

If that happened, he might as well send them an autographed, framed holopic of *387*, he thought glumly.

But for the moment, there was little he could do apart from curse his luck that *387* hadn't been thirty minutes earlier and hope that the Hammers were slow to reset their sensors. Mother would fine-tune the ship's active chromaflage coat to make sure the hull was doing what it was designed to do—look like an asteroid, closely enough, he hoped to fool the Hammer's infrared and optical analysis—but apart from that, they were relying on the power of prayer, sadly a notoriously unreliable nostrum.

Ribot hoped he'd done the right thing. Going active was always a risk, and like all warship captains, he hated taking risks until the shooting started. The alternative of relying on *387*'s stealthcoat to absorb the Hammer's radar was asking for trouble. The Hammer warship's grav arrays would tell it something was out there; when its radars couldn't see anything, there would be only one reason why: a stealth warship—so stand by missile attack.

"Command, sensors. Drop datum confirmed at Green 60 Down 1 at 200,000."

"Roger, Mother. All stations, Captain. We have a Hammer ship dropping 200,000 k's at Green 60, and we'll be within range of their sensors when they do. There's nothing much we can do, but if we detect a rail-gun or missile release, we'll be jumping immediately, so stand by."

Ribot took a deep breath. He'd allowed himself to believe they would get through this fly-by undetected. "Propulsion, command. Stand by emergency jump." The atmosphere in the combat information center was thick with tension as he sat back in his chair, fighting hard to look both confident and unconcerned. His father had often said that leadership was as much acting as anything else, and for once Ribot couldn't agree more.

As he waited for the inbound Hammer ship to drop, Ribot cursed long and hard under his breath. One decent radar paint, one decent grav intercept, one decent optronics image, and it was game over. Fleet would have little or no chance of getting the *Mumtaz* back.

"Command, sensors, contact dropping now. Datum confirmed Green 62 Down 2, range 210,000 kilometers. Stand by vector."

"Command, roger." Ribot wanted to do something, but he couldn't. There was nothing *387* could do. She just had to ride it out. The tension in the combat information center was palpable, and it wasn't just tension. It was fear as well, gut-churning fear, the product of decades of demonizing the Hammer, fear strong enough to drive *387*'s command team down into shapes hunched over workstations. Their ship was a long way from home, alone deep in Hammer space, and about to have a close encounter of the worst kind with what could only be a Hammer warship, and everybody knew it.

"Command, sensors. Contact confirmed as Triumph class heavy cruiser, *Carswell*. Vector confirmed. Inbound for Hell Central."

"Command, roger." Terrific, Ribot thought, just terrific. A goddamm heavy cruiser. A quick check. Yes, he'd remembered it right. The *Carswell* was one of the oldest cruisers in the Hammer order of battle, but she was an adversary to be feared nonetheless. Any slipup now and *387* was toast, and very badly charred toast at that. Sweat began to trickle cold and slimy down his spine. He shivered. He looked around; even through closed faceplates he could see the tension on every face.

Ribot turned back to the command plot, which now showed the red icons that marked the *Carswell*'s position and vector. It was not a pretty sight. The Hammer ship was way too close for comfort. And then the command plot blos-

somed with a new icon, a long stabbing line reporting the
fact that *Carswell*'s planar arrays had deployed and its long-
range search radar was painting the *387* with a torrent of
radio frequency (RF) energy.

Ribot sighed in fatalistic resignation. What would be,
would be. Right about now the Hammer command team
should be working out that the unknown contact 200,000
kilometers away wasn't all it seemed to be at first sight.

Thanks to *387*'s active chromaflage skin, *Carswell*'s optronics would report it as nothing more than another insignificant S-type siliceous asteroid, one of the countless
asteroids that wandered the cosmos. But even allowing for
the fact that 200,000 kilometers was a very long way even
for Fed gravitronics systems, especially against a small target like *387,* the mass analysis provided by the *Carswell*'s
grav arrays would tell her captain that the object's density
was way too low for an asteroid. First red flag. Then, to bang
another nail into *387*'s coffin, infrared would report the object as fractionally too warm. Second red flag. True, *387*'s
heat sinks were so good that it would be only by a tiny
amount, but together with the other inconsistencies, any warship captain worth his salt wouldn't ignore two red flags.
He'd dump a missile salvo down the threat axis, sit back, and
see what happened. Ribot knew he would.

Ribot's virtual finger twitched over the bright red virtual
emergency jump button. Any second now, any second now.
Barely breathing, he sat unmoving, waiting for the inevitable: the tightly focused beam of a missile fire control
radar followed by the infrared blooms of an inbound missile
salvo.

Time slowed to a crawl for Ribot, his shipsuit now cold,
saturated with sweat under a space suit suddenly tight and
constricted, the helmet ring digging into shoulders that were
taut with tension. "Jesus Christ," he muttered. Surely the
Hammers must have worked it out. What in God's name were
they up to? The most inexperienced captain would have
launched missiles by now. Hell, even a first-year cadet at
Space Fleet College would be on to them; they were fed sim-

ple tactical problems like the one facing the *Carswell* for breakfast.

If it were possible, time slowed down even more until Ribot began to entertain the hope that *Carswell* might just be more than an old heavy cruiser. She might be an old and unreliable heavy cruiser, and the more he thought about it, that was the only thing that made any sense. If *Carswell*'s sensors had been 100 percent online, *387* would have been on the receiving end of a missile attack long before now. She wasn't being attacked, so *Carswell* must be having problems. Sensors, maybe? Or the data analysis and integration software? Operator error? Anyway, it didn't matter why. The fact was, it was beginning to look very much like *387* had gotten away with it.

Ribot put a sudden burst of optimism firmly away. He'd wait another five agonizingly long and slow minutes before he'd allow himself that luxury. In the meantime, his virtual finger would stay firmly over the emergency jump button, his eyes locked on the plot for any sign of a Hammer missile launch.

It would be a long five minutes.

Michael and everyone else onboard heaved a huge sigh of relief as Mother downgraded the threat from the the aging and seemingly unreliable *Carswell*. The threat plot now was a mass of orange symbols and a reassuring change from the lurid reds of just a few moments earlier.

For one awful moment, like everyone else onboard, Michael had thought it was all over, sick at the thought that the Hammers might get not just him but Mom and Sam as well. He couldn't begin to imagine how his dad would cope with a disaster of that magnitude.

When Mother identified the new arrival as a deepspace heavy cruiser, it should have been game over.

But for some reason, they had survived undetected.

Anyway, it was all academic now, and Michael didn't have enough emotional energy left to worry why. The threat analysis teams back at Fleet would get the datalogs. Let them work out why *387* had gotten away with it. Getting safely through the outer ring of surveillance satellites that circled Hell at 3 million kilometers was the next job. In theory, that shouldn't be a problem because *387* would have to pass well inside 100,000 kilometers for a Hammer surveillance satellite to have any chance of picking up something that well stealthed and deceptive. Once well clear, *387* would maneuver to recover its surveillance drones and then jump to Eternity planet to confirm that part two of the Hammer plan was as reported. That should be a piece of cake compared to what we've just been through, Michael thought, unless it really is a trap. That was a possibility he'd found out was running at odds of fifty to one in the strictly unofficial book being run by Leading Spacer Miandad in propulsion.

But judging by the swarm of activity waiting for *Mumtaz* at Hell-13, it was no trap. Everything pointed to the *Mumtaz* being turned around and sent on her way to Eternity planet long before *387* got far enough out to jump out-system without being detected.

As soon as Holdorf stood the ship down from general quarters and restored its artgrav and atmosphere, Michael left the drone hangar. It was time to get out of his truly rancid, sweat-soaked, foul-smelling space suit for a long and well-earned shower followed by a good night's sleep. Six more days would see them fly by Eternity, an undertaking he earnestly hoped would be a great deal less stressful than the Hell fly-by if Fleet's THREATSUMs were to be believed. Then another week to get to Frontier planet and the job would be done.

It would be interesting, Michael thought as he went down the ladder, to see the effect Ribot's report had on Space Fleet and the politicians.

With *387*'s pinchcomms message confirming the hijacking of the *Mumtaz,* the full seriousness of the situation finally had sunk in. All of them, from flag officers on up, sat silent as they worked out the full implications of what the Hammer had done.

Up to that point, the frantic work of Battle Fleet Delta's hastily appointed staff had had a strange air of unreality about it, as if there still were some chance that the whole thing was an elaborate hoax and in the end the *Mumtaz* would drop out of pinchspace safely, on vector and decelerating into one of Jackson's two planetary transfer stations. Angela Jaruzelska also had felt the fear in everybody's mind, the terrible fear that once again the Federated Worlds would have to go to war against its most long-standing and bitter enemy.

At fifty-six, she was old enough to have been through the last round with the Hammer in the late '70s, and it was not an experience she would ever want to repeat. But then, she had chosen the Fleet and it had chosen her. With God's help, she would do her best to make sure that this time around the Hammers would be repaid tenfold for their stupidity and greed.

A glass of very fine Anjaxxian Pinot Noir cradled in her left hand, its heady perfume washing over her, Jaruzelska settled into her favorite chair on the broad timber deck that overlooked the sky-shaded lights of Foundation that were spread out below her.

Midnight was fast approaching. It had been another very long day.

Getting approval for the operation to recover the *Mumtaz*—Operation Corona it was now officially called—had not been easy. The preliminary concept of the operation had shocked the cabinet with its complexity, unavoidably so, given the mission objectives set. But what had really stunned the inner cabinet had been the risk assessment with its sobering estimates of the ships and lives that could be lost. For a moment, Jaruzelska had been surprised by the impact her casualty estimates had had.

What did they think?

That the Fleet could waltz into Hammer space, retrieve the hostages, and waltz out again while the Hammers sat on their big fat asses and let it all happen?

But in the end, the cabinet's go-ahead had been emphatic and unequivocal. She had thought there might be some of the weaseling around one expected from politicians, but there had been none. Jaruzelska strongly suspected that whichever Hammer genius had thought up the *Mumtaz* hijacking plan had completely misunderstood the Worlds in general and the ruling New Liberal government in particular. Despite the fact that it had ended nineteen years earlier and even though people no longer talked about it as much as they once had, apart from the Veterans of Interstellar Wars, of course, the most enduring legacy of the Third Hammer War was a deeply held hatred of the Hammer and total distrust of all its works.

So if she was to be totally cynical, maybe the politicians understood that and thought the idea of a nice clean war against a despised enemy on clear-cut and unambiguous moral grounds would be a good thing politically.

She sighed as she brought the wineglass to her lips. She was sure there was no such thing as a nice clean war. However, tomorrow she would have her staff rework the concept of operations to see if they could get a bit closer to a risk-free operation, something that could exist only in the minds of politicians.

Friday, September 18, 2398, UD
Offices of the Supreme Council for the Preservation of
the Faith, City of McNair, Commitment Planet

Chief Councillor Merrick leaned back in his chair as he finished reading Digby's latest report fresh from the courier drone.

As usual, it was brief and very much to the point. More important, it made Merrick happy for once. Unlike most of the self-serving rubbish that crossed his desk, it made for good reading. The holovid clips of the new base were good to see, too, and made it all real. Not only had Digby's team pulled it off, security remained tight. How had his long-dead father put it? Oh, yes, tight as a duck's ass. Merrick smiled as the half-forgotten phrase came back to mind. No, so far so good, and there was no sign of any leak to the Feds, and that was what mattered above all. If the news leaked, he was a dead man. But if all went well, he would be able to announce the successful start of Eternity's terraforming at a time and place of his choosing and with certain—how could he put it?—elements of the plan carefully concealed. The idea was intoxicating, and for a brief moment he enjoyed the thought of how it would feel as he announced to his fellow Hammers that there was hope for them, the hope of a new planet on which to grow and flourish under Kraa's beneficence.

Thank Kraa, Digby seemed rock-solid. The last report he had called for from DocSec had had nothing in it but the routine report of a man doing his job and getting the results he was expected to get. Merrick had had his doubts about the man. The departure of Digby's wife to visit family in some Kraa-forsaken outpost of Earth still didn't sit completely right with him, but to have turned down Digby's request might have unsettled the man just when Merrick wanted him completely focused. No, Digby was his man, and he was exactly where he was needed most: on Eternity, making sure that the grab bag of ex-convicts and Feds he'd been given got on with the job at hand. It hadn't been planned that way. In fact, his intention all along had been to eliminate Digby as soon as possible. The man simply knew too much to be allowed to go back to McNair, but given the way things were going, Merrick was happy to postpone the moment. But it was only a postponement, not a cancellation. If he'd learned anything in the viciously brutal school of Hammer politics, it was to eliminate any loose ends long before you needed to. That way, you kept control.

Anyway, enough of that.

It was still many months before the final phase of the Eternity plan, the bit that even Digby didn't know about, could be put in place. Pity to waste all that talent, but Merrick wanted no witnesses, Hammers or Feds, to what he had begun to think of as the miracle of Eternity. He only hoped that he'd be given the time, he thought sourly as he turned his mind to the increasingly serious problem of unrest on Faith. Merrick knew that Polk was going to have a go at him over the issue, and for the first time he felt a small twinge of unease. History showed over and over that civil unrest could rapidly become full-blown insurrection if it was not handled with the right balance of brutality and concession.

And history offered one more lesson: A chief councillor who allowed a serious insurrection to go unchecked never lasted long.

Within minutes of starting, the weekly meeting of the Supreme Council had degenerated from the routine into a vicious running battle with Polk over the situation on Faith. As he liked to do, Merrick had sat back to watch the battle unfold, unwilling to get involved just yet. "Eat shit, you miserable scumbag," he muttered as he watched Councillor Polk wilt visibly in the face of a furious attack from Claude Albrecht, councillor for foreign relations and probably the only man at the Council table he'd even come close to trusting.

"Kraa's blood, Councillor!" Albrecht said angrily, fist

pounding the table, "You know what the real problem on Faith is. It has nothing to do with heresy, not a damn thing. It's that corrupt piece of shit Herris, and you damn well know it! How can you call it an attack on the Path of Doctrine? It's all about corruption. Corruption, Councillor Polk, corruption. Kraa! And we know who's responsible, don't we? Herris, that's who. Planetary Councillor Herris! Come on, tell me I'm wrong."

Merrick watched with some enjoyment as Polk squirmed in his chair. The man might be a jumped-up parvenu, but he wasn't completely stupid. He'd know what everyone around the table knew even if they weren't all prepared to admit it. Put simply, the man charged with Faith's administration, Planetary Councillor Herris, was an irredeemably corrupt man with very extravagant tastes. Sadly for Herris, the patience and tolerance of the long-suffering people of Faith, the people who paid his bills in the end, were beginning to run out. It was as simple and straightforward as that, and heresy had nothing to do with it.

Merrick knew it, Polk knew it, everybody around the table knew it.

But Polk was not going to concede.

"Councillor!" he spit as Albrecht's attack finally ran out of steam, his voice dropping to a vicious whisper. "I'd be very careful if I were you. I would hate you to say something you might come to regret. Who knows," he said, his voice silky quiet, menacing, "what the future holds."

Merrick had to stop himself from laughing out loud. Still think you're going to be chief councillor, do you, you useless corrupt fool? Not a chance.

Albrecht shared Merrick's contempt for the man across the Council table and wasn't afraid to let it show. "Save it, Councillor Polk. It's your man, Herris. You know it, and I know it. We all know it. He's the problem, and he'll bring us all down if we don't do something about it soon."

Polk's face reddened with rage. It was obvious he knew where this was going. "I promise you, Albrecht—"

"Enough, Councillor!" Merrick sliced through Polk's response like a whip. "Enough," he said, looking Polk right in the eye until the man's head dropped in defeat. That's better, Merrick said to himself. You can bluff and bluster all you like, but you and I both know the truth. Herris is your man and you're his for the simple reason that your obscenely extravagant tastes are paid for by Herris, which Herris was happy to do in exchange for Polk's protection and patronage.

Merrick looked around the Council table. Now. His instincts urged him on. This was the time to strike.

"Let us not waste any more time," he said calmly, the faces of all present reflecting their uncertainty. Good. They knew he was up to something, but they didn't know what.

"We have a fundamental disagreement here which I would like to resolve. And I think it should be resolved in the interests of our people. Wouldn't you agree?" Merrick paused until Polk's head nodded in reluctant agreement. Yes, so you should, he thought.

"So Councillor Albrecht thinks the problem on Faith is . . . well, how can I put it? The fault of the administration, let us say. Councillor Polk does not. So it seems to me that the best thing to do is have Planetary Councillor Herris come here to tell us why Councillor Albrecht is wrong. So I propose to summon Herris to do just that. Any objections?"

Merrick stared intently at each councillor before turning his attention to Polk. Just try to force a vote, my friend, Merrick muttered to himself, confident that Polk didn't have the balls to take him on—or, if his instincts were right, the numbers.

Polk didn't, and his head dropped in defeat. And everyone knew it was a defeat. Safe back on Faith, Herris could duck and dive, could maintain the fiction that Faith's problems were the product of disaffected heretics. In person, in front of the Council, Merrick could nail him down, could wring promises from him that the situation on Faith would get better. And if it didn't, it wouldn't be long before Herris was on the wrong end of a DocSec firing squad, a prospect that Merrick enjoyed thinking about as much as Polk would bitterly resent losing such a key ally.

Eat shit, Councillor Polk, Merrick thought with quiet satisfaction. Think you can take me on? Think again, Polk.

After months of trying, he'd finally flushed Herris out of the safety of Faith, and there was nothing Polk had been able to do to stop him.

"Good. I look forward to seeing Planetary Councillor Herris at our next meeting. My secretariat will make the arrangements. Now . . . ah, yes." He paused for effect. For once, he had the Council where he wanted them, and he was going to ride them as hard as he could.

"Now," he said calmly, "since we're on the subject of the unrest on Faith, let me address a concern I've had for some time. As we all know, the Council can make the right decisions for the people of Kraa only if it has good information to work from. And I must say, Councillors, that for some time I've not been sure that we do have good information on what is really going on over there."

He paused again, this time to look at the councillor for intelligence. Albert Marek wriggled in his chair, the look of sudden panic on his face almost comical.

Merrick couldn't help himself. "Yes, Councillor Marek. Well you might look concerned."

"Chief Councillor!" Polk protested. "Where is this going? We have a huge agenda to cover today, and we have dealt with Faith. I suggest we move on."

"Oh, you do? Well, I beg to differ, Councillor." Merrick stared at Polk for a moment. Of course he had to step in; Marek was one of Polk's men, and he couldn't allow Merrick to attack him unchallenged. But the momentum was with Merrick today, and Polk knew it, an unpleasant reality acknowledged by a wave of the hand for Merrick to continue.

"Thank you. Now, Councillor Marek, I just wanted to point out that your department's most recent report on Faith paints Planetary Councillor Herris, well . . . Now, how can I put it? Almost," he said, his voice dripping with poorly concealed sarcasm, "as a saint in Kraa's eyes. To read your report, Herris has done nothing at all to contribute to the problems there. Once again, it seems that antisocial elements and heretics are the only cause."

Marek tried; Merrick had to give him that. "Yes, Chief Councillor," Marek said firmly. "That is the opinion of my people, and I stand by it." He stared defiantly back at Merrick.

"Good, good," Merrick said smoothly as he slammed the trap shut. "So if that turns out not to be the case, then of course you will not object if the Council asks for your immediate resignation."

Polk's objection was immediate, the anger obvious as he half rose from his seat, face working with rage. "Chief Councillor! I—"

Merrick wasn't having any of it. "Sit down, Councillor!' he roared. "I am speaking. Sit down or by Kraa, you'll regret it."

Polk stayed half standing for a long time before slumping down back into his seat. Merrick watched him for a moment. He had to be careful now. He had the Council where he wanted them, but it would take only one of the neutral councillors to object and the game would be over. Time to quit while he was ahead.

"So, Councillor Marek, you might like to consider the conclusions of your next report carefully," he said, his voice loaded with concern that Marek get it right. "Otherwise . . ."

Merrick didn't have to say any more. There wasn't a man present who did not know what happened to former councillors.

"Good, good," Merrick said exuberantly, much like a man receiving unexpectedly good news. "Let's move on, shall we. Ah, yes, Councillor Polk. Your report on industrial productivity, please."

Merrick sat back as the last of the councillors filed out of the Council room. Dear Kraa, when will they ever learn? he thought as the headache that had lurked half-felt throughout the Council meeting suddenly blossomed into full flower, the pain hammering at his temples. Why was every meeting the same? Why was the blindingly obvious so hard for Polk and his crew of misbegotten whores to accept? Kraa's blood! Each week they tap-danced around the simple fact that corruption was the core problem facing the Hammer and would destroy them all if they didn't do something about it.

Still, Merrick consoled himself as he massaged his aching head, in the end he'd gotten some of what he'd wanted.

Herris had been summoned, his first step to a short encounter with a DocSec firing squad.

Marek had been put on notice, his first step to dismissal from the Council.

And Councillor Polk had been given a very rough time over the Hammer Worlds' continuing problems with industrial productivity, allowing Merrick to remind him that the interests of the Hammer of Kraa would be much better served if he focused his attention on his own affairs rather than meddling in the business of other departments, intelligence, for example. Sadly, if he was honest, it was not much of a step to anywhere, but it was satisfying nonetheless.

Well, Polk was going to go on learning the hard way that Jesse Merrick was not a man to be fucked with. When the time was right, he had every intention of fashioning the miracle of Eternity into a very large blunt object that he would enjoy shoving right up Polk's ass.

Giovanni Pecora's neuronics chimed softly. With a quick apology to his dinner guests, he closed his eyes to take the comm.

It was the intelligence minister, Andres Suchapon. "Giovanni. Just thought I'd let you know. Department 24's people on Commitment have had a result on the *Mumtaz* business. They don't have absolute confirmation, but the agent's report confirms that there is only one large black Hammer project under Merrick's direct control involving a significant amount of off-planet activity. And Digby is the man responsible for day-to-day management. That all fits what we already know. Department 24 has graded the report Alfa-2."

Pecora was silent for a moment before he responded. Intelligence graded Alfa-2 was almost as good as it got. "Okay, Andres. Thanks. I guess we are marginally better off if the *Mumtaz* hijacking really is some lunatic scheme of Merrick's, so it's good to have that confirmed. But whether or not it really makes that much difference, I don't know."

Suchapon nodded sympathetically. The major risk of Op-

eration Corona was not the loss of life on that day. It was
what the Hammers might do in retaliation, and pinning the
blame firmly on Merrick was key to limiting their response.

"We can only hope that it does, Giovanni. In any case, I
don't think it changes anything at this end. We must get our
people back, and if the Hammer chooses to cut up rough afterward, so be it. We can take care of ourselves."

"Right enough, Andres. Okay. Valerie's up to speed?"

"She is. Not a happy woman. Anything else?"

"No, that's it for tonight. I'll see you on Monday."

"You will. Night, Andres."

"Night, Giovanni."

Monday, September 21, 2398, UD
Hell Central

Prison Governor Costigan stood on the low catwalk above
the milling group of orange coverall–suited prisoners.

The grim-looking man was flanked on either side by men
in closely woven black stab-resistant one-piece plasfiber
jumpsuits topped off with lightweight plasfiber close-
combat helmets, also black. Hard faces devoid of even the
slightest traces of emotion watched the mob over the barrels
of crowd-control stun guns, eyes flickering restlessly behind
closed plasglass faceplates.

One week, Costigan reflected. One week was all it had
taken to turn proud independent human beings into meekly
submissive convicts, feedstock for the driver mass mines and
plants that were Hell System's only reason to exist. The de-
personalizing combination of numbers instead of names,
convict haircuts, strip searches, confiscation of all personal
possessions no matter how innocuous, cold, sleeplessness,
hunger, and random acts of brutality, topped off with a cocktail of drugs that paralyzed the power of speech, never failed.
And for the group below, there were two added shocks. The

first was being dragged from the comfort and security of the *Mumtaz* without the time normal convicts had to adjust; the second was losing the feeling of connectedness that their neuronics gave them—now just so much electronic junk embedded in their brains. And perhaps there was one more. For these people, the Hammer was the devil incarnate, but here they were, helpless in the hands of the people they most feared.

The guards on the holding cage floor finally got the group into a semblance of order, and Costigan stepped up to the rail.

"I am Prison Governor Costigan." His voiced boomed from the huge flat speakers mounted on the wall behind him, and as one the heads of all the people below lifted to look him in the face. "I won't waste your time. You have work to do. But understand this. If you work well, you will receive two rewards: You'll stay alive, and you will eat well. If you do not, then you will die. That's all you need to know. Forget the future. You have none. This is all the future you have. And forget the past. It's gone, and you will never get it back." There was a moment's pause while he looked for dissent, for anger, but there was none, just shock, disbelief, and fear.

"Staff Sergeant Williams. They are all yours."

The large black-suited man beside Costigan, stun gun cradled casually in his arms, nodded. "Look down at your chests. All of you with a black tag around your neck, move to the door marked A. Yes, that's it, black tags to Door A. Yellow tags to Door B at the back. And red tags to Door C. Black to A, yellow to B, and red to C. Now move."

Williams paused as the group, encouraged by low-power shots from the stun guns, slowly separated into three smaller groups, each huddled around its respective door.

"Good. Now, when your door opens, walk through that door and keep walking until you come to the next door. When that opens, walk through. Keep going until you are told otherwise." With that, the doors silently slid open, and after a momentary pause the three groups slowly disappeared from sight, leaving behind only the faint sour smell of fear and six black-suited guards.

As the doors shut, Williams turned back to Costigan. "That's it, sir. A total of 160 altogether: thirty-five to Hell-5, twenty-nine to Hell-16, and the rest, ninety-six in all, to Hell-18."

"Ninety-six to Hell-18. That's a lot. Why so many?"

"They're a bit shorthanded, sir, ever since that incident with the runaway pellet processor."

Costigan nodded. He remembered, though there were so many deaths that it wasn't easy. He supposed it was a stretch to call the deaths of forty-three convicts, with another thirty-six so badly hurt that they had been euthanized, an incident, but in truth that was all it was in the greater scheme of things. An incident and one not even worth remembering. The Hell system held more than 57,000 convicts, so the loss of seventy-nine had caused scarcely a ripple. The head office back on McNair certainly didn't care. His weekly status report, complete with a short account of the incident, had been received without comment by the Prisons Administration Authority, and Costigan knew why: The magic phrase "without adverse impact on driver mass production schedules" never failed to demotivate even the most inquiring prisons administration bureaucrats, all of whom would have done almost anything to avoid having to come to Hell to follow up on a problem.

"Okay. Let's do the last group."

Williams muttered into his whisper mike, and Costigan, flanked by ever-watchful guards, made his way along the catwalk, pausing as the heavy security door slammed open before going through into the next holding cage. The crash of the door shutting solidly behind him was a reminder that this was a risky place to be.

As he came out onto the catwalk, Costigan could sense the difference. Despite the week's softening up, the group below him was still dangerous; that was not surprising given that every one of them was ex–special forces. Every man probably had been through worse in his training, much worse than anything Hell could dish out, Costigan realized. A quick glance at Williams told him that he wasn't alone in sensing the difference. Williams was visibly tense, and the guards down on the cage floor were, too, standing farther back with stun guns leveled at the group rather than cradled loosely. One guard stood even farther back with a knockdown gas launcher at hand in case things turned ugly.

As Costigan studied the group, one man stood out. Comonec, that was his name, the team leader. He could almost feel the hate blazing off the hard-faced young man with the dark gold stubble clinging tightly to his head.

He whisper-miked Williams. "The man at the front, in the middle."

"The fair-headed one, 381123-J, sir?"

"Yes. If he moves even so much as a centimeter, you have my authority to hit him and hit him hard."

"Sir."

Costigan launched into his standard speech of welcome, but he could see that his words had no impact. The *Mumtaz* group had been hunched, beaten men, every one of them. These men held themselves upright, loose but still alert and in control. Let them feel they are in control, Costigan thought as he finished up. They've still got no fucking chance, no chance in the world. A month on Hell-20, the toughest and least forgiving of all of Hell's sites and the only driver mass plant that had no production targets, would pound the fight out of them.

Until it had and until they'd won the right to be transferred to a softer mine, they would be given not the slightest bit of slack. Hell-20's regime was carefully designed to take hard men to the point of death. An eighteen-hour day, a punishing workload, barely adequate food, plascrete sleeping benches with no mattresses, and only one thin blanket even though the temperature barely rose above freezing would break even the strongest and best trained of them. That was, if they survived at all, and even with the best will in the world, many didn't. Not that he gave a shit. There were plenty more where these came from.

As Costigan stepped back and handed the group over to Williams to move them out, Comonec made his move. Even though he must have known how pointless it was, he made an explosive lunge for the nearest guard. He got surprisingly close before the guard, casually and moving with an elegant economy of effort, stun shot him full in the chest. Comonec dropped in agony, hands clawing at the plascrete floor in a vain attempt to get at the guard. Nice one, Costigan thought. Enough power to stop him but not so much that he was knocked unconscious. And he was pleased to see that Williams's full attention and that of the rest of the guards stayed on the group, not on Comonec.

Slowly, Comonec's tortured nervous system recovered from the gross insult it had received, and his writhing subsided. Casually, the guard dialed down the power and stun shot him again, left leg first and then right, ankles first, then calves, then thighs. A real artist, Costigan thought admiringly, such sadistic finesse. He liked that.

Five agonizing minutes later it was all over. Comonec's body had given up trying to stay conscious, and the man lay limp and unmoving at the feet of his tormentor.

Williams leaned forward, eyes running across the sullen faces in front of him. "Don't fuck with me, don't ever fuck with me. 712-M and 978-B, pick up that piece of garbage." A gentle tickle from his stun gun made sure 388712-M and 239978-B knew who they were.

"Now go to Door A, and when it opens, keep walking. You'll be told what to do next. Now move."

As the group shuffled out, helped on its way by a last touch from the guards' stun guns, Costigan nodded his approval. "Impressive, Williams, impressive."

"Thank you, sir. We'll escort this group all the way to Hell-20, so you can rest easy."

"I'll rest easy when they are actually on Hell-20, safely in the hands of Major Perkins, and not before."

"Sir." A short pause, and Costigan knew that the question Williams had been bursting to ask ever since he first had laid eyes on what were without doubt the two most unusual groups of convicts ever to be processed through Hell Central was coming. If he'd been Williams, he would have wanted to know just who those people were and where they had come from.

As Williams started to ask the question, Costigan's hand

went up, stopping him dead, his voice surprisingly gentle. Embittered and disillusioned though he was, Costigan was not all bad, and Williams had been one of the very few people he felt he could rely on. This was as good a time as any to repay the man for his unswerving loyalty.

"Staff Sergeant Williams. I know what you want to ask me, and I strongly advise you not to ask. I suggest that you forget the question. I suggest you even stop thinking about why you wanted to ask the question. It's not your business to know some things, and if you want to live a long and happy life, I advise you to forget that you ever even saw the groups we processed this morning. Understand?"

Williams's face changed, puzzlement replaced in an instant by the blank face of the professional survivor. A few beads of sweat were the only telltale signs of his sudden realization that he had almost crossed a very dangerous line. "Sir. Sorry, sir."

Costigan waved a dismissive hand. The man would do as he was told. "No problem, Williams, no problem. Just let me know when that particular consignment has been safely delivered."

Thursday, September 24, 2398, UD
HWS Myosan, *in Low Orbit around Eternity Planet*

Digby sat back in his chair, physically and mentally exhausted but strangely exhilarated after another grueling day.

By the time he was born, the pioneering days of terraforming new planets and mass migration were long gone and almost forgotten. But now, seeing the promise a brand-new planet offered, he understood for the first time the excitement and vision that had driven millions of Earth's people to look for a new beginning hundreds of light-years from home.

In front of him, the holovid showed Eternity in all its primal glory as it passed below the orbiting *Myosan*. Its atmosphere was the characteristic cobalt blue of all methane/nitrogen/carbon dioxide worlds, interrupted here and there by smeared orange-brown-gray stains of high-altitude photosynthetic methane smog shot through with dark streaks of hydrogen cyanide and other exotic organic compounds, all the product of the intense ultraviolet flux that flayed Eternity's upper atmosphere. Where clouds and methane smog permitted, Digby could see the planet's surface, a mass of blues and browns of every shade imaginable; to the south, a mass of swirling blue-whites and grays wrapped around a black core announced the arrival of yet another huge frontal weather system coming in off the ocean to dump its load of rain onto the raw and scoured rocks that made up Eternity's surface.

But after a lifetime orbiting the inhabited planets that made up the Hammer Worlds, Digby found it unsettling to see not even the tiniest speck of green.

That would change, Digby thought, wondering not for the first time at the extraordinary progress the Feds' technology had allowed them to make. If he hadn't seen it with his own eyes, he never would have believed the speed with which the former passengers of the *Mumtaz* were building Eternity Base, though he had to admit that if it were not for the AIs that managed and directed the entire process, progress would have been very slow. He thanked Kraa DocSec was not there to see the AI abominations at work, but it wasn't, and what DocSec didn't know wasn't going to hurt him.

The first day had been the worst; getting the first lander down safely onto a planet without a decent runway and no precision navaids was always an interesting exercise. But the ex-convict pilot had done a beautiful job, encouraged, no doubt, Digby thought cynically, by the considerable incentives he had not to fail.

To minimize weight, the lander had been stripped nearly bare, its only cargo a one-man survey team and two laser rock cutters together with their integral microfusion power plants and their two-man crews. After a series of careful low-speed fly-bys to confirm that he hadn't been given a swamp to land on, the pilot had put the massive machine down nearly vertically. Digby had watched with his heart in his mouth as the huge flier had touched down amid huge clouds of sand and gravel thrown up and out by belly-mounted hover control mass drivers firing vertically downward.

Within days and thanks largely to the brutal power of the Feds' massive laser rock cutters, Eternity was the proud owner of a fully serviceable spaceport, with a single vitrified runway, laser cut out of the living rock and capable of withstanding the huge shock of a fully loaded lander putting down, complete with a milled antiskid surface, a microwave precision landing system, runway lights, crude storm drains, and a small plasfiber shed housing the air traffic control team. From that moment on, the flow of materials dirtside had never stopped as night and day heavily loaded landers thumped down to be unloaded quickly and then sent back into orbit for the next shipment.

And now, not even two weeks into it, Digby had every right to be pleased with the progress. He was especially glad finally to have downloaded the last of the passengers and crew of the *Mumtaz*. While they never had posed a threat, Digby felt a lot more comfortable now that the Feds were planetside and finally off that damnable mind-control drug Pavulomin-V. Nasty stuff and not recommended for prolonged use, especially in kids. They were better off where there was real work to be done even if Eternity Base had little to offer by way of recreation other than spectacular sunsets, nice beaches, and safe swimming in a sea whose biggest life-form was harmless cyanobacteria.

No, it had been a good week, and things were going well.

Eternity Base was well advanced even if still a bit crude. The comsats, navsats, and high-definition optical and infrared imaging satellites were ready to be commissioned. Downloading the terraforming support equipment would start in two days. According to the master terraforming AI's schedule, the biomass plant responsible for the mass production of geneered bacteria, vastly more efficient at photosynthesis than their native cousins as well as the first of the methane-tolerant plant stock, would be operational in under a month. Even better, the carbon sequestration/oxygen production plant would be up soon, relieving the *Mumtaz* of the not inconsiderable chore of giving the 1,200 or so people now planetside the 2 to 3 kilos of oxygen they needed every day. It didn't sound like much, but it all added up to more than 100 tons of oxygen a month.

But perhaps the best news of all was Professor Cornelius Wang. Despite the appalling way the Hammer had treated him and very much to Digby's surprise, Wang appeared to bear no grudges and had thrown himself into the job of managing the terraforming project with a remarkable mixture of enthusiasm and drive. Digby was beginning to think that Wang might be a man he could trust to get on with it and not fuck up. Even the damn Feds seemed to respond well to Wang, which was a relief. They could be a stiff-necked bunch when they wanted.

Digby sighed as he turned his back on the almost hypnotic holovid. He could quite happily have watched it for hours, but if he didn't get his weekly report finished and into the courier drone for its pinchspace jump back to Commitment, Merrick wouldn't get it in time for the weekly Supreme Council meeting on Friday evening, and that would never do. The last thing Digby needed was to upset Merrick and be recalled. For the moment, Merrick seemed happy that he was staying here, though it was early days yet. To encourage Merrick to view his presence on Eternity as essential, he would slip a fictitious incident involving one of his security personnel—nothing serious, but disaster had been averted only because he had been there to manage it while his ex-Hell personnel got used to their new responsibilities—into his report. He might also talk up the amount of direction he was having to give poor Professor Wang.

Yes, he would paint a picture of good progress under difficult and demanding circumstances thanks to his firm leadership and control. That should do it.

Friday, September 25, 2398, UD
Offices of the Supreme Council for the Preservation of
the Faith, City of McNair, Commitment Planet

What a difference seven days makes, Merrick thought as he tried to massage another stabbing headache out of his temples.

Only one short week before, he'd had that rabble of a Council exactly where he'd wanted them. But now he knew his position was beginning to slip. He still had the numbers, but only just, and that meant making concessions to that Kraa-damned son of a bitch Polk. After working furiously behind the scenes to shore up his position on the Council by persuading some of the unaligned councillors that they had conceded too much to Merrick the previous week, Polk had slowly but surely moved the Council to support his view that the deteriorating situation on Faith demanded the immediate imposition of martial law to enable DocSec to hunt down and kill the heretics responsible for the problem in the first place. All, of course, without the usual constraints of the law and due process, weak and feeble though those things were in the Hammer scheme of things.

Polk had been relentless. With the worthless assurances of Planetary Councillor Herris, smooth and reassuring as ever, duly given, Councillor Marek, Kraa damn his soul, clearly deciding that Polk was the man not to upset, had presented his revised report confirming, without a shred of credible evidence, the view that dissident heretics were the cause of the problem. With his supporters visibly wavering, Merrick no longer could stall if he wanted to survive as chief councillor. Finally, reluctantly, he'd had to concede. The smug look on Polk's face as he did so had been almost unbearable, every head around the Council table nodding in enthusiastic agreement, the relief plain to see on the councillors' faces. The bit-

terness between Merrick and Polk had nothing to do with the
planet Faith and everything to do with Polk's barely concealed lust for the chief councillorship. Such fights were
dangerous affairs, and councillors on the losing side tended
to suffer heavy casualties as the winner settled old scores. So
even if everyone knew that the show of unanimity was a
sham, it was infinitely preferable to open conflict.

Within minutes, orders had been issued implementing
martial law on Faith and putting six battalions of marines on
standby in case DocSec was not able to control things.

Merrick had almost groaned aloud. Once again, the Hammer Worlds had set off down the bloodstained path of repression. Tens of thousands would die when only one needed
to die to solve the problem. And that one was that corrupt
bastard Herris. They never learn, he thought wearily. Failure
to remove excessively dishonest and greedy public officials
with friends in high places had always been one of the fundamental weaknesses of Hammer political governance, and
so it was this time.

Merrick knew the day of reckoning wouldn't be long in
coming.

Monday, September 28, 2398, UD
City of Kantzina, Faith Planet

As night fell, the insurgents erupted out of nowhere, their
momentum unstoppable.

Without regard for their own lives, young men and women
hurled themselves forward to overwhelm positions held by
nervous and increasingly demoralized DocSec troopers.
Each successful attack liberated the weapons needed to
fuel the next wave of attacks. As the night wore on with
violence flaring up all across the city and every DocSec
building outside the city center in flames, it became in-

creasingly clear that DocSec would not be able to contain
the situation.

To add to the problems facing a progressively more worried Kaspar Herris, who was holed up in the planetary councillor's residence, reports had begun to come in of incidents
in the towns surrounding Kantzina.

Csdawa's main DocSec barracks had fallen, and the body
of its DocSec colonel had been dragged out, stripped, and
hung by one foot in time-honored Hammer fashion from a
tree. The placard around his neck read "Traitor to the People."

In Jennix, panicked DocSec troopers had turned their guns
on peaceful demonstrators, killing and wounding hundreds
before the enraged mob, heedless of the risk, had turned on
their attackers, with the troopers going down under a tidal
wave of murderous humanity. In Fers, Morris, and Shiba,
mobs had trapped DocSec troops in their barracks and security posts. In the other towns and cities across the country,
anxious DocSec commanders reported steadily rising ten-
sions and begged for support.

Just before midnight, Herris admitted defeat and called in
the marines even though he knew he had just signed his own
death warrant. As he had left the Supreme Council meeting,
Merrick had made it abundantly clear to him what the consequences of failure would be, and if nothing else Merrick
was a man of his word.

Not that it would matter what Merrick wanted, he thought
with a humorless laugh, if the street scum got to him first.

The insistent bleating of the bedside phone dragged Merrick from the depths of sleep. Cursing softly, he checked the
time as he reached across to take the call. *Better be something damned important to wake me at 4:30 in the morning,*
he thought.

"Merrick!"

"Kato Miyasaki, duty secretariat officer, sir. I have a message from Planetary Councillor Herris. He's advising
that—"

Merrick cut the man off. "Let me guess. The situation in Kantzina has gotten out of control and he's called in the marines."

"Yes, sir. That's it exactly."

"Fine. I want you to call Jarrod Arnstrom and have him draw up a warrant for the arrest of Herris. I want the warrant and him in my office at 07:45."

"Yes, sir. What grounds for the warrant?"

"Oh, yes, good question, Miyasaki. Let's make it conduct prejudicial to the Doctrine of the Hammer of Kraa. That'll do for the moment. But say to Arnstrom that if he can think of any better alternatives, he can draw up warrants for those as well. I'll pick the one I like best when he briefs me. Got all that?"

"Yes, sir. Got it. Good night."

Merrick grunted and hung up, the faintest hint of a smile on his face.

He could accept the fact that Polk's star might be in the ascendancy and that his own days might be numbered, but by Kraa, he would take every chance he was given to cut away the bloody man's support. Let him explain to the Council why Planetary Councillor Herris had been a man to be trusted.

Anyway, with a bit of luck, Polk would soon be history. All Merrick needed was enough time for Eternity to come online, and he'd be untouchable. With a small sigh of satisfaction, he rolled over and was back asleep in seconds.

Tuesday, September 29, 2398, UD
DLS-387, approaching Space Battle Station 4, in Orbit around Jackson's World

As *387* decelerated in-system, Michael was almost euphoric at the thought that getting his mother and sister back could be only a few steps away.

In less than two hours, *387* would have completed a mission to remember. Not one but two Hammer of Kraa systems successfully penetrated, they had found what they were looking for, and more important, *387* had completed the tricky business of an underway remassing after it dropped into the Jackson system. But best of all, there was the prospect of some leave to look forward to, a chance to blow off steam and relieve some of the accumulated stresses of the last few weeks, and of course he'd be able to put Aunt Claudia's mind at rest about his mother and Sam.

How he could do that without compromising operational security he hadn't quite worked out, but there had to be a way.

Ribot had other plans.

As he walked around the ship, he realized that there would be a lot of unhappy people when he had to tell them the bad news that there would be no leave, a severe blow given Jackson's hard-earned reputation as one of the more fun places to be. But Fleet's pinchcomm had been emphatic and not open for debate.

Now Helfort had asked to see him. Even now, ten days after the *Mumtaz* had been declared overdue, probably lost with all souls, the holovids were full of tales of grief and anger that such a thing could happen in this day and age. Helfort would have assumed, not unreasonably, that he would have priority to get planetside to be with his stricken aunt and her family, and Ribot was not looking forward to telling him otherwise. But there was more bad news: So paranoid was Fleet about security, Helfort wasn't even going to be allowed to get a vidmail off to his father. There was no way that the needs of a junior lieutenant, however worthy, could be allowed to compromise operational security. Ribot had no doubt that Fleet would have put huge pressure on the Sylvanians to keep *387*'s arrival a secret.

So, as far as anyone who cared to inquire was concerned, it was situation normal and *387* was in pinchspace somewhere en route to the Kashliki Cluster.

For one moment Ribot wondered what had ever made him

want to be the captain of a Fleet warship. He sighed as he decided how to handle the most pressing issues on his plate: Michael first, officers and senior spacers second, and announcing the bad news to the troops third.

Ribot groaned. What an evening he had to look forward to, and no doubt Fleet had a full debriefing team standing by, ready to talk all night if need be. Wonderful.

"All stations, this is command. Hands fall out from berthing stations. Revert to harbor stations, ship state 4, airtight integrity condition zulu."

Strezlecki turned to Michael as the surveillance drone crew left without the high-spirited banter that normally accompanied berthing. "Not a very happy bunch of campers, sir."

Michael nodded. "Not surprising, I'm afraid, under the circumstances. But what I want to know is what Fleet wants us to do next. You saw the Fleet supply ship berthed ahead of us? The *Ramayana,* I think. I'm sure that's no coincidence."

Strezlecki smiled. "Well, sir, for what it's worth, I think the shit's about to hit the fan and little old *387* is going to be in the thick of it. We did a good job, maybe too good a job, to get in and out the way we did, and I'm sure Fleet will want more of the same."

"I won't give you odds on that, Strez, 'cause I think you're right. But let's just wait and see. Shit! I'd better get a move on. I'm officer of the day."

As Michael finished stowing his space suit, Mother commed him.

"For your information, Michael, Major Claudia McNeil is our Frontier Fleet liaison officer, and she'll be onboard in five to confirm that we have everything we need."

"Roger that."

"And Captain Andreesen from Fleet has just confirmed that he'll be arriving on the up-shuttle at 20:15. He should be here ten minutes after that."

"Okay. Captain got all that?"

"Yes."

"Thanks, Mother."

Strezlecki looked at him quizzically, left eybrow lifted inquiringly. "Developments?"

"Sure are. Fleet's sent OPS-1 to talk to us."

"Game on, I think, sir," Strezlecki said with half a laugh. "I'm sure Fleet hasn't sent OPS-1 to tell us to take a holiday."

"Know what? I think you're right."

With some relief, Ribot and Michael saluted the backs of Captain Andreesen and his two staff officers as they made the awkward and always undignified transition from *387*'s grav field to the space battle station's. Amazing, Ribot thought, how even senior officers refused to use the lubber's rail. Turning away from the enjoyable sight of one of the hardest men in the Federated Worlds Space Fleet on his hands and knees, Ribot stepped out of the air lock into the drone hangar. He waved Michael closer. "All officers, Michael. Wardroom in five."

Just as he was about to drop down the ladder, Ribot spotted Strezlecki huddled over one of the surveillance drones in the far corner of the hangar. Altering course, he wove a path across a crowded deck to where she was working. "Problem?"

"Oh, hello, sir. No, not really. *Bonnie* took some micrometeorite damage during her fly-by, and I was just double-checking the repairs. *Ramayana* has got hot spares if we need them, but I don't think there's any need. No damage, just cosmetic. The plasteel armor did what it was supposed to do."

"Pleased to hear it. Michael?"

"Sir?"

"What are you waiting for? Wardroom now. You can trust me with Petty Officer Strezlecki." Ribot's tone was mock serious, but Michael was too flustered to pick up on it.

"Yes, sir! Right away, sir!" With that, Michael shot across the hangar, dodging the closely packed drones before dropping down the ladder like a brick down a well.

He's a good officer, Ribot thought, and he's handled himself well despite what must seem to him an endless series of setbacks. Having to tell him that he couldn't go planetside to be with his family was bad enough. Telling him that there was a complete embargo on all outgoing personal messages and that as a consequence he could not even talk to his father must have broken his heart. But he just seemed to absorb the blows, burying the bad news somewhere deep within himself and moving on. Ribot didn't want to be the first Hammer that Michael met. It could be ugly.

He turned his attention back to Strezlecki. "Just a quick one, Strez. What's the mood below?"

"Pretty unhappy, sir. Lots of grumbling 'specially from the young and single. But I think that's no surprise. If the troops aren't complaining, then that's the time to be worried."

"True enough, but do they understand why?"

"They do, sir. Don't underestimate how they feel about the whole business. The idea that the Hammer would actually do what they've done is pretty hard to take. So as long as *387* is doing something to hit back, then things will be fine. And remember, sir, that there's more than one person onboard who lost family in the last war even if they are too young to remember the details. Reis, for one. She lost both of her parents. She would happily give up six months planetside on Jackson for the chance to kick a few Hammers to death, and she's someone the lower deck listens to. Mind you, the party animals are disappointed at missing out on the delights of Jackson, but they'll get over it."

Ribot nodded. It was what he had expected, but it was always good to get confirmation, particularly from a senior spacer as solid as Strezlecki.

"But sir, if I can add something?"

"Sure, go ahead."

"Everybody's figured out that Fleet has plans for us. The sooner everybody knows what's expected of us, the sooner they'll knuckle down and get on with things."

Ribot nodded. The advice was, as ever, solid. "Them and me both. As soon as I can, Strez, as soon as I can."

* * *

The wardroom felt crowded, the officers coming to their feet as one as Ribot entered.

"Okay, folks. Seats, please. Michael, close the door."

Michael watched carefully as Ribot sat down at the head of the mess table. Ribot paused for a moment while he gathered his thoughts. Something big was coming, and he was pretty damn sure he knew what it was. He looked around, forcibly struck by the look of hungry anticipation he could see on their faces. The last mission had welded them into a team, and it was a team that wanted to do more.

"Well, no prizes on offer tonight for guessing what comes next," Ribot said. "From what I've heard, everyone onboard has decided that Fleet has plans for us, and so they have."

"Pretty hard to explain away a bloody great supply ship the size of the *Ramayana* berthed immediately ahead of you as just one of life's little coincidences, sir," Armitage said with a half smile.

"True enough." Ribot smiled. "Well, anyway, enough tap-dancing around. We're going back to Hell as part of the covert surveillance team to prepare for Operation Corona, a full-scale Fleet attack sometime around late November tasked with the recovery of the *Mumtaz* and her people. We don't yet have exact dates."

Ribot paused in some amusement as Michael punched the air, his emphatic "Yes, yes, yes" giving vent to every ounce of stress, frustration, and anxiety accumulated over the last weeks. Michael was ecstatic. Involvement in what came next, yes. He'd expected that. But after one of the most hazardous missions ever undertaken by a Fleet ship in peacetime, to be put right back in the front line of a major planetary system attack, well, that really was a shock. Not that he cared. They'd be taking the fight right to the Hammers, and that was what he wanted.

"And before you ask," Ribot continued when Michael finally settled down, "let me just add that *387* has been awarded a unit citation for the last mission, which I think explains why we are going back. We are a known quantity to

Fleet. Given what's at stake, Captain Andreesen's made it abundantly clear that they want the A-Team right up front. Captain Andreesen asked me to pass on the commander in chief's personal appreciation for a job well done. And while we are on the subject, I'd like to add my own thanks. You all did well, and the unit citation is well earned, so thank you all."

It took an orgy of handshaking, backslapping, mutual congratulation, and excited chatter before the meeting settled down enough to allow Ribot to continue. Michael in particular, his face flushed with a mixture of pleasure and anticipation, his heart pounding at the thought that *387* would be right back in it, had bounced around the wardroom like some sort of demonic rubber ball until Armitage and Hosani, laughing out loud at his hyperactivity, had grabbed him by the arms, pulled him down, and told him to shut up.

Ribot struggled to keep from grinning as he tried to adopt a more serious tone of voice.

"Okay, okay. That's enough of that. We have a lot to do, and Fleet has scheduled us to depart in two days' time, first thing on Thursday morning. That basically gives us one working day to get everything turned around. I'm going to comm you the operations order for phase 1 of Operation Corona. I want a preliminary plan from the operations planning team in twelve hours, let's say at ten tomorrow morning." Ribot paused as three heads nodded in unison. Not much sleep for Armitage, Hosani, and Holdorf tonight, Michael thought.

"Cosmo. The usual. If you have any probs, call the *Ramayana*'s XO directly. He's been briefed to offer all the help you need, no questions asked."

Cosmo Reilly nodded. Fast turnarounds were nothing new, and he would get this one done as efficiently as he did everything else. "Will do, sir. I'll need some help with the stripdown of Weapons Power Bravo."

"Just ask. John, we'll be embarking a covert ops support team, and you'll be their liaison and support officer. Warrant

Officer Jacqui Ng is the team leader. Make sure they have everything they need. They are coming up on the 23:15 up-shuttle."

"I know Ng, sir. We were in the old *Zube* together. A good operator. The Doc, people called her, God knows why." Kapoor winced theatrically as he noticed the disapproving look on Reilly's face and held up a placatory hand. "Sorry, Cosmo, my dear chap, so sorry. My deepest and most humble apologies. Federated Worlds Warship *Zuben-el-Genubi*, DHC-775."

"That's better, you young puppy," Reilly said as laughter broke out around him.

"Ignore them, Cosmo. What do these babes know?" Armitage got her shot in while the going was good.

Reilly just snorted.

Ribot's hands went up. "Enough, enough. Finally, Michael, I think you've probably guessed what you've got to do," he said with a smile.

Michael responded with a look of mock horror. "I think I have, sir. Off-load all DefGrav's stuff and on-load all Warrant Officer Ng's gear."

"Give that man a banana. Got it in one shot. Right, that's about it for now from me. Any questions? No? Okay, then. Jacqui, I want all hands in the junior spacers mess in five minutes, officers included. It's time to tell the troops the good news."

Wednesday, September 30, 2398, UD
DLS-387, Berthed on Space Battle Station 4, in Orbit around Jackson's World

It had been a brutally long day, but finally everything had been done.

Michael's team had worked like demons to off-load the

DefGrav team's containers, replacing them with Warrant Officer Ng's stealth-coated containers plus something new from Fleet's development labs: an experimental small-scale driver mass manufacturing plant, the whole thing squeezed into two containers together with a microfusion plant. Neat, was the consensus of Michael's team, pleased with the idea that the boffins finally had done something about the perennial curse of independent light scout operations: lack of driver mass. Michael was even more pleased when Mother confirmed that Fleet had sent along two of the engineers responsible for the massive machine. Should maximize the chances of the damn thing working, he thought cynically, and give them someone to blame if it doesn't.

There was a bit under an hour to spare before the presentation of the final operations plan to Captain Andreesen. Michael lay back on his narrow bunk, watching his personal holovid, the sweat and the peculiarly sour odor that came from working hard in a space suit for hours on end washed away by a luxuriously long hot shower. In the absence of any vidmail, he had set the holovid to cycle between his collection of family holopix and those of Anna. As he watched, he realized, what with everything that had happened, how little he had thought about Anna; a brief feeling of guilt shivered its way up his spine. He froze the holovid on his favorite picture of her.

According to the notes attached to the picture, it had been taken at the height of Charlie Mbeki's birthday party in Year 2 and showed Anna, head back and face glowing with pure happiness as Michael buried his face in her neck. In a way that he couldn't begin to express, the holopic encapsulated everything about her that attracted him. Behind the two of them, the faces of the old team reminded him of the innocence they had all lost, he more than most.

The awful thought that he might lose Anna as well as his mother and sister at the hands of the Hammer crossed his mind for a moment before he firmly shoved the unwelcome thought away. You'll go mad if you think like that, Michael, he told himself, so don't. Anna was onboard the *Damishqui*, and a deepspace heavy cruiser was a good place to be in the middle of a punch-up with the Hammer. If anyone should be worried, it was Anna about him. He made up his mind that when this was all over, he would grab Anna with both hands and tell her that he loved her. And he did. Sure, the other girls who'd passed through his life had been fun, but that was all he had been to them and vice versa.

But Anna was different. In some way he couldn't fully define or express, she made him feel complete. Even if she didn't share the feeling, he knew he owed it to himself to say so, however inadequately.

Mentally squaring his shoulders, he swung his legs over the edge of his bunk and onto the narrow strip of plasfiber carpet tastefully decorated with a mottled purple, yellow, and brown pattern. The bloody designer must have been on something, Michael thought, if he or she imagined that the end result, used in every ship of the Fleet and known Fleetwide as the rat's vomit carpet, was in any way attractive or desirable. He dressed quickly in a fresh ship suit and within minutes had his tiny cabin squared away in best college style, the bedding immaculate, the plasfiber bedcover taut as a drum skin. Andreesen had a reputation for conducting unscheduled tours, and Michael did not want to be the one who let the side down.

Picking up his old-fashioned scriber and e-paper notebook—he had never gotten out of the doodling habit, though he did draw the line at using real paper, leaving that to the real diehards—he left his cabin to make his way down to the wardroom.

Hosani wanted him to run through his part of the operations plan, and Michael intended to get it 100 percent right. Andreesen was not a man to screw up in front of.

"And so to conclude, sir," Ribot said with a confidence that he didn't fully feel in the face of Andreesen's basilisk-like stare, "a standard covert ops approach and deployment. As ever, the primary risk comes from any late changes that the THREATSUM hasn't picked up or any unusual Hammer ship movements. But all factors taken into account, we have the right mission profile to succeed. That's all I have to say. Do you have any questions, sir?"

For fully twenty heart-stopping seconds, Andreesen said nothing, his stare unwavering. Ribot could only look him straight in the eye across the combat information center conference table. Then Andreesen did something that to the best of Ribot's knowledge had never been observed before. He stood up and leaned over. With the faintest hint of a smile on a face that was, considering the heavy responsibilities borne by its owner, surprisingly young and untroubled, he took Ribot's hand and shook it vigorously. "No, I don't. Excellent, Captain, excellent. Not something I say often, as you know. But good luck and may God watch over you all this day."

Even safely tucked away at his workstation as far away from Andreesen as he could get, Michael imagined he could hear Ribot's sigh of relief clear across a crowded combat information center.

But Andreesen had Michael's measure. He turned, and his eyes skewered him. "Helfort! I knew both your father and mother when they were in Space Fleet. Good officers, both of them, and a loss to the Fleet when they retired. My thoughts are with them and of course with your sister. We'll get them all back safely, I promise."

Michael could only nod as Andreesen turned back to face Ribot. "Now, Captain, let's have that drink you promised me and then I'll leave you in peace."

For a moment, Michael and everyone else present felt the full force of the Federated Worlds' commitment to resolve the crisis no matter what. It was an awesome and sobering statement of raw power, and Michael pitied any Hammer stupid enough to get in the way.

The transition from the cool air-conditioned comfort of the lander to Eternity's atmosphere was as sudden as it was brutal.

As Digby stood at the foot of the ladder, the raw heat and humidity of late morning wrapped itself around him and left him gasping as he struggled to make his breather seal to a face instantly slicked with sweat.

"So now you know what's it's like down here with us mud crawlers, General." Unlike Digby's, Professor Cornelius Wang's face was barely damp, his voice hardly distorted by the bright yellow breather mask that shrouded his lower face. This was his territory, not the general's, and his body language betrayed his inner confidence, his sense of command.

"Welcome to Eternity Base, General."

"Kraa's blood, Cornelius. Is it always as hot as this?" Digby said, his voice half-strangled, his left hand engaged in a futile attempt to keep the sweat beading on his forehead out of his eyes.

"Yes, I'm afraid it is, General," Wang said apologetically. "Just be thankful it's not raining, which it seems to do a lot. But a couple of days will have you acclimatized. The Feds' drug protocols are very effective at accelerating adaptation to heat and humidity. In a few days, you'll find it relatively comfortable, believe it or not."

"By Kraa, I hope so. I don't think this is something I'd want to put up with for very long. Anyway, enough of that. Let's get on. I want to see everything."

"Of course. And we have a lot to show you." With that, Wang waved Digby toward a jeep parked on an access ramp.

Despite the fact that it had been planetside for less than two weeks, the jeep's mud-streaked and battered sides betrayed the intensity with which Wang had been driving the terraforming project forward.

Beyond the jeep stood the skeletal frames of spaceport infrastructure as they emerged from the yellow-brown earth of Eternity's surface, an army of orange-coveralled figures and scuttling buildbots swarming over every part. To the left lay the lander maintenance hangars, and to the right the massive supplies warehouse, its vitrified rock floor so smooth that Digby could almost see the sky reflected in it as it waited for the roof to go on.

Directly ahead of Digby, the fusion plant was coming along, its roof of ultra-lightweight plasfiber panels now on, bright red primary power modules installed, and high-voltage power cables beginning to grow outward in every direction from the power distribution modules. Alongside the fusion plant sat the carbon sequestration and oxygen production plant, a mass of cryogenic gas separators and methane and carbon dioxide converters, and behind them was the liquid oxygen storage farm and raw carbon dumps.

Beyond it all stood the focus of this incredible display of Federated Worlds technology, the biomass production plant. Once it was commissioned, from this plant and others to follow would pour a torrent of fast-growing geneered biomass: photosynthetic cyanobacteria, diatoms, coccoliths, and other marine phytoplankton, together with methane-tolerant plants capable not only of surviving on Eternity's uninviting surface but of reproducing like wildfire.

As explained by Professor Wang, the process was simple, in principle at least.

Some geneered organisms converted water, carbon dioxide, and methane to free oxygen and carbon-based biomass. Others—high-energy crackers they were called, one of the keys to the Federated Worlds' terraforming technology—split hydrogen directly out of Eternity's superabundant methane. Eternity's excess methane was reduced further when, in the presence of oxygen, it was split by ultraviolet light in the upper atmosphere into yet more hydrogen, carbon dioxide, and oxygen.

The hydrogen escaped to space, and the carbon dioxide returned to start the process all over again, leaving a net increase in the amount of atmospheric oxygen and falling methane levels. The process was agonizingly slow to start with but would accelerate dramatically as methane levels fell, the planetary surface oxidized, the levels of dissolved oxygen built up in the sea, and less and less oxygen was lost into the planetary surface and oceans.

Easy, really, when you put it like that, Digby thought as he massaged a forehead that still ached with the mental gymnastics he was having to do to understand it all.

It was the sheer scale of the terraforming process that confounded him. The quantities involved were mind-numbingly huge. Wang's calculations showed that getting Eternity's atmosphere to a level at which humans could live comfortably at low altitudes would require close to 780 teratonnes—7.8^{14} metric tons—of free oxygen to enter and, more important, stay in Eternity's atmosphere. Or as Wang had kindly and more understandably put it, an average of 2.5 million metric tons of oxygen every second for ten years. In the process, Eternity's oceans, the source of all that oxygen in the first place, would drop by over 3 meters and would go on dropping until Eternity's atmosphere stabilized centuries in the future.

Digby's mind had been duly boggled as Wang had reeled off the statistics, but he was not a numbers man, and the very idea of a teratonne was more than he could grasp. To his way of thinking, the best part of the whole extraordinary drama, the only part he could get his mind around, was played by a family of FedWorld geneered plants unofficially called bursters, one of fifty or so geneered species that made up the land-based biomass program.

Bursters were a small, fleshy plant that pushed out long arms of reddish-green leaves studded with small bright purple flowers. Digby liked them in part because they were distant—to the point of being remote, it would have to be said—relatives of his wife, Jana's, favorite plant, the carpet sedums of Old Earth, *Sedum lineare*. The garden of their house in McNair was covered in mats of their starlike yellow, orange, and red flowers and gray-green-red leaves. Jana was constantly on the lookout for new varieties to plant.

But FedWorld geneers had taken the humble carpet sedum light-years from its modest origins. Not only would the sedums flourish in Eternity's appallingly hostile low-oxygen atmosphere, they would produce vast quantities of tiny seed pods that would burst to scatter tiny airborne seeds over a wide radius. Within weeks, those seeds would have germinated and grown into adult plants, each one producing new seed bursts to start the whole process all over again.

And so it would go on, the pace relentless, the timetable unforgiving, the progress awesome.

A single heavy lander run would drop half a million tiny burster and other seedlings in a precise pattern over an area 2 kilometers wide and 1,000 kilometers long. Within months, the entire area would be a flourishing mat of sedum and other plants busily churning out oxygen from the atmosphere's carbon dioxide, water, and methane feedstock. According to Wang, Eternity's land surface was just over 136 million square kilometers, and that meant—Digby's brow wrinkled as he struggled with the arithmetic—68,000 lander missions if the entire planet was to be carpeted, which of course it wouldn't be. Even the Feds hadn't been able to geneer a plant capable of growing on bare rock on the top of a 10,000-meter mountain.

That was how, according to the all-powerful project plan, phase 1 land bioseeding, paralleled by an equally aggressive ocean-seeding program, could be finished in under three years and the irreversible change from a methane/nitrogen/carbon dioxide atmosphere to an oxygen/nitrogen one would have started.

But it still belied belief, Digby thought. Such was the power of the Feds' bioengineering that the entire process, which on Old Earth had taken some 270 million years to complete, would take only ten years on Eternity. By then, the planet would have an oxygen-rich atmosphere, admittedly hugely unstable as its oxygen-depleted mantle and oceans soaked up their share of the free oxygen churned out by the trillions of tons of geneered land and ocean biomass but leaving enough to allow the hated breathers to be thrown away and serious migration to begin.

Left to Hammer technology, it would have taken a full century, maybe more, and even then the results could not have been guaranteed, so completely had all the terraforming skills and systems transplanted from Old Earth been lost. In fact, now that he had seen firsthand what was involved, Digby seriously doubted that the Hammer had what it took to manage a project of such mind-bending complexity that even the Feds couldn't do it without the assistance of literally hundreds of AIs. Just nursing Eternity through the tricky and, by geological standards, nearly instantaneous crossover from a methane- to an oxygen-rich atmosphere without having the whole lot blow up was a problem of such intricacy that Digby seriously doubted that even the mighty Professor Wang truly understood what would be going on.

As Digby settled himself into the jeep, he began to understand the power of Merrick's vision. For the first time he could begin to see the impact it would have on a people starved of hope.

The only problem with Merrick's vision, grand though it might be, was the price the Hammer would have to pay sooner or later. Any way he looked at it, it would be way too high. The Feds would see to that.

Oh, well, he thought philosophically as the jeep set off with a lurch and Wang launched into an enthusiastic and detailed account of every part of the massive undertaking that passed in front of Digby, that was a problem for another day.

Four hours later, the jeep was waved through the razor-wire security fence that surrounded the project control center, and they drew up in front of a drab two-story plascrete building.

Eternity's sun was a searingly bright point almost directly overhead, its harsh light turning the slight irregularities in the walls into a strange mottled mix of light and shade. Aes-

thetics was not high on the terraforming project's priority
list, and it had been a long time since Digby had seen a building so brutally functional, and he'd seen a lot of Hammer
government buildings in his time.

"Home sweet home," said Wang, his cheerful and exuber-
ant manner in stark contrast to Digby's as the general
climbed, exhausted and sweat-stained, from the jeep. "This is
the security block here." Wang waved a casual hand at a second plascrete building, which was identical in every way to
and every bit as ugly as the first.

"Yes, thank you, Professor, you've made your point. And
just so that we are in no doubt, I am impressed, very impressed, in fact, and you have every right to be proud of the
progress you've made.

"But"—Digby's voice hardened—"don't make the mistake of taking me for granted. It would be the last mistake
you ever made. So get the job done and done well and you
will be rewarded. But no games. Understood?"

Wang's face went white with shock. In his excitement and
enthusiasm, he had forgotten the brutality that lay at the
heart of every Hammer undertaking, big or small, the violence that underwrote the entire structure and fabric of the
Hammer Worlds.

"Yes, General. Understood," he said quietly.

"I hope so."

Digby truly hoped Wang did, if only because progress, bla-
tantly obvious uninterrupted progress and lots of it, was
probably the only thing that would keep Merrick from re-
calling him to a certain death. "Now, if you don't mind, I'd
like to clean up before I meet our unwilling guests. Which
shift do I talk to first?"

"Red, General. Blue is on-shift at the moment, and they
won't finish up until this evening. I've scheduled you to
speak to Red Shift this afternoon, if that's okay. It's 15:00
local now, so that gives you plenty of time. Blue Shift is
scheduled for tomorrow." Wang's tone was brisk but busi-
nesslike as he recovered his composure.

"Fine. Show me where to put my kit."

"Follow me, General."

* * *

"And so, let me finish by saying that for all of you, Eternity is now your destiny and what you put in will determine what you take out. This is your planet now, so make the most of it. That's all."

As Digby stepped down from the back of the jeep, a small sigh washed across the untidy throng gathered in front of him. If they hadn't worked it out before, they certainly had now, Digby thought. The one part of the Feds' standard ter-raforming package that Digby had not brought planetside—the food production plant—would ensure their cooperation, and Digby was now happy that they all knew where they stood.

At the front of the crowd, Kerri and Sam Helfort stood silent. Like everyone else ripped out of the comfortable and safe world that had been the *Mumtaz,* they had continued to hope that somehow, some way, this was all a horrible dream and that it would come to a happy end, just as the holovid soaps always did. But the man now walking back to the Hammer compound, his steps radiating power and authority, had dispelled every last ounce of that hope.

Sam was the first to speak. "Fuck" was all she said.

After a long silence, Kerri spoke. "Sam, please." Her voice was tired. She didn't have the energy to take Sam to task as once she would have done.

"I know, Mom, I know," Sam said, her voice flat, the uncertainty obvious. "But it's how I feel."

"Sam!" Kerri said fiercely, turning to look Sam right in the face. "Promise me. I know we have no reason to hope, but tell me that you will never ever give up. If we are to come out of this, we just have to stay fit and well until the Feds come to get us. And come they will, one day. These bastards can't keep it a secret forever, I know they can't."

"You're right, Mom, that's all we have to do. I know that's all we have to do." Sam's voice brightened. "Come on, the gang's going down to the beach for a swim, and I'm hoping that John and Jarrod are going to go along as well."

"All well and good but don't forget Arkady, young lady," Kerri said, getting only a grin in response, a grin that said,

"I'm only young once, for God's sake, and I intend to make the most of it!"

As they walked back to the open-sided hut that passed for home, Kerri marveled for a moment at how the young girl had been transformed in the space of a few short weeks. The steel in her voice, the determined look on her face, the ability to rise above the moment, were pure Helfort. For the first time in many weeks Kerri's mood lifted.

Perhaps it would all work out, though for the life of her she couldn't see how or when.

Thursday, October 1, 2398, UD
DLS-387, departing Space Battle Station 4, Jackson's World

As SBS-4 receded slowly behind *387* as she boosted out-system to make the jump back to Hell, finally and much to Michael's relief, the order to fall out from berthing stations came through.

In the whole history of humanspace, Michael was pretty sure, there had never been such a thing as a comfortable space suit. Worse for someone destined to see a lot of the inside of space suits, he doubted there ever would be. In front of and around him, Michael's team morphed from the large orange lumps that made up *387*'s EVA team into real people who, with suit turnaround complete, disappeared to do whatever spacers did when off-watch.

But no such luck for Michael, and after a few words with Spacer Karpov, the youngest member of the surveillance drone division, he and Strezlecki disappeared down the hatch, heading for the first planning meeting with the covert support operations team and its extremely taciturn and uncommunicative leader, Warrant Officer Jacqueline Ng, known as Doc but only to anyone prepared to take liberties with a woman who had a Fleetwide reputation as a thoroughly competent and tough operator.

As Michael entered the wardroom, Ng and her senior spacers—two chiefs and two petty officers—were sitting waiting, marked out as special forces by left shoulder patches embroidered with one of the most elusive and smartest alien animals yet discovered by man, the T'changa from Carr's World, an animal with the ability to adjust its skin pattern and color to blend into the background so fast and so effectively that it put marine-issue chromaflage suits to shame. But it didn't escape Michael's notice that the regulation acknowledgment of an officer's arrival was conspicuously absent.

Fuck that, Michael thought. He didn't care if Ng was a fucking legend.

"Doc. How are you? Ready to go?" Michael's voice was deliberately enthusiastic, as though they were there to swap bullshit war stories—of which he had a few now, come to think of it—over a few beers rather than review the difficult and dangerous business of landing a deepspace light scout on one of Hell system's outer moons right under the noses of the Hammer.

Waving Strezlecki into the seat alongside him, Michael sat at the end of the small table with a fixed grin on his face and waited a moment while the chunky woman, her hair streaked with iron-gray and her face expressionless, looked steadily at him for a good ten seconds. Then, as a tiny small smile turned up one corner of her mouth, she leaned forward and half stood up, followed by the rest of her team.

"My apologies, sir. We've quite forgotten our manners."

Michael couldn't help himself. He burst out laughing, less at the elaborate charade he and Ng had played and more because he successfully had navigated yet another trap that the people who ran the day-to-day business of the Fleet liked to set for young officers.

"Not a problem, Warrant Officer Ng, not a problem."

A tiny nod from Ng acknowledged Michael's small victory as he continued. "It's good to have you and your team onboard. I think you know we've seen a lot of the Hammer close up, and it seems we are going to do it again. Now, before we start, I've commed you all with the cargo manifests—all containers loaded and stowed as per the plan you sent up. And none bent or damaged, I'm happy to say."

"Pleased to hear it, sir. We get very unhappy when grunts—sorry, sir, regular spacers—damage our stuff." From the look on her face, Michael was prepared to believe her. "By the way, sir, could you give my regards to your parents when next you see them. I served with both of them way back when."

God's blood, Michael thought. Was there any spacer over the age of fifty who hadn't served with one or the other or both of his parents? "Of course I will." He paused for a second. "You know that I have a personal stake in this business?"

"We do, sir. Is it an issue?" Ng's face and voice were carefully neutral.

"No. Just makes me want to get the job done right, that's all. And I'm sure if it gets too personal, someone will take the time to let me know."

Ng put her head back and laughed. "I can tell you, sir, you are your parents' son. Now, shall we?"

"Yes, let's start. Captain Ribot wants a joint briefing at 20:00 this evening, so we need to get on with it. First, let me introduce my offsider, Petty Officer Strezlecki." Ng and Strezlecki exchanged frosty nods. She was what Ng was pleased to call a grunt, and it was no surprise that Strezlecki was no great fan of special forces; clearly, she wasn't going to make an exception even for a woman with Ng's fearsome reputation. "Second, have you gotten everything you need from *387*?"

"We have. Lieutenant Kapoor has gotten us everything we needed. We're well settled in, thanks."

Michael hadn't expected anything else. "Okay, they didn't tell us much about dirtside covert ops at the college. We always got the feeling that the powers that be didn't exactly approve. So this is all new to me, and Petty Officer Strezlecki tells me that she's done precious little dirtside herself, so I think we should hand it over to you. In all honesty, Warrant Officer Ng, I think we have to be guided by you."

The fact that there would have been a riot if he had tried to throw his weight around with people with the experience of Ng and her team didn't have to be mentioned. Everybody knew it. But there were plenty of fresh-out-of-the-egg officers who wouldn't have picked up on that.

"Okay. Makes sense. Anyway, meet my team. Chief Petty Officers Harris and Mosharaf, Petty Officers Patel and Gaetano. My two leading hands are prepping gear, so that's the lot. Now, from the latest intel, we are pretty sure we know what we are up against.

"Even though at about 60 k's in diameter it's not the smallest of Hell's moons, Hell-14 has no value as a driver mass mine on account of its relatively low density. Some sort of volcanic material riddled with gas bubbles and holes. It's also very rugged, though nobody's got a good explanation why, with peaks rising 200 to 300 hundred meters above the surface datum and depressions almost as deep. So the Hammer has no interest in it other than as a surveillance post, and even then not a very good one. Because installing a large array grav detector would have involved some very serious earthmoving, they have limited their sensors to two polar installations. Let's have a look."

The holovid behind Ng sprang to life with an image like no moon Michael had ever seen before.

Hell-14 was something out of a nightmare, with razor-sharp peaks lifting into the star-studded sky, their sides falling sheer into deeply fissured twisting ravines broken occasionally by depressions into which an eon's worth of dust had accumulated slowly. Some were easily large enough to berth an entire squadron of Fleet heavy cruisers.

The sensor installations were two large four-sided white towers protected by antipersonnel lasers and studded with passive sensor arrays and the large flat panels of phased-array radar. The tower was topped off with more phased-array panels and finally a small-array grav detector. To get the sensors up above the terrain, the Hammers had simply picked the two largest mountains at what would have been the poles if the moon had rotated and laser-sliced their tops off. The ground for kilometers around each installation was littered with the resultant debris, some pieces hundreds of tons in mass and held to Hell-14's surface only by its tiny gravitational field.

The overall effect was one of utter confusion. Michael could immediately see the problem: how to get through what was in effect a hugely complex three-dimensional maze without being detected by the polar arrays. That was, of course, assuming that they'd gotten in undetected in the first place.

"Um" was all Michael could say. He couldn't begin to think how to solve a problem like this. He looked helplessly at Strezlecki, but she, too, was stumped.

"Well, the good news is that the surface approach is always the primary problem in these missions. Once we are close enough, it's pretty straightforward. But getting close enough without being detected and bringing the wrath of the Hammer down on all of our heads, well, that's the tricky bit."

"But you do have a way to do this, don't you?" Michael asked somewhat anxiously. For one awful moment, it occurred to him that Ng wanted to use the surveillance drone team as sacrificial lambs. As quickly as Michael dismissed the thought as ridiculous, Ng put him out of his misery.

"Let me introduce you to a little toy we use a lot, the optical terrain analysis vehicle, but known in the trade as OTTO. And very nifty they are, too. Here's one."

The holovid switched to show a rough uneven lump of rock. It could have been any one of trillions of bits of rock floating around in space except that Michael imagined he could see the hands of the design engineers in the careful sculpting of the surface.

"It's a surveillance drone just like ours but without the stealth coat and a lot smaller," said Strezlecki.

Ng laughed. "Well, yes and no. The difference is inside. What it does is produce a very precise map of the surface terrain using only optical sensors feeding into the mother and father of all quantum computer–based AIs. No active transmissions at all, and it produces a surface map that's as accurate as anything from a high-definition 3-D mapping radar. Don't ask me how, but it does. And all you need to know is that we have had a number of these babies do the necessary fly-bys to get us the terrain maps we need. And not only do we get a map, OTTO's AI produces the recommended routes from *387*'s landing site to the poles, taking into account the threat sensors we are up against, load sizes, and so on."

Ng switched the holovid back and zoomed it in. In a small depression almost exactly midway between the two poles and shielded from them by massive curtains of rock sat an image of *387*. From it ran two colored lines, one to each of the polar sensor stations, each twisting and turning through the fractured terrain like the tracks of a Saturday night drunk.

Ng finally broke the silence that followed. "Bastards, I think it's fair to say, but they are the best routes we've got. Route North comes in at 69 kilometers, and Route South at 57. Could be worse."

Michael and Strezlecki stared at the holovid, appalled. Sixty or so kilometers didn't sound far, but neither one knew of any suit that would do the job, and some of the gaps were decidedly tricky for sleds to get through. Then it clicked with both of them simultaneously.

"Sherpas," Michael exclaimed. "Mountain climbing," said Strezlecki, as one.

Ng laughed, but this time openly and from the stomach.

"Well, bugger me. You'd be amazed how long it takes some people to get the answer. So yes, we have to use your team plus a few others to stage supplies up the line and set up the habs along the routes so that my team can get there safely, do the job, and get back. Now that we've worked out the strategy, let's work out the details."

Ribot sat back in his chair. "Looks good to me. Anyone have any questions or issues?" He used the pause to look at each of his team members in turn. This was too tricky an operation for anyone to sit on a possible problem, and he wanted everyone to know it. The response was a succession of shakes of the head.

"Last chance to speak up. Anybody? No? Okay, then. Well, you all know me well enough by now, so I want the sim scenario set up by tomorrow morning. Maria, I'd like you and John to lend a hand on that, please. Once it's up, I want as many run-throughs as we have time for. Michael, Warrant Officer Ng is the one with the experience here, so she'll be mission commander, of course. Any problems with that?"

Helfort actually looked surprised. "God, no, sir. That's absolutely fine."

"Good. By my rough calculations, the entire mission will take five days, so I want the first run completed by"—he paused for a moment while he worked it out—"October 7. Let's schedule the debrief for 20:00. That okay with you, Warrant Officer Ng?"

"Fine, sir. We'll look forward to it."

"Right, then, I'll stay out of it until then. Michael, you and your team are exempt from all duties with the exception of general quarters, of course. Talk through the people you need with the XO, and then Jacqui, can you make sure the gaps in the rosters are covered? Any more? No? Thanks, everybody."

Friday, October 2, 2398, UD
Offices of the Supreme Council for the Preservation of the Faith, City of McNair, Commitment Planet

Councillor Marek pushed his microvid screen away after presenting a summary, mercifully short, of his report.

Merrick felt a momentary stab of fear. What in Kraa's sacred name were the Feds up to? Marek's people could make no sense of the apparent link between Operation Corona, whatever that was, and Vice Admiral Jaruzelska. But vague though the intelligence was, it had come from four sources, all consistently asserting that something big was up, it was called Corona, and Jaruzelska was in charge.

So the Feds were up to something. But what?

For a moment he considered the awful possibility that the

Feds had uncovered the truth about the *Mumtaz*. Just as quickly, he pushed that thought away. No, operational security had been as tight as the ass on his father's proverbial duck. If the Feds had found out, Merrick would have staked his life that the Hammer would have heard from them by now with all the usual moaning and complaining from that dickless wonder of an ambassador of theirs. But maybe he'd better stall just in case, he told himself.

No, he had a better idea, a much better idea and one that had been germinating for weeks. Now its time had come. Time to cut the head off the intelligence department. Together with Faith's seemingly unstoppable slide into chaos, the inevitable confusion that followed would keep everyone's head down, probably for months. He looked benignly down the Council table at Marek.

"Thank you, Councillor. For my part, I don't think we should read too much into the reports. Those Kraa-less Fed bastards are always up to something that never comes to much, so unless anyone has anything to add, I suggest that intelligence keep an eye on things and we leave it at that. Councillor Marek?"

"Yes, Chief Councillor." Marek struggled to keep the relief out of his voice. No doubt, he had expected Merrick to dish out his usual thrashing for bringing vague and unsubstantiated rumors to the Council table, but not this time, it seemed. "We'll see if anything turns up, but as you say, the Feds are always chasing after some shadow or other, so that's probably all it is."

"Fine. And that brings us to our last agenda item, the situation on Faith." Merrick's voice, which had been amiable and relaxed in the exchange with Marek, hardened into steely sarcasm as he turned to look directly at his nemesis.

"Well, Councillor Polk! It seems that the marines have taken the situation under control with only at last count, let me see, 426 civilian, 231 DocSec, and 32 marine deaths and Kraa only knows how many thousands of wounded. Oh, and I forgot, Planetary Councillor Herris. I'm not sure what category we would put his imminent demise under, but I think we can add him to the list. Councillor Khan?" Merrick looked down the table at the man responsible for the internal security of the Hammer Worlds.

Khan nodded. "Yes, Chief Councillor. Herris was tried this morning and sentenced to death without leave to appeal. Sentence has been confirmed by the Supreme Tribunal and will be carried out tomorrow morning."

Merrick smiled broadly. "Well, that's what happens when you treat this Council with disrespect." He could barely keep the triumph out of his voice. "You must be as relieved as the rest of us are, Councillor Polk, not just that the situation on Faith is back under control but that Planetary Councillor Herris has paid the price for his incompetence and corruption."

The impotent fury in Polk's eyes lifted Merrick's spirits no end. He enjoyed impotent fury as long as it was in other people.

"Yes, Chief Councillor," Polk muttered reluctantly.

What else could the spineless bastard say? Merrick thought.

"However," he continued, "it must be said that the situation on Faith is far from secure. I don't think I need to remind anybody of the Great Schism. The Supreme Council thought they had that under control, and look how it ended up. And I'm not just talking about the heretics, either."

A small shiver ran down the back of every man at the table. The power and wealth that accrued to councillors were substantial, but they were well matched by the risks. Within days of the end of the Great Schism, James MacFarlane had overthrown the Council and had installed himself as chief councillor before hunting down and hanging every councillor by one leg from the nearest tree in time-honored Hammer mob fashion, with the people howling their triumph over the corpses as they swung slowly in the wind.

Merrick watched and enjoyed the fear so visibly obvious in the eyes of all present. "Yes, well. Now that I have your attention, let me just say this. Councillor Marek!"

Marek jerked upright.

"Ah, good, Councillor Marek. You are paying attention. Now, I am sure it's abundantly clear to everyone here that you made the situation worse by refusing to provide the Council with honest reports on the causes of the unrest on Faith and the resultant heavy loss of life. So"—Merrick dropped his voice to a sibilant whisper, forcing the men around the table to lean forward to hear him—"I believe it is impossible for you to continue. I require your resignation. Now, if you wouldn't mind."

As Merrick slipped the knife in, the shock on Marek's face was instant and total, but he could only sit there immobile, unable to believe what he had heard. As the full import of Merrick's demand finally sank in, he turned in desperation to his patron, mouth working but saying nothing.

Polk said it for him. After a moment's indecision, he was on his feet, his mounting fury visible to all. "I will not allow this! I insist you withdraw. I—"

Merrick's hand went up to silence Polk.

"Well, Councillor Polk. Some might say that I should hold you personally responsible for the situation on Faith. Some might say that for months you resisted any and every attempt I made to have that corrupt pig Herris removed before the situation got completely out of hand. Some might say that perhaps it is you who should be asked to resign. But for the moment at least, I wouldn't suggest such a thing. But if you wish me to open the matter up for debate, I will be happy to do so."

Polk stood silent for a second as Merrick watched him run the numbers in his head. True, if it came to a ballot, the pro-Polk faction might have the votes if Merrick tried to remove him; he was the only man on the Council able to restrain Merrick in any way. But that didn't make seeing one of his own get the ax any easier to swallow.

Slowly Polk sank back into his seat, the bitterness of defeat obvious to all. "No, Chief Councillor. That won't be necessary."

Marek just stared at him, sudden terror stretching his face taut, his eyes wide and staring, a thin sheen of sweat across his face. He couldn't speak. It was obvious to everyone that Polk had just decided to abandon him, and without Polk he was nothing but a dead man. He looked desperately to Polk's men, but there was no support there.

Merrick's smile of satisfaction was cold and cruel. "Resign, Councillor. Resign now! Or I shall put the matter to secret ballot. Believe me when I say that I think it would be most unwise to do that. And remember, if you are tempted to count votes, you cannot vote on your own removal."

For a long minute, nothing was said. Nobody spoke in defense of Marek, and no one would. It was over, and they all knew it. Finally, Marek, taking a huge breath to steel himself for what would come next, got slowly to his feet, turning to look Merrick right in the eye.

"Chief Councillor. I hereby tender my resignation. I have served Kraa to the best of my ability, and all I ask is that I be allowed to live out my days in peace."

No fucking chance, Merrick thought viciously. You know the rules, you corrupt self-serving bastard. Former councillors who died peacefully in their beds were a rarity, and Merrick had no intention of allowing Marek to be one of them. Former councillors knew too much. Former councillors were owed too many favors by too many people to be anything but trouble. And history showed that even if they intended to live out their days in peace, former councillors were always drawn back into the maelstrom of Hammer politics. They owed and were owed too much to stay out of things. But there was time to deal with Marek later.

There was nothing more to be said, and as the silence stretched into awkwardness, Marek slipped from the room, a shrunken shadow of the man who had sat down at the Council table barely an hour earlier.

They came for him in the early hours of the morning.

Herris had not slept, ignoring the tray of slop pushed into his cell in favor of watching the sky through the tiny cell window. As the cell door banged open, he turned, standing unafraid and surprisingly calm, lit from behind by the sun as it burned its way into the bleak plascrete cell. The young DocSec lieutenant seemed nervous, the hand holding the death warrant shaking slightly as he began to read, his voice a near gabble under the stress of the moment.

"To the governor, McNair State Prison, Commitment.

"By my authority, you are hereby instructed that Kaspar Anjar Herris, 5300-718994-91F, now in your charge and having been found guilty by the investigating tribunal of conduct prejudicial to the Doctrine of the Hammer of Kraa and sentenced to death without leave to appeal, which sentence has been duly confirmed by the Supreme Tribunal for the Preservation of the Faith, is to be executed in the manner authorized by law at 05:30 Commitment Standard Time on the third day of October 2398.

"Given under my hand and seal this second day of October 2398 at McNair, Commitment. Carlos J. Ferenici, Deputy President, Supreme Tribunal for the Preservation of the Faith."

The lieutenant paused long enough to wet his lips before continuing. "Kaspar Anjar Herris, 5300-718994-91F. Do you have anything to say?"

"No," Herris said curtly. It had been good while it lasted, and he had always known the risks he was running. "For Kraa's sake, get on with it."

As the DocSec officer backed out of the narrow cell, two

DocSec troopers, covered by two more with stun guns, grabbed Herris, spun him around, and secured his wrists with plasticuffs. Then, blindfolded and gagged despite his protests, he was hustled out of the cell, down the corridor, and out into a small dirt-covered yard. As he was strapped to the single post set against the high wall at the back of the yard, the lieutenant, now briskly efficient in an effort to get the whole awful business done with, called the firing squad to order.

Seconds later it was over except for two last pieces of ritual.

First, the doctor, casual, disinterested, and as always visibly unhappy at being out of bed at such an early hour, checked that the firing squad had done its job. The lieutenant held his breath. He did not want to have to administer the coup de grâce, and it was with heartfelt relief that he acknowledged the doctor's curt nod of confirmation that the firing squad had done its job.

As Herris's body hung in its straps, shattered and still bleeding, the blood stark against orange prison coveralls as it dripped slowly to the dirt, the DocSec lieutenant stepped forward and in a clear firm voice called out the words that had followed countless victims of the Hammer of Kraa into darkness.

"Kaspar Anjar Herris. So die all enemies of the peoples of the Hammer of Kraa."

Dismissing the firing squad and leaving the body of what once had been one of the most powerful men in the Hammer Worlds to the burial detail, he left the yard to get some breakfast, his appetite powerfully restored by successfully completing his first execution without a single fuckup.

"I think to call that a debacle is being a bit unkind to debacles. And Michael, I hold you largely responsible." Ribot's face was as unsympathetic as his voice.

Michael squirmed in his seat, miserable and embarrassed. "Sir" was all he could say.

"Three points to make," said Ribot. "First, there is no excuse for not liaising closely with Warrant Officer Ng's teams. If they run into unexpected problems, it is you who has to adjust, not them. They are, after all, the whole reason why you are there. You support them and not the other way around. Now look." Ribot brought up the holovid of Hell-14, the two tortuous routes to the poles marked in livid red.

Ribot's fingers stabbed at the display. "Route South first. Here, here, and here. Three times, same problem. You should have shifted resources from Route North to compensate for the extra work needed to get past these bottlenecks. OTTO's maps are good, but they're not that good, and there will always be parts of the route that are narrower than we expect, and that means finding a way around or cutting rock to get Warrant Officer Ng's equipment through. Route North, same problem. So be prepared."

Michael nodded. Much as he hated being dressed down in public, everything Ribot had said so far had been fair enough.

"Second problem is AI overdependence. It takes time to truly understand their limitations, but we don't have much time, so learn fast. There is no substitute for the human brain, well, not yet, anyway, so don't take Mother's advice uncritically." Ribot paused as Michael's finger came up. "Yes?"

"Understood, sir," Michael said cautiously, "but part of the problem is that we haven't given Mother enough learning time and Hell-14 is a unique problem. Such a problem in fact that the standard libraries of AI rules for covert operations haven't been much use. I've spoken to Lieutenant Hosani and Warrant Officer Ng about the problem. What we are going to do is set up secondary sims running in parallel. Two of Warrant Officer Ng's team will oversee those while the rest of us concentrate on the primary sim. That way, Mother will see multiple attempts at the problem. That way she'll get more exposure to the issues we'll face as well as the benefit of the real-life experience from Ng's people at the same time. Hopefully, that means Mother will be better at supporting us when the real thing happens."

By the time he finished, Michael's voice reflected a confidence he didn't feel. Managing the support teams—sherpas, as Ng called them—had proved surprisingly difficult. Not only was wrestling the recalcitrant sleds very hard work physically, the problems came thick and fast, the timetable was unyielding, and the adjustments were never ending. Michael and his team had to get Ng's teams to their targets on time, and that was that.

"Neat, Michael. Neat. But is the experience Mother gets from sim on sim, as it were, going to be useful?" A shadow of doubt tinged Ribot's voice.

"We think so, sir." Ng sounded confident. "Lieutenant Hosani has split Mother's experiential base into two, one taking input from all three sims, the other from the primary sim only. We'll analyze and compare the two as they grow, and if we see inconsistencies between them, we'll trash the one using the secondaries. But I don't think we'll have to do that."

"Oh?" Ribot didn't look convinced. "Why?"

"Well, because the secondaries get the benefit of my people's contribution. In the primary sim they are really nothing more than pack mules, there to move gear from A to B. But in the secondaries my people work at the command level.

That way Mother's experiential base not only grows faster, it gets multiple command inputs."

Ribot thought about it for a while before nodding in agreement. "Okay. Makes sense, so let's see how it goes. Maria, the comparative analysis has to be good, and I'd like to understand the methodology as well as the results. Can you talk me through what you plan to do on that front?"

"Sir."

"Okay. Where was I? Ah, yes. Lightly roasting Mr. Helfort." Michael could manage only a half frown, half smile as laughter rippled around the room. They'd all been there, and Warrant Officer Ng knew that her turn was coming fast. Ribot paused for a moment. "Michael, for fuck's sake, don't take this too seriously. The reason we have sims is so that we can get most of the mistakes out of the way first. You know that."

Michael nodded. "I know that, sir. But there's a lot at stake and a lot to think about."

"There is. So let's get back to it. I'm happy on the AI front, so here's my last point. Michael, I've told you before, and I'm sure I'll tell you again. You get too involved, too close to the action. You must remember to stand back. If you don't, nobody else will, and we risk the operation if that happens."

As Michael acknowledged the point with another nod of his head, Ribot turned to Ng.

"Warrant Officer Ng, two points. It's taking far too long, as I'm sure you know, but hopefully the next run-through will benefit from lessons learned so far. And second, some of your team are too casual, it seems to me, about concealment discipline. We all know that the Hammer's sensor technology is crap compared to ours, but that's no excuse for pushing the envelope." Once again Ribot paused as the holovid bloomed. "Here and here, overaggressive cutting. Too much debris too quickly, and hot debris at that. And here, moving too fast too high. Asking for a radar paint and we can't afford that."

Ng nodded. "Fair points, sir. We'll do better next time."

"Okay. Now, any comments from the teams? Michael?"

"No, all covered, sir."

"Warrant Officer Ng?"

"Yes, sir. I'd like to see if we can beef up the sherpa teams supporting Route North. I know there's not a lot of room and that more bodies do not necessarily give us a better result, but it's well protected. If we can save some time, we may need it. I think it's worth a look, and I'll talk to the XO about where we get the bodies to do it if that's all right."

"Fine by me." Ribot looked across at Armitage, who nodded her agreement. "Any more? Okay, then we're done. Twenty-four-hour stand-down and if all goes well, we'll run the next sim after we've dropped into normalspace."

As the meeting broke up for a moment, Michael sat back with his eyes closed, his mood flattened not just by fatigue but by knowing how much had to be gotten right if the whole sorry *Mumtaz* affair was to be sorted out and his mother and Sam recovered safely. That they might not make it didn't bear thinking about. He opened his eyes to see Warrant Officer Ng looking at him in the uncomfortably direct way that was one of her trademarks.

"Oh! Didn't realize you were still here."

"I am. And I'm just hoping that you aren't taking this all too much to heart, sir. That would be a worry." Ng's face betrayed her concern.

"You'd be right to, but no, I'm not. It's just . . . Well, it's just that I've never been part of anything that mattered so much before, and that takes a bit of getting used to, I suppose." He rubbed his face as Ng's eyes seemed to bore right into his soul. Not a woman to bullshit, he thought.

Ng's eyes softened. "That's why sims aren't the answer, sir. Never forget. They've got a fatal flaw. No risk. Nothing to lose. So keep it in perspective. Let me tell you something. I've always found that the real thing is easier somehow. Don't really know why; never been able to work it out. But my theory is that some people perform better when it comes to the real thing precisely because it is risky. And I suspect that you are one of those people."

"I hope you're right, I hope you're right," Michael said doubtfully.

"Well, I think I am, and I'm not usually wrong. Anyway, that's it for me. A shower, something to eat, and then a solid eight hours will do me. I'll see you in the morning."

Tuesday, October 6, 2398, UD
DLS-387, *Hell System (Revelation-II) Farspace*

With its usual stomach-churning lurch, *387* dropped out of pinchspace 19 million kilometers out from Hell system.

In seconds, Mother had begun to build up the normalspace tactical picture of Hell system, the threat plot blossoming with hundreds of red Hammer intercepts.

"This all seems very familiar." Armitage grunted as the threat plot filled up with red symbols marking the mass of long- and short-range radars, lasers, and radio frequency and other emitters that infested the Hell system. One by one, Mother analyzed each intercept and downgraded the threat it presented, turning the symbols to orange as she did so. The tension in the combat information center visibly decreased as the threat plot finally changed to all orange.

"Captain, sir. Command. Threat plot is orange, ready to conduct vector alignment and deploy pinchcomsats." Hosani didn't try to keep the relief out of her voice. Dropping out into normalspace was bad enough. Dropping into hostile normalspace was ten times worse.

"Approved. Stand the ship down from general quarters and revert to defense stations. I'm going for a walk-around and then to my cabin."

"Sir."

Extravehicular activity conducted while the ship was doing 150,000 kilometers per hour was never popular, and this time it was even less so. Michael and his team were denied the protection of *387*'s short-range defensive lasers, which normally were tasked with picking off any space debris that got too close to the drone team. The chance that Hammer sensors would pick up laser fire was simply too great. The risk was very real. The death of three of *Bombard*'s crew doing a routine drone launch five years earlier— the spacers had been drilled through one after the other by a single fragment of rock only millimeters across that had been let pass by a defective short-range laser—was all the reminder Michael's team needed that what they were doing was a very risky business.

It was from the heart that Michael heaved a sigh of relief as the surveillance drone team finally maneuvered the last pinchcomsat out of its protective container and clear of *387*.

"Command, Alfa. Pinchcomsats deployed. Containers closed and secured. Returning," Michael commed as he and the team scrambled to get back inside *387*.

"Alfa, command, roger."

Ten minutes later, the six pinchcomsats were boosted on their way to take up their positions in orbit 4 million kilometers out from the gray-black mass that was the planet Revelation-II. Their tiny low-power pinchcomms arrays had been locked successfully on to the pinchcomms carrier wave transmitted by a temporary tactical pinchcomms relaysat drifting in deepspace 2 light-years out from the Revelation system.

Thursday, October 8, 2398, UD
29:37 Local Time
Eternity Base

For a moment Kerri Helfort struggled to remember where she was.

It didn't take long; the hated breather mask cutting into her face saw to that. She rolled onto her back and checked the time. She had twenty minutes before midnight and reveille for Red Shift. She hated getting up in the dark and, along with everyone else, had been more than happy with Digby's announcement that the much-disliked system of two back-to-back shifts seven days a week would end on Friday. Even the stupidest Hammer, and Kerri hadn't taken long to work out that Digby was far from stupid, understood that you couldn't work people nearly fifteen hours a day every day of the week forever.

And so this Saturday would be a big day for the mostly unwilling inhabitants of the Hammer's newest settled planet.

Not only would it be their first free weekend, it also would mark the end of phase 1 of the terraforming project with all the primary infrastructure well on its way to completion. With the massive methane/carbon dioxide converters now in final testing, the next day would see the carbon sequestration and oxygen production plant commissioned, all of which was something of a relief to Kerri and everyone else dirtside. Nobody liked the idea of depending on the breather oxygen supplies being ferried down from the *Mumtaz*. Speaking of which, she saw that her oxygen supplies would get marginal during the shift, so she'd need to get replacement cylinders. And while she was at it, she thought, she might as well cycle the breather's molecular filters.

But far more important to Kerri was Sam's welfare. Not surprisingly, Sam had taken the hijacking very hard. But things were looking up. Thankfully, the biomass plant was only days away from final acceptance, and once it was onstream, seeding the planet with geneered plants and cyanobacteria would start in earnest. In the absence of anything better to do, Sam had secured a position on one of the crews that would be responsible for field biomass management and atmospheric monitoring. Kerri said a small prayer of thanks for the experience Sam had gotten back on Ashakiran at the Manindi Center for Oceanic Research. Even though it was largely irrelevant, it had sounded impressive enough to land her the job.

And the job was a good one.

Sam would be a member of Doctor Jack Loudon's atmosphere monitoring team. Despite his cultural heritage, Loudon seemed different from the rest of the Hammers who had been brought dirtside. Most unusually, he did not seem to share the view held by most Hammer men that all women were good for was sex, reproduction, and housekeeping and that if they really had to take paid employment, it had to be doing the crappy jobs that men or cheap labor imported from Scobie's World couldn't be persuaded to do. In fact, Kerri strongly suspected that Jack Loudon's three or so years as an unwilling guest at the Hammer's premier prison facility had made him think long and hard about what the Hammer of Kraa really stood for.

To top it all and thanks to Sam's holding a basic grade flier's license, a sixteenth birthday present, she had been selected for flight duties. That was not really a big deal given the power of the average flier's AI and the fact that almost everyone had a fliers' license of some sort, but nonetheless it was not something offered to everybody. She strongly suspected that Doctor Loudon's promotion of Sam had been motivated by more than professional interest, but she didn't care. For a Hammer, he seemed like a nice guy, and if he wasn't, it was time Sam learned to handle herself.

Finally, there was the icing on the cake. One of the guys from the project planning office had told her over lunch the previous day that he had overheard two of the Hammers discussing the possibility that they would get their neuronics back. *Mumtaz* had an entire planetary neuronics system sitting in containers somewhere, and because the entire project was being run by AIs, Kerri could see that it made no sense not to bring the power of neuronics-based decision support to bear as well. She hoped Professor Wang could persuade Digby to relent on the matter. It would be nice not to have that awful empty, blank feeling in her head anymore.

Not that it was as simple as not having neuronics.

Like all the older *Mumtaz*ers she spoke to, she felt the awful certainty that everything they had spent their entire lives building—careers, homes, families, friends—was gone forever, every atom of it vanished. The loss hung over all of them every waking minute of the day like a black cloud, and no matter how hard she tried, it was always there—an immovable monument to everything she'd never see again.

And Andrew. How she missed him. There wasn't a waking moment when she didn't think of him, and the thought that they would never hold each other close again tore at her heart with an intensity that was almost physical. Not to mention Michael. How must he be feeling? If it were not for Sam, she feared she might have given up completely. Some already had, retreating into a world of drug-soaked might-have-beens. By God, it was hard to get up every day, to work up alongside those Hammer swine, to keep going hour after hour.

In truth, she did it only because of Sam.

Worst of all was knowing that without the goodwill of the Hammer, they were all dead. Digby had made sure of that by keeping the food plant in orbit, and there was no sign of its being brought dirtside. In the days immediately after being dumped on Eternity, the very small number of people with some claim to military experience naturally had coalesced around Kerri; she was by far the most senior service officer around. But every way the group looked at it, they were jammed. All the early talk of violent action against Digby and his goons had foundered on the rocks of cold hard reality: They had no weapons, they had no way of sustaining life, and they had no way of getting off the planet, and even if they somehow did, they had nowhere to run to and no one to call for help.

The group, now self-deprecatingly called the escape committee, still met regularly, but the focus had shifted to intelligence gathering and to planning what they would do in the unlikely event that the cavalry arrived to rescue them. Despite her private fears that the whole process was a waste of time, Kerri played her part—strong, firm, and resolute—and tried to keep alive the few embers of hope she still had left.

Another quick check of the time told her that she had three minutes to Red Shift reveille. If she got going now, she would beat the rush through the showers and be first in line for breakfast. Sitting up, she grabbed her towel and washing kit and set off down the still-dark shed that was home to almost a hundred fellow *Mumtaz*ers, their sleeping forms quiet and unmoving around her.

Ribot was tired. Everyone was tired.

It had been a long run in, and with every kilometer the tension and pressure had mounted. This was no fly-by, safely in and out at a brisk 300,000 kph like the last time, with the option to jump to the safety of pinchspace always available.

No, this was a drop right into the Hammer's backyard, and as *387*'s speed fell away and the distance closed, the risk increased exponentially. Ribot and everyone else onboard knew only too well that *387* was a sitting duck if it was detected by a stealth Hammer. Even the slowest rail-gun crew would have no problem picking them off. But so far, so good. They had come millions of kilometers since dropping out of pinchspace, and only intermittently had the threat plot gone to red, and then only for a few seconds as a newly switched-on Hammer radar came online.

"Captain, sir." Leon Holdorf had the watch, and the strain was showing in his drawn and lined face.

"Yes, Leon."

"One minute to main engine cutoff, sir. Vector nominal. 2.2 million kilometers and 98 hours 43 minutes to run to Hell-14."

Ribot nodded. If the tension was bad now, it would be ten times worse as they closed in on Hell-14 and its massive arrays of sensors. Still, that was what stealthed ships such as *387* were built to do even if that still left the problem of the gravitronics array. It was the one sensor that the Feds had yet to work out a sure way of defeating, though the Hammers had done what they could to make things easier for *387*: The dumb fucks hadn't put new grav wave detectors up to replace the unreliable antiques that had been on Hell-14 for decades. As the arrays measured the rate of change in the fabric of space-time caused by a moving mass, the only tactic that worked was to make the approach as slow as possible, and even that was no guarantee of success.

"Main engine cutoff, sir." Holdorf's comment was a formality. Even when the ship was operating at very low power, the sibilant whisper of its main engines had penetrated every corner, and the sudden silence as it fell in toward Hell-14 seemed almost deafening.

"Roger. Michael's team ready to go?"

"Yes, sir. Deploying now."

Two decks above the combat information center, Michael and his team cycled the air locks and moved toward the upper container stowage area. Michael moved to port, and Petty Officer Strezlecki to starboard.

As they moved aft, *387* was visible below them only as a formless black void razor-cut out of the billions of needle-sharp stars that littered the sky. Michael's stomach twitched as he moved across the empty nothingness. On his left side sat the Revelation system's distant orange-red dwarf star. A miserable excuse for a star it was, too, Michael thought. At only 0.65 sols in mass and 0.28 sols in luminosity, it was barely noticeable across 6 billion kilometers, shedding no useful light on Michael and his team as they moved aft across the formless abyss that was *387*'s hull.

As they reached the cargo bays, Michael comforted himself with the thought that at least they weren't doing 150,000 kph like the last time, an experience neither he nor his team had much enjoyed. In deference to their proximity to the Hammer, this exercise saw the team secured to the ship by fiber-optic comms tethers. Even at ultralow power, the risk of suit comms being intercepted was deemed too great, so tethers were the only answer even if the damn things were a pain in the ass. They appeared to have a mind of their own, and no matter how carefully Michael and the rest of the team maneuvered, the thin black cables, almost invisible in the nearly total darkness, seemed to be determined to wrap themselves around everybody and everything.

It was a frustrating five minutes later before Michael and

Petty Officer Strezlecki had gotten their teams positioned safely and were ready to start.

"Command, Alfa. Open upper cargo doors."

"Roger, opening."

Slowly the massive doors swung open, the interior of the cargo bay barely visible in the small helmet lights of the team. Michael wasted no time. Open cargo doors and exposed containers compromised 387's stealth capability, and Ribot had made it abundantly clear that time was absolutely of the essence, a sentiment wholly shared by Michael and his team.

As soon as the gap was large enough, the drone team was in, their target the two forwardmost containers. In seconds, the container seals were off and the doors were opened to reveal an array of what looked like elongated black eggs, four to a container, the formless blobs in their stealthcoats just over a meter long. One by one, securing straps were released, protective packaging removed and safely stowed, and tethers attached, and the eggs floated out to drift a few meters off 387's hull. Once they were clear and had taken the time to check that all loose packaging had been accounted for, the container doors were closed and secure, and all tethers were clear, Michael ordered the port cargo doors shut.

"Command, Alfa. Ready for system tests."

"Command, roger. Stand by."

Within seconds, Michael's neuronics confirmed that all eight intercept bots were nominal. Without further delay, the tethers were disconnected, and with a gentle shove, the eggs were pushed clear of 387. His team's job done, Michael commed Strezlecki.

"Strez, Alfa, sitrep."

"Roger, Alfa. Krachovs Alfa and Bravo deployed and mounted. Fifteen minutes to deploy the rest."

"Roger, Strez. Need any assistance?"

"Negative."

"Roger, Alfa and team returning to ship. Out."

Michael was happy to leave Strezlecki to it. The Krachov shroud generators were very large and could be difficult to mount. But if Strezlecki could get two mounted in the time it took Michael and his team to deploy the intercept bots, she certainly didn't need any help from a novice like him.

He took a final look down the length of the ship in an optimistic attempt to spot the Hell system. Even though he'd commed Mother to put the planetary datum on his heads-up display to tell him where to look, there was nothing to be seen against the dazzling array of stars spread out before him. Not to worry. He was damn sure he'd see more than enough of the Hell system before they were finished, he thought as he dropped down the air lock.

Fifteen minutes later, Petty Officer Strzelecki and her team were finished and *387* was safely buttoned up, much to the barely concealed relief of all onboard.

Michael sat at the back of the combat information center and watched as Mother, communicating over ultra-low-power frequency-jittering whisker-beam lasers, sent the interceptbots on their way. Everyone onboard, from the most junior spacer up, understood the crucial importance of the insignificant-looking black eggs. They had a lot to do. First, they had to locate and tap into the laser and microwave backbones that formed the administrative comms network used by the Hammers to run every nonmilitary element of the Hell prison system. Second, they had to crack the low-grade encryption used by the network. Third, they had to drop autonomous softwarebots into the system to try to search out where the *Mumtaz*'s crew, its male military passengers, and the hijackers had been taken. Fourth, they had to report back.

As always, there was a fifth, the key to light scout covert ops: Don't get caught.

And if they didn't succeed, this part of the operation would be a bust, and God only knew how many people would be condemned to rot on Hell. It didn't bear thinking about.

"Okay, everybody. Now it gets interesting, so on your toes."

Ribot's tone was carefully controlled. Hell-14 and its sensor arrays lay only 5,400 kilometers ahead of them, and as the sims had pointed out, this was the point of maximum risk. Unavoidably, *387*'s stealth integrity was slightly degraded by the Krachov shroud generators even though they were mounted as far aft as possible to get the maximum protection from the flare of the hull. Ribot felt uncomfortably exposed even if Mother was sure that the risk was minimal.

To make things worse, it needn't have been that way. Fleet had only gotten as far as installing the smaller tactical shroud generators for antilaser defense. Integral Krachov shroud generators big enough to shield a light scout's main engine burn had long been promised, but relatively modest though the generators were, the work needed to put them into existing ships was significant and was done only during major quarter-life refits. That put *387*'s shroud generators at least seven years away, which was no help to him right now.

Ribot cursed softly. He, like every other light scout captain, was obsessive when it came to keeping his ship stealth, and the sooner he could get the protective shroud out and the damn Krachov generators stowed, the happier he would be.

"Captain, sir. Ready to deploy Krachov shroud." For the benefit of a crowded combat information center, Armitage's voice sounded firmly confident, but Ribot knew better. Krachov shrouds big enough to shield a ship safely were relatively new, and though they had performed well in trials, they had never been used for real, certainly never when the cost of failure was so high. Not for the first time, Ribot shivered at the thought of what an ambushing Hammer warship could do to them.

"Deploy."

And with that, the eight Krachov shroud generators began to spew out what in broad daylight would have looked like a gigantic swarm of tiny flies. In fact, they were small wafer-thin disks, hundreds of thousands of them. Each was carefully designed, some to absorb the radar energy thrown at the ship by the Hammer's phased-array radars, most to diffuse and deflect the infrared signature of *387*'s main engines as they braked the ship for its rendezvous with Hell-14.

The shroud's job was simple: to stop the Hammer's sensors on Hell-14 and elsewhere from seeing *387*. Easy to say and very hard to do, so hard that the Krachov shroud had been in development for more than ten years before the hard-nosed men and women of Fleet's operational acceptance board would allow it to be used in earnest. And *387* was the guinea pig, the first warship to take the system into a hostile environment.

Within minutes the shroud began to take shape. The sheer scale and complexity of the task were huge as the shroud's master AI carefully choreographed an elaborate space dance across a dense spiderweb of ultra-low-power laser comms, with hundreds of subordinate AIs manipulating each disk's tiny onboard processors. In response, minute explosive puff thrusters fired to move the disks into a complex three-dimensional set of disk clouds; the overall shroud was many hundreds of meters across and perfectly constructed to put a thick layer of disks between *387* and every known Hammer sensor in Hell nearspace. If the engineers had gotten it right, the radio frequency energy thrown at them by the Hammer's radars would be absorbed and the thermal energy produced by *387*'s main engines would be contained by the Krachov shroud—just like pissing into a bottle, as one of the development team had delicately explained it to Ribot—allowing only a tiny, undetectable fraction to leak through. Ribot hoped that the technical intelligence reports about the sensitivity of Hammer radars and infrared sensors were correct.

If the TECHINT reports weren't . . .

As the shroud was being shaped to the master AI's satisfaction, Michael and his team had been deployed, working frantically to recover the now-useless shield generators. Finally, with the generators safely secured, all was set and the master AI gave the word. As one, the disk clouds making up the shroud began to accelerate gently away from *387*. With a final check to make sure the shield was far enough away not to be disrupted by main engine efflux, Mother carefully turned ship and fired up the main engines. *387* began its slow deceleration down to Hell-14, its modest exhaust plume safely hidden from the Hammer's infrared sensors behind the Krachov shroud.

Not one to miss an opportunity to do some housekeeping, Ribot extended the heat panels, which quickly turned a bright cherry-red as they dumped the excess heat load accumulated during *387*'s long run in to Hell-14.

After desuiting in record-breaking time, Michael returned to his usual position behind the goofers line at the back of the combat information center to watch as the holovid tracked the shroud swarm as it moved away, blotting out the stars as it did so.

He was beyond tired. Ribot's endless sims had seen to that. But tired as he was, Michael could see the sense in Ribot's relentless pursuit of perfection. Even in the final run, with every possible problem thrown at them to slow them, Michael's sherpas had gotten Ng and her team to the poles on schedule and, more important, without being spotted.

Now all Ribot had to do was get the ship down safely.

Knees sagging with fatigue, Michael decided to call it quits. He and the rest of his team were now officially off duty until *387* touched down on Hell-14, and that was over a day away before *387* would drift in to Hell-14 at a snail-like— he'd checked the navplan with Mother—5 kph.

There was absolutely no point hanging around. If things went pear-shaped, he'd know about it pretty quickly. He would take the longest, hottest shower he could bear, get some food inside him, and then get some badly needed sleep.

Heart pounding and mouth dry, Michael woke with a start, for a moment completely lost. The gray plasfiber deck head above his bunk was no help as he tried to orient his tangled mind in the dark.

When he'd checked the time, he'd been astonished to see that he had slept for almost the full fourteen hours he'd given himself. And he'd slept through the shutdown of *387*'s artificial gravity, something he'd never been able to do before. Must have needed the sleep, he thought with a grin as he pulled himself out of his bunk and into the 0-g shower before changing into a clean set of coveralls, grabbing some food, and hurtling into the combat information center.

There was no way he was going to miss *387*'s arrival on Hell-14.

As he did that, he cursed as he remembered an unfinished vidmail to Anna. He would have to finish it later. He'd started it more than a week earlier, along with one for his father, not that they would see their vidmails until the punch-up with the Hammer was over.

He just hoped his father was all right, though God knew he would have no reason to be. The pain of not being able to talk to him, to tell him that Sam and Mom were all right and that if all went well they would all be home soon, cut deep into him.

And then there was Anna onboard *Damishqui*. Michael had a horrible feeling that she would be in the thick of it since that was what heavy cruisers were specifically built for. Even if the Feds had a technology edge over the Hammer, in the end a rail gun was a rail gun and there wasn't a heavy cruiser that could take too many hits, heavily armored though it was. Michael had seen the holovids of a full swarm attack, the tiny slugs smashing into the bows of *Fidelity,* an old Arcturus class deepspace heavy cruiser, during the final Fleet acceptance trials of the new ultra-high-velocity Mark 56 rail-gun system.

It had not been a pretty sight. Michael and the rest of the audience of second-year cadets had winced as the iridium/ platinum alloy rail-gun slugs had smashed into the hapless cruiser at better than 1,000 kilometers a second, her bows disappearing behind a firestorm of exploding ceramsteel armor, the outermost layer of high-explosive reactive armor able to deflect only grazing impacts. Less than a microsecond after impact, each slug had turned to plasma, an incandescent mass of ionized gas cutting a tunnel deep into the cruiser's heavy frontal armor. A few microseconds later, the slug had done its job, its enormous kinetic energy, equivalent to more than a ton of conventional explosive, completely transformed by the ship's armor into heat, with the resultant thermal explosion blowing a broad flat crater deep into the cruiser's bows.

The cruiser was doomed. Slug after slug blasted away its armor, ceramsteel spewing off into space in colossal swirling clouds of gas until huge sections of its bows had been stripped down to the inner titanium hull. Then it was the turn of the second salvo, just a matter of time until a slug got lucky and scored a direct hit on the exposed inner hull, with the tiny mass of plasma blasting into the ship to smash indiscriminately through everything in its way. The damage was almost unimaginable as the shock wave from the slug spalled shards of metal off ship and equipment alike to drive a cone of destruction through the ship. Michael shivered as he tried not to think about what a slug would do to any human unlucky enough to be in its way.

If the plasma ball survived long enough, and some did, it would explode out of the hull to disappear into deepspace, its lethal job done as all around it its swarm siblings finished the job of turning the inside of a once-proud ship into a shambles of molten metal, shattered equipment, and ionized gas, the ship's hull visibly rippling as wave after wave of energy release shocked its fabric. You didn't have to be a genius to see why bow-on penetrations were so deadly and why all warships had heavy frontal armor many meters thick.

Michael had to give himself a mental shake.

It wasn't all doom and gloom. On the plus side, slugs worked well only at relatively short ranges and in large swarms, mixed in with plenty of decoys. They could maneuver no better than a shotgun pellet, and the Hammers' swarm geometry computers were as poor as the Feds' AIs were good at winnowing out slugs from decoys and choreographing the maneuvers needed to get ships out of the way of an incoming attack. Even better, the Hammer's rail guns had a muzzle velocity of only 778 kilometers a second, and their rail-gun slugs were slightly smaller. But on the minus side, Hammer decoy technology was improving, and that made picking the slugs out of the incoming swarm increasingly difficult.

But all things considered, *Damishqui* should be all right. No properly handled Fed warship would ever have to withstand what the *Fidelity* had endured. *Damishqui* had very good close-in defenses, a carefully integrated triple layer of lasers, missiles, and chain guns, so she should have no trouble handling whatever the Hammer could throw at it. That was the theory, anyway, and at the rational level, Michael believed it. But at the emotional level the thought of Anna on the receiving end of a serious Hammer rail-gun swarm made his guts knot.

As he hung unnoticed at the back of the combat information center, he comforted himself with the thought that at least Anna wasn't in a light scout like *387* completely on its own millions of kilometers inside Hammer space. The trials that had destroyed the *Fidelity* also had targeted a light scout. The holovid footage showed the ship literally being gutted by a single slug coming in at an angle steep enough to defeat the armor's best efforts to absorb the slug's impact, hitting just where the armor thinned back from the bow and releasing enough energy to blow the hull apart. Not a pretty sight and one that rumor had it was shown to all prospective light scout captains to remind them why they should stay well away from rail-gun-fitted opposition. And here they were, deep in Hammer nearspace thick with rail-gun-fitted warships and, what was more, for the second time in a matter of weeks.

Michael dismissed the thought that it might happen to them and turned his mind to the command plot, with Ribot switching the massive holovid over to *387*'s aft-mounted holocams. What they showed was the stuff of nightmares.

Every detail of the shattered, twisted surface of Hell-14 was clearly visible. Job done and done well in Mother's opinion. The Krachov shields, now switched from passive to active star-simulation mode to defeat Hammer holocams searching for stars occulted by a stealth ship, had opened out to cover *387*'s final approach. She now was only 500 meters above the dust-filled depression that would be her hiding place until the operation was complete, closing in at a shade under 1.4 meters per second, viciously sharp ridges surrounding her landing site, reaching up as if to grab the ship.

The combat information center was deathly quiet; the entire crew watched as the dusty gray-black surface crept closer. So intense was their concentration that Michael visibly jumped when Mother triggered a final brief main engine burn to bring *387* to a dead stop, with the efflux driving plumes of ancient dust writhing up into the sky and just as quickly vanishing from sight.

"Hope it really does resemble a meteorite strike like it's supposed to," Michael whispered to Warrant Officer Ng, who was standing silently beside him. A burn that close to the moon's surface wouldn't be missed by the Hammer's sensors.

"We're fucked if it doesn't, that's for sure," Ng muttered.

So precise had been its final burn, *387* hung motionless for a few seconds only meters above the surface.

All around her, massive rock walls rose hundreds of meters from the shallow basin, their faces shimmering in the low-light holovid display, splintered spines of rock etched sharply against a dazzling star-studded sky, the dirty gray-black cliff faces fractured by huge cracks. The place was completely alien and totally dead. Hostile, harsh, and utterly pitiless, Michael thought. They were a very long way from home, and all around them were the forces of the most ruthless regime in human history. Michael knew full well that they wouldn't get any second chances. He suppressed the shiver of fear that ran through him, turning his attention with a conscious effort back to the holovid.

With infinite patience and care, Mother gradually spun the ship on its axis to roll its stern away from the landing site below, putting the hull parallel to the moon's surface, ready to touch down. Mother let Hell-14's microgravity do the rest, the moon gently pulling *387* to ground.

Seventy-two seconds later, *387* settled with barely a tremor onto the surface of Hell-14.

"Landed, sir." Armitage's face was split by a broad grin, a mixture of triumph and relief, as the ship erupted in cheering. In penetrating a heavily defended system to put down on Hammer real estate, *387* had done something no Fed ship had done in twenty years, and the pride in the accomplishment was tangible.

"Thank you, Jacqui," Ribot said with a smile, "though I'm sure Cosmo will have something to say about the damage to our stealthcoat." Ribot's smile got even broader. "Now, not to rain on anybody's parade, but we're not quite home yet. Jacqui, deploy the anchor team and let's get the chromaflage covers up. If no one knocks on our door in the next six hours, I think we can say we've cracked it. Oh, and get the artgrav back on."

Armitage nodded and commed the necessary orders.

Below and aft of the combat information center, the massive lander hangar doors swung open, and the EVA team, barely visible in their space suits now that combat gray had replaced high-visibility orange, poured out onto the moon's surface. Effortlessly, Bienefelt, huge in her bulky space suit, maneuvered the rock bolt gun out of the hangar. Michael watched in admiration as she flew the unwieldy metal cylinder along *387*'s starboard side, coming to a dead stop in precisely the right place under the ship's starboard bow and at

precisely the right attitude to fire an explosive bolt deep into
Hell-14's crust. That's what thousands of EVA hours does for
you, Michael thought enviously.

As the bolt went home, Bienefelt was off to the next anchor point, and it was only a matter of minutes before *387*
was securely tethered fore and aft, short cables pulled out of
hidden recesses in her hull holding her firmly to the moon's
surface. Arguably, tethers were overkill. Even Hell-14's microgravity was more than enough to keep *387* in place. But
tidal stresses made Hell-14 earthquake-prone, and so, to
comply with Fleet standard operating procedures, tethers
were required. It took five more minutes to attach and arm
the explosive cutters that would be needed if *387* had to leave
in a hurry, and the job was done.

While Michael and his team had been concentrating on
tethering the ship, the XO's team had not been idle. Bulky
rolls of chromaflage net were unloaded and ranged hard up
against the foot of the massive cliff rising above them. As
Carlsson and Leong fired small pegs into the rock wall, the
XO's crew secured the end of each roll before running it out
and over the ship to the cliff face on the other side, the chromaflage rolls twisting and turning as creases from long storage were shaken out. Bit by bit, *387* disappeared from sight
under the gray micromesh net.

Once *387* was fully covered and with the XO's instructions not to allow his fucking body to get above the surrounding rock cliffs ringing in his ears, Michael was
dispatched to hover 200 meters over the ship to provide an
image feed to Mother as she carefully adjusted the shape,
color, and texture of the chromaflage net to match the original surface. It was a surprisingly long process as Mother
slowly and carefully blended the net into the background.
With nothing more to do than hang motionless and keep his
helmet-mounted holocam pointed in the right direction,
Michael felt very vulnerable and very alone. By the time
Mother had finished, he might as well have been the only
human being in millions of kilometers. Apart from a slight
hump where the chromaflage nets crossed over the top of
387's hull, the landing site looked like the original basin

floor, dust and all. The ship had completely vanished, and provided that the Hammer didn't deploy high-power ground-penetrating radar, it would stay that way.

Finally called back by Armitage, a relieved Michael and his crew still had much to do. Remote heat sinks, remote holocams, low-power whisker laser comms relay stations, and Ng's equipment as well as the surveillance drones needed to act as *387*'s long-range eyes and ears as she lay cut-off under her protective chromaflage net—all had to be moved out of the ship, ready for deployment. There was also the experimental driver mass production plant to be moved carefully out of its containers and secured to the basin floor alongside *387* under the watchful eyes of the two project engineers who had been sent along by Fleet to make sure the damn thing worked as advertised. In itself that was no small challenge given the very substandard feedstock that Hell-14 gas-riven rock would supply.

But eventually everything got done to Ribot's satisfaction, and a very impatient Warrant Officer Ng and her team were able to start the long haul to the north and south poles of Hell-14.

As Ng's team led the four heavily loaded sleds away from *387*, heading for the narrow cut identified by OTTO as the only safe way out of the rock-walled basin, Michael's sherpas struggled to keep the heavy awkward sleds on track and away from the rock walls. Ribot began to relax for the first time since they had left Frontier. There was not a lot more he could do now. It was up to Ng.

Ng knew her stuff, and Michael had done particularly well in the final mission sim; his suggestion that they parallel run multiple sims to maximize Mother's experience base had produced a marked improvement in the quality of Mother's advice. Even better, the threat plot, fed by sensor data streams from *Bonnie* and *Clyde,* the two surveillance drones now carefully positioned on the basin rim above *387*, showed only orange intercepts. There were no angry red symbols to show a Hammer force boosting out-system to investigate *387*, and for that Ribot offered a small prayer of thanks. The plan called for Warrant Officer Ng and her team to reach the poles by no later than midday on 23 October and to have the two massive Hammer sensor arrays sterilized no more than twenty-four hours after that.

Ribot stretched to try to get the kinks out of a tired body.

He hoped that Mister Murphy would stay away. Even hundreds of light-years from Vice Admiral Jaruzelska, he felt all too keenly the enormous pressure on him to provide the up-to-date operational intelligence she needed to make the final commitment to the operation. The consequences of failing her were too dire to contemplate, and he was going to do everything in his power not to do that.

Thursday, October 22, 2398, UD
Hell-14

Ng's language was unprintable as she and her team tried for the umpteenth time to maneuver the bulky sled around an impossibly tight bend in the 30-meter-deep cleft of rock slashed into the nightmare that was Hell-14's surface.

But it was not to be. Any way she tried, the sleds were too big and the corner too tight to pass through. Ng's frustration was understandable. Over four days, Michael's sherpas had performed flawlessly, and the routes to the poles had matched those mapped by OTTO perfectly. But now, when they were almost there, their luck had run out and at a point where going over the choke point and picking up the route again on the other side was not an option: The surface above their heads was in clear view of the Hammer's sensors.

Ng knew when to admit defeat. "Okay, boys, it's not going to go. Get the rock anchors out and the sled safely tied down while I call Helfort. When that's done, start unstrapping the gear. We're going to have to backpack this lot in."

As her team set to work breaking down the sled's load, Ng found the fiber dispenser mounted on the back of the sled and quickly spliced in a comms node. Seconds later, her neuronics were patched in and she had Michael Helfort on the line.

"Problem?" Michael's voice betrayed his concern. He'd begun to allow himself to think that the mission actually might go according to plan.

Ng nodded. "Afraid so, sir. OTTO's let us down, and we have a choke point we can't go around or over this close to the pole. At this late stage, there's no alternative route in. So it's backpack time, and I'm going to need more than my fair share of your sherpas even if it means slowing down the northern team."

"Any chance of cutting the choke point away?"

"No. Not this close. Too much risk. All it would take is one gas pocket and we'd have a rock plume that the Hammer couldn't fail to see."

Michael scowled in frustration. "Fair enough. That's one less thing to bring up. Okay, I'll start diverting people up the line to you. The northern team's in good shape, and in any case standard operating procedures require both sensor installations to be attacked at the same time, so we can afford to slow them up a bit."

"Good. We've secured the sleds and are making up the first loads now. I'll send Chief Mosharaf and Petty Officer Gaetano on ahead to set up the habs at the 32-k mark. That's as far as we can go this shift."

"Done. I'll be back to you with a revised schedule as soon as I can."

"Good. I'll leave it to you to brief the captain if that's all right."

"Okay."

Shit, Michael thought. Left to his own devices, he would have forgotten to do that, and Ribot was not a man to be left in the dark. "Thanks," he said. "I would have missed that."

"Thought you might," Ng said with a chuckle.

Two hours later, the elaborately choreographed, hugely complex dance that kept a long line of space-suited humans alive across 60 kilometers of unforgivingly hostile terrain had been transformed to accommodate the choke point.

Michael had pulled people back from the northern route and pushed them up the line, heavily loaded with the additional habs and supplies needed to support the greatly increased number of sherpas working the southern route.

Frantic, scrambling, desperate hours later, things settled down and Mother was able to take control of the logistical minutiae: marrying the right sherpa with the right load at the right time in the right order, making sure that every one of Michael's team was spaced out along the route like beads on a necklace, and stayed within limits for oxygen and water.

As Mother took the weight, Michael offered a small prayer of thanks and vowed to buy Leading Hand Kazembi a beer. No, a case of beer. In one of the final sims, it had been Kazembi who had pointed out that assuming OTTO would get everything 100 percent right was probably not a sensible thing to do, and as a result the team had run sims involving the very problem confronting them now. He didn't like to imagine the chaos that might have been if they had not de-bugged what was in retrospect something that almost inevitably was going to happen.

Time to update the skipper and then he could stand down for six hours and let Hosani take the strain.

Friday, October 23, 2398, UD
M-5 Motorway, Faith Planet

Fourteen hundred kilometers east of Faith's capital city, Kantzina, the Clearwater Hills lifted into a dramatic sandstone ridge known locally as Gordon's Ground. The Kantzina–Schadova motorway left the riverbank, swinging up and into a long tunnel that would emerge on the other side of the ridge to run down to a fertile floodplain that ran on in an endless carpet of blue-green forest, rising and falling all the way to the city of Schadova and beyond. Thousands of kilometers across the continent the rain forest flowed, right to the shores of Marulian Sea, the rich soil studded with the massive tropical trees that made Faith famous for its timber.

It had been a long journey for the 2nd Battalion, 22nd Regiment of marines. The convoy of trucks was a frantic last-minute response to a sudden increase in heretic activity in Schadova.

Seconds after the last truck entered the long tunnel, the sensorbots leading the convoy detected a suspect laser transmission. Their futile warnings screamed out unheard as massive explosions brought tons of rock down onto the roadway. Plastex charges painstakingly concealed in the roof of the tunnel, in maintenance tunnels, and in safety recesses exploded ahead and behind the convoy.

The 2/22nd's commander, Lieutenant Colonel Mitchell, only had enough time to utter one last curse, damning brigade intelligence for its stupidity in declaring the Kantzina–Schadova motorway safe for truck convoys before his half-track, brakes locked and tracks screaming in tortured protest, smashed into a pile of rubble strewn across the roadway and turned over, its plasteel armor screeching and ripping as it came to rest against the tunnel wall. It was still for a few seconds before the rest of the convoy smashed home in quick succession, the bored drivers too slow to react as truck piled into truck, the screams of injured marines echoing in the sudden silence as metal and rock came to a shuddering, wrenching halt. The tunnel filled with smoke and dust in the half-light cast by the few headlights still burning.

Ten seconds later, crude homemade fuel-air bombs mounted in the center of the tunnel exploded with exquisite timing, the deadly aerosol of solvents and air igniting to turn the tunnel into an inferno and the living into the dead.

Chief Councillor Merrick put his head in his hands and for one of very few times in his life felt like weeping.

Two hundred sixty-nine marines, for Kraa's sake. Killed. In one attack. And only thirty-four survivors, most so badly burned and their lungs so badly seared that they wouldn't survive the night despite the frantic efforts of the regen techs. How the fuck could it have happened? And he was responsible because he had not done what had to be done, what had screamed out to be done when that Kraa-damned son of a whore Herris had first crossed the invisible line between modest corruption, long an inevitable and accepted part of Hammer life, and rampant uncontrolled graft. No, not graft. That was far too kind a term for what in truth had been unrestrained looting.

And all because he hadn't wanted to take on Councillor Polk. Polk was the man whose influence protected and nurtured Herris. Polk was the man who made sure that all his parasitical fellow travelers enjoyed the huge dividends from Herris's uncontrolled pillaging of Faith. What had made Polk think that the people of Faith, always the most difficult and independent of the Hammer Worlds, would put up with having their wealth confiscated, husbands and wives cheated, sons conscripted or arrested, daughters corrupted, homes despoiled, and institutions pillaged by DocSec? DocSec! The guardians of the Path of Doctrine, and all under the direction of the very man appointed by Kraa to watch over his people on Faith, Planetary Councillor Herris.

Merrick sat back in his chair, his mind a churning, confused mess.

At every point in his life he had known what he had to do and where he had to go, but not anymore. The *Mumtaz* project, his master plan, the biggest risk of his life, was the only piece of his world that was going according to plan, and he thanked Kraa for giving him Digby to make it all happen. But as the moment approached when he could reveal the project to an amazed and grateful Council before telling the tired peoples of the Hammer that there was hope for them and their families, that there was room to grow and flourish, that there was a new planet to take the pressure off the Hammer Worlds, Faith looked like it was about to go over the cliff. And if it did, it would drag the Hammer into another Great Schism and him to his fate in front of a DocSec firing squad.

So what was he doing now? He was getting ready for yet another Kraa-damned useless Supreme Council meeting.

As Merrick scanned the agenda, he could see nothing but bad news. Faith of course, as usual, headed the list, followed by the even worse than expected economic results for the July–September quarter. Unemployment up, consumer confidence down, business investment down, inventories up, and capital markets fragile as Faith's battered economy, in theory the Hammer Worlds' second largest, went into free-fall.

Then there was the arrest of a senior DocSec officer for a particularly nasty rape-murder on Fortitude that had brought the people of the capital, Mardoz, out in the streets in protest. Thank Kraa, DocSec had been sensible for once and had not indulged in the usual brutal street-clearing tactics. Must find out who the incident commander was and promote him, he thought in passing. Then there was the usual industrial unrest in the star shipyards of Commitment, the spiraling cost of the subsidies for unprofitable interplanetary space lines, allegations of corruption in the contract administration branch of the defense department.

On and on it went, a never-ending nightmare. By Kraa, he was tired.

Worst of all, he couldn't begin to think how to make things work anymore. He sighed deeply. More of the same, it would have to be. Maybe things would settle down; they always had in the past. But Faith was a real worry. Perhaps he could remove some heads, especially the moron who had sent the 2/22nd to their deaths. What was his name? Oh, yes, Brigadier General Abinse. A spell on Hell would fix him. Might even have the useless bastard shot. And Abinse's senior staff officers as well. Why not? Why not indeed?

Somewhat cheered by doing what he enjoyed best—the brutal exercise of his authority—Merrick picked up the phone.

Michael watched as Chief Petty Officer Mosharaf raised his right hand in victory, the remote holovid feed picking up the broad grin that split his face.

A herd of space-suited elephants could now tap-dance in lead boots in front of the massive sensor tower, and the Hammer's operators would see only what the Feds wanted them to see: nothing but shattered rock and a star-studded sky.

Safely tucked away under a broad chromaflage net secured to the rock walls of a deep depression well out of sight of the tower and its deadly array of sensors, Michael and his team of sherpas had looked on in horrified fascination as Mosharaf and his team had worked with infinite care and patience to place suppressors on the tower's infrared sensors and holocams, their every move in full sight of the tower's antipersonnel lasers. Michael had practically died as he'd watched them cross the open ground, protected by nothing more than a smart screen, a milky-gray net supported by hair-thin gas-filled ribs tuned by its onboard AI to blend perfectly with the rock surface around it; surface-mounted emitters had adjusted the screen's signature until it did not exist even to the most discriminating eyes.

As Ng's people completed the laborious process of installing the massive active radar suppressors, Michael and his sherpas began the weary process of recovering all the equipment used to get Ng and her teams safely up to the towers. As the last load began its long trek back to *387*, Michael completed his final task—putting in place and arming demolition charges, enough boosted chemex to flatten the tower and destroy everything on it—before he, too, with one last tired look around, set off.

Back onboard *387* and with no reaction from the Hammer

to indicate any problems, Ribot flashed a pinchcomms message to Fleet to report Ng's success. That'll cheer them up, Michael thought as he turned in for a well-earned rest.

Tracking through deepspace 120 million kilometers out from Hell at a sedate 150,000 kph, Lieutenant William Chen, captain of *DLS-166,* smiled broadly as he read the latest pinchcomm broadcast from Fleet, his pride mixed with anxiety at the thought of the mission that lay ahead. Ribot's team had done the job, and finally *166* was on its way in.

Comming the officer in command to finalize *166*'s vector, he made his way to the combat information center for the microjump that would drop them a safe 18 million kilometers from Hell-14 en route to his rendezvous with Ribot and *387*.

After dropping out of pinchspace 18 million kilometers from Hell, *DLS-166* coasted in unseen.

Even though *387* had done all the heavy lifting, the nerves of all onboard were stretched tissue-thin as the pressure of dropping so deep in Hammer space built up. Thank Christ he didn't have to do it like *387,* Chen thought gratefully. Going in second was bad enough: hour after hour of slow deceleration right into the face of the Hammer's sensors, not knowing if at any moment a great Hammer heavy cruiser would go active and smash the ship into a cloud of battered and twisted metal.

"Captain, sir. Krachov shields deployed and in position. Final deceleration burn in two minutes ten seconds."

"Roger that."

Two minutes later, with *166*'s driver efflux safely blocked from view by Krachov shields positioned with exquisite care top and bottom, left and right, and now by Hell-14 itself, so close directly ahead so that every possible intercept angle between *166* and the Hammers' surveillance satellites was blocked, Mother fired the main engines. The ship bucked and heaved in the face of the sudden deceleration, the drivers pouring hundreds of kilos of ionized mass per second out into space, the pencil-thin plume of plasma reaching out toward the waiting moon.

Finally, Mother shut down the main engines. *166* hung motionless for a few seconds before Hell-14's tiny gravitational field took hold of her; the ship drifted down to the moon's surface with painful slowness as Mother rolled it belly down in preparation for landing. Long minutes later, *166* had settled down alongside *387,* and Chen felt his breathing and heartbeat return to normal.

Friday, October 30, 2398, UD
Offices of the Supreme Council for the Preservation of the Faith, City of McNair, Planet Commitment

Merrick massaged temples split by the sudden onset of yet another in a long line of shockingly intense headaches as the Council erupted around him in a storm of furious argument.

The issue of the moment—what else did they talk about these days? Merrick thought morosely—was Faith's continuing slide into anarchy. Merrick watched through pain-slitted eyes as Polk defended himself furiously against the charge leveled by Merrick's supporters that the entire situation had been caused by Polk's protection of Herris and the stinking web of corruption that Herris had woven through the entire fabric of Faith's economy.

Merrick cursed quietly to himself as Polk refused to be moved. Polk's association with the late and unlamented Herris was the only chink in the bloody man's armor, and Merrick had tried every way he could to exploit that weakness. But Polk had not given an inch and wasn't going to.

Time to call off the dogs, Merrick thought. This is going nowhere.

He smashed his hand down on the table, the noise cutting through the argument. "Enough! The situation on Faith has clearly deteriorated to a point where I intend to establish a formal inquiry into the causes of the problem. We need to know why we've ended up where we have and what we can do to avoid further outbreaks. I'm sure I have your support on this."

Nice try, you old buzzard, Polk said to himself, but there was no way he was going to let Merrick off the hook. Polk loaded his voice with what he fondly imagined to be equal parts sincerity and doubt. Merrick thought he just sounded sarcastic. "Well, Chief Councillor, I'm not sure we need one. We—"

Merrick could not contain himself. "Not sure?" he shouted, voice crackling with anger. "Not fucking sure? What was I just watching? A bloody high school debate? Nothing is more obvious than the fact that we need an inquiry. If the Council cannot agree to that, then what good is it?"

"I'm sorry, but I am afraid I cannot possibly agree," Polk said smoothly, eyes flitting across the faces of the rest of the Council as he double-checked that he had the numbers. He was pretty sure he did; he wished he could be absolutely sure. His heart pounded at the terrible risk he was about to take.

Pushing any doubts aside, Polk forced himself to radiate confidence. "No, as I say, I cannot agree, and I think you'll find if you put the matter to the vote that the Council does not agree, either. It is of course up to you, but I do think we have talked enough."

In the face of Polk's cool assurance, the brief glimmer of hope that had sprung into Merrick's eyes as Polk had made the challenge died as quickly as it had come. Shit, Merrick thought. He thinks—he knows he's got the numbers. A quick look at the faces around the table confirmed his worst fears. Kraa damn it. The nonaligned councillors refused to look at him, so they were gone, and even his own supporters looked shaky. He'd lost.

Merrick's voice was quiet, barely concealing his bitterness at the defeat he'd just been handed by Polk. "No, Councillor. I don't think that will be necessary. Unless anyone thinks it should be voted on right now, why don't we sleep on it? I'll put it on the agenda for next week."

Polk's triumph was obvious. Got you, you Kraa-damned

son of a bitch, he thought. He'd taken Merrick to the edge, and the bloody man hadn't liked what he'd seen. But Merrick had better get used to it because the next time he wasn't going to let him back away.

With a stomach acid-bitter with defeat, Merrick had no option but to move the meeting on. He had needed that inquiry to give himself the best possible chance of shifting the blame away from himself and onto Herris and, by extension, Polk. But Polk knew that as well as he did, and so did the rest of the Council. Much as they hated Polk, they needed him if only to keep Merrick in check.

Merrick cursed silently.

He shouldn't have been surprised. Things had changed, and maybe Jesse Merrick was no longer a man to be feared. But Polk was.

Saturday, October 31, 2398, UD
DLS-387, Hell-14

No matter how hard he tried, Ribot's neuronics refused to let him sleep. The piercing comm alarm relentlessly dragged him up from the depths of a wonderfully dreamless slumber, his first in a long time.

Groggy, Ribot commed his bunk light on, oriented himself, and accepted the call.

Helfort had the watch. His voice was hoarse with stress, and his avatar made him look like shit. "Captain, sir. Officer in command. Sorry to bother you, but I thought you would like to know."

"No problem, Michael," Ribot muttered groggily. "What is it?"

"The interceptbots, sir. They've finally broken in, and we have just begun getting good-quality datastreams. The intercept AI is just starting its analysis of the Hammer's data structures, and we'll have a definitive data model shortly to allow us to attack the knowledge base. I'll draft a message to Fleet for your release, sir."

Ribot's mind was a mass of wet concrete, and he had to struggle to think straight. "Uh, no, Michael," he said after a moment's thought. "Wait. Hang on for a moment. I'd like to go to Fleet with specific data rather than the promise of specific data, in particular the first of the *Mumtaz*ers we can identify, where they are, and so on. Otherwise, we'll just get another damn pinchcomm urging us to try harder. You know how twitchy they're getting."

"Oh, okay, sir. That'll take us at least three or four days, maybe more. Makes sense, though. They have been nagging us somewhat."

"Understatement, Michael. No, sit tight for the moment. We'll put a pinchcomm through to Fleet as soon as we have something specific. Anything else now that I'm awake?"

"Not really, sir. The Hammer's pretty quiet tonight. The light escorts *Regan* and *Bates* moved from Fleet base to Hell Center two hours ago and are now alongside the planetary transfer station. *Verity* and the rest of the Hell flotilla are alongside at the flotilla base, though Mother thinks that at least four of them are preparing to get under way. The usual premission stuff: sensor testing and so on. There's one light cruiser, two heavy escorts, and a heavy scout doing a lot of systems testing, all fire control systems but not much else, so Mother's not sure what they're up to, but we'll know more in the morning. Hammer ships tend not to unberth much before 08:00. Loads of commercial traffic as always, but Mother's watching the vectors pretty closely, and there's nothing unusual going on."

"Okay. Let me know if we get anything specific out of the interceptbots. Night."

"Night, sir."

Ribot commed the light off and lay back. For once, sleep came quickly, and in minutes he was down somewhere deep and black, snoring lightly.

"The Feds have done what?" Merrick roared. "Put a ship into orbit around one of our planets? And sent a lander dirtside? I don't fucking believe it! What in Kraa's name do those stupid bastards think they are doing? I want a full report together with your recommended response within the hour!"

Merrick slammed the phone down on his long-suffering councillor for war and external security. As if he didn't already have enough to worry about.

Kraa-dammed Feds. The bastards had put an Abydos class deepspace heavy patrol ship in orbit around Hammer 14-1. It was way too big for a genuine survey operation, as the Feds claimed it was, but not small enough to be pushed around.

Why, for Kraa's sake, why? What were the Feds up to now?

Maybe he'd missed something. Merrick grunted as he pulled up the file on the planet 14-1. He snorted derisively as he quickly scanned the data. No, he hadn't missed anything. It was a miserable apology for a planet. Thanks to a severely elliptical orbit, it was a frozen inhospitable waste most of the time, scoured by endless storms that ripped its methane/nitrogen atmosphere apart, the sky thick with the sulfurous smoke and dust belched out from the thousands of active volcanoes that punctuated a planetary surface wracked with endless earthquakes triggered by two massive moons orbiting far too close for comfort. A worthless piece of dirt.

And yet, and yet. Slow down, Merrick, and think this through, he told himself.

It was becoming harder and harder for him to ignore the possibility that somehow the Feds had found out about the *Mumtaz* and were about to do something about it. In fact, that was the only scenario that made sense. The problem was that all he knew for a fact was that the Feds were mounting an operation code-named Corona under the command of a Vice Admiral Jaruzelska. Exactly what Corona was, nobody could tell him. But if Corona really was about the *Mumtaz,* he was stuck. The mountain of deceit he had erected around the whole affair had trapped him. To admit that he knew what the Feds might be up to would be to put a bullet in his head.

Polk and his gang would see to that.

So why should he take the chance unless he had to? There was always the possibility that the Feds were simply trying it on. They had been known to put pressure on the Hammer for no good reason at all. No, he had no choice. He had to keep quiet and try to hold things together until the time was right to announce the success of the Eternity project and reap the enormous political and social rewards that would follow. In fact, maybe it was time to call Digby back to start constructing the elaborate cover story that would be needed if he was to be able to claim that it was the Hammer and the Hammer alone that was responsible for the successful and speedy terraforming of Eternity. And if word had leaked . . .

The more Merrick thought it through, the clearer the way forward became. Get something heavy to Hammer-14 to make it clear to the damn Feds that they'd be blown to hell if they didn't withdraw. In the meantime, get the usual pointless exchange of protest notes going and use the incident to take people's minds off what was going on in Kantzina. But stretch things out. Kraa's blood. He needed as much time as he could get.

The necessary calls having been made to put the wheels in motion, Merrick turned his attention back to the unhappy subject of the civil unrest on Faith. Despite its impressive bulk, the report from Major General Barbosa, COMGEN-MARFOR-3, was unable to conceal the simple fact that even with the dispatch of an additional battalion of marines, the situation on Faith was slowly but surely sliding out of control. Resistance was hardening as the locals began to realize that although marines were tough, very well trained, and very dangerous, they were not invincible. With thorough preparation, good leadership, and a bit of luck, all under-written by a willingness to accept heavy casualties, they could be taken on with some success.

The previous week had seen a major heretic assault in Kantzina's eastern suburbs, the first attack that showed signs of careful planning based on accurate intelligence supported by good staff work. Even though the attack had had no chance against the well-dug-in marines of 5 Brigade, for once prepared with their own accurate and timely intelli-gence, the butcher's bill had been too high, with the heretics leaving no fewer than 245 marine casualties behind them as they were finally thrown back in bloody confusion. That had happened only because 5 Brigade's reserve armor had sliced deep into the northern flank of the attack to leave the heretics, cut off and isolated, to be pounded into dust by the marines' ground attack fliers.

But 5 Brigade's casualties in that particular encounter weren't the end of it. They were on top of mounting DocSec casualties in Ksedicja and, worst of all, in Cascadia, home of the Great Schism. Merrick knew it would get worse before it got better. He suspected that whoever was behind the latest Kantzina assault wouldn't make the same mistakes the sec-ond time around, and that meant many more marines shipped home in body bags. But 5 Brigade's commander seemed to have his shit together, so maybe he was being too pes-simistic. Even so, it was damn hard to be anything else.

Not for the first time he cursed Polk and his willful stupid-ity. "Chief Councillor Herris is a trusted servant of Kraa, and he would not tolerate corruption and cronyism." Polk's words came back to him as though they had been spoken only yesterday. "Well, they'll see," Merrick muttered sav-agely. Herris had rightly paid the ultimate price, and maybe Polk would, too. All he had to do was somehow keep a lid on Faith and on the *Mumtaz* affair and hope to Kraa that the Feds hadn't found out, and maybe, just maybe, he'd get through things.

Maybe more marines was the only answer, short of walking away, that was. He had to bring the unrest to an end. He turned his attention back to the mound of papers on his desk, his decision to recall Digby forgotten for the moment.

Tuesday, November 3, 2398, UD
Offices of the Moderator and Cabinet, Terranova

The moderator, Valerie Burkhardt, sat back in her chair, trying to stretch the kinks out of her back without being too obvious. It had been a long cabinet meeting. "Giovanni, I think I know why you are looking so smug. So do tell."

The federal minister of interstellar relations was indeed looking smug, and for good reason. "Yes, Moderator, I suppose I am. As you all know, the heavy patrol ship *Delphic* duly entered orbit around Frechaut-I, or perhaps I should say, in deference to our Hammer friends, Hammer 14-1, two days ago and successfully landed its survey party shortly thereafter. Since then, we've had only routine pinchcomms, but that's to be expected until the Hammer gets a ship there. Fleet tells me that thanks to Corelli Reef, a particularly large and unpleasant grav anomaly between the Hammer and Frechaut, the earliest a warship is likely to get there is tomorrow morning sometime.

"We've just received the standard protest from the Hammer government. Ambassador Carlyle was summoned to the Department of Foreign Relations this morning and presented with this protest by none other than the councillor for foreign relations, Claude Albrecht himself. They helpfully pinchcommed the protest to us at the same time. The formal hard copy is on a courier drone on its way to us now. A copy is in your in-box if you'd like to have a quick look at it."

Moderator Burkhardt snorted derisively as she read the protest. "Hammer scum" was all she said.

"And so they are, Moderator. But the good news is that

they have given us one week to comply, which suits our purpose well. We want if at all possible to keep *Delphic* on station around Frechaut until just before Corona kicks off in earnest. Hopefully, that will keep the Hammer looking firmly in the wrong direction."

"Good. So that means that for whatever reason, the Hammer has given us seven of those sixteen days, which is very helpful of them, I must say. So what now, Giovanni?"

"I'll get the Hammer desk to put together the usual bullshit response and run it past the lawyers before getting onto a courier drone to Commitment. No pinchcomm summary in advance this time. That should stall things a bit further, and we'll see what happens. The Hammer will be upset, but that's to be expected."

"Not so upset that they would do anything, well, stupid?" Moderator Burkhardt's concern was less for *Delphic* than for the hugely complex military operation now gathering pace as they talked. It would be hard enough for Jaruzelska to do what had to be done without the Hammer jumping the gun, shooting up *Delphic,* and then going to a state of high alert just as Battle Fleet Delta launched its attack.

Pecora shook his head emphatically. "No, I don't think so, Valerie, and neither do my people. And believe me, we've looked at this very hard. Despite their reputation, the Hammer are much more considered in their actions than people give them credit for. They have enough on their plate at the moment with the situation on Faith and will be very concerned that by upsetting us we would start covert support for the rebels dirtside. Not hard to slip stealth carrier drones past their sensors, and they know it. We think worrying about that will slow them down, which is of course exactly what we want right now."

"Okay, Giovanni. We'll leave that to you." Burkhardt's tone made it clear that the issue had been dealt with. "Well, everybody, if there's no other business, I think that's enough for now."

Angela Jaruzelska sat, as she did every morning, nursing a cup of tea at the back of the massive strategy simulation building's main combat information center.

For her, it was the best time of day.

It was too soon for the pressure of other people's agendas to clutter up her thinking but not too early to put the new day into the proper perspective. A good time, she always found, for thinking through the issues the day would bring while below her the pace of activity began to pick up as the operations and planning staff got themselves organized for the first formal event of the day, the daily operations conference otherwise known as morning prayers.

"Admiral, sir."

"Yes, Bian?"

Jaruzelska's flag lieutenant, who she would have sworn got younger by the day, nodded nervously. Jaruzelska was well known for treasuring the first part of the day as her thinking time, and interruptions had better be for something important.

"Flash message from *DLS-387*, sir. Can I forward it to you?"

Jaruzelska nodded. Seconds later, the message popped into her neuronics, its old-fashioned format and extreme brevity marking it out as a pinchcomms message.

As she read it through, Jaruzelska had to restrain herself forcibly from leaping to her feet. At last, she thought, at long last. *387* had found the crew and passengers of the *Mumtaz*. Now her staff could fine-tune the operations plan for Corona and begin the final simulation exercises before the battle group deployed.

Comming her chief of staff to come to her office as soon as he arrived, she turned her attention back to her cup of tea. Finally, she thought exultantly, finally, things were coming together.

Wednesday, November 11, 2398, UD
Hut 2, Eternity Base Camp

Kerri Helfort awoke with a jerk. A scream was building behind her breather mask as a black-gloved hand kept her head down on the pillow until the quietly spoken message, the FedWorlds accent unmistakable, penetrated her sleep-soaked mind.

"Commodore Helfort, sir! Wake up! And for Christ's sake do it quietly. Commodore Helfort, sir. Wake up!"

Kerri did, and in a hurry. Signaling the black shape, which was almost invisible in the faint night-lights that lit the long hut and its rows of silent sleeping forms, to let go, she turned slowly onto her side, struggling to get her breath back.

"Who the hell are you?" she whispered, her voice shaking with the suddenness of it all.

"Corporal Gupta, sir, 1/24th FedWorld Marines, and we are here to get you out, but not yet. We need to do some work to get ready. You are the senior service officer here, so we thought we'd start with you."

Kerri could only gape into the matte-black faceplate of the marine crouched on the floor beside her bed as the fear and tension of the last weeks welled up inside her, the tears streaming down her face past her breather mask to drop onto the tattered black T-shirt she wore in bed. She couldn't speak, only stare, as hope burst into flame inside her, her mind racing with insane joy. She wanted to leap to her feet and tell those Hammer fuckers that their days were numbered, but years of service discipline kept her under control.

Kerri took a deep slow breath. "What do we need to do, Corporal?"

"For the moment, do nothing but think about what it's going to take to get every one of your people out of here safely when the time comes. We'll meet you 400 meters northeast of the camp tomorrow night at midnight. Make your way across the creek and wait there. We'll find you, but you must come alone. Any problems with that?"

"No. There's nowhere to run to. This is the only place dirt-side to get oxygen and food, so the Hammers don't care about perimeter security. That's why there're no fences. Well, except around their compound, and that's only to make sure we don't strangle them in their beds. Lots of people like to get away from the camp for an evening, so there's nothing unusual about that. No, it'll be fine. Midnight, 400 meters northeast, wait just across the creek."

"That's good, sir. But tell nobody just yet. Let's work out the details first. Are there people you trust? Absolutely trust?"

Kerri nodded. "Sure are. We have a committee. We talk about escape, but not with much enthusiasm of late, I have to admit."

"Good. Bring their names and the names of any others who can be trusted. We'll need at least one group leader for every twenty of you when the time comes. Say fifty people and grade them one to three, with one the most reliable. Okay?"

"Fifty names, graded one to three. I'll have it for you when we rendezvous."

"Good. And I want a second list. Let's call it the red list. Anyone you can't trust, anyone who might betray the escape."

Kerri's face twisted. Sad to say, there were more than enough of them. Cowardly, treacherous bastards. "Will be done. Anything else?"

"Yes. We've broken into the Hammer's comms net, and we see that they've reenabled neuronics. It made it much easier to find you."

"Thank God, yes."

"Fine. Are they monitoring the neuronics datastreams, do you know? We couldn't find evidence, but we didn't probe too deep—mission security is top priority."

"We don't know for sure. The network architecture and software shouldn't allow it, but they've got some smart software people, they control all the network hardware, and they've had both time and incentive, so they might be. We've assumed that they wouldn't have enabled it unless they thought they could break in. So we don't use it for anything, uh, serious."

"Okay. Good. Let's keep it that way. When the time comes, we can use it to coordinate things, but until then we'll need to depend on your core cadre of fifty. Commodore, that's it. Moonrise is in less than an hour, and we have to go."

"Where are you holed up?"

"Sorry, Commodore, you don't need to know."

"Oh! Yes. Sorry. Stupid of me. How do I contact you if I need to?"

"Tomorrow night we'll put a patch into your neuronics software to set up a secure network operating in parallel. It'll talk to us through a small short-range infrared transceiver we'll pin to your breather assembly. You'll codephrase switch between networks. Until we get some infrared rebroadcast units in, you'll need to stand outside the camp to talk to us. But we'll explain all that to you tomorrow. We must go. Midnight tomorrow. Don't be late."

"I won't. Oh, wait. Sorry. One more thing. Maria LaSalle, the one responsible for a lander accident. She's gone walkabout, and we're concerned about her."

Gupta grimaced. "Supplies?"

"Enough for a week, we think. She was last seen late Monday."

"Okay. Leave it to us. We'll go through the holovid records and see if we can work out when she left and where she went—when the time's right. Now I must go, Commodore. See you tomorrow night."

And with that the shapeless phantomlike form of Corporal Gupta was gone as though it had never existed. Twisting in her bed, Kerri thought she saw a flicker of movement across the ground outside the open-sided hut, but that, too, was gone in seconds.

Saturday, November 14, 2398, UD
Eternity Camp

As the sun set, the western sky turned a riotous blaze of scarlet and gold struck through with purple-green fingers of methane smog.

As the deepening blue-black of night began to overwhelm the last remnants of the day, small oases of light started to appear around the camp as *Mumtaz*ers sought privacy away from the pressures of daily life in Eternity Camp. Digby had promised that work would start on building a small township on the slopes of Mount Kaspari to the north, but it would be months before people would be able to move out of the cramped sleeping huts whose open sides and lack of internal partitions provided an absolute guarantee of no privacy.

In the meantime, *Mumtaz*ers who wanted to be alone had no choice but to take a coldlamp and head out into the darkness. Each night many did, and this night was no exception.

As Kerri waited for the last members of the escape committee to straggle into the circle of light thrown by the small lamp set on a rock 200 meters downstream from the camp, she was struck by how quickly a new etiquette had grown up, in this case a strict rule that nobody should approach a coldlamp any closer than 100 meters unless previously invited. Not for the first time as she watched the lamps wandering out of the camp, she wondered at the incredible adaptability of human beings.

Because she couldn't tell them why, it had taken considerable cajoling on Kerri's part to get the escape committee together. The very idea of escaping had become more ludicrous as each day passed, as the vision of a green and fertile Eternity took root in the minds of more of the *Mumtaz*-ers, as lives past were written off and consigned to the rubbish bins of history, as the sheer impossibility of escape had finally sunk in.

But she had persisted quietly but emphatically until, with great reluctance, the escape committee had agreed to meet.

As usual, they had been waiting for Colin Mendes, former FedPol chief inspector on Anjaxx and a man so incapable of being on time for anything that Kerri often wondered how he had survived in the police service. But he'd finally turned up with his usual mumbled apology before taking his place in the circle around the coldlamp. While the group settled, Kerri reached into her coverall and pulled out a small gray box, placing it on the rock next to the lamp and pressing a small switch.

It took only a moment for the implications of that simple and outwardly unremarkable action to start to sink in. Everyone present knew an electronic shroud when he or she saw one. More to the point, they knew that Kerri hadn't had one before. In an instant there was pandemonium as the sharper members of the group worked it out, and it took a while before Kerri, a broad grin splitting her face under her breather mask, was able to quiet the group. But finally she had the undivided attention of the escape committee.

"Well, everybody, I still have trouble believing it, but it's true. All being well, we'll be going home and . . ." Kerri couldn't continue as emotion overwhelmed her and every other member of the group. All were of an age at which they had too much invested in the past to contemplate a new life, at which it was too late to start again, and the thought that all that was precious and dear to them might be restored was almost too much to take.

But finally, the group settled down and Kerri was able to start again. She was pleased this time to see emotion slowly replaced by a steely determination to do whatever it would take to make their escape from Eternity happen.

"Okay. Here's what we have to do, and we don't have a lot of time to do it in, so pay attention. First up, meet a friend of mine."

The shock was total as the leading edges of two small mounds of rock just outside the pool of light lifted to reveal the smiling faces of two marines. The mouths of the escape committee members were hanging as far open as breather masks would allow, and the silence was total.

Major Anschar Shao, Federated Worlds Marines (retired), was the first to recover.

"Christ," she said, "chromaflage certainly has come a long way since my day. But it's good to see you, by God. I can't tell you how good."

"Likewise, Major," replied the first marine, "Lance Corporal Jensch and Marine Maziz at your service, sir. Now, please, our time is limited because we need to be safely tucked up by moonrise. Two things. We need to get all of your neuronics modified so you can talk securely among yourselves and to us. When that's done, we've got some holocams we'd like placed and some whisker laser rebroadcast units to cover some blank spots in our neuronics network, and when that's finished, we'll hand over to Commodore Helfort. That gives us less than three hours, so if I could have you, Major, and you, Captain Zuma. Just sit down with your backs to us and leave the rest to us."

Monday, November 16, 2398, UD
Task Force 683, Revelation System, Hell Outerspace

One after the other in quick succession, the four deepspace heavy patrol ships of Task Force 683 dropped into normal-space over 30 million kilometers out from Hell, their arrival announced only by the briefest flashes of ultraviolet.

The *Atsumi*'s combat data center was quiet as Commodore Kawaguchi and her staff watched the ship's three consorts—*Almohades*, *Ashanti*, and *Akkad*—take loose station 2,000 kilometers apart, the ships invisible on the holovids against the brilliant tapestry of stars that curtained the skies. Within one minute of dropping, BattleNet was up and *Atsumi,* using the 6,000-kilometer baseline provided by the four ships' sensors, started the slow and painful process of scanning the huge volume of space ahead of them before slowly rotating the line to cover the space to port and starboard of the original line.

This was a very unpopular maneuver, with captains understandably concerned about exposing their ships' poorly armored sides to any loose rock or debris in their path as the ships coasted in-system at 150,000 kph. But it had to be done.

Slowly the ships' sensors sucked data from every part of the electromagnetic spectrum and from every direction. The massive sensor AIs crunched terabytes of data a second as the threat plot located and displayed every ship, every satellite, and every fixed installation in the Hell system, all prioritized by proximity and threat.

Kawaguchi could see it all, feeling godlike as she looked down on the Hammers going about their business, unaware that they were being watched.

Even from more than 30 million kilometers away, she could see the characteristic signature of a Hammer mership. Judging by her vector as it boosted out-system en route, it was bound for the planet Faith in the Retribution Star system 3.75 light-years away. Farther out, a Hammer warship boosted out-system. It was an old Constancy class light escort judging by its electromagnetic profile and was identified by Mother as the *Conciliator.* Not a problem.

The long drawn-out process went on, the sensors gradually sorting the electronic chaos into an orderly picture of Hammer activity across trillions of cubic kilometers of space. Most important, Kawaguchi was relieved to see the threat plot turn and stay a uniform orange. Her orders were very specific. She was to jump back into pinchspace immediately irrespective of vector the instant the threat level escalated to red.

"Command, command AI."

"Go ahead."

"Threat plot is orange. Mission prime directive met. Ready to commence deployment."

"Command, roger. Deploy."

For five minutes, the local plot showed nothing more than the four warships, now back in a loose line abreast, coasting in-system. And then, from each ship there began to emerge a growing line of little dots, each dot representing a single Sandfly deepspace starship simulator, all shepherded clear by unseen EVA teams.

With a flattened, stealth-coated ovoid cross section broadening sharply out into a blunt bow making it look like a hammerhead shark, the Sandfly was the Federated Worlds' latest and most sophisticated deepspace ship simulator. It was able to replicate any ship, from the most dilapidated tramp mership running the trade routes to the Far Planets up to and including the Feds' latest, the Seagirt class deepspace heavy cruiser.

The Sandfly came complete with a boost engine aft, double redundant microfusion plants amidships, and banks of transmitters forward capable of simulating almost any active emitter ever built, from the 10-meter VHF radio band through all the radar and satcomm bands, military and civilian, up to 400-nanometer ultraviolet comms lasers. Together with Krachov microshrouds, active jammers, radar echo enhancers, AI-controlled voice spoofers, pinchspace drop simulators, and all the other tricks of the electronic countermeasures world, the Sandfly was an impressive piece of equipment.

Today, Task Force 683's job was to send 120 of them straight down the throat of an unsuspecting Hammer.

Not that the starship simulators would look like FedWorld warships when the time came. No, that would be too obvious. When they went active, they would look like no warships the Hammer had ever seen, and then, when their job of thoroughly confusing matters was done, they would explode into dust. Probably the most expensive dust ever, Kawaguchi thought cynically.

Three hours later and the deployment was complete. The

starship simulators were arrayed in a rectangle 8,000 kilometers across and 2,000 high, the classic heavy battle fleet formation for a direct attack on a heavily defended planetary system.

As the starship simulators took up station, they were followed by a cluster of pinchcomsat killers, each one a small football-sized black sphere mounted on top of a small boost engine and carrying a fuel cell, a close-range attack laser, an integrated star/inertial navigation system, and a tiny low-power optical targeting system.

"Command, command AI. Ready to launch."

"Command, roger. Launch."

And with that, 136 stars flared into existence as booster rockets smashed the starship simulators and pinchcomsat killers on their way toward their targets and then, just as quickly, winked out, their job done.

"That was pretty," Kawaguchi murmured.

Five minutes later, Kawaguchi and her ships jumped into pinchspace.

Thursday, November 19, 2398, UD
Eternity Nearspace

The usual gut-wrenching jump delivered the seven ships of Rear Admiral Kzela's Task Force 681 safely into Eternity nearspace 525,000 kilometers out. That was far enough for the low-grade sensors on the only Hammer military warship in orbit to have no chance of detecting their arrival.

Kzela sat in the flag combat data center deep inside his flagship, the deepspace heavy cruiser *Seagirt*. With its sister ship *Searchlight*, *Seagirt* was one of the Fleet's newest heavy cruisers, both ships having been accepted into Space Fleet service from the massive orbital starship yards of Suleiman's World only months earlier. It was so new in fact that Kzela would have sworn that he could smell the fresh paint. He had little to do but watch as, without any fuss, the task force quickly and efficiently came online and within seconds had rebuilt the threat and tactical plots.

"Good," Kzela grunted, pleased that the threat plot confirmed that everything was as it should be, that nothing had changed.

Kzela zoomed the *Seagirt*'s massive holocam array in on the only Hammer threat, the *Myosan*. For all the world so close that Kzela could reach out and touch it, the Hammer ship hung in low orbit around Eternity like a brilliant silver and gold pebble. Its highly polished hull, its gold trim, and the massive gold Kraa sunburst on the upper side of the bow vouched for its membership in the chief councillor's personal flotilla. The only signs that the ship was alive were the brilliant orange anticollision lights that flashed from every side and the occasional flicker-flash as *Myosan*'s Ka-band radar-controlled short-range lasers vaporized another small piece of space debris in its course.

Stupid bastards, Kzela thought. *Myosan* wasn't even bothering to radiate its long-range search radar. Well, they'd find that was a mistake before very much longer. Its India band search radar would have no chance of picking up the ships of the task force so far out, but Kzela couldn't begin to imagine not at least trying. Too damn confident, that was what they were. Either that or they didn't care.

"Sloppy," said Kzela's chief of staff from the seat alongside, as if reading his mind, "though I'm happy to have it so. He won't see either of us until it's much too late for him to do anything about it."

Kzela nodded. "No, he won't."

A small tremor in the holovid as the flag AI switched holocam arrays was the only indication that *Seagirt,* the best military warship technology in humanspace, was rolling ship in preparation for its scheduled deceleration burn. As the *Myosan* slipped out of sight behind Eternity, the faintest of tremors marked the firing of *Seagirt*'s main engines, the maneuver intended to put the heavy cruiser in a position to bring its main rail-gun and missile batteries to cover the heavy scout *Groombridge* as it ran in on *Myosan*. After a quick check with the flag AI had satisfied Kzela that all was going according to plan, he switched the holocams in quick succession to the rest of the task force, which was pulling slowly ahead of *Seagirt* as she began to decelerate.

There was little for him to do now but watch as the heavy cruiser *Firnas* headed into low orbit carrying the main ground assault force, the 2nd and 3rd Battalions of the 78th (President's Own) Regiment of Marines. Farther back, the heavy scouts *Draconis* and *Aquila* ran in to intercept *Mumtaz* while the three remaining heavy cruisers, *Regulus, Ishaq,* and *Recapture*, adjusted vectors to put themselves into high orbit, the first line of defense if Eternity turned out to be the trap many still feared it might be.

Kzela felt like a spectator as he watched the elaborately choreographed movements of his ships.

He sighed as he reminded himself that if he had done his job right, he should feel just like a spectator. Contrary to popular belief, an admiral's role was mostly before the event and not during it. His job was to make sure that the operational planning was sound, the sims were realistic and relevant, all possible scenarios had been assessed, and his subordinate commanders were both able and willing to discharge the responsibilities they had been delegated. The idea that modern space warfare with all its speed and three-dimensional complexities might allow him to pace some metaphorical quarterdeck while directing the activities of the thousands of men and women under his command in real time was utterly ludicrous.

More to the point, Space Fleet spent a great deal of time and effort ensuring that its senior commanders were able, as one of Kzela's peers had memorably put it after a particularly harrowing command sim, to watch as everything went to shit and then, against all instinct and intellect, do nothing about it because there was nothing they could have or should have done.

That was not to say that admirals and their staffs didn't have to step in now and again; they did. It just didn't happen quite as often as the action-adventure holovids would have you believe.

So Kzela did his job, switching endlessly between the flag AI and the subordinate AIs controlling each of his ships with one eye watching the command, local, and threat plots like a hawk. But that was all he and his flag staff did. His captains knew what they had to do and needed no nagging from him to do it and do it well.

But nobody had ever said it was easy just sitting there.

Thursday, November 19, 2398, UD
Hell-14

As the final ops conference broke up into the usual noisy disarray, Michael waved Gerri Mangeshkar, his opposite number from *166,* clear of the throng.

"Hey, Gerri. One for the road?"

"Damn straight, Michael! I feel like I've done nothing else but work since God knows when, so that's just what I need right now."

Michael followed Mangeshkar as she turned right out of *166*'s combat information center and down the narrow passageway to the wardroom. She waved him into a violently patterned armchair that had pride of place in the cramped compartment.

"This is, without doubt, the ugliest fucking chair in all of humanspace, Gerri," Michael said as he stretched out a grateful hand to take a small glass of Gabrielli single-malt cut with a dash of Jascarian spring water. It was pure mother's milk, and Michael treasured every precious drop as it slipped down a throat dry and scratchy from a diet of too much recycled air.

"So you say, Michael. But I'll have you know it's a treasured family heirloom belonging to our esteemed navigator."

"Balls, Gerri! Your previous skipper left it behind. I know. I checked."

"Bastard" was all Mangeshkar said as the two settled into

a companionable silence. Michael and Mangeshkar were happy for the moment to do little more than stare into the depths of their drinks and let the seconds tick by unwatched.

Michael finally broke the silence. "Four hours till the kick off, Gerri. How do you think it'll go?"

"Well, like you, I've been through the sims God knows how many times, and any way I look at it, I think Battle Group Delta is going to kick the Hammer back to join that damned Kraa of theirs." Mangeshkar paused to take a long drink from her glass. "No, all in all I think that side of it's fine. Jaruzelska should pulverize them, no problem. It's us I worry about."

Michael nodded. "Funny you say that. The skipper was just saying how heavily we've drawn on our luck. Christ, I just hope it holds up another—what?—six hours. That's not too much to ask, surely to God."

"I feel the same way, Michael. It's almost like we've been tempting fate being here. Who would have thought it two months ago? Two light scouts spending nearly five weeks sitting on a piece of Hammer real estate only a couple of hundred thousand kilometers away from an entire Hammer flotilla. Shit, we've done exactly that, and it's still hard to believe!"

"It is. Still, we live in hope. Anyway, Gerri, much as I love you—and I do—we've got work to do, so I'll say thank you." Michael climbed out of the armchair, finishing his drink as he went. He took Mangeshkar's outstretched hand. "It's been an honor, Gerri. Truly it has, so let's get through this, and hopefully I'll see you on the other side."

"Take care, Michael. Let's hope that the bastards are so busy fending off Jaruzelska and her overpaid staff that we can slip away without being seen."

"Let's hope so. See you." With that, Michael was gone.

Mangeshkar poured herself another small drink and sat back down. Her department was well and truly under control, and if *166* wasn't ready to lift off on schedule at 04:15, nobody would be pointing a finger at her. But the strain was killing her. She could see it in Michael, too. They'd both lost a good five kilos since Corona had started, and their faces sported the same dark black smudges under both eyes and the same tense, stretched look. The rest of *387*'s officers didn't look much better. Michael's skipper in particular looked like a man about to be hanged, his face a drawn gray-tinged caricature. God only knew how he was coping. The final approach to Hell-14 must have been a killer.

Mangeshkar gave herself a metaphorical shake. Fuck this, Mangeshkar, she chided herself. You're getting far too maudlin. A final check of her department, a couple of hours of sleep, and then up to be ready for liftoff. Decision made, she downed her drink, slapped on an alc-suppressor patch to neutralize the two drinks she'd just enjoyed so much, and was on her feet, heading for the surveillance drone hangar.

Thursday, November 19, 2398, UD
Flag Combat Data Center, Onboard FWWS Al-Jahiz,
Revelation System Farspace

As Vice Admiral Jaruzelska settled into her seat to wait out the minutes until the final pinchspace microjump into Hammer nearspace, the flag combat data center was hushed. The only sounds were half-whispered conversations and the ever-present murmur of the air-conditioning.

All around them, hunched over holovid screens and watched over by her chief of staff, the relentless Commodore Martin Li, a man she was convinced slept less than one hour a night, Jaruzelska's flag staff checked and rechecked the final details of the attack.

Not that there was anything that she or her staff could profitably do now, she reminded herself.

Her job was the operations plan, and that had long been completed, worked and reworked, until every possible risk had been identified—eliminated if possible and managed if not. Now it was up to her captains, their ships, and the thousands of spacers under their command. If they got it right, she would be the hero of the hour. If they didn't, her fall from grace would be savagely quick. Deservedly so, she thought. Everything she had asked for, she had been given. In return she had given her assurance that the mission would succeed, and she knew full well it was a bargain she would be held to.

All of which was well and good, but it did nothing to suppress the nervous churning that was beginning to make its presence felt in a stomach she had been too busy to fill as often as she should have. She commed the galley for one last cup of coffee.

The huge holovid screen that dominated the entire flag combat data center told the story.

In loose formation around her were the seven heavy cruisers—*Sina, Revenge, Damishqui, Zuhr, Arcturus, Searchlight,* and *Orion*—which, together with the *Al-Jahiz* and eight light cruisers whose main responsibility was missile defense, made up Task Group 256.1, the primary assault force for the attack on the Hell system's flotilla base, home to one Rear Admiral David Pritchard and the twenty warships of his Hell flotilla. To starboard and astern were the two light escorts attached to the *Al-Jahiz* task group, *Crossbow* and *Bombard,* providing casualty recovery and there to pick up the pieces if the cruisers made a mess of things.

Ranged across hundreds of kilometers of space were the rest of her ships.

The Hell Central attack force consisted of the four heavy cruisers *Rabban, Al-Battani, Resilient,* and *Retaliate,* together with two missile defense light cruisers and their casualty recovery ships, the light escorts *Carbine* and *Arrow.*

The Hell-5 hostage recovery force was led by the heavy cruiser *Repudiate* and the heavy patrol ships *Deflector, Democracy, Hatshepsut,* and *Fu Xi,* followed up by *Arbalest* for casualty recovery, a ship so new that she had completed fleet acceptance in June and the fleet workup and operational readiness inspection in early October.

There also were the ships tasked with recovering the *Mumtaz*ers from the outer mines together with the hijackers responsible for their capture: three heavy cruisers—*Ulugh*

Beg, Resolve, and *Khaldun*—twelve heavy patrol ships—
*Ban Chiang, Akrotiri, Anjar, Eidetic, Denouement, Ecesis,
Elegant, Hiradokoro, Djagaral, Dong Yi, Bampur*, and *Beau-
maris*—and the three light escorts for casualty recovery—
Rifle, Destrier, and *Mangonel*.

It was one hell of an outfit, Jaruzelska thought with considerable pride.

Together with the two light scouts *387* and *166*, she would
command fifty-two ships for the attack on the Hell system,
the best warships, combat systems, and spacers the Federated Worlds could assemble.

And that wasn't all of Operation Corona.

Add in the heavy scouts tasked with dropping surveillance
satellite killers and pinchspace drop decoys, the ships of
Corinne Kawaguchi's Task Group 683, whose swarm of
pinchcomsat killers and ship simulators even now were driving their way into Hell nearspace, and the ships of Admiral
Kzela's Task Force 681, tasked with recovering the passengers and crew of the *Mumtaz* from Eternity, and Battle
Group Delta was a hugely impressive force.

All of which was well and good, but numbers never had
been enough to ensure success. She hoped that the Hammer was impressed enough to get out and stay out of her
way.

Thursday, November 19, 2398, UD
Ministry of Interstellar Relations, Foundation City,
Terranova Planet

Giovanni Pecora stood up as the perennially sour-faced
Hammer ambassador was shown into the small meeting
room that adjoined his office.

Ambassador Yoon was well-known for his view that the
Federated Worlds were nothing more than a filthy degenerate
cesspit of heretics. From the day he had stepped unwillingly

onto Fed soil, he had made little attempt to conceal that opinion from his unwilling hosts, an attitude that accounted for the open contempt in which he was held.

"Sit down, Ambassador." Pecora kept his voice as courteous as he could, even though in all his years of public service he had yet to deal with anyone as unappealing as the squat gray-haired man sitting in front of him. The only reward for his courtesy was a grunt as Yoon planted himself in the armchair on the other side of the small coffee table, with the registered observer seating herself unobtrusively to one side. Fuck you, then, Ambassador, Pecora thought, canceling his commed order for coffee.

There was a moment's silence. Pecora had seen more than enough of Yoon during the *Delphic* affair, though he had enjoyed Yoon's obvious befuddlement over the ruse. Yoon sat in silence, obviously wondering what the Fed heretics were up to now.

Pecora had no intention of keeping him waiting. "Thank you for coming, Ambassador."

Yoon's face actually managed to turn even more sour.

"The matter we wish to discuss is very serious, so perhaps the best thing I can do is to hand you"—Pecora paused to pick up a heavy bound document from the small table beside his chair—"this document. I think it will tell you everything you need to know. It makes our position quite clear." Even to ill-mannered, superstitious primitives like you, Pecora thought as he settled back.

Yoon half grabbed the document from Pecora's outstretched hand. He rolled his eyes at the heft of the bundle. It was much too thick to be the usual complaint about some Fed commercial spacer being handled roughly by DocSec. Yoon sat back in his chair and started to read.

From under hooded eyes, Pecora greatly enjoyed watching the blood drain from Yoon's face as the implications of the diplomatic note and its declaration of limited military action sank into his shocked and disbelieving mind.

At last, Yoon finished reading. He looked up, mouth working but unable to get the words out. Pecora just sat and watched, his eyes pitiless, his stare unwavering, as he saw

Yoon struggling to come to grips with the enormity of what he had been given.

Finally, Yoon managed to collect himself, clearly unable to believe what he had just read.

"This cannot be true!" he blurted out. "You cannot be serious. Attacks on two Hammer systems! For an alleged hijacking? This is just lies. Unprovoked aggression. I don't think you—"

Pecora cut him off, rising to his feet, his voice brutal with barely controlled anger.

"Frankly, Ambassador Yoon, neither I nor my government cares what you think. It's all there in the statement of facts, chapter and verse, as required by the New Washington Convention. So unless you have any questions that the note does not answer, I suggest you leave now. I am sure your government would like to know of our declaration sooner rather than later. My staff will show you out. Goodbye."

With that, Pecora was out of his chair and gone. Yoon just sat, shocked into paralyzed immobility, the cheerful floral pattern of the armchair hugely at odds with the high drama of the moment.

Thursday, November 19, 2398, UD
The Palisades, Ashakiran Planet

High in the mountains above the upper Clearwater Valley, the old man sat staring into the distance, the stress showing in stark lines cut across a face that had aged a decade in only weeks.

The midday sun beat down relentlessly, bleaching the color out of the timber deck that looked toward the distant Karolev Ranges. The trees and mountains that framed the house were shimmering visibly as the heat of the day began to build up, the air trembling as it started its long climb thousands of meters into the sky. Behind the house, clouds already were building up as humid air started to fight its way across the Tien Shan Mountains.

Andrew Helfort knew there might be a serious storm later in the day. The air was thick and heavy with the promise of it, but he did not care.

Many minutes passed before he turned back to the young man sitting patiently beside him at the well-used table that had pride of place on the deck. The deeply varnished surface was immaculate, the deck around it pristine, kept that way by the habits of a lifetime of Space Fleet service. In the end, it had been all that had held the tortured mind, body, and soul of Andrew Helfort together.

Andrew Helfort could barely speak, his voice coming out as a half-strangled croak. "You couldn't be wrong about this, could you?" His voice cracked with doubt. The terrible, aching fear that the news of Kerri's and Sam's survival might not be true wracked his body.

The immaculate young officer, his formal dress blacks at odds with the rough informality of the setting, shook his head emphatically. "Not a chance, sir, I can assure you. Federated Worlds forces are right now moving to recover your family and the rest of the passengers and crew from Eternity. Everything we know is available through the Corona persona. You have priority access, so please, see for yourself. Take all the time you need."

Andrew Helfort finally allowed himself to believe.

The nightmare that had started that awful day when a police flier had arrived unannounced finally started to clear. The process was as slow and uncertain as the morning mist burning off the hills that surrounded the Palisades, tendrils of fear and doubt and grief coming back to wrap themselves around his mind, blotting out any newfound hope before disappearing as hope reasserted itself.

He nodded.

Reluctantly he commed the Corona persona. He half smiled as its avatar appeared. This one was a middle-aged woman clearly designed to radiate both sympathy and confidence in equal measure. He didn't stay talking long. The holovids of *Mumtaz* in orbit around Eternity and the list of passengers and crew transferred dirtside, the names of Kerri and Sam there with all the rest, were all he needed. He broke the comm.

"No," he said. "There really doesn't seem to be any doubt." He took a deep breath to steady himself. "When do they come home?"

"The operation to recover them is under way now, and allowing for debriefing, they should be home in a bit over a week. But we'll let you know an exact time as soon as we have one. But there'll be no delays. We'll be as quick as we can."

"Thank you, Lieutenant, thank you. With all my heart, thank you."

"My pleasure, sir. Believe me."

But then Andrew Helfort's growing happiness collapsed as he suddenly realized that the Federated Worlds were in the middle of the biggest military action against the Hammer in almost twenty years and he had no idea where Michael was. His last message had been just before *387* had left for the Kashliki Cluster, and that had been weeks earlier.

His mouth was suddenly dry, his heart thudding. "My son. What of him? Is *DLS-387* involved? Tell me."

The young officer's eyes skidded off Andrew Helfort's face to look into the far distance. He couldn't help it as he was asked the one question he dreaded. "Well, sir, as you know, operational security means I cannot say . . ."

The young lieutenant's voice trailed off under the full force of Andrew Helfort's best "I'm a Fleet captain and you're not, so don't fuck with me" look.

"Er, yes, sir," he stammered unhappily. "Well, as I was saying . . ."

Andrew Helfort threw his hands in the air. "Young man, for God's sake, get to the point. Is *DLS-387* directly involved in Corona. Yes or no?"

"Yes, sir," the man said reluctantly.

"Right. Are you allowed to tell me in what role?"

"No, sir."

"Fine. I don't like it, but I do understand. When can I expect confirmation that *DLS-387* is all right and on her way home?"

"The operation is scheduled to complete no later than 09:00 UT. I can tell you that Fleet will be in touch with you as soon as they have received *387*'s jump report."

Andrew Helfort nodded. He knew that was the best he could expect. "Thank you, Lieutenant. Now that the business is over, can I persuade you to stay and have some lunch?"

"No, thanks, sir. Another time maybe. This is a great place you've got here."

"It might be, Lieutenant, it might be again one day," Andrew Helfort said softly. But not until the whole family was back sitting alongside him. Which, God willing, they would be soon.

Thursday, November 19, 2398, UD
Eternity Base

Digby settled down in the thinly padded seat of the big half-track as it swung out of the security compound and made its way down the road toward Eternity Base.

The half-track splashed through the puddles of water left over from the day's torrential downpour. What little twilight there was was fading fast, the setting sun obscured by thick gray-black clouds scudding across the sky, driven by a blustery swirling easterly wind; the humidity was about as bad as it ever got. Digby didn't much care. Bad weather or not, it was now part of his routine to drive around the base, making sure that all was as it should be before climbing Humpback Hill to think about the day that just past and what the next day might bring.

Therein lay the problem that was taxing him. He could not understand why the Feds had done nothing. It had been weeks now, and the Feds had to know that the only thing stopping them from walking in was the *Myosan,* and that was not much of a threat. Anyway, there was nothing more he could do except sit and wait and hope that Merrick didn't decide he was past his use-by date and call him back.

Fifteen minutes later and with the routine slow drive-by of the base finished, Digby's driver stopped the half-track at the foot of Humpback Hill.

"Back in thirty, Corporal."

"Sir," said Erdem as he and his partner, Lance Corporal Korda, settled down to wait for Digby's return.

Digby made short work of the shallow slope of Humpback Hill, settling himself down on his favorite rock, looking across the western end of the lander runway; the rock's wind-sculpted surface provided a perfect support for his back. For once his mind was not on work but on Jana, unimaginably far away and gone now for almost three months. Well, at least she'd seemed happy in her last vidmail. Thankfully, he had three months before she would even think of coming back, so all being well, that would give him enough time to secure his own position and work out how he was going to get out of the mess he was in.

His breather squeaked in protest as Digby sighed deeply in frustration.

The comm jolted Kerri upright in her chair, her heart beginning to pound as adrenaline flooded her system.

"Commodore Helfort, Lieutenant Kerouac."

Oh, thank God, Kerri Helfort said to herself. It's time. The awful dragging wait was almost over.

"Yes, Lieutenant?"

Kerri's voice gave no hint of the terrible churning in her stomach as every fiber of her body cried out for this to be over and for her to be at home with Andrew. Her fingers were tightly interwoven with Sam's as they sat waiting in Hut 1 for the word to move.

"Everything is in position, sir. The landers are on their way in and will be here on schedule. So start moving people out now. What about the red list?"

"We have the red list nominees under control."

"Roger that. Start autojecting them now. Good luck." With that, Kerouac was gone.

Kerri stood up, pulling Sam to her feet with her.

"Come on, Sam, let's go," she said, her attention focused on getting the guides moving and, most important, getting the red list nominees autojected so they could be herded out of the camp like the sheep they'd be until the binary mind-control drug wore off.

A quick check to confirm that the coldlamp groups were where they should be, blinding the holocams, and she was able to wave the first groups through, out from under the low eaves of the wall-less hut that had been home for so long and on into the darkness and the welcoming arms of the waiting marines.

Every so often, a group was diverted to the end of the hut and given a coldlamp to make things look normal, but soon the trickle of people became a flood to the point where Kerri and the guides had to hold them back physically, so strong had the urge to flee become.

Twenty minutes later, everyone except Kerri, Sam, and half of the escape committee had vanished into the night. For a moment, Kerri marveled at how easily and quickly almost a thousand people could disappear. Even the four occupants of the makeshift camp hospital had been extracted without incident, carefully maneuvered clear of the camp, out of sight of the Hammer's holocams.

"Okay, everybody. Our turn. Sam, grab a lamp. Let's go."

And so with no further fuss and no regrets, the last non-Hammer occupants of Eternity Camp moved into the night, the ground ahead speckled with pools of light cast by almost a hundred lamps scattered through the darkness. No more than 50 meters out, the chromaflaged shape of a marine reared up so suddenly that Sam and Kerri flinched in surprise.

It was the familiar face of Corporal Gupta, his face crinkled by a wide grin.

"Sorry about that, Commodore. Just to confirm, you are the last ones out, so keep going and please make sure that everyone stays put at the rendezvous point until we come to get them."

"Will do, Corporal, and thanks. I can't tell you how much this means."

"You don't have to, sir. I think we know."

Kerri nodded, and the pair hurried on. Once they were across the stream, which was a lot deeper than usual because of the rain earlier in the day but still fordable without too much difficulty, she picked a dark spot to put down the lamp. Then, their hands still tightly locked together, she walked with Sam up the banks of Base Creek as fast as a dangerous blend of gloom and broken ground would allow.

Seven hundred meters farther on they were at the rendezvous point, joining the huge throng of *Mumtaz*ers waiting nervously in the dark, the night air sibilant with half-whispered conversations.

Kerri hoped they wouldn't have to wait long.

High on Humpback Hill, Digby had stayed alone with his thoughts for much longer than usual. His driver would be wondering what in Kraa he'd been up to. Screw it, he thought, that's enough for tonight. As he levered himself up off his rock, his comms unit chirped, announcing a priority call. Odd, he thought. The camp was quiet, so why the priority call? Everything looked okay.

And then it hit him and hit him hard.

The Feds were coming, and they were coming now. Nobody needed to tell him. He just knew.

As he took the call, Digby turned and started to half walk, half run down the hill.

Even as the alarm came through on his earpiece, Corporal Erdem sat bolt upright in his seat, boredom gone and heart pounding as he brought the half-track's gyro-stabilized low-light holocam to bear.

It took seconds for him to identify the black shapes coming in from the west on final approach as military assault landers. They definitely weren't commercial. The holocam was zooming in to pick up every detail of the lead vehicle, its wings flexing alarmingly as it bounced and shook and drove its way down through the rough air rolling off the hills. They'd been caught, he thought as he locked the holocam to autotrack the incoming lander, and now there would be hell to pay.

Erdem didn't hesitate as years of military training kicked in. The only time to hit a lander was before it landed, and even if he had only a single 30-mm hypersonic light cannon, he was going to have a go. Shouting to Korda to get set up, he gunned the half-track sharply forward, swinging it south toward the runway to get clear of the long ridge that ran down from Humpback Hill.

As Erdem hammered the half-track down the slope toward the runway, Korda's microvid told him the system had a firing solution on the lead lander. It was closing rapidly, wheels coming down as it approached the threshold, nose pitching up as belly-mounted mass drivers fired to slow the massive ship for landing. Without waiting, Korda opened up, the laser-guided fire control system putting him precisely on target, the high-explosive cannon shells smashing into the lander's belly armor, splashes of red-gold stitching their way across the hull. For a moment, Korda would have sworn that the lander flinched before it settled again. Erdem actually cheered as Korda hammered away, the cannon shells spalling thin shards of ceramsteel armor off the lander, the pieces whipped away by the airflow howling turbulently past the lander's less-than-aerodynamic hull.

But Erdem and Korda had forgotten that landers were built to survive much worse than 30-mm cannon and not simply by absorbing whatever was thrown at them.

Within seconds, an escorting ground attack lander had tracked the shells back to their point of origin and had passed the data to its fire control system. Microseconds after that, it had a valid firing solution, and then, happy that there was no more pressing threat that needed looking after first, it directed the full fury of its forward laser batteries onto the hapless half-track and its crew, pausing only to switch targets to hack the last few shells out of the sky as they raced in toward the lander Korda was trying so hard to bring down.

Moments later, all that was left of the half-track was a charred wreck. Even the wreckage didn't last long as the half-track's microfusion bottle gave up the unequal struggle to hold on to plasma hotter than any sun before exploding in a shattering, searing blast that picked Digby up and threw him brutally onto his back as he ran in.

Seconds later the first lander thumped down on the runway. The liberation of Eternity Base and its unwilling guests was just a matter of time.

For more than an hour, almost a thousand *Mumtaz*ers had huddled miserable and afraid in the darkness of a damp Eternity night as all hell had broken loose to the east and south, the darkness lit by the flashes of grenade explosions and the ripping sound of small arms fire.

Kerri Helfort, with Sam never farther than a foot away the entire time, had walked through the group, settling people down, calming the nervous, reassuring everyone that all was under control even if the flow of information from the marines who'd slipped them out of the camp right under the noses of the Hammer had dried up completely.

To Kerri's relief, the wait finally came to an end.

A group of shifting, shapeless blurs emerged cautiously from the broken ground between her and the huge slab sides of the bioplant supplies and driver mass buildings. Close as they were, they were barely discernible even under the floodlights that swamped the base in orange light. It took them no time at all to get to her position, but as they got close enough for her to make them out, Kerri was pleased to see that just as they were quick, they were also watchful; their heads and carbines swung ceaselessly from side to side, and from time to time they turned to walk backward.

As the marines approached, Kerri rose slowly to her feet. She saw the marines spread out to take covering positions around the *Mumtaz*ers, chromaflage reducing them in seconds to just another part of the rock-strewn ground that surrounded Eternity Base. One of the leading marines, flipping his battle helmet's visor up to reveal a disarmingly young face, made his way over to where Kerri and Sam were standing.

"Commodore Helfort? I'm Major Krasov, sir. Colonel Musaghi's compliments. It's time to go home."

Kerri just nodded.

Holding Sam tightly by the hand, she waved the watching *Mumtaz*ers to their feet. "You heard the man. Let's get out of here!"

Without a look back, they set off down the long road home.

The last two FedWorld heavy assault landers sat patiently on the apron, anticollision lights on full power throwing splashes of orange light across the ground.

The air was thick with tension as Colonel Musaghi and his battalion staff watched the infuriatingly slow process of herding the last of the Hammers in sullen flexicuffed silence up the ramp of *Clarion Call,* a well-used assault lander with plenty of scars to show for it.

Musaghi snorted disapprovingly. Where did the Fleet get its lander names from? The second lander rejoiced in the sobriquet of *Nervous Nellie,* for Christ's sake. No such nonsense allowed in the marines, thank God.

"Not a happy bunch, Colonel." Musaghi's operations officer, a tall lanky Suleimani, waved a dismissive hand at the dejected line of men.

Musaghi nodded. He'd have much preferred to leave every single one of the Hammer scum dirtside, but orders were orders. "Not quite what the bastards expected, I'm sure. How many to go?"

"That's the lot, Colonel. Apart from the dead ones."

"I'm sure as hell not taking them," Musaghi said, lifting his breather mask for a second to spit on the ground for effect. "Sterilization teams?"

"On schedule, sir. All the major facilities have been seeded, and those teams are back; just the minor support systems to go and we're done."

Musaghi grunted.

Not for one second had he allowed himself to forget that they were deep inside Hammer space, and the minute they pinchjumped out-system wouldn't be soon enough. In the interests of completing the operation sooner rather than later, he had wanted simply to blow up the entire base, but he had been emphatically overruled. Some lunatic, probably some useless seat polisher in interstellar relations, clearly thought that Eternity Base would be reactivated some day, and to that end teams had fanned out to seed every system in the place with software that would turn millions of FedMarks worth of AIs into so much solid-state junk. Never in a thousand years would the Hammer be able to reactivate the enormously complex systems that could turn a dirtball of a world like Eternity into a place fit for humans in a matter of years.

Musaghi grunted again, this time much more emphatically. He didn't give a toss for Eternity, and it would be one hell of a long time before the Hammers would allow anyone back to pick up where Brigadier General Digby and his unholy crew of jailbirds had been forced to leave off. If ever.

A flurry of comms interrupted his thoughts. Eternity Base was now officially useless, and the last of the sterilization teams, job done, were pulling back, the protective wall of marines surrounding them following them into the landers.

As the last techs disappeared up the ramp of *Nervous Nellie,* Musaghi followed them into the cavernous hold. A final head count and they could go, their job done and done well.

The lander climbed out of Eternity Base at an impressively steep angle under full military power.

An impassive Digby sat unmoving, eyes fixed on the holovid, which was still locked on Eternity Base fast disappearing into the dark behind them. He'd been the last to board, kept on the lower deck well away from the rest of the Hammers, surrounded by an impressively large honor guard of marines. From the safety of Humpback Hill, he'd been watching the systematic takeover of everything he had built when a snatch team had emerged from the ground around him, carbines emphatically making the point that this was not the time for heroics. Slowly, reluctantly, Digby had raised his hands as, for the second time in his life, he had surrendered to the enemies of the Hammer of Kraa.

But this time, he had the blood of innocents on his hands, and the Feds knew it. For a moment his resolve had failed as he wondered whether he'd ever be allowed to walk free again.

As the lander thundered its way into orbit, Digby closed his eyes and put his head back, the helmet ring of the survival suit biting into his neck. He'd done what he could; he'd done his best. If that wasn't good enough, then so be it. All he wanted was to be able to hold Jana one last time, and then the Feds could do what they liked with him. As he drifted off to sleep, he knew somehow that even if the Feds chose to treat him like a common criminal and hang him from the nearest tree, he finally had laid the ghosts of his past to rest.

Thursday, November 19, 2398, UD
DLS-387, Hell-14

387's long wait for the start of Operation Corona came to a shattering and totally unexpected end.

"Command, this is Mother. I have a positive gravitronics intercept. Six vessels. Grav wave pattern indicates pinchspace transition imminent. Estimated drop bearing Red 30 Up 5. Initial drop vector suggests ships inbound for Hell Flotilla Base."

Ribot's heart turned in an instant to a block of ice. He struggled to breathe. Just as he had begun to hope that Mr. Murphy would not crash the party, the son of a bitch had arrived with a vengeance. He'd always known that it might come to this. Hell-14 was close to the primary approach axis for ships transiting from Commitment, and there had always been a chance that the two light scouts would have to do more than provide forward surveillance, precisely why they'd been on Hell-14 in the first place. But where the hell had six Hammer ships come from? Not from Commitment, that was for damn sure; otherwise he'd have been told, been given plenty of time to deploy his missiles to ambush the warships as they dropped and then get the hell out.

"Shit." Ribot paused to think for a second. "All hands to general quarters, Maria. And depressurize as well."

Hosani shot him a worried look as she commed the necessary orders through the ship.

Ribot commed Chen, whose anxious face gave him all the confirmation he needed.

"Bill, are you thinking what I'm thinking?"

"I suspect I am. We can't just sit here and let the Fleet Base attack group just drop into their laps."

"No, we can't. We've gone to general quarters, so let's get our heads together and see what we can do. We've got a little time before the bastards drop. Though I think it's going to be real simple. Throw ourselves at them and pray that they can't shoot straight."

"I'm rather afraid that's right. Wonder where they came from."

"God knows. The surveillance reports from Commitment nearspace showed no ships boosting out-system for Hell, and we've had no reports of military traffic inbound from any of the other planetary systems." Ribot sighed in frustration. "I suppose they've been in deepspace somewhere. God knows there's plenty of it, so I guess we can't blame fleet intelligence for not knowing. Reconvene in five. Ribot out."

"All stations, this is the captain. We've gone to general quarters early because we have Hammer ships dropping at Red 30, six of them, and from the quality of the grav array intercept, they look to be dropping very close. I'll be honest with you all. It's going to be rough, very rough. But God willing, we'll come through. That is all."

"All stations, command. Ship will depressurize in five, repeat, five minutes."

* * *

Michael and his surveillance drone team were struggling into their suits, chromaflage skins already darkening from their normal Day-Glo orange down to combat gray-black.

Michael felt like a marathon runner closing in on the finish line only to be told that he had to run another 40 kilometers. The whole business had gone on for so long that he could barely remember any life other than the waking nightmare he was in. If all had gone well—and Michael had spent hours obsessively going through the Corona time line to the point where he knew the plan down to the second—the marines would have Mom and Sam safe by now and soon Dad would know that. But just as he had begun to think about getting home, this had to happen. For the life of him he couldn't begin to imagine how two light scouts were going to be able to hold up six Hammer ships, and for an instant a terrible icy hand clamped itself around his heart at the thought that death for him and everyone else onboard *387* might be only minutes away.

Michael pushed the fear away with a conscious effort as he settled his helmet onto the neck ring, the seal locking with its usual quiet hiss. With a final quick look at the tense faces of his team, Strzlecki's deep brown stress-narrowed eyes staring deep into his, Michael smacked his visor down, commed the nitro-purge autoject, and started his suit checks. He consoled himself with the thought that even if they weren't going home, they might take some of the Hammers with them.

He quickly said a little prayer for Anna, who'd be dropping in-system in *Damishqui* in fifteen minutes or so, and then concentrated on the job at hand.

"Command, this is Mother. Sensors confirm pinchspace drop of hostiles at 68,500 kilometers Red 30 Up 5. Six ships: one Hammer City Class heavy cruiser provisionally identified as *New Dallas*, two Panther Class deepspace heavy escorts, *Cougar* and *Shark*, and three heavy patrols, *Gore*, *Arroyo*, and *MacFarlane*."

Anonymous behind the visor of her space suit and struggling to steady her ragged breathing, Hosani flicked Ribot a glance. Fear had soaked into every fiber of her being; her heart was pounding, and her breathing was shallow and ragged. Somehow, and she couldn't work out why or how, she knew this was it for her. She wouldn't be going home. She wondered how Ribot felt sending *387* and *166* and all onboard to an almost certain death, and she thanked God it was he and not she making the decisions. She wasn't sure she could have done what he was doing.

As the last suit check came in, she forcibly turned her mind to business.

"All stations, command. Depressurizing in one minute, repeat, one minute."

"Permission to step across, sir?" The unexpected voice of Warrant Officer Ng cut across Hosani's thoughts.

"Yes, of course, Warrant Officer Ng. What can we do for you?"

"Word with the captain, sir."

"Sure. Captain, sir? Warrant Officer Ng."

Ribot nodded. Hosani was happy to have her captain doing something better than worry about the less than encouraging results of Mother's latest quick and dirty sim. The prohibition on nukes set by Corona's rules of engagement were reducing to zero what little chance the two light scouts had of causing the Hammers some grief.

Ribot waved Ng across the thick yellow and black goofers line.

"Warrant Officer Ng. Desperate business," Ribot said flatly.

Ng nodded her agreement. "It is, sir. I realize my team are just supernumeraries now, but from what I can see, you're going to need all the help you can get. So I'd like to spread them around. With the damage control parties would probably be the best."

"Good idea, Doc. Should have thought of it first," Ribot said apologetically. "Talk to the XO and tell her it's fine by me so far as your team is concerned. But I want you to walk the ship for me. You know, steady people down, that sort of thing. They're very young, most of them, and I don't think any of them ever thought this would be happening to them."

"No problem, sir. I'll do that."

* * *

387 and *166* had not wasted the precious few minutes that had been given them.

Ribot had slowly pulled the ships back away from Hell-14. With a bit of luck, he hoped to be able to convince the Hammer after-action analysis teams that the two light scouts had been drifting slowly in-system rather than sitting dirtside right under the Hammers' noses the whole time.

And then a lot happened in a very short time.

First, the Hammer sensors were fed carefully crafted dummy data telling them that two light scouts had gone active, apparently to launch four Merlin antistarship missiles directly at the installations that had been so carefully and painstakingly neutralized by Warrant Officer Ng and her team; the sensor towers duly disappeared in a searing blue-white flash as the massive demolition charges laid by Michael's teams were fired by tightbeam laser command. Ribot smiled for a second as he imagined the Hammer after-action analysis teams struggling to work out just how *387* and *166* had managed to get so close without being detected by Hell-14's sensors. The bastards would be even more puzzled as they tried to work out how two light scouts had apparently each gotten four Merlin antistarship missiles onboard. After all, everyone knew that Federated Worlds light scouts could carry only a maximum of twelve of the smaller and much less capable Mamba missiles.

Even as Ribot enjoyed the prospect of angry and confused Hammers, hatches whipped open on the flanks of the two ships, and in a matter of seconds hydraulic missile dispensers had deployed *387*'s full complement of short-range Mambas. Moments later, the two ships deployed a small cloud of active ship decoys, each one mimicking the emissions profiles of *387* and *166*.

Forlorn though it might be, the attack was on.

Ribot grunted in satisfaction as he watched the holovids blank out as the intense light of a swarm of exhaust plumes momentarily overwhelmed the holocams, mass drivers lighting off to accelerate the salvo and its decoy cloud toward *New Dallas*. He knew full well that it wasn't much of a salvo as salvos went, but at least they'd give the Hammers in *New Dallas* something to think about.

Mother's emotionless tones reported the launch. "Missiles away. Target *New Dallas*."

Ribot intervened. "Mother, hold lasers until they've woken up. If we go active now, they'll pick us out of the decoy cloud." Fed active ship decoys were very good but not so good that they could mimic the awesome power of an antistarship laser.

"Mother, roger."

Then it was time for *387* and *166* to show their hands.

Flanked by ship decoys doing their best to look like the real thing, the two ships erupted into life, main engines spewing blue-white tails of driver efflux, speed rapidly building under the thrust of a maximum-g tactical burn.

With his neuronics patched into the command plot, Michael waited, suited up with nowhere to go and nothing to do. All he could do was sit and worry, watching anxiously as the four antiship lasers mounted by *387* and *166* slowly chewed away at *New Dallas*.

He sighed in frustration as Mother faithfully reported the near futility of it all. The lasers were doing their job, burning off heavy frontal armor, but only by the centimeter, and the Hammer ship had meters of the damn stuff. All the while, *New Dallas* was turning ponderously toward them, untroubled by the light scouts' attack. The x-ray antiship lasers carried by light scouts were good, and their beam diffusion was minimal at such close range. But Hammer ceramsteel armor was also good, and the heavy cruiser had plenty of it to spare.

Well, Michael consoled himself, all *387* had to do was keep the Hammer ships' attention away from the incoming Fed warships and it would have done its job.

The good news was that the lights scouts' armor was holding up well despite the best efforts of the Hammer ships to burn their way through it, which by rights they should have been well on their way to doing. By Fed standards, the performance of the Hammers' lasers was very poor, to the point where, as Holdorf put it, they were giving *387*'s bows only a light all-over tan rather than the third-degree burns they should have been dishing out.

To cap it all, *387*'s Krachov microshrouds, pumped out in a never-ending stream from forward-mounted dispensers, were having some success in attenuating the lasers' destructive force even if the tiny disks lasted only seconds before the lasers overwhelmed them. But thankfully, there were an awful lot of disks.

That man Krachov was a fucking genius, Michael thought gratefully. He would make a point of buying him a beer if he ever emerged alive from what was beginning to look worryingly like a suicide mission. Michael felt powerless as nail by nail the Hammers slowly banged down the lid on *387*'s coffin, a strange sense of resignation coming over him as he faced the inevitability of his death.

Mother broke his thoughts. "Command, Mother. Missile launch from *New Dallas*. Estimate twelve missiles plus decoys. Initial vector analysis shows salvo split equally between *166* and *387*."

"Command, roger." Ribot's confusion was obvious to Michael. "Confirm missiles twelve."

"Confirmed. Missiles twelve. Six on *166* and six on *387*." Mother was emphatic.

Michael banged Petty Officer Strezlecki on the shoulder. "Stupid Hammer fuckheads have split the salvo, Strez. And the salvo's badly underweight. Only twelve missiles. They could have launched hundreds of the damn things, for God's sake. I wonder why." Michael couldn't conceal his relief. Six missiles gave them a chance at least, whereas without a miracle, a full missile salvo from *New Dallas* would have been the end.

Then it hit Michael. A small split salvo might be Hammer stupidity, but there was another, much less encouraging explanation.

Obviously Ribot had just had the same awful thought. "Mother, command. Could these be nukes?"

"Negative, command. Best estimate is conventional warheads. Hammer standard operating procedures preclude use of nuclear warheads this close to friendly installations. Electromagnetic pulse and residual radiation unacceptably high."

Michael gratefully offered up a silent prayer of thanks. *387* might be small, but she was very tough, her inner titanium hull shock-mounted and her artgrav and active quantum-trap radiation screens good enough to shield the crew from the transient shock and radiation produced by a nuclear warhead burst as long it wasn't too close. But nobody liked nukes, and if one got close enough, it was all over.

Ribot had watched impassively as the Hammer ships had finally swung bows onto *387*.

Now we're in for it, he thought. Any moment now, any moment now. It looked like the heavy patrol ship *Gore* would be first to get a rail-gun firing solution. She was, followed a good twenty seconds later by *Arroyo* and *MacFarlane*. But *Gore*'s command team, clearly at one and the same time overexcited and overconfident, couldn't wait. They should have.

"Command, Mother. Rail-gun launch from *Gore*. Target *387*."

"Why *387*?" Ribot mumbled as fear crunched his stomach into a tightly packed ball. This was getting horribly serious. "Command, roger."

"Command, Mother. Rail-gun launches from *Arroyo*, target *387*, and *MacFarlane*, target *166*."

"Command, roger. I don't think they like us," Ribot said, mouth dry and heart pounding at the thought of what the rail-gun swarms launched by *Gore* and *Arroyo* could do to *387*.

Hosani nodded. She could hardly think given the terrible certainty that she was eking out her last minutes, that she and everyone onboard were doomed. It was only by an enormous effort of will that she kept going. "You can say that again, skipper. I have the horrible feeling that we are going to get more than our fair share," she said shakily.

"Command, Mother. Multiple rail-gun launches. *Shark*, target *387*. *Cougar*, target *166*."

"So where the fuck is *New Dallas*?" Holdorf asked rhetorically. "Surely she doesn't want to miss the party."

"Give the fat bitch time, Lucky, give the fat bitch time. I'm sure she'll get to us." Maria Hosani's voice was tight. By her calculations, they had six Hammer missiles and hundreds of thousands of rail-gun slugs inbound, all due on target in a matter of minutes. Each slug had a kinetic energy equal to damn near 600 kilograms of high explosive and was focused on an area considerably smaller than the end of her little finger. That made—her brow furrowed as she did the math—200 kilotons of high explosive give or take, and all heading for her. She cursed silently. With the best will in the world, she couldn't see how *387* was going to get out alive, a conclusion absolutely reinforced by an unshakable conviction that even if *387* made it, she wasn't going to.

Hosani damned her Iranian ancestry. Too many mystics in the bloodline.

"Command, Mother. Speed now 80,000 kph. At pinch-space jump speed in three minutes."

"Command, roger. Warn propulsion that I'm going to jump *387* and *166* together as soon as we can."

"Mother, roger."

"If we live that long, that is," Hosani commed Holdorf.

"I'm not called Lucky for nothing, Maria, so have faith," Holdorf commed back.

"Command, Mother. Vector analysis of incoming salvos confirms very low probability of slug impact. *166*'s AI concurs. Time on target has been inadequately synchronized. Ripple timing and swarm geometry are very poor. Confirms THREATSUM assessment that Hammer fire control discipline is weak."

"Command, roger."

Ribot took a deep breath to try to slow his body down. Hammer fire control discipline might be weak, but just how *387* was going to duck and weave its way clear of the incoming rail-gun slugs was a question he could only hope Mother had a damn good answer to. Apart from a nearly overwhelming urge to run away and hide, he sure as hell didn't.

In her flag combat data center deep within the heavy cruiser *Al-Jahiz,* Vice Admiral Jaruzelska came to her feet as she cleaned up after the pinchspace drop, her eyes fixed on the command plot as the flag AI got the tactical situation settled down into some semblance of order.

She couldn't believe what she was seeing, but there it was, plain as day.

Her chief of staff interrupted her shocked study of the command plot. "Do you see what I see, sir?"

"I do, and I don't believe it. The crazy, crazy bastards." Jaruzelska could not keep the intense pride she felt out of her voice as she watched the hopelessly one-sided battle unfolding on the other side of her primary target, Hell's flotilla base.

"But thank God for it, Admiral. If they hadn't gone in, those fuckers might have had us on toast. We could have dropped right into a rail-gun swarm. I've ordered the task group to engage with lasers. The rail guns and missiles can take care of the flotilla base."

"Concur. I just hope it helps."

Any hope that *New Dallas*'s rail-gun swarm would be delayed until after her missiles had arrived died as the huge ship finally completed its turn.

Eyes fixed on the *New Dallas,* Michael felt like a small child watching a cobra. The laborious and painfully slow maneuver had taken a lifetime, the maneuvering systems spewing furious jets of reaction mass as they pushed the ship's unwieldy bulk around to bring her forward rail-gun batteries to bear on *387* and *166.*

Heavy cruisers had many advantages in the business of space warfare, but agility was not one of them, Michael thought.

As the huge black bulk of the *New Dallas* settled onto her attack vector, brief flashes of reaction mass spurting out as she fine-tuned her rail-gun launch, Ribot zoomed *387*'s holo-cams in close. He could see every detail of the two pinlike rows of rail-gun and decoy ports stretching from one side to the other across the otherwise black nothingness of the Hammer ship's stealth bows. They were all pointed directly at *387* and *166.* Ribot's heart pounded. Who's going to get it? he wondered. Then *New Dallas* fired the swarm, searing blue-white dots rippling out from the ship's centerline.

"Command, Mother. Rail-gun launch from *New Dallas*. Swarm split to target *387* and *166*."

"Thank you, you Hammer motherfucker, thank you very much," Michael cursed under his breath. But at least the stupid bastards had split the swarm, and that meant that only 96,000 slugs were heading their way, spread out by the time they arrived at *387* across a 40-square-kilometer front. Taking them for granted? he wondered. How stupid could you get. Try that in a Fed command exercise and you would get your ass kicked hard and justifiably so. Nonetheless, add in thousands of decoys and Mother was going to have her work cut out to keep *387* out of trouble.

Holdorf's excited shout beat Mother to it. "I don't believe it, skipper," he yelled. "They're turning; the bastards are bloody well turning away. They've fallen for Kawaguchi's decoy attack."

Ribot's heart thudded in his chest as hope flared for the first time since the Hammers had dropped. "Shit, Leon! Are you sure?" Ribot stared at the command plot, desperately praying that *387*'s navigator was right. "By God," he said finally. "I think you're right. Mother, you confirm?"

"Confirmed, command. But not *Gore*. She remains on targeting vector."

"Command, roger. Mother, any chance the *New Dallas* and the heavy escorts will get off a salvo from their stern batteries?" Ribot tried unsuccessfully to keep the edginess out of his voice. Together, the three heavy ships in the Hammer group could fire close to 400,000 slugs from their after rail-gun batteries. Even if they targeted both of the light scouts and got their swarm geometry and ripple timing only half-right, it really would be all over.

"Stand by, command . . . Negative. They are having to pitch up to get a firing solution on the decoys, so they'll be off vector for us by the time they are stern on."

"Command, roger. Let's hope we can ride it out, and with

a bit of luck the task group can help us finish off *Gore*."
Ribot's voice resonated with new hope.

"Confirmed."

"Roger. Keep the lasers on *New Dallas*. If she shows us
enough of her big fat ass, we may get lucky. Mother, what are
our chances?"

"Probability of mission abort level of damage is 7 percent.
Probability of hard kill is negligible."

"Bugger." Ribot sighed in disappointment. "Not great
odds. Okay. Priority mission is own ship defense. Second
priority, *166* defense. Third, *New Dallas*."

Michael shared Ribot's disappointment.

For one wonderful fleeting moment, he had thought, had
hoped, they might have a chance of killing *New Dallas*. But
with the rail-gun swarms now coming thick and fast, *387*'s
lasers weren't getting enough time on target to have a chance
with a warship as big and tough as *New Dallas*. That was a
hell of a shame, as the distance and angle of attack were
good and getting better by the minute as *New Dallas* swung
her stern into *387*'s and *166*'s lines of attack.

Add yet another tactical screwup to the Hammer's already
long list, Michael muttered, even if it looked like one *387*
and *166* wouldn't be able to exploit.

"All stations, command. First rail-gun salvos due in one
minute."

They were in Mother's hands now. For Christ's sake, do it
well, Michael thought.

In the end, the rail-gun swarms hurled at them by the two
Hammer heavy patrol ships were an anticlimax. Mother was
easily able to maneuver *387* down and away out of the path
of *Gore*'s and *Arroyo*'s onrushing slugs. The attack was too
poorly targeted, the swarm too small, the rail-gun slugs
spread too far apart and leaving too many holes for Mother
to exploit. The ship barely registered the impact of the lightweight thin-skinned decoys intended to confuse its sensors
as they smashed uselessly into the ship's thick frontal armor.

Then it was all over, and the slugs were gone. Two light

scouts had survived the first Hammer rail-gun attack in twenty years. A miracle, that was what it was, Michael told himself, a bloody miracle.

Ribot didn't think it was a miracle at all. Nor did Holdorf.

"Stupid, impatient bastards," he said. "If the whole lot of them had hung on and fired as one, they'd have had us on toast. And if they'd taken us one at a time instead of trying to kill us both . . ." Holdorf's voice trailed off into silence as the thought of *387*'s destruction at the hands of a Hammer rail-gun attack struck home.

"True enough, Lucky. But it's not over yet," Ribot said as Mother flung *387* almost onto her back under emergency maneuvering power as she desperately tried to get the ship out of the way of the next swarm. The artgrav howled in protest as Mother struggled to get *387*'s bulk clear of *Shark*'s slug rail-gun salvo. Ribot winced as Mother took the terrible risk of presenting her thin upper armor to three objects on a collision course.

Christ on the Cross, Ribot prayed desperately, his heart pounding as fear threatened to swamp him. They'd better be decoys and not slugs. If they were slugs . . .

Ribot breathed out raggedly as Mother reported three decoy impacts and no damage. Jesus, he thought, this is tough. There were still more incoming slugs, not to mention missiles, than he cared to think about.

"Command, Mother. Report from Commander Task Group 256.1. First rail-gun and missile salvos away. Target Hell system Flotilla Base fixed defenses and warships on station."

"Yes! Yes! Yes!" Ribot shouted, slapping the arm of his command chair.

Ribot couldn't help himself; a broad smile split his face behind the visor of his space-suit helmet. That was more like it, and with a bit of luck, the Hammer might leave them alone now that Admiral Jaruzelska and her cruisers had joined the party.

From the moment the sixteen cruisers that made up Task Group 256.1 had dropped into Hammer normalspace, Admiral Jaruzelska and her entire flag staff had watched the deadly game being played out by the two massively out-gunned Fed light scouts in horrified fascination. The flag combat data center was deathly silent as the task group's holocams tracked *387* and *166* as they writhed and twisted their way out of the path of the rail-gun swarms from *Gore, Arroyo,* and *MacFarlane.*

Their concentration was broken only when *Al-Jahiz* shud-dered with the characteristic heavy metal-on-metal crunch-ing thud of rail-gun mass drivers punching a full swarm of slugs and its decoy cloud toward the hapless ships berthed at the flotilla base at over 3.8 million kph, the salvo flanked on all sides by the slug swarms and yet more decoy clouds from the other ships. The attack was massive, the kinetic energy thrown at the Hammers equal to three megatons of high ex-plosive.

"Flag, flag AI. Force rail-gun salvos away."

"Flag, roger," Jaruzelska said mechanically as she switched half her brain away from her two smallest ships and back to the big picture.

She shivered as she thought of what the salvo was going to do to the unprepared warships of the Hell Flotilla and its fixed defenses. She wouldn't want to be on the receiving end of a ten-slug salvo, let alone one with millions of the mean ugly bastards. For all their massive bulk and enormously thick frontal armor, the flotilla flagship *Verity* and its sister heavy cruiser *Integrity* were doomed, and the two light cruisers *Cordoba* and *Camara* wouldn't be long in follow-ing. It was just a matter of time, and with a bit of luck the Hammers would soon be without the massive phased-array radars that provided targeting data for the base's missile and antiship laser systems and would have to fight back half-blind.

Five seconds after the rail-gun swarm had departed, the characteristic ripping-metal buzz of a full missile salvo launch ran through *Al-Jahiz.* The ship's massive hydraulic missile dispensers rammed a full salvo of Merlin heavy mis-siles clear of the ship in only a matter of seconds.

"Flag, flag AI. Force missile salvos away."

"Flag, roger." Jaruzelska could do nothing now but watch the flag combat data center's command plot as the task group's two salvos reached out toward the Hammer, their vectors thin green lines of death stark against deep black.

No, that wasn't right. There was something she could do, and she should have done it long before. If she didn't, *Gore* would be the death of *387* and *166*.

"Flag AI, flag. Hostile *Gore*. Engage with force lasers."

The flag AI didn't even blink at the sudden change in mission priorities.

Within seconds, the cruisers had turned their antiship lasers away from *New Dallas* and onto the distant form of the *Gore*. The intense beams of coherent light quickly began the process of tunneling a hole into *Gore*'s ceramsteel side armor; high-definition targeting holocams were focusing the task group's antistarship lasers down onto a single point on the Hammer ship's hull.

It took a desperate combination of high-g maneuvering and good work with the ship's defensive systems to save *387*.

Close-range rail-gun engagements had been described as something akin to high-speed four-dimensional chess, with swarm after swarm trying to checkmate the target, herding it into a position where it had nowhere to move except into the path of the oncoming slugs. Then it was just a matter of the weight of metal as the slugs ripped away armor to allow the slugs following them to punch through into the hull. At that point it was checkmate.

But Ribot knew full well that there was a lot of space out there and how very small warships were in the grand scheme of things. Therefore, a well executed rail-gun attack, as much a matter of art as of science, needed very precise timing, close coordination of the swarm patterns, and good swarm design, all based on what could only be described as an intuitive understanding of how the target would behave. Those were all things the Hammers had yet to demonstrate they were capable of. The simple fact that *387* had survived a 96,000-slug rail-gun attack was all the proof needed that the Hammers didn't have their shit together. One thing was for sure: If the ships attacking *387* and *166* had been Feds, they'd be dead by now.

Even so, it was scary stuff. Ribot couldn't remember being so terrified. Ever.

Leaving *387*'s long-range antiship lasers on target as long as possible in the hope of doing some serious damage to *New Dallas,* Mother finally brought their awesome power to join the ship's short-range defensive lasers in time to try and fend off the few slugs from *Shark* that posed any threat. *Shark*'s swarm had been bigger, better aimed, and more carefully timed than those from *Gore* and *Arroyo,* forcing *387* to move down and across the path of the final four slugs to the point where Ribot would have been prepared to swear on his life that three of the four had passed close enough to graze *387*'s outer stealth coat.

But the fourth was luckier. It hit *387* almost directly where her armor was thickest. The slug vaporized in a nanosecond to blow a huge crater in *387*'s armor, the massive explosion smashing the ship down and into a slow spiraling turn, spewing rolling, twisting clouds of vaporized ceramsteel. Great gouts of reaction mass poured from her maneuvering thrusters as Mother struggled to bring the ship back on vector, artgrav screaming as it absorbed the shock waves that racked it from end to end.

"Christ Jesus protect us. That was way, way too close," Holdorf said, desperately wishing he could unsuit and wipe away the ice-cold sweat running down his spine.

"Maria! Get Helfort and one of his team out there. I want that impact damage repaired."

"But sir," Hosani protested, "the next salvo's due any minute now."

Ribot's voice was brutal. "I know, Maria. But if we get another slug where that one hit, it'll go through us end to end and we'll all be dead. And it's too close to Weapons Power Charlie. I can't take the chance. That crater has to be filled." He held a hand up even as Hosani started to protest his callous indifference. "Okay, okay. Hold them back until the next salvo's passed. There's not time for them to make a difference, anyway."

"Sir." Hosani sounded relieved as she commed the warning order to Michael.

Ribot sat back. He'd come as close as he could to condemning Helfort and his surveillance drone team to death, but what choice did he have?

"Command, Mother. *166* reports single grazing impact. Minor damage only to hull armor, no loss of hull integrity."

"Command, roger." Bastards. Ten points to the *Shark* and *Cougar*. It seemed that the Hammer might actually be getting its act together.

"How long, Maria?"

"Fifteen seconds, sir."

"Warn the troops."

"All stations, command. Stand by next rail-gun swarm. Ten seconds. Out."

As the incoming swarm had approached, Michael had unconsciously pulled his head down into his shoulders, his already tense stomach contracting even further into a tight knot. He'd never seen a command plot, even in the worst tactical exercise scenarios thrown at him during his college time, as bad as the one he was looking at now.

The instant *Shark*'s swarm had passed, Mother had thrown the ship even farther off vector before the cone of 96,000 slugs buried somewhere inside a huge cloud of decoys from *New Dallas* shut down her options even more. But with only seconds between salvos and a lot of mass to shift, Mother didn't have enough time and maneuvering power to get it right. Her desperate attempt to get *387* clear between salvos was not enough to move the ship completely clear of danger.

Michael cursed wordlessly as Mother updated the command plot, the primary threat vector turning a deep red as the impact probability approached 100 percent. This couldn't go on. If rail guns didn't get them, missiles might. And if missiles didn't, the lasers slowly chewing away at *387*'s hull eventually would break through, and people would begin to die. The frustrating thing was that they would be at jump speed any minute now. So close and yet so far.

But maybe he should be thankful for small blessings,

Michael thought as he stared almost mesmerized at the time-on-target clock counting off the seconds. *Gore* must have a problem with her rail guns; she still hadn't fired again. This early in an engagement, she should have gotten her second rail-gun salvo away in under two minutes or so if her crew and systems were up to scratch, but it was now well past that. If *Gore* didn't fire soon, *387* and *166* would jump, provided that they weathered the incoming storm of slugs from *New Dallas*. If they could do that, the ships would vanish into pinchspace, leaving the one and only missile salvo fired at them nothing more than an ultraviolet flash to home in on.

Michael started to pray really, really hard. They were so close to safety, it hurt. The wait was pure torture. And now, as if the wait wasn't bad enough, Ribot wanted him outside to fix the damage caused by the last slug. Heart pounding, he could only stand and wait.

By nature and duty physically active people, the surveillance dròne team suffered in silence as the seconds dragged by, the weight of space suits and full EVA gear dragging them down, with only the occasional update from Ribot and Hosani in the combat information center to tell them what was going on. Michael tried to shut out the terrible images of what a rail-gun slug could do to him, concentrating with furious effort on the gray plasteel deck of the harshly lit hangar and its clutter of infinitely deep black holes that were *387*'s eight surveillance drones, Michael's pride and joy. Fat lot of use they were now.

That didn't help much, so Michael eased himself back into the surveillance drone air lock. There were a couple of small comms boxes at just the right height to take the weight of his EVA pack if only he could find them. In the end, it wasn't hard: Bienefelt had gotten there first. Michael smiled. He should have known better than to think he could ever be a step ahead of her.

Unnoticed by Michael, now busy twisting around in an attempt to find somewhere else to rest, Warrant Officer Ng had made her way up from below. She stuck her head through the open air lock door and leaned her helmet against Michael's. He jumped as she spoke.

"How's it going, sir?"

"Oh, um, hi. Yeah, okay, Warrant Officer Ng. But nobody told me that Space Fleet life was a combination of pure terror dished out in random dollops along with long periods of stupefying boredom. You know, the old cliché."

"Well, so it is, but I must say that it has been a long time since I was quite so scared shitless. And for Christ's sake, call me Doc."

"Er, right. Okay, Doc," Michael said, feeling like someone who'd just been blessed. "Was it like this last time around?"

"As best as I can remember 'cause it was a very long time, yes, it was. Though I was in big ships then. Must say, I don't remember being in a situation quite as bad as this."

"All stations, Command. Stand by next rail-gun swarm. Ten seconds. Out."

"Don't exactly tell us a hell of—"

Michael thought that the world had come to an end.

Frantically winnowing out the decoys, Mother had successfully deflected three high-risk slugs. *387*'s massive antiship lasers hit the platinum/iridium slugs, ionized metal imparting sufficient energy to shift the slugs' vectors fractionally away from them.

But it wasn't enough.

New Dallas had done it well even if she'd made the elementary tactical error of splitting her salvo between two targets. She'd carefully fashioned the 96,000 slugs into a cone-shaped swarm, with the point of the cone leading the way, forcing *387* to commit, to move out into the path of the rest of the swarm as it lagged fractionally behind.

And so *387*'s luck began to run out.

Ninety-six thousand slugs buried inside a well-designed and well-timed swarm all wrapped up in a mass of decoys was simply too many for the little ship to deflect or evade. As Mother tried desperately to roll *387* in a dive out of the path of the last of the swarm, the ship shuddered as three slugs hit home. The massive impacts, only microseconds apart, wracked the ship with terrible violence until the entire fabric of the hull screamed in protest.

Moving at nearly 800,000 meters per second, the first slug

hit the lower starboard side of *387*'s bow at a fine, almost grazing angle. Another meter farther out and it would have missed altogether. With the slug only meters and microseconds away from hitting home, *387*'s hull-mounted microwave sensors had computed its precise impact point and predicted its vector through the hull before firing the ship's last-ditch defenses of ultra-high-gain explosive reactive armor nested in hexagonal titanium cells. The armor's shaped charges fired in a carefully calculated pattern, at best to drive the slug away from the ship, at worst to diffuse and spread its kinetic energy wave front.

This time *387* was lucky; the slug's angle of attack was sufficiently shallow to allow the reactive armor to deflect it slightly away from the inner hull. Even so, the slug gouged a gaping furrow across the hull before erupting violently back into space in a cloud of shattered ceramsteel armor and platinum/iridium plasma. The ship rang with the shock as high-explosive-packed armor exploded against the shock-mounted titanium that formed its inner hull.

The second slug met the same fate.

As it smashed into *387*'s upper bow on the starboard side, again the reactive armor did what it was designed to do. High explosive blasted out with enough force—barely, but enough—to turn the tiny slug out of the hull to disappear back into space, its short path through the hull a white-hot smoking scar cut deep into the bottomless black of the ship's stealth coat. But this time real damage was done, the slug taking with it much of *387*'s short-range laser capability as it gouged its way across the ship's outer armor.

387 had spent all the luck it had been given. Slug swarm tactics were a numbers game, and the Hammer had the numbers.

Unlike the others, the third slug hit *387* well aft of the bow, at the forward end of the surveillance drone hangar, just where the ship's titanium frames locked the forward upper personnel access hatch to the main structure of the ship, an unavoidable weak spot in the ship's armor. This time, the slug came in at an angle steep enough to overcome the reactive armor's efforts to turn it back out of the hull. Even as the armor exploded vainly underneath it, the slug kept coming, its trajectory only marginally flattened as its plasma sheath vaporized the entire air lock.

Within microseconds of hitting, the slug was pure plasma and had reached the inner hull. The titanium armor vaporized in an instant to let the plasma into the ship, the shock of its entry driving viciously high-energy metal shards from the ship's titanium frame through the Kevlar splinter matting bonded to the inner hull. Each shard was a deadly missile pushing a growing cone of destruction deep into *387;* the ship's hull around the entry point peeled back in tangled sheets like wet cardboard.

Without warning, the surveillance drone hangar exploded into a searingly bright maelstrom of ionized gas and flying metal splinters. The lethal shroud of plasma came down through the small personnel air lock to cut across the hangar at an angle, vaporizing the drones in its path before exiting through the aft end of the hangar. It took out the aft personnel access hatch and the pinchcomms antenna in the process before finally leaving the ship, its path marked by a lethal firestorm of incandescent metal and swirling high-energy plasma.

The massive overpressure from the slug's plasma blast wave was enough to smash Michael back into the surveillance drone air lock. For a moment he could only half stand, half kneel there, unable to move as waves of pain racked his body, his tortured back and ribs screaming at him, until the urgent shrieking of his suit alarm and a tightness in his chest told him that he'd lost suit integrity and had better do something about it quickly. He couldn't work out why Warrant Officer Ng was half sitting crumpled in her heat-seared suit at his feet, helmeted head hanging awkwardly to one side, her suit front gaping open and strangely slick in the swirling murky aftermath of the slug's passing.

Then he got it. Ng was dead. Somehow, it didn't mean anything, so Michael pushed the unresponsive Ng away and quickly slapped bright red suit patches out of the dispenser on the bulkhead behind him. In seconds, his fumbling efforts guided by his suit AI, he had sealed a gaping hole in the upper left leg of his suit, a smaller one lower down, and a small but dangerous-looking crack in his plasglass visor. The hole in the left leg of his suit was strangely shiny, surrounded by a sort of crystalline sheen that some dim recess of his mind told him must be heat-carbonized blood. But apart from a numbness in his leg, he felt no pain. With a huge effort, he forced his mind back to work and tried to decide what to do next.

With no air to hold it up and only residual hot spots spewing metal vapor into the compartment, the plasma fog filling the hangar cooled and cleared quickly. It revealed a scene of utter devastation, the sight so awful that Michael saw it without understanding any of it. Evidence of the fury of the slug's passing was everywhere, with almost every surface, every bit of equipment, every fitting, baked by intense heat and scarred and slashed by the metal splinters that had been thrown up as the slug had passed. Collapsed in untidy stiff heaps on the deck was his team, the last tendrils of gas spewing from ripped and torn space suits.

Only Bienefelt had been left standing, her suit a mass of hurriedly applied red patches.

Michael forced himself to put the comm through to Mother. "Medics and crash bags, surveillance drone hangar. Quick, for God's sake."

And then, pulling another wad of suit patches from the nearest dispenser, he made his way out of the corner that had shielded him from the full fury of the slug's passing, climbing over Warrant Officer Ng. A quick check confirmed that she was dead, and he started trying to seal endless gashes in suits, ignoring the stinging prickle of wound foam as his suit tried to stop the bleeding in his leg.

Even as he did that, medics erupted from the hatch.

In seconds, helped by Michael and Bienefelt, the worst of the casualties were shoved unceremoniously into crash bags, zipped up, and pressurized before being manhandled hurriedly down the hatch on their way to the ship's tiny sick bay, the only part of the ship still with pressure inside its triple thickness of ceramsteel armor.

Numbly, Michael watched as the shattered remains of Ng,

Strzlecki, Leong, Carlsson, and Athenascu were taken below. Their suits were so badly ripped that he knew in his heart that they weren't ever coming back.

Finally, Maddox and Karpov, both clearly in pain and badly hurt but at least with suits more or less intact—Michael couldn't begin to work out how—were helped down the hatch. He began to tremble as the awful shock of it all hit him as he stood there with Bienefelt amid the metal-splintered, flame-seared, black-blood-spattered wreckage of the hangar.

Michael was shaken out his trance by Ribot, his voice soft but firm. "Michael, this is the captain. Your people are in good hands now, so it's time to do what you're paid for. I want that slug crater over Weapons Power Charlie fixed before the next attack, so get moving. Main propulsion's been shut down, but watch out for no-notice maneuvers. I'll keep things steady for as long as I can, but Mother's going to do whatever she's got to do to keep us out of trouble, so make sure you're well clipped on."

"Sir."

With a heavy heart but grateful that he had something better to do than stand around waiting for the ax to fall, Michael commed Bienefelt to follow him. At least, he thought, he didn't have to wait for any damn air lock to open. There wasn't one anymore, just a fucking great big hole. Wearily and more scared than he'd ever been in his life, he clipped his safety line onto a handy stanchion. With a deep breath, a kick, and a heave, he was safely past the ripped and torn remnants of the forward personnel air lock and out into the awful darkness, heart pounding and mouth dry.

"Command, Mother. *166* reports two hits. Moderate damage only, hull has lost integrity in two places; all combat systems nominal but unable to jump. Casualties. Three dead and twelve injured but none critical. Time to repair, ninety minutes maximum."

"Command, roger," Ribot said. Shit, shit, shit. Now neither of them could jump. This couldn't go on. But it could and it would, and with a conscious effort, Ribot forced himself to face whatever would come next.

"Command, Mother. At pinchspace jump speed."

"Roger," Ribot said with a heavy heart. Too late.

With both *166*'s and *387*'s hulls ripped open, it was all academic now, anyway. The mass distribution model used by the nav AI to compute *387*'s pinchspace jump parameters was hopelessly compromised by the gaping holes in *387*'s hull. The ship was hours away from being jump-capable; any jump now would destroy it and kill them all. Ironically, they were safer staying put, where the chances of death and destruction weren't quite 100 percent.

"Command, Mother. Rail-gun launch from *Gore*. Swarm of 48,000-plus decoys. Target *387*."

Good old *Gore*, Ribot thought. It finally got its act together. Better late than never. But what the Hammer was doing still didn't make sense.

"Mother, Command. Why no missiles? *Gore*'s got missiles and plenty of them. Why doesn't she use them?"

"Command, Mother. Uncertain. Only clue is given by the missile salvo from *New Dallas*. I believe it confirms orders to conserve missile reserves for the decoy assault, which is now their primary objective."

"Makes sense, I suppose."

Ribot pulled up the standard incoming salvo report. It was not good reading.

Shit, Ribot thought, get a grip, man. He was definitely losing his edge when he forgot that *387* and *166* weren't just receivers but givers as well. For a few seconds he felt good about what his missiles might do to the Hammer ship. *387* and *166* weren't just sitting there like sacrificial lambs waiting for the ax to fall. Ribot zoomed the holocam as far in on *New Dallas* as it would go, the ship's size losing nothing in the process.

His feel-good moment didn't last long. "Don't think our missiles are going to hurt that big bastard very much." Ribot's voice reflected his pessimism.

"Can but try, skipper."

As ever, Holdorf's voice was bright with optimism, and
not for the first time Ribot wondered how he managed it in
the circumstances. Space warfare had often been compared
to standing with one's feet stuck in concrete boots, watching
a homicidal maniac walk slowly toward you, meat cleaver in
hand, with every intention of hacking you to pieces. And so
it had turned out. Waiting as death rushed toward you was
the hard part, the entire process made worse for *387* and its
crew by knowing there was almost nothing they could do to
hit back. How Holdorf always managed to sound so damn
cheerful was a real mystery.

And then the holovid began to flash as, too fast to count,
the missiles and decoys from *387* and *166* began to die useless deaths at the hands of the Hammers' defenses. But just
as Ribot gave up hope that any would get through, there was
a single red-yellow bloom on *New Dallas*'s upper hull, a
short-lived plume of ionized gas marking the impact point.

"Got the fucker! And it was one of ours." Hosani's voice
rang with triumph. "Suck that, you Hammer bastard! They
must be asleep over there."

The combat information center team watched the holovid
with furious concentration, hoping against hope that the missile's shaped charge warhead had shot its plasma lance far
enough into the huge ship to reach something vital.

But it was not to be.

The Mamba antistarship missiles carried by light scouts
were too small and had too small a warhead to have any
chance against a Hammer heavy cruiser. Even hitting the
New Dallas had been a minor miracle. In seconds the bloom
had darkened, and then just as quickly it died, leaving only a
tiny hot spot on the ship's hull. *New Dallas* continued on as
though nothing had happened.

Ribot sighed in resignation. "Can't win them all. Mother,
tell *166* to close on me for mutual support. How long until
the missiles from *New Dallas* arrive?"

"Command, Mother. Two minutes."

Ribot grunted. Two minutes before they lived or died, assuming of course they survived *Gore*'s rail-gun salvo, which
was due in—he did a quick check—less than a minute.

"Roger that. Tell—"

Ribot could only watch open-mouthed as *Gore*'s port side, flayed by the enormous power of FedWorld long-range anti-ship lasers, suddenly ripped open. It was almost as if somebody had taken a huge knife and cut the ship open from stem to stern. A huge plume of incandescent gas and debris spewed out into space as the shattered hulk began a slow spiraling tumble to nowhere, automatic distress alarms sounding frantically in Ribot's neuronics until he commed them off.

Jesus, Ribot thought. Jaruzelska's ships must have cracked the armor and hit a fusion plant. Big one, too. Main propulsion by the look of it. Great targeting considering the range.

"But we can win some," Ribot said jubilantly. "Maria, tell the troops. I suspect they could do with some good news. And get the XO to confirm when she expects to have the drone hangar foamsteeled. I'm sure I don't have to remind her that we can't jump with it ripped open."

"Sir."

As Mother confirmed that *166* was closing in, Ribot settled down once again to wait. At least there were only two more rounds to go, and neither would be as bad as what they had gone through before. Maybe, just maybe, they'd get out of this.

He was quickly disabused.

"Command, Mother. Final vector analysis on *Gore*'s railgun salvo indicates very high probability of impact."

"Command, roger. Maria, how's Michael doing?"

"It's slow, sir. That's one hell of a big hole out there. They've got the emergency ceramsteel generator secured and are putting the supply feeds in place now. Michael estimates another two minutes will see the job done."

"Tell him he doesn't have two minutes."

"He knows, sir."

Desperately aware that they were standing directly in front of an oncoming rail-gun salvo, Michael and Bienefelt had dragged the ceramsteel generator and a bolt gun out of the forward emergency repair stowage. Their back-mounted personal maneuvering units were working overtime as they manhandled the awkward heavy lumps of metal across the hull to the lip of the huge crater that had been blown deep in *387*'s armor, its walls still glowing with residual patches of red heat. As Bienefelt worked desperately, punching explosive bolts deep into *387*'s hull to hold the generator in place, Michael, struggling to connect the generator to its high-pressure supply feeds, took a moment to marvel that *387* had been able to withstand the violent explosive release of so much energy. Finally, Bienefelt got the last bolt home. Working with frantic controlled haste, Michael helped Bienefelt run hoses into the crater. The armored hoses were awkward and stiff to space-suited hands, and a terrible feeling of panic threatened to overwhelm him as the seconds ticked remorselessly away.

But finally, all the feeds were in place. Bienefelt's massive frame was braced against the crater wall as she tightened the last connector.

"Done, sir," she said laconically.

She could have been talking about the damn weather, Michael thought. One last check and Mother brought the generator online, gray-black ceramsteel sludge already pouring out of the generator ports to bond instantly with the walls of the crater. Looking good, Michael thought as the crater began to fill at an impressive rate.

"Okay, Benny. Let's get the fuck out of here."

"Not before time, sir."

As they cleared the rim of the blast crater to start their frantic dash back to safety, Mother ran out of time. As she simultaneously fired main propulsion and rolled the ship, Michael and Bienefelt were hurled back along the hull until, with a vicious slamming snap, their safety lines brought them to a dead stop before the recoil threw them back where they'd come from, skidding and sliding uncontrollably along *387*'s hull before swinging out into space and back again to hit the ship full on with a sickening crunch that tested their suits' crashworthiness to the fullest. With a despairing lunge, Michael grabbed Bienefelt as she cannoned into him and snap-hooked his suit harness onto hers, all the while desperately fighting to reel in his safety line.

A quick check with Mother, and Michael saw that *387*'s violent maneuvering had destroyed any chance of getting back inside the ship. They didn't have time to get back to the personnel air lock; they'd have to snap into the nearest hard point, secure their safety lines, and wait it out. There was nothing more they could do. They were going to ride out the next attack locked out of *387*, hanging on the end of monofil safety lines with only combat space suits between them and God knew how many oncoming slugs.

If their monofil safety lines failed, at least they'd die together.

And then they waited. As Michael hung there, Bienefelt's massive bulk tightly locked alongside him, he knew he was about to die. He had never been more certain of anything in his life.

Ribot glanced across at the XO, who had just arrived from the surveillance drone hangar to report. He hoped she had good news. Restoration of jump capability in the next ten seconds would qualify.

But he waved her back. She'd have to wait.

The final rail-gun salvo from the now-crippled *Gore* hurtled toward *387,* the bright red icons on the plot closing the gap with remorseless intent.

Mother did her best, driving *387* up and to port to escape the slug swarm. But the task was nearly impossible. With the *Gore* and *387* now barely 60,000 kilometers apart, the battle geometry was heavily weighted in favor of the rail-gun attacker, the slugs having a time of flight from launch of only eighty seconds.

And eighty seconds did not give Mother enough time to shift *387*'s bulk out of the way before turning the ship back to put her heavy bow armor facing the slugs. Worse, and probably more by luck than good judgment, the *Gore*'s rail-gun targeting team, probably dead now, had gotten it right. The slugs in the swarm were perfectly lagged and spread, and the decoys were well positioned to confuse and overload *387*'s sensors. *387* had nowhere to run.

And one slug's vector was exactly right.

Even as *387*'s short-range lasers belatedly flayed it, the killer slug's surface literally bubbling as platinum/iridium boiled off into space, it smashed into the ship's starboard upper bow, precisely where one of the slugs from *Shark* had gouged a crater in *387*'s frontal armor. The metal slug smashed through the still-setting emergency ceramsteel repair and the remaining armor as though they didn't exist, turning to plasma as it sliced through the inner pressure hull and down into Weapons Power Charlie. Microseconds later, the plasma containment bottle erupted in an enormous secondary explosion that ripped the upper bow of *387* apart into a mass of shredded ceramsteel and twisted titanium frames.

The slug, now a concentrated lance of pure energy, plunged unopposed down into and through *387*'s combat information center and then on into the hangar, through the bows of *387*'s lander, and finally out into space.

Michael didn't remember much of what had happened.

Gore's attack was over in seconds. Afterward, all he could recall was a smashing impact as the blast wave hit, a ripping, tearing blur of heat and intense white light, a hoarse scream from Bienefelt followed by a soft bubbling moan, and then a crunching collision with *387*'s hull that bounced the two tangled spacers out into space before their safety lines jerked taut. Michael's head was driven forward hard into his armored plasglass visor and snapped forward nose first onto his collar ring with brutal force.

And then silence. Deathly, deathly silence.

Oh, Jesus, he thought, Bienefelt's dead. She should be breathing, but she's not. Frantically he spun her massive frame around, and there it was, a long rough-edged gash ripped across the lower back of the suit, moisture-laden gas spewing ice crystals out into the black night. Even as he slapped suit patches out of his thigh-mounted dispenser onto the gash, he knew he couldn't help her.

Calling for help and with an urgency born of desperation,

Michael unclipped from the sorely tested hard point and reeled in his safety line, the inertia of Bienefelt's body making the process agonizingly slow. As he got to the gaping hole in *387*'s hull that had once been its forward upper personnel access hatch, a first aid team emerged. Within seconds, Bienefelt had been crash-bagged and taken below.

For a moment, Michael just hung there. He didn't care too much anymore what happened next. He went below only when the coxswain grabbed his arm and dragged him bodily down through the wickedly sharp-edged hole in *387*'s hull.

Only later did he find out how lucky they'd been. The curve of *387*'s hull had been just enough to protect him and Bienefelt from the worst effects of the Hammer attack.

The flag staff's increasingly heated debate about what to do with the *New Dallas* task group was rudely interrupted.

"Flag, flag AI. Missile launch from flotilla base fixed defenses. Stand by vector and attack profile."

"Flag, roger."

"Taken them a very long time, Admiral," her chief of staff said. It was what they'd all been thinking. All the sims had assumed that the Hammers would get their fixed missile defenses into action inside the thirty-second launch window laid down by Hammer standard operating procedures. Something had to have gone very wrong, not that anybody on Jaruzelska's team was complaining.

Jaruzelska nodded absently.

At that moment, she was more concerned about whether her ships were ready to deal with the incoming Hammer attack. They looked to be, and with minutes to prepare, they'd be even more ready when the attack arrived. The good news was that the delay meant that the Hammer was unlikely to be able to get another missile salvo away. The task group's massive rail-gun attack would see to that.

Jaruzelska turned her attention back to the issue at hand. After a further short discussion with her flag staff, she made up her mind.

She hated overruling her flag AI, but there were times when it had to be done. The task group's second missile salvo would be ready to launch in less than thirty seconds, and if she was going to change the plan, she needed to do it now.

"Flag AI, flag. I don't think the decoys are going to keep the attention of the *New Dallas* task group much longer. Now that we have the main Hammer force on the back foot, I want *New Dallas* and her escorts taken out before they give us too much grief."

The flag AI's consideration of Jaruzelska's proposition was noticeably prolonged as it digested the implications of her orders. "Flag, flag AI. Missile salvo on *New Dallas* task group. Confirm."

"Confirmed." Jaruzelska's tone was very emphatic even as she keyed a marker into her neuronics as a reminder to have the AI boffins look at the flag AI's inability to see that the *New Dallas* group was every bit as big a threat as the flotilla base ships. A bigger threat, in fact, as the task group's relentless assault slowly ground the Hell Flotilla and its base's fixed defenses into dust. Even if the *New Dallas* and her escorts weren't shooting at them right now, they would be soon.

"Flag AI, roger. Missile salvo on *New Dallas* task group. Stand by, stand by . . . away now."

That was one thing she liked about AIs, Jaruzelska thought. Unlike some of the prima donnas on her staff, they never sounded hurt when you overruled them.

Before Mother, safe in her meter-thick shock-mounted ceramsteel box, commed him, Michael had been sitting amid the shattered wreckage of the surveillance drone hangar, watching but not seeing the frantic efforts of the ship's damage control teams to seal the damage to *387*'s hull. The hangar was a mess of emergency foamsteel generators, steel bracing, and welding gear. Bienefelt had been crash-bagged and taken below to join Karpov in regen. There was nothing more he could do for any of them now except watch. He'd patched his neuronics into the sick bay's holocams and, with his head a mass of white-hot agony, watched as the medics struggled to stabilize the surviving members of his team and get them into the regen tanks in time. Worst of all were the ones the medics had lost, their crash bags laid out neatly against the sick bay bulkhead. Michael struggled to remember the faces of Ng, Strezlecki, Leong, Carlsson, and Athenascu.

But he couldn't. They were just blurs behind a thick red-gray fog of hurt.

It was all he could do just to sit there slumped on the deck as pain poured through his system. He was a mess. His neuronics told him he had lost a fair bit of blood and that there had been a whole lot of other damage involving bones, muscles, and tendons that didn't sound too good, but he didn't care.

Through the red haze and with blood pouring down his face and into his suit, Michael finally answered Mother's increasingly insistent comm.

"Yes, what?" He winced. Just talking hurt.

"Michael, this is Mother. I know you are hurt, but you'll be okay." Mother had firmed her voice to a point just short of being brutally direct. "But I need you and I need you now. You are now the senior line officer, and you must take command."

"Senior line officer? Command? What do you mean?" Michael struggled to concentrate. The blood around his neck was getting sticky as it congealed, but thank God the bleeding was stopping. "Command? Why?"

"They're all dead, Michael. Ribot, Hosani, Holdorf, Armitage, Kapoor. All dead. That last slug took out most of the combat information center crew and the lander as well. Reilly's okay. He was in propulsion control."

Michael nodded painfully, not fully understanding what Mother was saying to him. All in all, it was much easier to do what the insistent voice was saying and not argue. Arguing required thought, and thinking hurt. "Okay. Where do I go?"

"Wardroom, Michael. Best I can do and the only large holovid screen left intact. And please be quick. The next attack is due in under ninety seconds."

Michael forced himself to his feet with as much speed as his bruised and battered body would allow and made his way down to 2 Deck and past the combat information center. It was no more. It had been blown apart, its forward bulkhead a shattered and shredded curtain of plasteel opening onto a nightmare vision of pure destruction.

The slug's deadly shroud of plasma and its escort of metal splinters spalled off Weapons Power Charlie had passed right through the center of the combat information center, with the blast wave smashing people and equipment with indiscriminate disregard. Now the compartment was a scene of appalling carnage and frantic activity as overworked medics and damage control crews struggled desperately to crash-bag the survivors and get them below and into regen.

Michael couldn't see much, and what he could see did not look good.

There was very little left of Ribot, Hosani, and Holdorf, only a few pathetic shreds of shattered flesh and pieces of heat-seared gray-black space suit slowly turning back to orange as combat chromaflage settings wore off. On the port side, he recognized Armitage, whose suit looked surprisingly intact, though the body was slumped over at an awkward angle. Armitage was being ignored by the medics, so she must be dead, Michael thought without emotion.

As he pushed past the shattered chaos that once had been *387*'s combat information center, he could see no sign of Kapoor. Must have been in the hangar, poor bastard, he thought.

It took all the willpower he possessed, but finally Michael was settled in the wardroom, itself badly damaged both by the slug as it had torn through one bulkhead en route to the combat information center and by the shock from Weapons Power Charlie going up on the other side of the heavily armored bulkhead. Thank God for blast venting, Michael thought, and for the designers and engineers who had put it in *387*.

As Mother ran Michael through the tactical situation, his heart sank as his badly battered brain slowly came to grips with what was happening to *387* and, even worse, what was about to happen. With much of the ship's forward armor now stripped, most of her short-range laser capability destroyed, and her long-range lasers degraded by the loss of Weapons Power Charlie, even six missiles and their attendant decoy swarm would be a handful.

Despite the pain and after a careful look at the tactical plot, Michael knew instinctively what had to be done.

He commed Chen. *166*'s skipper was the boss now that Ribot was gone, so it would be his call.

Jaruzelska watched the command plot, her thoughts a mix of professional satisfaction and private pity.

No matter how hard she tried, she could never take any pleasure from the spectacle of spacers dying in the pitiless hard vacuum of space, whether they were Hammers or not. She sat back in her chair struggling to get comfortable, her combat space suit heavy and uncooperative. Christ on the Cross, she thought, I'm getting too damn old for this sort of thing. She watched in silence as the task group's first rail-gun salvo finished its 150,000-kilometer journey to drop a hailstorm of platinum/iridium death onto the Hammer's fixed defenses and the hapless ships of Rear Admiral Pritchard's flotilla as they struggled to get going.

Jaruzelska hissed through clenched teeth as the slugs smashed home, the surface of Hell-8 disappearing behind a roiling, churning mass of pulverized dirt. The Hammer ships, their shapes sharply black against massed stars, were spewing clouds of ceramsteel and reactive armor into space.

"Caught the bastards asleep, Martin." There was no triumph in Jaruzelska's voice.

Her chief of staff nodded somberly. "True. But I doubt that even our ships could get going from a cold start in ten minutes, never mind four."

"God, is it only four minutes?" To Jaruzelska it felt like hours.

Oblivious to all else, Jaruzelska watched as the damage assessments flowed in. If she didn't think too much about the human cost of it all, the news was good. The heavy cruisers *Verity* and *Integrity* and the light cruisers *Cordoba* and *Ca-*

mara had been damaged but were still assessed as combat-effective. The heavy escort *Titov* had been hit hard and probably was combat-ineffective. So, she thought, it's really started.

"Sir, priority vidlink from *166*. Will you take it?"

"Of course."

Two seconds later the vidlink connected.

"Jaruzelska."

The tortured face of Lieutenant Chen filled her neuronics as he made his request for help. Jaruzelska reviewed with mounting horror the damage and threat assessments commed through to the flag AI by *166* and *387*.

"Chen, okay. Stop. I'll do it," she said, cursing herself for losing sight of the big picture to such an extent that she had forgotten the unequal struggle being waged by two of her ships. It was a classic example of why people were still in command, not AIs.

Her ships, her people, her responsibility.

She wasted no time, and in seconds the task group's massive laser batteries had switched away from the *New Dallas* and the *Shark* to fill the void between the two light scouts and the onrushing missile salvo with a lethally focused curtain of light. The lasers first blinded and then shredded the missiles into pieces as their microfusion plants were turned into spectacular balls of rolling white-yellow light.

The threat to *166* and *387* was over.

With a final prayer that the two light scouts would get home safely, Jaruzelska turned her attention back to the Hammer ships.

As the cruisers switched their heavy antiship lasers back to *New Dallas* and *Shark,* the next round of damage assessments scrolled across Jaruzelska's neuronics.

Titov was confirmed destroyed, the ship having erupted in an enormous ball of flame, probably as a result of a direct hit on her main engine fusion plant as it powered up to get the ship under way. The flotilla base's fixed missile batteries and phased-array missile control radars had almost all been destroyed. *Verity, Integrity, Cordoba,* and *Camara,* no change: damaged but combat-effective.

The news from Hell Central was even better.

The administrative center of the Hell system was lightly defended and stood no chance against the four heavy and two light cruisers of Commodore Molefe's task group, its fixed defenses wiped out in the first seconds of the attack. Two Hammer light scouts unfortunate enough to be caught alongside had fared no better. They had disintegrated as rail-gun slugs had ripped them apart, their fusion plants erupting in huge secondary explosions to send two shattered hulks spinning off into space. As they tumbled away, the hulls began to spit out a pathetically small cluster of life-pods, their characteristic double-pulsed orange strobes winking like demented fireflies; the international distress band was busy with radio beacons pumping out cries for help.

"Flag, flag AI. *Shark* combat-ineffective."

"Flag, roger." The light cruiser *Shark;* that was good. *New Dallas* could ill afford to lose her and her firepower. And it was a surprise. For all the awesome power of antiship lasers, they did not have a high kill probability against ships as large as light cruisers. Too big, too much armor, and, in this case, at 320,000 kilometers getting very close to the maximum effective range of the system. But the *Shark* had been turning, and the task group had been able to catch her side on where her armor was thinner. Good laser beam formation and tight coordination had done the rest. And for that she had the *387* and the *166* to thank, a debt of gratitude she hoped they would survive long enough to be repaid.

Jaruzelska sat back to watch the arrival of her second rail-gun salvo.

The Hammer's last missile attack disintegrated around Michael and his scratch command team.

With *387*'s short-range lasers largely inoperative and its chain guns overwhelmed, a few of the missile fragments made it through. The laser-shredded, heat-warped remains of the Hammer's heavy missiles and their decoys smashed into *387* at over 280,000 meters per second, their kinetic energy strong enough to punch deep gashes in the ship's armor. The ship's hull shuddered as the last of its battered and torn reactive bow armor struggled to protect the inner hull.

But finally all was quiet, and for the first time in what seemed like hours the plot showed no immediate threats to the battered hulk that was *387*. Michael slumped back in his seat, so tired that he wanted to crawl somewhere quiet and sleep. He forced himself back to the task at hand.

"Command, Mother. *Shark* combat-ineffective."

Michael sat up. "Command, roger. Put it up."

Michael and his team watched in awe as the holocams zoomed in on the huge bulk of the light cruiser *Shark,* one of the Hammer's newest warships. Its bottomless black shape was riven along one side by a long gash, venting ship's atmosphere to space; the humid air turned instantly to an ice cloud that was visible in *387*'s low-light holocams as a scintillating plume writhing its way into nothingness. Then, as Michael watched, a secondary explosion racked the stricken ship, a huge cloud of yellow-red plasma boiling out of the hull.

"Jesus," Michael muttered, suddenly conscious that he had a ship to command, a ship to get out of Hell nearspace with all onboard. It was now his personal responsibility to bring them to safety.

"Mother, Command. Main laser battery power status."

"Seventy-five percent. I've switched targeting back to *New Dallas,* and *166* has done the same. We're on a stern-crossing vector, so the angle of attack is very good. I am rerouting power from propulsion and will have both lasers back to 100 percent shortly."

That was what Michael wanted to hear, and with the much simpler and more straightforward tactical situation firmly in Mother's capable hands, he turned his mind to what had to be done to get *387* out of its current mess. First, he needed to talk to Chen, now senior officer of a very battered two-ship task group. Second, he needed an XO to look after getting the ship jump-worthy. Then he needed to make sure that Cosmo Reilly was getting on top of the enormous job of producing a ship capable of getting them home safely.

The comm to Chen was short and sharp, and Chen's plan was simple: Keep lasers on *New Dallas* for as long as they could, make *166* and *387* jump-worthy, and then get the fuck out of the Hell system as soon as possible.

Direct orders from Admiral Jaruzelska, Chen said, and Michael saw no reason to argue. In the meantime, Chen was bringing *166* alongside to get his medics onboard to help clear *387*'s backlog of casualties.

After a brief pause to watch as *387*'s and *166*'s lasers reignited the glowing red speck on *New Dallas*'s stern just outboard of her starboard heat dump, Michael commed the medics to expect help any time now. Then he commed the next most senior person left alive in the chain of command and, effective immediately, his new XO, Chief Harris from Warrant Officer Ng's team, to meet him in the surveillance drone hangar.

Mother commed Michael as he and Chief Harris started their survey of the battered wreck that was *387*.

"Command, Mother."

"Command, go ahead."

"Patch neuronics into primary holocam."

"Roger, patching."

Mother didn't need to tell him where to look. What he saw staggered him.

What had been just a small, dull red speck, a mere pin-prick on the vast expanse of *New Dallas*'s stern, had grown in the space of only a few minutes into a searingly bright spot. Even as Michael watched, the spot began to spew a small jet of plasma, molten metal, and debris out into space as the ships' lasers chewed their way remorselessly into the hull. Shit, Michael thought. He was seeing ship's atmosphere venting to space.

"By Jesus, their hull integrity's breached," he said. Michael could hardly breathe, the tension of the moment gripping his heart like an iron band. He had trouble believing what he was seeing, but something deep inside told him there was more to come.

"Mother, I have a feeling about this. I want everyone who can to watch."

"Roger."

When the end came, it came horrifyingly fast. In a matter of seconds, the jet of material pouring out of the hole in *New Dallas*'s stern exploded into a searing plume of incandescent gas hundreds of meters long as the lasers finally broke through deep into the ship's hull.

And then, in a single searing flash, the antiship lasers finally connected with something big, and the entire starboard quarter of the huge ship erupted in a massive explosion. Its force punched *New Dallas* into a slow, tumbling stern-over-bow spin, furious jets of reaction mass spewing fore and aft as maneuvering systems struggled to bring the heavy cruiser back under control.

Mother provided the commentary this time. "According to the TECHINT briefings we've been given, there's an auxiliary fusion power plant aft of the propulsion power compartments that feeds the after rail-gun batteries. I think that's what's gone up. She won't be destroyed, but she will be combat-ineffective for a while until they sort things out."

Michael could hardly speak, wishing that Ribot and all the other *387*s could have been there to witness something that would go down in the record books.

Chen commed him.

"We did it, Michael, we did it."

"Hard to believe, sir. But by God, we've paid a price." Michael stopped, choked with emotion.

"You did. I'm calling a halt. It's time we got jump-worthy and went home. And Michael!"

"Yes, sir?"

"You're *387*'s skipper now, so for fuck's sake stop calling me 'sir.' It makes me nervous. Call me Bill," Chen said, his voice soft with compassion.

Michael managed a laugh. "Sorry, sir—er, Bill."

"And one more thing, Michael. Get yourself to the sick bay. You need attention."

"All in good time. There are things I need to do first."

Flanked by her senior staff, all standing dumbstruck, Vice Admiral Jaruzelska stared open-mouthed at the holovid.

She'd known that *387* and *166* had kept up their laser attack on *New Dallas* but had tucked that information away in the back of her mind, where she parked stuff that wasn't significant, bits and pieces that didn't matter in the grand scheme of things for which she was responsible.

Therefore, it took a good long time before she and the rest of the flag staff believed what they were seeing: a huge ship slowly falling out of the line of attack, the massive explosion on her starboard quarter pushing her into a slow spiraling spin to nowhere.

And then the cheers from the ship's company of *Al-Jahiz* and from her own flag staff drove home the extent of what the two little ships had achieved. "By God, that was one for the record books," Jaruzelska muttered, disabling a ship hundreds of times their size. Finally, order prevailed and the flag staff turned their attention back to the rest of the battle now under way across hundreds of billions of cubic kilometers of Hell nearspace. The command plot was now showing the Hell nearspace component of Operation Corona in its entirety. Along with the two heavy assault forces tasked with reducing the flotilla base, Hell Central, and any warships unlucky enough to be on station to dust, the command plot now tracked Task Group 256.3, under the command of Commodore Pinto in the heavy cruiser *Repudiate* together with four heavy patrol ships as they ran in on Hell-5, one of the three moons holding those of *Mumtaz*'s passengers and crew who had not been sent to Eternity.

Much farther out, Commodore Yu Genwei in the heavy cruiser *Ulugh Beg* and the fourteen other ships of Task Group 256.4 had dropped out of pinchspace on schedule and were tracking in toward three of Hell system's outer moons. Hell-16 and Hell-18 held the rest of the *Mumtaz*ers, and the third, Hell-20, held the overly trusting and no doubt thoroughly disillusioned hijackers of the *Mumtaz*.

Satisfied with the big picture and after a final check that the Hammer forces in orbit around the system's home planet of Commitment were still showing no signs of moving, Jaruzelska collected her thoughts. "Flag AI, flag. Message to the captains and crews of *DLS-387* and *DLS-166*."

Graham Sharp Paul

She paused for a moment, conscious that what she said would go down in history and wanting to get it right. Not for her own sake but for the sake of those who needed to understand, to know at what a terrible price the freedoms long enjoyed by the Worlds came.

She took a deep breath. "In the face of appalling odds, crippling damage, and severe casualties, your unrelenting attack on vastly superior forces is in the highest traditions of the Federated Worlds Space Fleet. With you, we mourn the loss of your comrades. The ultimate sacrifice they have made to protect the freedoms we all hold so dear will never be forgotten. I and every other member of Battle Group Delta salute you all. Signed, A. J. Jaruzelska, vice admiral, Federated Worlds Space Fleet, Commander, Battle Group Delta."

Jaruzelska braced herself for what was to come as she counted down the seconds to the arrival of what the flag AI assured her would be the first and last missile salvo launched at her ships from the shattered flotilla base.

Jaruzelska hadn't much enjoyed missile engagements with the Hammer the last time around and didn't expect to now. It had been nearly twenty years since she'd been shot at seriously by the bastards, and she wasn't looking forward to repeating the experience, a view shared by her chief of staff as he exercised his authority to shut down the excited chatter and get the flag staff to focus on what came next.

"All stations, command. Missile salvo inbound. One minute."

Only half-aware of what she was doing, Jaruzelska hunched down in her seat and struggled to bring her breathing under control, if only to give her fogged-up visor a chance to clear. As always, her space suit was uncomfortable, the helmet neck ring heavy on her shoulders as she watched the massive attack make its way inexorably toward them.

Jaruzelska completely approved of Captain van Meir's caution in going to full suits. Unlike some heavy cruiser captains, the *Al-Jahiz*'s skipper insisted that visors be closed and suit checks completed as an attack became imminent. Heavy cruisers rarely depressurized for combat. They were too big and too tough, and the loss of personal communication was too keenly felt, particularly by command teams under pressure. But not shutting up suits as an attack approached risked the lives of anyone caught in a compartment suddenly open to hard vacuum.

As Jaruzelska checked and rechecked that nothing had been overlooked, the tactical plot showed an ugly and menacing sight.

The flag AI's latest estimate was that there were upward of 750 Sparrowhawk missiles in the attack, though based on what she'd seen so far, Jaruzelska thought that the AI's assumptions about Hammer missile availability were too pessimistic. She snorted dismissively. The Sparrowhawk was so old that it used hypergolic fuels for its launch stage, for God's sake. But it didn't matter who was right. They'd soon find out one way or the other. What really mattered was how well the task group's sensors had separated the missiles from the myriad decoys and jammers sent along to confuse, baffle, and divert the attention of the antimissile defenses.

If the task group got that right, they'd come through this pretty much unscathed. If they didn't . . .

After a quick check that everything on the command plot was as it should be, Jaruzelska forced the grim prospect of a successful Hammer attack out of her mind as she turned her attention back to the tactical plot.

The Hammer had adopted what the missile attack tacticians called a standard doughnut formation, or do-form. The doughnut formation was exactly what it sounded like. After the launch and second stages burned out, the missiles would open out into a thick ring of missiles around an open center, with the attack axis running right through the middle of the hole. As the range shortened, the missiles would fire their third-stage maneuvering engines to collapse the doughnut inward onto the Fed ships, accelerating fiercely as they closed. The do-form was standard Hammer tactics for anti-starship missile attacks, and Jaruzelska was not surprised to see it coming at her. It was exactly what the THREATSUM had predicted. Well done, boys and girls at Fleet intelligence, she thought.

That was fine up to a point. They had simmed such attacks to death, so Jaruzelska had little to do but sit back and watch as her warships closed in to a tight, closely packed ring, the ships' heaviest armor facing outward at the approaching missiles. In a missile-only attack, it was a good defensive formation, although it took only one ship in the ring to fumble its defense and missiles would slip past to smash directly into the thin upper armor of ships in the rest of the ring. Not for nothing was the formation considered a great test of mutual trust, Jaruzelska thought.

But despite all the sims, facing one for real was a very different matter, as the fist of fear and tension that gripped her stomach proved.

All of a sudden, the tactical plot erupted as the Hammer missiles reached the maximum effective range of the task group's medium-range area defense missiles. In seconds, the command plot was thick with tracks as missiles streaked out, eating up the 50,000-kilometer gap at better than 330,000 meters per second.

Barely more than two intensely frightening minutes later and with hundreds of missiles and countless decoys and jammers expended, the Hammer attack was over.

But not without cost.

A power failure on an overloaded weapons power fusion plant deprived *Damishqui* of an entire battery of close-range defensive lasers just as flag AI handed over two Hammer missiles that somehow had made it through the outer defensive cordon wrongly classified as decoys, and as such well down the pecking order, for the attention of *Damishqui*'s close-in weapons. The belated efforts of *Damishqui*'s chain guns had been too late to destroy the missiles, and despite her enormous bulk, *Damishqui* had shuddered as the first missile hit home, the armored warhead combined with the missile's massive kinetic energy punching effortlessly through the upper armor, cutting right through the ship before venting its fury to space. The result was nine compartments breached, four dead, and twenty-seven injured, but no mission-critical systems degraded. The second missile had scraped through, impacting *Damishqui*'s bows at a shallow angle almost exactly where the armor was thickest. Apart from an enormous gouge across *Damishqui*'s hull, the damage was minimal.

Two missiles made *Al-Jahiz* suffer, though not close to the extent to which *387* and *166* had suffered. Losses on that scale in a ship the size of *Al-Jahiz* would have been unthinkable.

With its warhead's circuitry fried by lasers and a close-range antimissile missile ripping its third stage apart in a brilliant flash of blue-white, the tattered fragments of a single Hammer missile had squeezed past the task group's defenses to crash into *Al-Jahiz*'s bow armor. But the second missile got a better result.

A serious datastream error allowed the missile to get lost in the flood of data being handled by the task group's AIs, an error that in theory couldn't happen but did, one of the hazards of volume defense using laser-based high-speed datastreams to shuffle information between ships. The missile slid down a gap between *Zuhr* and *Searchlight* before crashing into *Al-Jahiz,* the warhead reaching into the ship to destroy an auxiliary fusion plant, with the massive explosion shaking *Al-Jahiz* bodily as the blast vented to space. A few anxious moments followed until the warship's damage control crews sealed off the damage and reported no mission abort problems. Considering the enormous forces unleashed when a magnetic plasma containment bottle ruptured, casualties were relatively light at nine dead and sixty-six injured.

As Jaruzelska ran her eyes across the final damage assessments, she was relieved to see that the rest of the task group had gotten off lightly. Any missiles that had made it past the area antimissile defenses had been ripped apart by the carefully crafted layers of close-in point defense weapons systems, short-range missiles, then antimissile lasers, and finally, for last-ditch defense, chain guns. Apart from *Blue-*

fish, which had lost its long-range search radar to an inert missile, the only damage suffered was from missile fragments chewing up small sections of hull armor.

The Hammers' next effort turned out to be a total waste of ordnance. Close to half a million rail-gun slugs fired from extreme long range in three separate salvos gave the flag AI enough time to calculate vectors to enable the task group to slide effortlessly out of the way. In the end, it was all a bit of an anticlimax. The relief in the flag combat data center was reflected in a sudden upsurge of nervous chatter as the task group maneuvered to allow the slugs to pass harmlessly clear.

As the task group moved relentlessly in, Jaruzelska sat and watched, grim-faced and silent, as her attack ground the Hammer forces into dust. It didn't take long, and then it was all over. Rear Admiral's Pritchard's two bases and his twenty-strong flotilla were no more, their only monuments blackened, slowly tumbling wrecks of ships. Hell nearspace was thick with the orange anticollision lights of rescue and recovery craft as they started the long process of gathering in the scores of lifebots spewed into space by the stricken ships.

What came next would be the Hammer's last throw of the dice, a moderately serious missile attack compared to their first effort, which even she would call serious. Jaruzelska's neuronics scrolled through the list of incoming attacks, The report showed seven missile salvos on their way in from the *New Dallas* task group, thousands of missiles in all. They wouldn't be as easy to avoid as the rail-gun swarms had been. Jaruzelska sucked her teeth.

The command plot was not a pretty sight as it tracked the onrushing salvos.

Not for the first time that day, Jaruzelska cursed her luck that five Hammer heavies had chosen that morning to drop in-system. In all the sims they had done, it was not far off the worst-case scenario, and it was only the desperate attack by *387* and *166* that had diffused the threat they posed. Also, they carried the new Eaglehawk antistarship missile, not obsolete Mohawks. By Fed standards, the Eaglehawk was still a relatively crude piece of engineering, but it was a big improvement on its predecessor. It was faster, had a much improved terminal guidance system, had good antijamming capability, and was topped with a high-gain shaped-charge warhead: a very nasty piece of work and definitely not to be taken for granted.

But there was some good news.

The salvos were well separated and minutes apart. There was only one threat axis, and Hammer ship-launched missiles had no better off-bore capability than did Fed ship-launched missiles. That meant Jaruzelska could place her sixteen cruisers in a loose wall, the ships in two tiers in line abreast, bows and bow armor facing the missiles coming at them but positioned close enough to provide overlapping fields of fire even if the Hammers had been smart enough to focus their salvos onto one ship or maybe two. If the Hammers went for two ships, and that was the flag AI's prediction based on what she'd observed so far, that left plenty of firepower in reserve. The greatest risk was that the Hammer would be smart enough to go for only one of the light cruisers and lucky enough to pick one that she had been stupid enough to leave exposed and unsupported on one flank.

That was something she had no intention of doing.

"All stations, command. Missile salvo inbound. Two minutes."

"Here we go. A small one to get us started and then some serious stuff," Jaruzelska muttered.

And then, in a flash, *Verity*'s missiles were upon them, every one targeting *Al-Jahiz* as she rode at the center of the task group. But the combined firepower of sixteen cruisers was more than enough to rip the missiles out of space, leaving *Al-Jahiz* to be troubled only by scattered fragments of missile debris, with the impacts triggering only tiny puffs of reactive armor.

Jaruzelska settled her breathing down. Her turn now, she thought, and a short pause in the action while her missiles fell on the unfortunate ships of the *New Dallas* group.

"Flag, flag AI. Missile salvo on *New Dallas* group in one minute."

"Flag, roger."

Jaruzelska watched as the missiles from her ships, their arrival carefully timed and their final vectors orchestrated to stretch and overwhelm the defenses of their targets, did what they had been sent to do.

For a brief few seconds, the holovid was filled with brilliant white flashes as the Hammer ships' close-in defenses reached out to destroy the early arrivals before the sheer weight of numbers allowed missile after missile to smash home, burying warheads deep into armor. Plasma jets reached inside until one by one hulls were ripped open, spilling debris and molten metal into space. The crippled *New Dallas* was the last to go, but eventually, for all her enormous size, the numbers were against her and she, too, succumbed.

Jaruzelska felt sick as she watched.

It had to be done, and she had no doubts about doing it. In any case, the Hammer was still trying to do to her what she had done to the unfortunate *New Dallas* and its task group. But it was still butchery, and she didn't have to like it.

"All stations, command. Missile salvo inbound. Two minutes."

And so it started again, only this time the salvos were larger, and just as the flag AI had predicted, all were targeted on just two ships. The first three salvos were aimed at *Damishqui,* and the last three at *Al-Jahiz,* though Jaruzelska and the flag AI could find no logical reason why they had been picked other than that they rode in the center of the task group. But the missile attacks were doomed to failure; the enormous defensive firepower of sixteen cruisers was simply too much to overcome.

Then the Hammer attack was spent. After more than half a million rail-gun slugs and thousands of missiles, it was all over. Jaruzelska settled down with little more to do than watch as the four task groups responsible for the rescue of the *Mumtaz*'s passengers and crew swept in on their targets.

As the order to relax visors came through, Jaruzelska leaned back in her suit and squirmed her body around to try to relieve a persistent itch in the small of her back. She hoped that there would be no more surprises like *New Dallas*.

* * *

Jaruzelska cursed the Hammer for its willingness to sacrifice good ships and spacers for no possible gain. Unbelievably, Commitment had dispatched the heavy cruiser *Ascania* and the heavy escort *Perez*. Picked up by surveillance drones in orbit around Commitment, the two ships jumped out of pinchspace directly into Jaruzelska's missile salvos.

She had taken no pleasure in what followed. It was far too close to cold-blooded murder for her liking. The two Hammer ships never had a chance.

Still struggling to set up after the drop, the Hammers saw the missiles coming only when it was far too late to do anything effective. The space around the two ships turned into a blazing mass of defensive laser fire, with missiles and chaingun fire clawing at the Merlins as they raced in, the sheer size of the attack overwhelming the Hammer ships' tracking and fire control systems. The space around the two ships sparkled with the red-gold blooms of their few successes.

Ascania took the brunt of the attack. Close to a hundred Merlin antistarship missiles slipped past her defenses, hitting home in the space of only two seconds. *Perez* did better but not well enough, absorbing forty-two direct hits, a nearly impossible number for a cruiser to deal with, never mind a heavy escort. The two doomed ships heaved as nose cones of vanadium/tungsten-hardened steel cut deep before explosive warheads unleashed a storm of white-hot gas and shrapnel that scoured the life out of every compartment; the hapless crews were incinerated where they sat.

Sickened, Jaruzelska watched as the warheads finally found what they were looking for: the fusion plants that powered the ships' propulsion and weapons systems. The appalling energy within them was unleashed as the magnetic bottles containing the fusion plasma gave way, successive blasts ripping huge holes in the sides of the two ships.

"Abort remaining missile salvos," Jaruzelska said flatly. The butchery was done.

Jaruzelska rubbed her face wearily. She now had status reports from all of her subordinate commanders. Thankfully, they'd gotten what they'd come for: the 158 passengers and crew taken from the *Mumtaz* and 22 of the 30 hijackers. The rest were dead. And she'd had the pinchcomm from Rear Admiral Kzela confirming the successful recovery of the *Mumtaz*ers marooned on Eternity.

Could have been a hell of a lot worse, she thought, though the price paid by *387* had been far too high. But considering that the premission sims had shown a strong chance that Battle Group Delta would lose at least one major fleet unit with heavy casualties, they had been lucky. She shivered. With only a pair of heavy cruisers close to any one of the battle group's four drop points, the losses could have been even worse. Still, the only real surprise had been the *New Dallas* and the ships of her task group. Thank God they'd dropped well short and, even more important, that *166* and *387* had been there to lure them into turning away for those critical few minutes as the battle group dropped.

But that didn't help *166* and *387,* which were still a good two or more hours away from being jump-capable. Jaruzelska had no intention of leaving them alone in Hammer space. A minute's consideration and she knew what she would do. She'd keep *Al-Jahiz* and *Sina* together with *Crossbow* and *Bombard* back in support of *166* and *387* until they jumped.

For everyone else, it was time to go home.

Thursday, November 19, 2398, UD
Offices of the Supreme Council for the Preservation of the Faith, City of McNair, Commitment Planet

Merrick had been dragged from sleep by the news of the Feds' attack on Hell, and it had taken him only a few sleep-befuddled seconds to work out precisely why they were doing what they were doing.

From that moment on, he knew he was a dead man.

Desperately, he scoured his mind to work out some way, any way, of surviving the storm that was about to break over his head, but there was none. He'd gambled, risking everything he'd had to play with, and the gamble had failed. That was it, and there was no way back, no way out.

Now the moment of judgment had come, and Merrick could do nothing but sit at the Council table and await the executioner's ax. He would at least go with as much dignity as the circumstances allowed, fighting every step of the way as he'd done all his life.

The hastily convened meeting of the Supreme Council finally came to order as Polk and Albrecht hurried into the room. Close on their heels followed a disheveled and very anxious Councillor Kando the newly appointed councillor for intelligence. He was obviously half-panicked by the early hour and worried sick that something had happened that his department should have known about but hadn't. Merrick managed a wry smile in spite of himself.

Let the charade begin, Merrick thought as he looked down the table. Time for one last bluff. "Good morning, everyone. We are here to decide what immediate actions we must take in response to the unprovoked attack by the Federated Worlds on the Hell planetary system. I suggest we start by asking the councillor for war and external security for an—"

Polk held a hand up, stopping him dead. "I think not, Merrick, I think not."

Merrick couldn't stop himself, half rising to his feet as he spoke. "How dare you, Councillor Polk," he barked, "how dare you! I am the chief councillor, and you will address me as such or you will face the consequences."

Polk's voice was silky smooth, "I don't think so, Merrick. And what consequences might those be, anyway?" He waved a hand dismissively in Merrick's general direction. "I don't care what you think anymore. What we should do is hear from the councillor for foreign relations about what you have been up to behind the backs of the Council."

The assembled councillors could do nothing but stare open-mouthed. Something terrible was about to happen and they had absolutely no idea what it was. In the circumstances, all they could do was sit, their minds desperately trying to work out how best to survive the coming storm.

Claude Albrecht, the councillor for foreign relations, looked like he was trying to bring up a half-digested meal of broken glass. "Thank you, Councillor Polk. I have here," he mumbled, waving a single sheet of paper, "a diplomatic note from the Federated Worlds which I shall read to you in its entirety. It goes as follows."

Albrecht paused, his extreme discomfort obvious to all.

"Get on with it, you Kraa-damned bastard," Merrick muttered.

"To the Government of the Worlds of the Hammer of Kraa." There was another pause as Albrecht struggled to stop the quaver in his voice. With a visible effort, he got himself back under control.

"You are hereby served Notice that a State of Limited War is hereby declared and shall exist between the peoples of the Federated Worlds and the Worlds of the Hammer of Kraa with effect from 04:15 Universal Time on the nineteenth day of November 2398 Universal Date.

"In accordance with the New Washington Convention, you are hereby advised that the Affirmed Basis of this Declaration is the hijacking of the Federated Worlds Commercial Ship *Mumtaz*, registration number FWCS-700451-G, hereinafter known as the *Mumtaz*, on the eleventh day of September 2398 Universal Date for the express purpose of diverting its cargo to the terraforming of the planet Judgment-III, hereinafter known as Eternity. This illegal act was directed by Brigadier General Digby, Hammer of Kraa Marines, under the direct orders of Jesse Merrick, Chief Councillor of the Worlds of the Hammer of Kraa.

"Further, as required by the Convention, you are hereby advised that the objectives of the Limited War are the rescue of the passengers and crew of the *Mumtaz* from illegal detention on Eternity and various moons of the Revelation-II planetary system, the arrest of Brigadier General Digby and all other persons reasonably believed to be responsible for the planning and execution of the hijack to face trial in the courts of the Federated Worlds, the safe recovery of the *Mumtaz* and as much of its cargo as possible, and the safe departure of Federated Worlds forces from Hammer space. Upon the satisfactory achievement of these objectives or 07:00 Universal Time on the nineteenth day of November 2398 Universal Date, whichever is the later, the State of Limited War shall cease. Thereafter, a Demand for Financial Restitution shall be served.

"As required by the Convention, the Statement of Facts relating to this matter is attached to the Declaration, having been attested to by Corinne Bhose, Chief Observer of the Federated Worlds.

"Delivered to the hand of Tae Uk Yoon, Ambassador of the Worlds of the Hammer of Kraa to the Federated Worlds, at 04:05 Universal Time on the nineteenth day of November 2398 Universal Date by my authorized delegate, Giovanni Pecora, Federal Minister of Interstellar Relations.

"Signed, Reshmi Diouf, President, Federated Worlds, and dated the nineteenth day of November 2398 Universal Date."

Councillor Albrecht put the piece of paper down on the table. Probably Merrick's most committed supporter, he was the first to break the stunned silence that followed. His voice was harsh and his face grim as he looked up the table directly at Merrick.

"True or not, Jesse? True or not?"

Merrick sat there, unmoving.

Fear and frustration that the man on whom his life depended could have been so stupid drove Albrecht's voice into a cracked scream. "True or not? Tell me, Kraa-damn it! Is it true?"

"Answer the question, Merrick." Polk was unable to keep the satisfaction out of his voice.

The pause was a long one.

Finally, Merrick nodded once and sat back in his seat as if to say, Do what you want. He could have argued the point, tried to bluff his way out of it. Ten years earlier, he would have. Polk as usual overestimated the strength of his position even if it was probably strong enough to see Merrick at the bottom of a DocSec lime pit. No, he was tired, bone-tired, utterly spent. He really didn't care anymore.

Despite the fact that his own life had been put in jeopardy by the unilateral actions of the man at the head of the Council table, Albrecht's voice softened. He had always respected Merrick, and certainly the man had been better than most chief councillors of recent times. "Why, Jesse? Why? This is not how we do business. You should know that better than anyone."

Merrick waved a hand uncertainly. "I . . . I had my reasons, but I suspect that most of you don't want to hear them," he muttered as Polk looked on, his face hard with triumph.

Polk knew there would never be a better time, and he struck. "No, we don't, Merrick. You can explain it to Doc-Sec. I move that Jesse Merrick be removed as chief councillor and held for trial by the investigating tribunal. All those in favor."

The vote was a formality, with every hand in the air within seconds. Polk's lip curled in a half sneer; they had good reason to be quick, he thought, especially Merrick's men. He would take his time about it, but they would know the meaning of the word *fear* before many months were out.

The next step followed as surely as day follows night. As Merrick was bundled away, hands tied behind his back with the ubiquitous plasticuffs so loved by DocSec, with three heavily built troopers towering over the bent and broken figure, the councillors were not able to keep the shock and surprise from their eyes. Moments later, the motion to appoint Polk as chief councillor was carried unanimously.

Polk savored the moment for a long minute, the shattered remnants of Merrick's supporters silent and still, faces white with shock at the awful suddenness of it all. Then the orders flowed: the immediate announcement of Merrick's arrest for dereliction of duty, his replacement by Polk, full holovid coverage of the outrageous Fed assault, military funerals for those killed, an immediate purge of the senior ranks of the military, a board of inquiry to look into the disaster, and a warrant for the arrest of Brigadier General Digby.

If there had been any doubt about who was in control, there was none anymore.

Then the meeting was over. As councillors fled with unseemly haste, Polk moved to the chief councillor's chair at the head of the Council table. He sat down, exultant, his victory complete. The one order he hadn't given—to hunt down and exterminate every influential supporter of Jesse Merrick—could wait until tomorrow. He was inclined not to talk up Merrick's role in the Fed attack. He had a feeling that the more he could portray the Feds as unprincipled aggressors, the more pressure he could bring to bear on the insurgents who plagued Faith.

If the Feds thought that the fallout from the *Mumtaz* affair was now a matter for the diplomats, they'd badly underestimated Jeremiah Polk. After all, centuries of human history had shown that there was nothing better than an external threat when it came to crushing internal dissent. He didn't think he would have much trouble convincing his people— he liked that, "his people"—that the Feds' real agenda was the destruction of the Hammer Worlds. And even if it took ten years, he would make sure the Feds suffered for the humiliation they had heaped on the Hammer of Kraa.

The tiny fires lit by the news of Merrick's arrest and transfer to McNair State Prison smoldered for a while before bursting into life and spreading like wildfire.

Within the hour, people began to emerge onto the streets of the sprawling industrial suburbs to the south of McNair, small groups coalescing first into large groups and then into mobs, the anger building as leaders emerged to whip emotion into action. The message was the same, hurled out by angry and defiant men at angry and defiant people in hundreds of impromptu street meetings: Merrick was one of them, he'd come from the same mean streets as they had, and they'd be damned if they would allow an off-worlder like Polk to take over.

By late morning, smoke began to darken the sky over McNair, the air split with the sirens of DocSec convoys deploying to cordon off the city center. Their instructions were clear and simple: Stop the mobs converging on McNair State Prison. At any cost.

Thursday, November 19, 2398, UD
DLS-387 and DSLS-166, Hell Nearspace

Michael and the tattered remnants of his crew had worked like they'd never worked before.

With *166* alongside, the crash bags of the living had been ferried across to *166*'s sick bay and those of the dead had been transferred to external storage containers for the long ride home. Michael's heart was sick as his neuronics updated the casualty list as medics worked feverishly to stabilize the injured and get them into regen for the long ride to the base hospital. The toll kept mounting as the casualties from *387*'s combat information center were triaged.

The list was awful; Michael had to struggle to understand the enormity of the disaster that had hit *387*.

Ribot, Armitage, and the rest of the officers except Cosmo Reilly were all gone. Strezlecki, Leong, Carlsson, and Athenascu were gone. Ng was gone. Most of the combat information center crew, gone. Half the galley crew, unlucky enough to be caught at their damage control station in the cross-passage just outside the combat information center, gone. The entire crew of *387*'s lander, *Jessie's Hope,* gone. Two engineers working on a trivial problem with Weapons Power Charlie's local AI as it went up, gone. There'd barely been enough of them left to put in a coffee cup.

Chief Kemble interrupted. "Command, sick bay. We're done here, sir, and *166* is almost finished with our overflow. I've commed you the final casualty list: twenty-eight dead, sixteen seriously injured, but according to the regen AIs, they'll all be okay, though I'm still a bit worried about Biene-

felt and one of Warrant Officer Ng's team, Petty Officer Gaetano. And twelve walking wounded, you included."

"Thanks, chief. Let me know if there's any change. A bad
business."

"It is, sir. Didn't think I'd ever see something as bad as this.
One more thing, sir. I know Mother's given up nagging you,
but you really must come down so we can take a look at you.
You're not going to drop dead on us or anything, but you've
lost a lot of blood despite the best efforts of your suit, and
woundfoam's only good up to a point, especially if you won't
stay still. So, sir! For the last time or I'll send a team to get
you, sick bay now!"

Michael had to laugh at Kemble's earnest firmness. "All
right, all right. Just give me ten minutes. I need to see how
my new XO is doing with the ship repairs, then I've got to
talk to the skipper of *166,* and then I'll turn myself in.
Promise."

Kemble grunted. "If you can do all that in ten minutes,
fine. If not, I'm coming to get you."

"Yes, chief," Michael said meekly.

Harris and his team, more *166*s than *387*s, Michael noted,
were hard at it. Emergency generators were pumping white-
gray foamsteel to secure the footings of a crude framework
of steel crash beams that had been jury-rigged across the
huge hole blown out of *387*'s hull when Weapons Power
Charlie had lost containment. The hole now was jammed
with spacers welding steel bracing into place, the brilliant
blue-white light from the welding arcs bleaching the color
out of their orange suits.

"How's it going, chief?"

Harris waved an arm at the chaos around him. "It may not
look like it, sir, but we are getting there. This is the bad one,
but Mother's confirmed that the design of our repair is good
even if it looks like something kids dreamed up. She's happy
that the steel crash bracing will hold the foamsteel plug in
place. We've just got to get it all in there, and that's a slow
process, what with cutting the braces to size and all. The rest
aren't so bad. I never thought I'd have anything good to say

about a rail-gun slug, but at least they don't leave huge holes like this. *166*'s XO is down sealing the lander hangar now, and then we'll do the surveillance drone hangar. Another two hours, tops."

"Good. If you need anything, let me know."

"Sir."

As promised, Michael made it to the sick bay inside Chief Kemble's deadline after a short comm with Chen. The captain of *166* had sounded relieved to get a finish time for the repairs to *387*. Clearly, hanging around in hostile Hammer space was not something he wanted to do any more than Michael did. Cosmo Reilly had cleared *387* to maneuver, the final rail-gun slug shaking the main engines up a bit, but nothing that a bit of recalibration couldn't fix. Even better, Reilly and his team were well on the way to getting the ship jump-capable. With detailed designs for the emergency repairs uploaded to Mother, she should have the new ship mass distribution model completed within the hour. Terranova might be a distant 270 light-years away, but Michael was beginning to allow himself to believe that they'd be dropping in-system inside six days.

As he looked into the sick bay, the thought of going home almost overwhelmed him, and at that instant he would have given almost anything to be in Anna's arms, to be home with the people he loved. He'd felt physically sick when he saw that *Damishqui* had been hit, but thank God, Anna had not been on the casualty list. Please God, get her home safely, he prayed.

As the sick bay air lock safety lights switched to green, Michael firmly shoved all thoughts of Anna into a distant corner of his mind. Like it or not, he was the skipper of *387*, and he had a ship and what was left of *387*'s crew to get home safely first.

The instant he stepped into the sick bay, Chief Kemble and her team were on him like a rash. Michael had been dreading what he might find, so he was pleased to see that the crash bags with the ship's dead had been moved to the cargo containers for the trip home. The way he felt, it was bad enough just thinking about them. Seeing the physical evidence, seeing a line of crash bags, would have been too much.

It was the work of only moments for Kemble's team to strip Michael's suit off, leaving him standing in a ship suit saturated with a gruesome mix of reddish-black blood and bright green woundfoam. As he looked down at himself, he found it hard believe that he'd lost so much blood. He was drenched in it. But he stood only for a second until the accumulated insult and injury done to his long-suffering body finally overwhelmed him.

With a tired sigh, Michael's eyes rolled up into his head, and he crumpled like an empty sack to the deck.

Michael was swimming in a strange sort of pool, the water deep, thick, and red. Something heavy was holding him back.

Slowly, doggedly, he fought his way to the surface, and as he did, the everyday sounds of a ship began to seep into a head stuffed full of cotton wool. But eventually he made it, opening his eyes to see Chief Kemble leaning over him, her face a mixture of amusement and concern.

"Hello, sir. The AI said you were coming back to us."

"Try and keep me away," Michael mumbled, his mouth thick.

"That's what I said. Okay. How are you feeling?"

"Like shit. And sore all over."

Kemble nodded sympathetically. If it were up to her and the medical AI, she'd have had Michael in a regen tank immediately, but she wasn't going to waste her time asking. If her years in the Fleet had taught her anything, it was not to try to persuade a ship's captain to put self first and duty second.

"You will be, I'm afraid. You have very severe bruising to your lower back and ribs and a lot of tendon damage. That will account for most of the pain. You managed to break your nose, but not too badly, but the rest of the face is just bruised. The base hospital will take care of that and make it look pretty again. Your left leg is the real problem. It's a real mess,

and I'm not at all sure how you've even been able to walk.
Pity we didn't get to it a lot sooner. It's been sliced up pretty
badly, so the medibots have been busy putting it all back together again, and we've transfused repairbots in to try to repair the muscle and tendon damage. It's going to hurt like
hell, but it'll mend in time. You'll just need to go easy on it.
I've held off the painkillers until you surfaced, but we've
loaded you up with drugbots, so just comm them when the
pain gets to be too much."

Michael nodded as he tried to take it all in. All he knew
was that the longer he was awake, the more everything
seemed to hurt.

Kemble offered him a large beaker with pale blue fluid in
it. "Now drink this. We need to get you rehydrated. You'll
feel a lot better in a moment."

Gratefully, Michael brought the large beaker of fluid that
Kemble was holding up to his mouth, suddenly craving
every sweet drop. "More. Please."

Two more beakers later, Michael did indeed feel better.
Much better, in fact, to the point where as Kemble turned to
put the beaker back, he sat himself up. Wincing, he quickly
wished he hadn't, bruised ribs and back screaming in protest
as the movement pulled at torn ligaments and ripped muscles. Ignoring the pain, he swung himself off the bunk to
stand, swaying slightly, looking around for his suit, his left
leg sore and stiff under the plasfiber bandages. He commed
the drugbots to give him painkillers and sighed in relief as
the pain evaporated almost instantly.

"Hey, hey, hey," Kemble protested as she turned back and
saw what he was up to. "Where are you going, sir?"

Michael stared at her in astonishment. It had never occurred to him to do anything other than get back to work.

"Things to do, chief. What time is it?"

"Time? It's 08:20. Now get back on that bunk. That leg's
not good for much just yet."

Michael shook his head. "Chief, I'll get back on the bunk
if you swear to me that I'll do myself irreparable damage by
walking on it, but if not, then I've got things to do."

"No, I can't swear to it, but you'll see more of the inside of the base hospital than you'll like if you don't give the leg time to recover. As it is, you should be in regen. Moving it is going to undo a lot of what we've had to do."

"Sorry, chief, you'll have to forgive me. But I do promise to take it easy." And with that Michael, pleased to see that someone had thought to bring him a new one, was struggling to get a very uncooperative left leg into his space suit.

"Fuck's sake, sir. Let me give you a hand," Chief Kemble said resignedly. "And let me see if I can find you something to lean on."

The minutes dragged past, and Michael was acutely aware of the growing risk that the Hammer would finally get off their asses and do something about them.

Despite the best efforts of Commodore Kawaguchi's pinchcommsat killers, the Hammers clearly had a working pinchcomms data channel with Commitment, so a response had to be coming soon. But the work had been frustratingly slow as Harris and his teams struggled to fill the holes punched in *387*'s hull. The gaping void left by the failure of Weapons Power Charlie was proving to be a real problem as bracing, bracing, and more bracing was tap welded into place to try to give the foamsteel plug the strength it would need to hold back thousands of kilograms of air pressure.

Michael was smart enough to know that hassling Chief Harris wouldn't cut one second off the time needed to make *387* jump-worthy.

Foot up, as firmly instructed by Chief Kemble, he sat, surrounded by the shattered remnants of *387*'s command team, and watched the tactical picture on the holovid. The vectors marked the last three groups of ships left in Hammer space inching their way slowly forward, the seconds running down to Chief Harris's best estimate of when *387* would be jump-ready with painful slowness. Michael stared obsessively at the countdown timer in the bottom left-hand corner of the holovid, willing the digits to change faster with every ounce of willpower he possessed but without any effect. If anything, the damn things seemed to go more slowly.

It was a relief when Chief Harris interrupted his zombielike focus on the timer.

"Command, XO."

"Go ahead, chief."

"The team from *166* has completed testing the hangar breach, and it's 100 percent; with your permission, I'd like to return them to their ship. I'm sure Lieutenant Chen will be happy to have them back. I've got everyone I need."

"Make it so, chief. How's the rest going?"

"Pretty good, sir. The damage to the surveillance drone hangar has been sealed finally, and we are just running the ultrasonics across the plug to make sure there are no flaws, but so far it's looking good. Say another ten minutes and we should be done. I've sent the foamsteel generators up to the blowout from Weapons Power Charlie to get started up there. We've started to get the final bracing in place, so I'd say we're looking good for being jump-ready by 09:30 at the very latest. Should be earlier with a bit of luck."

"Well, the engineers have got everything right at their end, so earlier would be good, chief."

"Working on it, sir."

Thursday, November 19, 2398, UD
DLS-387, Hell Nearspace

Michael's heart lurched in shock at the news. For the first time that day, the Feds could expect some serious opposition.

The surveillance drones in orbit around Commitment had just reported the departure of twenty-three Hammer ships led by a heavy cruiser positively identified as the Hammer Warship *Bravery*. It had taken the Hammers an inordinately long time to get a proper response together, but finally they had. And contrary to plan, it looked like *387* would still be in Hammer space when the bastards dropped in-system.

"Damn, damn, damn," he muttered as he commed Mother

to run a formal threat assessment even as Jaruzelska ordered *166* and *387* to turn away from the threat.

Fear mixed with frustration in equal measures whipped his stomach into a mass of churning acid bile. *387* wasn't that far away from being ready to jump, and now this. Well, there had to come a time when the Hammers finally got their shit together, and maybe he should be grateful that it had taken them this long.

"Not what we wanted, sir," said Cosmo Reilly. The voice of *387*'s chief engineer was thick with concern as he and Michael watched Mother's threat assessment. Her conclusions were brutally simple. The last Fed ships in Hammer space were very badly exposed, and their destruction was assured if they didn't jump into the safety of pinchspace soon. The two heavy cruisers *Al-Jahiz* and *Sina* were beginning to run short of missiles. Even with the *Crossbow* and *Bombard* in support and assuming they had time to get two salvos away, the four ships could put only 1,300 missiles down the throats of the Hammers. That wouldn't be enough even if they got lucky and timed a rail-gun salvo to hit the Hammers as the missiles closed in.

Not that rail-gun slugs fired across hundreds of thousands of kilometers at a drop datum of extremely doubtful accuracy would make the Hammers sweat. Things were not looking good.

Michael looked across at Reilly. "Are you thinking what I'm thinking, Cosmo?"

"I'm afraid I am, sir. We can't hold everyone back just to save our skins."

Michael nodded, the fear and frustration turning to fatalistic resignation. He'd been through too much to waste energy on things he couldn't control. "I'll make the call. You go. Do what you can to speed things up."

Reilly nodded. He paused for a moment, patted Michael on the shoulder, and left without another word.

Michael took a deep breath as he put the comm through to Chen.

"Bill, I'm not going to fuck around on this. You cannot wait for *387* any longer. Mother tells me that you'll be ready to jump any moment now. So jump when you're ready. For God's sake, don't wait."

Chen's tortured face filled Michael's neuronics.

"Michael. I can't do that. *387* is one of my ships now."

Michael laughed. He hadn't expected Chen to behave any differently. "Thought you'd say that, so it's only fair to let you know that my next call is to Admiral Jaruzelska."

Chen couldn't quite conceal the faint flush of relief that crossed his face. "Okay, Michael. Make the call. Your right as a captain in command."

"Go with God, Bill."

Michael put *166* out of his mind as he put the comm through to Jaruzelska. He didn't waste words as her face, gray-tinged with fatigue and stress, came up on his neuronics.

"Yes, Helfort."

"Admiral, sir. As you know, our battle damage is pretty severe, so we're going to be around for a while. Sir, I cannot allow the rest of the task group to be put at risk just on our account, so please, jump. We'll take care of ourselves. The Hammer is bound to drop short, and I've got full driver mass bunkers, so catching *387* will be hard for them."

Jaruzelska's eyebrows shot up as Michael spoke. As a rule, junior lieutenants were not in the habit of telling vice admirals what they would or would not allow. But on this occasion, she'd make an exception. Helfort was absolutely right. Sacrificing four capital ships for the sake of one badly battle-damaged light scout and its already depleted crew was not a sensible option. But in her heart she knew full well that abandoning *387* to the Hammer would be the right decision only if *387* survived. If it was destroyed, she would be known forever as the commander who left a defenseless ship to the Hammer. She took a very deep breath. So be it. The ability to make the hard decisions was why she was a vice admiral.

"I agree, Helfort. I'll comm orders to *166* to jump as soon as she's ready. I'll hold my ships back until we can get full missile and rail-gun salvos away, and then we'll jump. You'll be on your own then."

"Sir, I understand. It's the only sensible option. Let's do it."

Jaruzelska had to smile. Helfort might only be a junior lieutenant, but he had balls like titanium coconuts. Even better, he thought straight under pressure. She hoped to God he survived.

"Thank you, Helfort," she said wryly. "I do appreciate your endorsement."

Michael flushed as he realized that he'd been speaking to a full vice admiral rather more firmly than protocol allowed. "Oh fu— Uh, sorry sir. Shit. I, er—"

Jaruzelska cut him off with a smile. Her voice softened. "Enough, Michael. Do what you have to do and you'll get home safely. Go with God."

"Thank you, sir."

With the comforting presence of Jaruzelska and her ships gone, Michael had never felt so alone. Judging from the faces of his scratch combat information center crew, the rest of *387*'s crew probably felt the same way.

Jaruzelska's final efforts on his behalf had come to nothing. A coordinated rail-gun salvo from the four heavy ships had duly ripped through the Hammer's predicted drop point datum. The only small problem was that the Hammer commander, clearly no fool, had neutralized the salvos by dropping short and low and splitting his ships into two groups. The swarm was now just another forgotten entry in the knowledge base of space navigation hazards as it disappeared at 3.6 million kilometers per hour into the void.

The follow-up missiles were no more effective. Three salvos in all, they were too spread out, too small, and too far from the drop point to trouble the Hammer ships much. But worst of all was the fact that for once that day the Hammers seemed to know what they were doing. A good clean drop, warships well positioned, sensors up smartly, and their first salvo away quickly—all spoke of a commander who could be relied on to get things right.

Time was running out for *387* and fast, Michael thought, and the worst thing about it was the simple brutal fact that he personally could do absolutely nothing more to get *387* jump-ready. Chief Harris and his damage control teams were doing as much as any humans could do, and no amount of nagging from him would or could speed things up.

Michael was discovering that the hardest thing for any commander to do was nothing when that was the right thing to do.

"Command, Mother."

"Go ahead."

"Hammer forces redeploying."

"Roger," Michael said, now resigned to his fate. "They're going to try to box us in, I suppose."

"Confirmed."

Michael nodded. Mother had been driving *387* hard away from the Hammers, but in the end, they had the numbers, and now, with only one small target to focus on, the Hammer commander could afford to spread his net wide. That was exactly what he was doing, the holocams picking up the flaring of main engines as the Hammer ships began to open out.

"How much time?"

"Estimate thirty minutes. They'll have us enveloped then. I expect a single coordinated rail-gun salvo."

"To finish us off," Michael said, completing Mother's sentence for her. He commed Chief Harris, who took the news impassively. Michael successfully resisted an almost overwhelming urge to tell him to hurry up.

The minutes ticked by as *387*'s every change of vector was matched instantly by the Hammers, the deadly net closing inexorably around the fleeing ship. Michael toyed with the idea of surrendering to the Hammers but dismissed it almost as quickly as it had come. History showed that the Hammers never accepted such offers when they had the upper hand, and Michael was not going to give them the satisfaction of refusing. Now they had less than two minutes before the Hammers were in position. The Hammer ships already were turning to match bearings. Allowing five minutes' time of flight for the rail-gun salvo, and *387* had less than seven minutes to live.

"Command, XO." It was Harris, and Michael began to pray harder than he'd ever prayed before, his heart pounding in his chest as he struggled to steady his voice.

"Go ahead, chief," he said, barely able to squeeze the words out.

"Sir, we've finished. The hull is jump-worthy. The engineers are running the final numbers into the mass distribution model now, so it's up to them."

Relief flooded through Michael like a warm wave. "Chief, you are a fucking star. Oh, and thanks."

"Any time, sir, any time," Harris replied matter-of-factly.

"Okay. We might have to jump without the mass distribution model 100 percent right, in which case it might be a rough ride, so I want everyone and everything battened down real tight."

Michael grimaced. A rough ride. That was an understatement. If the navigation AI got the ship's mass distribution wrong by more than one part in a hundred thousand, *387* would never make it home. Where it would go, Michael had no idea, nor would the navigation AI. Nobody had ever come back from a badly set up jump, and for all he knew, *387* would tumble through pinchspace for eternity. He put that awful thought aside. He'd take his chances in pinchspace because one thing was sure: At least they might survive, whereas staying in Hammer space would be 100 percent fatal.

He commed Reilly and was not reassured by his chief engineer's worried face.

"Cosmo, just to let you know. We've got five minutes or so and—"

Mother's urgent tones cut across him. "Command, Mother. Multiple rail-gun launches from Hammer task group. Vector analysis confirms target *387*. Time of flight four minutes twenty-four. Probability of survival zero, repeat, zero."

Oh, sweet Jesus, Michael thought, so soon. "Cosmo, did you copy?"

"I did, sir."

"Okay. I'm going to jump anyway whether you're happy with the mass distribution model or not. We have to take the chance. But I'll leave it as late as I can. I'll execute a crash jump from here, so make sure everything's ready to go."

Cosmo's face seemed to crumple as he worked out that

387's survival now depended on him. He visibly caught his breath before replying.

"Well, sir, I guess that's all we can do. We're pretty close now, and I'll run the numbers as long as we can. If I don't see you again, it's been an honor."

"Same here, Cosmo. Same here. Command out."

Michael commed Mother to adjust vectors to set *387* up for a jump direct to Terranova, gave command authority to override the safety locks that in normal circumstances would never have allowed *387* to jump, and then sat back. He felt strangely calm as he commed his crew for the last time.

"All stations, this is the captain. We'll be jumping shortly, ready or not. It'll be rough, so hold on. May God watch over us this day. Captain, out."

Michael waited as long as he could, the wait agonizing as he watched the incoming Hammer attack remorselessly close in. Then he could wait no more. *387* jumped.

Five seconds later, the Hammer's massive rail-gun swarm ripped through a small knuckle of tangled and warped space-time, all that was left to mark *387*'s presence in Hammer space.

Under the arch of a velvety star-speckled sky of a beautiful Commitment night, high-intensity floodlights streamed into the execution yard, drenching the small group of Doc-Sec troopers in a harsh white glare.

On the other side of the yard from the firing squad, two men stood beside a slumped figure tied to the execution post, his orange prison coveralls drenched in blood.

The prison doctor looked up at the young DocSec officer standing impatiently in front of him and shook his head. With a muffled curse, the DocSec officer drew his pistol to put the finishing shot into the head of Jesse Merrick.

"Jesse Arthur Merrick. So die all enemies of the Peoples of the Hammer of Kraa."

The deed done, the DocSec lieutenant turned away, a sick feeling lying very heavy on his stomach. He knew full well that he might have signed his own death warrant with that single pistol shot. He could only hope that Polk stayed chief councillor long enough for the memory of Merrick to fade and for his part in the man's death to be forgotten.

Monday, November 23, 2398, UD
City of McNair, Commitment Planet

McNair had simmered for three days, a lethally unstable stew of sullen resentment flaring without warning into vicious brutality.

It had taken a declaration of martial law and the news that Merrick had been executed for crimes against the Peoples of Kraa before a major offensive by DocSec supported by marine light armor had been able to push the mobs roaming the streets back behind shuttered windows and locked doors.

With control reestablished, it was only a matter of hours before DocSec swung back onto the offensive, doing what it did best. Black-uniformed snatch squads fanned out across the riot-wrecked city in an endless stream of trucks. By midday, the city had been swept clean of anyone even remotely connected to Merrick's political machine. His once-mighty organization was destroyed as thousands of people were dragged out of their houses and thrown into trucks, the first step on the long road to some Kraa-forsaken labor camp if they were lucky or a DocSec firing squad if they were not.

DocSec didn't worry about just the human elements of the Merrick machine. Their orders were to destroy everything. Before the day was out, every Hammer of Kraa party office in McNair had been stripped down to bare furniture, with every file, every document, and every workstation ripped out and taken away for analysis.

Chief Councillor Polk had watched the progress reports with grim, silent satisfaction. Commitment in general and McNair in particular were the wellspring of Merrick's political strength, a source so ably exploited by Merrick during his long years at the pinnacle of Hammer political power. Well, Polk thought, not anymore, and this day's operations in McNair were just the start. The pustulant boil that was Merrick had been lanced, and his power base had been damaged seriously. Over the coming weeks anyone and anything even remotely capable of lending aid and succor to the Merrick/Commitment faction would be dealt with with the same deadly efficiency.

It was Polk's intention that there would be nothing left to challenge his authority by the time order was fully restored. If it took an ocean of blood and hordes of fatherless families for that goal to be achieved, that was the price that McNair and the planet of Commitment would have to pay.

Chief Councillor Polk was here to stay.

Thursday, November 26, 2398, UD
Space Battle Station 1, in Orbit around Terranova Planet

If Fleet protocol was any guide, it wasn't supposed to happen, but it did.

Throughout the vast bulk of Space Battle Station 1, work rapidly ground to a halt as word got around, the news spreading like wildfire. In a matter of only minutes, every holovid had been switched over to watch the incoming ship as it decelerated slowly in-system.

Now every living soul on SBS-1, from the commodore in command down to the lowliest spacer, was focused on the tiny flares of ionized driver mass as *387* dropped in toward the station, safely secured fore and aft by the salvage tugs that had rescued her shattered hull after it had dropped, spinning uncontrollably, out of pinchspace.

It seemed to take a lifetime, but finally, the tugs' main engines shut off and *387* was in position for her final approach. Slowly, the tugs began to roll *387* to line up her main hangar door for berthing. As they did, a shocked gasp swept through the station as the damage to the ship's hull became obvious. The white-gray patches of emergency foamsteel repairs stood out starkly against the deep blackness of the scout's hull; everywhere gashes and gouges had been torn, ripped, and punched into the ceramsteel armor. Then, as *387* made its final approach, the massive foamsteel-filled hole that seemed to take up almost all of the ship's starboard bow came into view.

"Holy Mother of God," breathed Commodore Perec, his morning staff meeting in ruins around him, the chairs around the conference room table pushed back as his staff unconsciously moved to stand in front of the holovid. Perec had been through the last war and had seen some pretty badly cut-up ships, but the only time he'd seen them this bad, they'd been complete write-offs.

Perec turned to his senior engineer, a tall gray-haired captain. "I don't believe it, Marta," he said. "How did they survive that?"

"By good engineering design, I'd say, Commodore," she replied, shaking her head in amazement. "She's been hit right above Weapons Power Charlie. Looks like the blast venting really does work."

Perec nodded. "Well, after all the ships we lost last time around from poorly contained fusion plants going up, they had to do something, and it's good to see that it really does work." He turned to the rest of his staff.

"This meeting's canceled. I'm going down to meet them."

As Perec strode from the room, nobody even noticed the fact that he was doing something unheard of. Commodores in command of space battle stations never met ships as small and insignificant as a light scout. They just didn't.

After a short pause as *387*'s cruelly torn lander was off-loaded into the care of the station's cargobots, the salvage tugs started *387*'s slow move in to berth. Her brilliant orange anticollision lights were the only signs that the scout was a operational warship and not just some battered and abandoned hulk.

* * *

Michael had received two vidmails that mattered.

One was from Anna, who, miracle of miracles, was already berthed and somehow had wrangled leave from *Damishqui* from 18:00. The second was from his father, reporting the imminent arrival home of his mother and Sam.

Michael sat in his makeshift combat information center bathed in a wonderfully warm glow of happiness. Surrounded by his scratch command team sitting incongruously on the cheerfully patterned chairs of the wardroom, Michael watched as the bulkhead-mounted holovid showed the meters running off as *387* made her final approach. As instructed by Chief Kemble and in no uncertain terms, Michael had his foot up as he tried hard not to keep thinking about Anna, though with little success.

None of them had much to do except keep an eye on things as the salvage tugs slowly and with infinite care maneuvered *387* alongside and then into one of the station's berthing stations. Hydraulic locking arms reached out from SBS-1 to hold the ship firmly on the pad that would frame and seal its entire hangar door.

"Command, Mother. Berthed."

"Command, roger. All stations, this is command. Hands fall out from berthing stations. Revert to harbor stations, ship state 4, airtight integrity condition zulu."

"Command, Mother."

"Yes, Mother?"

"Message from the station, Commodore Perec is on his way down."

Michael went pale. Somehow it had never occurred to him that anyone apart from the station's engineers would be interested in poor old *387*. "What? The commodore? Oh, shit. Tell the XO. We'll—"

Mother interrupted Michael's moment of panic at the thought of having to organize the ceremony that normally accompanied a commodore's visit, the scale of the crisis magnified in Michael's mind by a complete lack of notice and magnified again by Space Fleet's enduring love of and abiding commitment to ceremony.

"Command," Mother said patiently, "the commodore has

specifically instructed that there be no ceremony, and he'll wait until the medevac teams have gotten all the regen tanks off."

Michael whistled with relief. "Oh, ah. Right. Okay. Thank God for that. Warn Chief Harris anyway and get him to meet me down in the hangar. Oh, and by the way, enough of the 'command' stuff. We're alongside now, so it's Michael. Just Michael please."

"Yes, Michael."

Michael got painfully to his feet. By Christ, he was sore all over, and his leg was worse today. There was no use comming painkillers, as the drugbots had run out the previous night and he hadn't gotten around to getting more from Chief Kemble; that probably was the least smart thing he'd done all week. Add that to the list of things to do, he thought ruefully, still amazed at how much the captain of a ship had to stay on top of even with all the help that Mother provided.

Not that the routine things bothered him, not at all.

In fact, he quite enjoyed them. They could be listed, prioritized, and dealt with, each humdrum task a small reminder that there was an ordinary world out there somewhere.

No, it was the painful task of putting together the personal vidmails to the families of *387*'s lost crew. Every one had hurt more than he had ever thought possible, and though Michael did his best, working and reworking each one for hours, he never felt that they were right. In the end, sheer exhaustion, the million and one other things he had to attend to, and the stress of running a ship badly shorthanded had forced him to finish the job, well or poorly. With the forlorn hope that they might in fact be at least all right, he had commed them through to the station's next of kin support team and prayed for the best.

Michael finally made it to the hangar, white-faced and glistening with sweat from the pain of dragging an increasingly aching leg past the shattered wreck that had once been *387*'s combat information center and down two sets of ladders into the hangar. Without the lander, the huge space was echoingly empty, its deck a buzz of activity as station work crews carefully maneuvered the heavy and awkward regen tanks through the forward air lock door, down to the hangar deck, and out across the grav interface; the whole process was managed by a spiderweb of AI-controlled winches and lines.

Michael stood back out of the way in the door leading aft out of the hangar and into the power control room, the sight of the regen tanks bringing back to him what he'd lost, what he might lose even now. Despite Kemble's assurances that Bienefelt was indestructible, she was still worried about her, and it didn't escape Michael's notice that Kemble had watched like a hawk as Bienefelt's regen tank had left the ship. Don't die now, cyborg woman, Michael prayed, don't die.

"Michael, Mother."

"Go ahead, Mother."

"Warrant Officer Morgan and the casualty-handling team are here. He requests approval to commence transfers."

"Yes, tell them to go ahead. No, no . . . Wait."

Once the shock of having to cope with a visit by the resident commodore had faded, Michael's happiness at the thought of seeing Anna and knowing that Sam and Mom were safe had come flooding back. Now it disappeared in an instant, replaced by a feeling of dread that hollowed out his stomach. He was left with a sick, empty feeling, part loss and part fear. It didn't seem right that the people who had been such an important if short part of his life should leave the ship this way, unseen and unacknowledged, like so much cargo to be off-loaded.

"Mother."

"Yes, Michael?"

"How many more regen tanks to go?"

"The one going off now is the last."

"Okay. Tell the casualty-handling team this from me, and it's nonnegotiable. I want to know the name of each person before, and I mean before, they move them from the ship. Understood?"

"Yes, Michael."

"And I want them to wait. I'll tell them when to start, and please, ask them if they can arrange it so that Warrant Officer Ng is second to last off and then the captain."

"Understood. Stand by . . . The casualty-handling team confirms that's understood."

"Good. Okay. I want all of *387*'s crew in the hangar, now. No exceptions. There's nothing that can't wait, agreed?"

"Agreed, Michael."

"And get the external cameras to cover the transfers, please. Put the feed up on the hangar holovids."

"Will do."

Michael quickly commed the commodore, who had been waiting patiently but grim-faced outboard as the regen tanks came aboard his station in an awful procession.

"Commodore Perec, sir, Junior Lieutenant Helfort, acting captain in command, *DLS-387,* reporting."

"Welcome home, Captain. Request permission to come aboard."

"Please, sir, come aboard. That's the last of the regen tanks. But sir, I have a request. I'd like to muster my crew. My casualties are about to leave the ship, and I want to acknowledge that fact, so you'll have to bear with us for a while."

"My boy, it will be an honor to stand beside you. Coming aboard now."

Five minutes later Perec watched the pathetic remains of what was left of *387*'s crew and Warrant Officer Ng's covert operations support team, two ranks of gaunt-faced and hollow-eyed men and women, with the rocklike figure of Chief Harris out front fussing over the lines until they were just so.

Once he was satisfied, Harris called the crew to attention before turning to face Michael and, flanking him, Cosmo Reilly and Commodore Perec. Harris stepped smartly forward. His salute was textbook in its precision and timing. "Deepspace Light Scout *Three Eight Seven* present and correct, sir!"

Michael came to attention and returned the salute, desper-

ately trying to keep the weight off an increasingly painful
left leg. The hiss of a sharp intake of breath as a jagged stab
of agony shot up into his heavily bruised back and ribs was
not unnoticed by Commodore Perec. Michael was beginning
to rethink his decision to trust a left leg that was showing
every sign of giving up on him. Maybe he should have
brought Chief Kemble's makeshift cane along, after all, he
thought, even if it didn't feature anywhere in the dress code
for Space Fleet officers.

"Very good, chief." He paused to take a deep breath before
lifting his head high to look at the tattered remnants of his
crew full in the face.

"*387*s. There is nothing about this in the Manual of Space
Fleet Ceremonial. But when I thought about the people we'll
never see again, I just couldn't let them leave without saying
goodbye, and I was sure you'd feel the same. That's why I
wanted you all here. Let's not forget them."

Michael took another deep breath. "Mother, the casualty-
handling team can start."

They stood stiffly to attention, Michael calling out the
names one by one as the casualty-handling team with infinite
care and patience slowly unloaded *387*'s awful cargo. To
Michael, the terribly slow process as crash bags were extracted from the cargo bays seemed to take hours to complete. Tears ran openly down his face and the faces of every
one of his crew as the names of people who had been so
much a part of them were read out one by painful one.

Finally, there were only two names left for Michael to call.

"Warrant Officer First Class Jacqueline Pascale Maria Ng,
officer in command, Covert Operations Support Team
Twelve. Go with God."

The final, agonizing wait was almost more than Michael
could take, the pain in his left leg, now a mass of white-hot
agony, nearly impossible to bear. But then it was almost over
as the last crash bag was brought slowly out into the harsh
glare of xenon floodlights.

"Lieutenant Jean-Paul Gerard Augustine Ribot, captain in
command, Deepspace Light Scout *Three Eight Seven*. Go
with God."

As Ribot left the ship, his anonymous crash bag escorted by the two spacers, the bulky space-suited figure of Warrant Officer Morgan turned to make a stiff-armed but nonetheless regulation salute before silently following the heart-wrenchingly sad train of bright orange crash bags away into the darkness.

With a deep breath, Michael got himself under control. "Chief Petty Officer Harris!"

"Sir."

"Dismiss *Deepspace Light Scout Three Eight Seven*."

"Aye, aye, sir."

For a man well-known for his no-nonsense approach to life, Commodore Perec had been deeply moved, much more than he ever would have expected. As he'd watched in silence, he'd had to blink away the tears that had welled up in his eyes. The unadorned tragedy spelled out by the terrible procession of crash bags had hit him hard.

But now it was time once more to be Commodore Perec, commodore in command, Space Battle Station 1.

As Michael turned away from his crew, his left leg dragging noticeably, Perec took him by the arm, moving him out of the way of the engineering teams flooding onboard to start the formal damage assessment and take over what remained of *387* from its exhausted crew.

"Michael, I don't think you are going to like what I am about to say. But at the end of the day, I'm a commodore and you're not, so pay attention."

Michael nodded. He was so tired, so emotionally drained, that all of a sudden nothing mattered anymore.

"Captain Baktiar, my principal medical officer, tells me that you are in very bad shape. The delays in getting your leg treated are causing real damage. He wants you in the base hospital for treatment, and he wants you there right now. Now, I can't order you off your ship. You are the legally appointed captain in command and supreme under God until relieved by proper authority. However, you are doing irreparable harm to yourself, and I'm not prepared to allow you to do that. So even though I can't order you, I strongly suggest that you do as Captain Baktiar suggests. And unless you don't particularly want a long and successful career in the Fleet, I can assure you that listening to the requests of commodores is generally considered to be a very good thing."

Michael had to smile at Perec's forthright use of carrot and stick. "It's all right sir, say no more. I'm convinced. To be honest, sir, I actually don't think I can stand up much longer."

"Good man. I'll tell Captain Baktiar that you are on your way. I know your XO. Chief Harris is a good man. He'll manage fine until the base teams have taken over, and I'll make sure that *387* gets everything it needs."

"Thank you, sir," Michael said quietly with a half smile.

He stood there for a second. As he turned toward the station, his left leg finally gave way and he crumpled unceremoniously to the deck.

Monday, December 7, 2398, UD
Federated Worlds Space Fleet Barracks, Foundation,
Terranova Planet

Michael's stomach was a churning mass, and the fact that he hadn't been able to eat anything for days didn't help settle the worst attack of nerves he had ever experienced.

Michael had taken up position well clear of the milling mass of spacers crowded onto the huge parade ground that lay at the heart of Foundation's sprawling Space Fleet barracks. He watched in silence as Chief Harris, aided and abetted by the ever-imperturbable Cosmo Reilly, quickly and efficiently brought order out of *387*'s tiny part of the chaos. The morning sun of another brilliant Terranova day struck dazzling shards off medals and gold badges stark against dress black.

A firm hand on his shoulder brought him back to earth.

"For God's sake, Michael, try not to look so nervous!"

Bill Chen's cheerful face was the best thing Michael had seen all day. His dress uniform was immaculate, the deep crimson ribbon around his throat supporting the gold Valor in Combat starburst, the award bright with newness and brilliant against the black of his dress uniform. In comparison, the silver Hell's Moons campaign medal hanging on a blue and yellow ribbon studded with a tiny gold command star that hung on his left breast looked washed out. On his left sleeve, a thin gold hash mark close to the cuff recorded *166*'s unit citation for the Corona operation, and on his right was stitched his first combat command hash mark, also in gold.

Michael took a deep breath, his right hand moving without his knowing it first to check that his own Valor in Combat starburst was in place and then down to the two unit citations on his left arm. Truth was, he felt very overdressed, almost gaudy.

"Oh, hello, Bill. Can't help it, sorry. Don't much like crowds, and my damn leg still hurts."

The captain of *DLS-166* smiled indulgently. "Hang in there. It'll all be over before you know it."

Michael sighed deeply. "I know. I just wish *166* could be up front alongside us. God knows you earned it."

"You know the rules, Michael. Order of ships in parade is determined by losses, so you'll forgive me when I tell you I'm happy to be well back in the parade with most of my crew intact. We were lucky, damned lucky, and to this day I still don't how I lost so few when that Hammer slug came inboard."

"I wish we'd been lucky. None of this"—Michael waved an arm across the assembled spacers—"makes up for it."

"No, it doesn't and it never will," Chen said, his voice heavy with sympathy. He couldn't begin to understand what Michael had been through. "Michael, I'd better go. We're behind the *Al-Jahiz* and the *Damishqui*, and the funeral AI's getting fractious. I'll catch up with you afterward."

"Will do, Bill," Michael said as Reilly and Chief Harris, finally satisfied that they had the surviving crew members of *387* where they needed to be, made their way over.

In deference to the occasion, Harris's salute was stiff and formal, the silver-gray T'changa badge on his left shoulder bright in the morning sun, the ribbon holding his gold Valor in Combat starburst glowing richly in the yellow light. "*Deepspace Light Scout Three Eight Seven* present and accounted for, sir."

Michael's salute was equally formal. "Thank you, chief. And thanks for sticking with us."

Harris nodded. "No problem, sir. No problem at all. It's been an honor, and I think it's what the Doc would have wanted."

Michael looked across at Reilly. "Cosmo, you okay?"

"Well enough, skipper. Though it's damned hard. I never thought I'd miss them as much as I do."

Michael could only nod. There was a short awkward pause.

"I'm not looking forward to this, either," Michael said, bobbing his head at the mass of Federated Worlds spacers neatly formed up behind the *387*s.

Reilly and Chief Harris both smiled.

"As if we couldn't tell," Reilly said. "We'll be right behind you, and the AI will make sure it all goes off all right. Don't worry."

Michael nodded. Easy to say, but in a few minutes he'd be the one out in front of hundreds of thousands of Worlders. And thanks to World News Network's epic four-hour holovid of the entire Corona operation screened in prime time and reportedly watched by nearly every FedWorlder able to stand, every one of them would know who he was and what he'd done. It was not a thought he relished; the idea that he might be somebody famous was completely at odds with his natural inclination to blend into the background. He'd never been one to seek the spotlight. The opposite, in fact. His mother always used to say that if you wanted to know where Michael was at any public occasion, look behind the back row. And now he would be at the head of the biggest public display the Fleet had put on in decades.

"You're right as usual, Cosmo. Okay, chief. Let's do the final walk-around and then we'll be set."

"Sir."

It took only minutes for Michael and Harris to check that the *387*s were as they should be, the spacers precisely arrayed in a few thin ranks, a gap in the last rank serving as a stark reminder of those missing.

"Very good, chief. Stand the crew at ease."

"Aye, aye, sir."

As Harris turned away to give the order, huge double gates to Michael's right began to swing slowly back. Michael's heart sank as the gates opened to reveal an old-fashioned column of horse-drawn gun carriages.

He'd been dreading this moment.

To Michael's way of thinking, black-plumed horses and the deeply varnished wood, polished leather, and burnished brass of gun carriage and harness struck an oddly discordant note. Their primitive simplicity was out of place in a world of neuronics, AIs, mass drivers, and pinchspace travel. But as his father often had pointed out, the archaic traditions of military ceremony were dear to every Worlder's heart. So whatever he might think, horses pulling gun carriages would play their traditional part in carrying the ashes of those fallen in battle to their final resting place.

On a sudden impulse, Michael left his *387*s and made his way across the yard to the column of gun carriages. The pungent earthy straw smell of horses in the warmth of the morning sun hit him as he walked over.

The gray-uniformed Planetary Service warrant officer at the head of the column snapped to attention and saluted as Michael approached.

"Chief Warrant Officer Kamal, officer in charge. An honor, sir."

"Thanks, Mister Kamal. I . . . I just . . . I just wanted to see them before we left. I . . ." Michael's voice trailed off as the emotion rose, choking his throat shut with sudden intensity.

"Go ahead, sir. We've got time." Kamal's voice was gentle. "And I think the captains of the *Al-Jahiz* and *Damishqui* want to do the same. And Lieutenant Chen. Behind you, sir."

Befuddled for a second as protocol and emotion short-circuited his brain, Michael recovered in time to half turn and salute as the two four-ring captains stopped in front of him; his salute was returned by the pair with military precision. Bill Chen stood a pace behind with a half smile on his face as he watched Michael recover from his momentary confusion.

The older of the two, Captain van Meir of the *Al-Jahiz,* a broad-shouldered woman with startlingly deep blue, almost violet eyes set in a dark face the color of aged teak, was the first to speak, reaching across as she did to shake Michael's hand. "Helfort. It's an honor to meet you."

"It is indeed," said Captain Chandra, his grip painfully strong, clear hazel eyes boring right into Michael's. "You did well, very well."

"Thank you, sirs. But what a price." He nodded at the line of gun carriages. "I still have trouble coming to terms with it all."

Van Meir nodded sympathetically. "We all do, believe me, we all do. I really hoped we'd taught the Hammer enough of a lesson the last time around, but apparently not. Sadly, there are times when we have to stand up and be counted, and this was one of them. But it still hurts, especially when you knew the people. Chief Kazumi was one of mine on *Warhammer,* and Corporal Meritavich was with me on *Qurrah* when I was her XO. I'll miss them. They were good people."

The small group stood in silence for a moment as memories crowded in, the clinking of harnesses and the soft breathing of horses the only sounds breaking the intensity of the moment.

Chandra brought the group back to earth. "Helfort, good to meet you. If you are passing the *Damishqui,* please step aboard for a drink. It would be an honor, and I'm sure a certain junior lieutenant of your acquaintance would be more than happy to see you as well."

In an instant, Michael's face was bright pink with embarrassment. How the hell had the captain in command of a heavy cruiser found the time to know about him and Anna?

Chandra smiled indulgently. "Now, I have some people I wish to say goodbye to, so forgive me."

"Sir."

Michael and Chen followed the two captains as they made their way past the depressingly long line of 387's gun carriages to those of the *Al-Jahiz, Damishqui,* and finally *166.*

As Chen walked on, giving a brief pat to Michael's shoulder to steady him, Michael slowly moved past gun carriage after gun carriage, all draped in the gold and purple flag of the Federated Worlds. Mounted in the center of each gun carriage was a simple mahogany plinth cradling a small gold funeral urn in front of which was a cushion, its deep crimson fabric decorated with a pathetic spread of medals, with a small brass plaque being the only clue to each urn's identity.

Not much to show for a life, Michael thought bitterly as he wondered if the win was worth the pain. None of it felt real to Michael as he struggled without success to connect brass plates to the faces of the people who once had been his fellow 387s.

Michael stood alongside the last of the carriages, the one carrying the pitiful remains of Spacer Vignes, killed only weeks after his twentieth birthday and the youngest of 387's crew. His neuronics chimed softly.

"Yes?"

"Junior Lieutenant Helfort, this is the AI. My apologies for interrupting, but we move off in five minutes. Would you mind taking your position."

"On my way."

Michael's left leg had begun to ache, a vicious stabbing pain, only minutes after the cortege had left the Fleet barracks. True to form, he had forgotten to renew his supply of drugbots.

The strain of the march through Foundation streets packed solid with an unbroken mass of silent Worlders, their faces bitter with grief and anger, began to tell. The slow, measured pace pulled mercilessly at muscles and tendons that despite the best efforts of FedWorld medical technology were not fully recovered from the slashing damage inflicted by the Hammer slug. The human body still kept some secrets, and how to quickly repair the damage inflicted by high-velocity projectiles was one of them. As for all of human history and despite the enormous advances in geneering and trauma medicine, getting well mostly took time and lots of it.

By the time Michael had covered the seemingly endless kilometers that separated the Fleet barracks from Braidwood National Cemetery, the final resting place for the ashes of all spacers killed on active service, his leg was molten agony. So bad was the pain that the huge crowd of silent Worlders that had flanked the route from the very start had become a blur.

As the cortege turned into Remembrance Avenue for the final approach to the massive gilt gates of the national cemetery, the deep hush broken only by the chinking of gun-carriage harnesses and the uneven beat of horses' hooves on the ceramcrete road, Michael cursed himself for not taking the basic precaution of getting some painkiller drugbots inside him just in case. You are a fucking idiot, Helfort, he railed at himself, conscious that his left leg was beginning to drag and embarrassed that there was nothing he could do about it apart from gripping his sword so tightly that the pain in his hand and wrist would distract him, praying all the time that he made it and that the holovid commentators didn't think he was playing to the crowd.

At last, the cortege passed the gates. Guided by the AI, without which he would not have the slightest idea of where to go or what to do, Michael led *387*'s crew and the sad column of gun carriages up a gently sloping hill away from the main access road and the rest of the cortege. The narrow road was surrounded by achingly beautiful trees and shrubs, their leaves and flowers bright with color in the late morning sun.

And then there it was, the sight bringing a lump to Michael's throat and tears to his eyes: the final resting place for the *387*s he was there to bury that day. When the engineers had finished making the ship safe for its return dirtside, it would be the last resting place for *DLS-387* also. The torn and blasted ship would be set into a sandstone-walled recess cut back into the hillside above the small hollow that would cradle the ashes of its fallen crew, almost as though it were looking down in sorrow at the people it had failed to protect.

The marine honor guard and firing party stood to attention as Michael led the surviving *387*s past the waiting burial plots, turning them off the road to halt opposite the temporary stand with the families and friends of the dead. Tears fell unashamedly down their faces as the gun carriages came to a halt one by one, to be relieved of their pathetically small burdens by the marine burial parties.

For a moment, Michael had to smile to himself as a picture of Athenascu, objecting strenuously that the marines she so loved to hate were handling the last of her mortal remains, flashed across his mind's eye.

Michael watched the sad sight of golden urns one after another being put in position alongside each of the burial plots. As the last one was set in place, he looked across the little hollow to where his family was standing, his parents rigidly at attention in the front row of the stand. Between them stood Sam, her face a frozen mask as she struggled to absorb the full meaning of this, the final act in a tragedy that had been unthinkable just a few short months earlier. Her plain gray-black dress stood in drab contrast to the dress blacks, loud with medals, unit citations, combat command stripes, and rank badges, that flanked her. Behind his family, Michael picked out Vice Admiral Jaruzelska and, with a shock, the president herself, her mass of chalk-white hair standing out starkly like a beacon in a sea of Space Fleet black, marine green, and the dark grays and blacks of the crew's families. Also there were Moderator Burkhardt, Minister Pecora, and most of the cabinet. But Anna, the one person he most wanted to see, the one he most wanted to have with him, was not there. Her place was with the *Damishqui* spacers who had fallen. Michael ached to be with her.

As the last gun carriage pulled away, the senior spiritual guide to the Federated Worlds Space Fleet stepped forward. In somber tones, she recited the formal address for the fallen in battle, its archaic language and complex sentences somehow exactly right for the occasion. But it mostly washed over Michael as he enjoyed the simple pleasure of standing still, careful to keep almost all his weight off his tortured left leg.

Finally, the spiritual guide had finished. Michael stepped forward to perform his final duty as captain in command of *DLS-387*.

At precisely midday, he removed his dress cap and in a voice firm with a confidence he didn't feel gave the order that would consign what little remained of *387*'s lost crew to the ground. Marine burial parties moving with careful precision interred the urns before lifting plain granite slabs inscribed with the names of the fallen into place. Then the firing party raised its carbines, and with a sudden shocking violence, the air above the burial plots was ripped apart with volley after volley of carbine fire.

It was all but over. Michael replaced his cap and, saluting, gave the final blessing.

"*Deepspace Light Scout 387*. May God watch over you this day."

He was finished. With *DLS-387* now formally decommissioned, he was no longer a captain in command.

He was plain ordinary Junior Lieutenant Michael Wallace Helfort again.

And even if part of him yearned to be just plain ordinary Mr. Helfort, he knew that when the day of reckoning with the Hammer came, and it surely would, he would be there to do his part.

Monday, February 15, 2399, UD
Conference Room 24-1, Interstellar Relations
Secretariat Building, Geneva, Old Earth

As Giovanni Pecora looked across the table at his Hammer counterpart, he knew in his heart that the chances of settling the *Mumtaz* affair on anything remotely like reasonable terms were slim.

The Hammer's councillor for foreign relations, the unlovely Claude Albrecht, sat directly opposite Pecora. He was flanked on one side by Pius Sodje, his undercouncillor for Federated Worlds relations, and on the other by Viktor Solomatin, officially the undercouncillor for departmental security but in fact the man put into Albrecht's department by Doctrinal Security to keep an eye on things. According to the latest intelligence briefings, Solomatin was under Polk's control now that the head of DocSec, Austin Ikedia, reportedly had jumped ship, abandoning what little was left of the Merrick/Commitment faction.

Given the typically ruthless way Polk had been consigning Merrick's followers to DocSec lime pits, Pecora had been surprised to see Albrecht still holding his position. He shook his head in despair. Trying to understand the Hammer was made nearly impossible by the endless infighting that went on as faction struggled with faction for supremacy, as the winners took advantage of their position to cull as many of the losers as they could until, inevitably, the tables were turned. Then losers became winners, winners became losers, and the whole ghastly blood-drenched process started again.

Pecora sighed. Hammer politics could best be described as a blood-soaked mass of lies and deceit liberally laced with treachery, backstabbing, and appalling brutality. Exactly what was going on inside the Hammer was anyone's guess.

Pecora turned his attention back to the group in front of him.

When not participating in the role-play sims so beloved of Fed management experts, he had spent much of the previous week reviewing everything the Feds knew about the trio on the other side of the conference table. It had been a depressing exercise.

The three men were survivors, the fittest that Hammer society could produce, God help it and its oppressed citizens. They had clawed their way to the top of the Hammer heap over the broken and bleeding bodies of ordinary Hammer citizens, with the corpses of more than a few competitors tossed in for good measure.

Solomatin in particular was a nasty piece of work. His file was full of examples of his sadistic and brutal approach to

DocSec business. He was rumored to have personally shot more than two hundred so-called heretics during his time as DocSec commander on Fortitude, but never with one clean shot. No. That would have been too easy. Solomatin preferred multiple shots: two to wound, one in each thigh, and then, after an agonizing wait as the victim writhed in agony on the ground, another shot to finish it all when Solomatin got bored and it was time to move on to the next victim, who was invariably kept close at hand to heighten the terror of those last few awful moments of life. Pecora felt sick as for probably the tenth time he wiped his hand down the side of his trousers as if to rub away the contamination from Solomatin's clammy handshake.

And even if Sodje and Albrecht weren't as bad as Solomatin, it was probably only for lack of opportunity. Pecora had little doubt that they, too, would have just as little compunction about putting a bullet into the back of his head.

As he waited for Nikolas Kaminski, the Old Earth Alliance secretary for interstellar relations and as decent a man as Albrecht and his crew were psychopathic killers, to bring the meeting to order, Pecora knew deep down that the ten weeks set aside by the Hammer and Federated Worlds governments for mediation brokered by Old Earth were going to be the longest weeks of his life. He just hoped that they wouldn't be the most wasted.

A small cough from Kaminski announced the start of the meeting, and with a sigh Pecora settled back in his chair to listen to the mediator's opening statement. Pecora knew it would be a worthy speech. It would be full of pleas for common sense to prevail, for the standards of civilized behavior to apply, and so on. But no matter how worthy the sentiments, Pecora's view of the Hammer would not change. They were so far beyond the bounds of decency that Kaminski might as well piss on a forest fire for all the good it would do.

Happy for once not to have to stand on a leg that still ached when he put his full weight on it, Michael hung back and watched the painfully slow process of moving *387* out of the orbital repair station's maintenance dock and into the cavernous hold of the huge ultraheavy planetary lander.

387, tiny against the orbital heavy repair station's vast bulk, was being maneuvered with infinite care to line up with the lander's gaping cargo hold. An army of orange-suited spacers shepherding a swarm of heavy-duty cargobots, anti-collision lights flashing like demented orange fireflies, fussed around the scarred and torn hull, which had been cleaned of the tons of foamsteel and bracing that had been used to get the ship safely home. All classified equipment had been stripped out, and fusion plants shut down and decommissioned.

A moment of sadness struck Michael.

387 once had been a living thing and, through Mother, almost a friend, or at least a comrade in arms. He'd miss her quirky, deadpan sense of humor. But now *387* was just another dead warship hulk, and Mother had gone on to other things. She was the latest in a long line of warship AIs safely downloaded into Attila the Hun, the massive AI that powered the Fleet's StratSim Facility at the Fleet College. Michael knew that some warship captains liked to reminisce with their old AIs, but he didn't think he'd ever be one of them. For him, *387* was something that had happened in the past, and there it should stay.

As the bows of *387* nosed slowly into the lander's hold, Michael could look directly down into the hole that marked the point where Weapons Power Charlie's plasma containment bottle had blown out most of the starboard bow. The hole was huge, a mass of twisted titanium frames and shredded ceramsteel. The edges, torn, twisted, jagged, and razor-sharp, had been masked off with Day-Glo plasfiber for the trip. Down through the hole, its sides etched out of the darkness by *387*'s internal lighting, Michael could trace the path of the platinum/iridium slug inside its deadly shroud of plasma as it had cut its way down through the ship, taking the lives of so many of the crew on the way.

Farther aft on the port side, the entry point for the slug that nearly had taken Michael's life was framed untidily by yet more orange plasfiber. Less dramatic, the pear-shaped puncture was surprisingly small. The slug's awesome kinetic energy, with little armor to slow it, had been focused as it hit on a single small part of *387*'s hull.

And then, farther back, there was another hole. The slug's exit from the hull aft had been much more dramatic, its plasma shroud by that stage blooming into a lethal blast wave that had opened up the ship's ceramsteel armor like a tin can. The hole was much bigger, now rimmed with yet more orange plasfiber to mark the place where the slug had finally cleared the ship, taking with it *387*'s pinchcomms antenna, leaving only the stump of its hydraulic ram to show that it ever had existed.

Michael smiled as he tried to picture the surprise of some poor spacer crew centuries down the track as they tried to work out just what the hell a pinchcomms antenna was doing floating in interstellar space.

As Michael watched, performing his final duty as excaptain of *387* and with orders posting him to Fleet freshly received, something made him look up. Across the massive hangar, a substantial orange figure emerged from a small personnel air lock and with considerable verve shot across the gap that separated them before coming to an impeccably judged halt only centimeters from Michael. The spacer barely had to move to touch helmets.

Michael only knew one very large spacer that good.

"Junior Lieutenant Helfort, sir. Leading Spacer Bienefelt reporting for duty, sir."

"Benny, you are a fucking rogue," Michael said with a broad grin. "Last time I checked, they said two more days."

"I know, sir. I am a fucking rogue, and they didn't want to let me go. But I can be very persuasive when I have to. I had to see *387* one last time before she went dirtside."

Michael laughed.

He'd always believed that Bienefelt would make it, and even though it had taken months in regen, the news that she would be fine had set the seal on his own slow recovery.

Saturday, April 3, 2399, UD
Offices of the Supreme Council for the Preservation of the Faith, City of McNair, Commitment Planet

Chief Councillor Polk wearily rubbed his eyes. They felt like someone had poured sand into them.

He'd always wondered why Merrick had aged twice as fast as his peers. Now he knew. The pressure was unrelenting, the workload enormous, the torrent of issues that poured into his secretariat so huge that he felt like he was drowning.

But he was making some progress. It had taken time, but he now had people he was prepared if not to trust at least to let handle much of the day-to-day work he'd been forced to take on in the days after Merrick's fall from power.

Day-to-day work! One crisis after another was more like it. He ran through the list in his mind.

The Hammer economy was completely stuffed. In truth, it was always stuffed, so maybe he shouldn't classify it as a crisis; no change there. In any case, his handpicked successor at the Department of Economy and Finance, Tobias de Mel, was pretty competent, so Polk was happy to let him get on with it.

The riots in McNair provoked by his predecessor's departure and execution were finally over. The city and the rest of the planet were simmering in unhappy silence, which was just fine with Polk. Let them simmer.

The situation on Faith was coming under control. DocSec's ruthlessness backed by marine firepower was slowly grinding the life out of the heretics, the ground having been cut out from under their feet by a carefully stage-managed upsurge of xenophobic anger and resentment after the Feds' attacks on Eternity and Hell.

Of the really big issues, that left only what to do about those Kraa-damned and insufferably arrogant Feds.

Polk picked up the latest report from the negotiating team on Old Earth from a paper-cluttered desk. He snorted derisively as he reread the document. Councillor Albrecht thought the Feds might agree to let Brigadier General Digby carry the can for the *Mumtaz* affair. In return, Albrecht wanted the authority to agree to the Feds' long-standing demand for a formal public apology before any further discussions took place. Polk snorted again. Stupid bastard. They might as well agree to what the Feds really wanted: referral of their outrageous demand for financial restitution to the interstellar court for determination, because they sure as hell were not going to stop at an apology.

Well, Polk thought as he flicked Albrecht's report back onto his desk, many things might come to pass, but agreeing to Feds' demands was never going to be one of them. Not while he was chief councillor.

In any case, he didn't much care what Albrecht did, thought, or said. Short of complete capitulation by the Feds, whatever Albrecht achieved would not be enough to save him no matter how well he'd done under the circumstances. On his return from Old Earth, Albrecht would be arrested the second he stepped off the down-shuttle; the carefully doctored holovid of him in unwisely close proximity to known agents of the Old Earth Alliance would be more than enough to take him down. If the bastard lived for another week after that, he'd be Kraa-damned lucky, thought Polk with a small shiver of pleasure. He made a note to himself. He must be sure to get holovids of Albrecht's execution. That would seal the moment. Yes, he'd enjoy that, he thought, as he jotted down a short note to get it arranged.

Flicking on his voicewriter, Polk pushed back in his chair and closed his eyes. His response to Councillor Albrecht was not going to be what the man wanted to hear.

Two minutes later a blunt, short, and dismissive note was on its way to Albrecht. Polk felt good, very good in fact. Telling Albrecht to tell the Feds to fuck off always made him feel that way. Knowing that Albrecht was finished made him feel even better. Of the remaining Merrick appointees to the Council, that left only Khan and al-Hamidi. Unknown to Khan, the case against him being put together by a secret DocSec task force was almost finished. Very compelling it was, too, Polk had been pleased to see when presented with a preliminary draft.

But al-Hamidi wouldn't be so easy, far from it. Shifting him would be hard.

Unique among Merrick's appointees to the Council, al-Hamidi was not from Commitment, and winning his support had been one of the keys to Merrick's success. Al-Hamidi had a deep-rooted power base centered on his home town of Providence Sound. From there, he controlled the huge continent of South Barassia, the center of the Hammer's substantial defense industry. Needless to say, it was a matter of considerable frustration to Polk that even after years of effort, his supporters, whose control over the rest of the planet Fortitude was total, had been unable to shake al-Hamidi's grip.

Well, Polk thought, he'd be interested to see how well al-Hamidi coped now that Merrick was gone, along with control of DocSec. History showed that no single individual could stand up against DocSec, and in the end, that was all al-Hamidi was. Just one man, and like all the others, his time would come.

Polk sat for a while, comfortable in the warm glow of self-congratulation. The more he thought about it, the closer he was to securing his domestic power base, so maybe this was the time to start thinking about making the Feds wish that they had left the *Mumtaz* business alone. Yes, he decided, it was time, despite unanimous agreement at the last Defense Council meeting that the matter was probably best left alone. Fact was, he didn't give a flying fuck what the Defense Council thought. They would do as they were damned well told.

He reached for the intercom. "Singh!"

"Sir?"

"Contact Fleet Admiral Jorge. See if he's free for lunch tomorrow."

"Sir."

Polk flicked off the intercom.

By all accounts, Jorge was a good man. He was an off-worlder, which meant he probably wasn't much of a Merrick supporter, though according to DocSec, he had taken scrupulous care throughout a long and competent career to stay well clear of factional politics, so who would know? Much more significantly, Jorge owed his appointment as commander in chief of Hammer Defense Forces to Polk, and Polk had made damn sure he knew it. He had plucked Jorge out of relative obscurity as the flag officer in command of Space Fleet research and development, promoting him two ranks over the heads of those Polk judged to be largely responsible for the Hammer's spineless and incompetent response to the Feds' attack.

Most of those men, Polk was happy to remind himself, were now anonymous bodies among the thousands in some DocSec lime pit somewhere.

The purge of Space Fleet in the weeks after the attack on the Hell system had been merciless. Senior officers had been cut down in the hundreds without appeal, the executioner's bullet reaching deep into the organization to root out anyone even remotely connected to the humiliation dished out by the Feds at Hell's Moons.

From Polk's perspective, the daily reports from DocSec summarizing the previous day's arrests, convictions, and sentences—all but a tiny minority of those arrested going to the firing squad the next day—had been profoundly satisfying. It was very simple. Most if not all of those condemned must have been tacit supporters of Merrick. Otherwise, how could they have flourished during Merrick's time as chief councillor? Add in their contribution, actual or inferred—it didn't much matter which—as Fleet's senior management to the defeat at Hell's Moons and it was pretty straightforward if you thought about it.

Polk's enjoyment of the moment was interrupted by the carefully neutral tones of Ramesh Singh, his longtime confidential secretary. "Chief Councillor?"

"Yes, Singh."

"Fleet Admiral Jorge would be delighted to meet you for lunch tomorrow, sir."

I bet he would, Polk thought. As if he had any choice in the matter.

"Good. I'm so pleased to hear it," Polk said sarcastically.

"I'll arrange lunch for 13:00 at the residence."

"Yes, that should be fine. What else do I have tomorrow?"

"Photo opportunity at 12:30, sir. Front lawn, weather permitting. Medal ceremony for crew members of the *New Dallas*. Ten minutes."

"Ah, good. Will Jorge be there?"

"Not planned to be, sir. It's a Space Fleet–sponsored affair, so Admiral Kseki will be there, and he's hosting the lunch afterward."

"Okay. Fine." Admiral Kseki. Another one of his recent appointments.

As the intercom clicked off, Polk smiled a grim smile of satisfaction.

If necessary, Jorge would be left in no doubt that any reluctance on his part to commit body and soul to what Polk was beginning to think of as a righteous crusade against the Feds would be a career-, not to say life-threatening move on his part.

But somehow Polk didn't think it would come to that.

Three hundred forty light-years away from the Federated
Worlds, the late-afternoon sun of an Old Earth day threw
long bars of golden sunlight into the small conference room
on the top floor of the Interstellar Relations Secretariat
building on the outskirts of Geneva.

The room was empty except for a small table and a scattering of chairs. Two people were seated at the end closest to
the window, the spring sun enjoyably warm on their backs.
Giovanni Pecora had his head in his hands, the frustration
obvious.

"You know, Marta," he said despairingly, "I don't think a
single fucking word we've said here today to those Hammer
bastards has had the slightest effect. They really are the most
stiff-necked and obstinate people in all of humanspace.
We've always been prepared to consider compromise, but
the Hammer? Never. I was afraid that this mediation might
be a waste of time, and so it's turning out. I'd give it another
week, maybe two, tops."

Marta Diallo, Pecora's deputy secretary responsible for the
Hammer Worlds and one of the very few people in the Fed
Worlds with a deep understanding of the Hammer psyche,
nodded. Her frustration was obvious.

"Well, Giovanni, there was a chance, I suppose," she said.
"Small one, maybe, but there was a chance. If the Hammer
had publicly blamed the whole affair on Digby and made the
necessary apologies, then they might have been able to save
enough face to look at the compromise positions we pro-
posed." Diallo sighed deeply, running her hands through
thick black hair as if to push away the problem. "But I'm
afraid that Polk's intervention has blown that chance out of

the water. Why he wouldn't blame Digby is beyond me. He had his boss put up against a wall and shot, after all, and we've got Digby locked up, so who the hell's going to argue?"

She paused for a moment before continuing. "No, stupid me. We know why, and it's the age-old reason. Domestic politics is why he wouldn't put Digby in the frame. Digby was a Merrick man, and everyone knows it. Blaming Digby is as good as blaming Merrick. But putting the blame on us gives Polk his best and probably only chance to gut the opposition and rally support behind himself as leader of the Hammers. I hate to say it, Giovanni, but unless we get something positive out of them at tomorrow's session, and I don't believe we will, I think there is a real risk that this is going to slide into full-scale war."

"I'm very much afraid you are right, Marta," Pecora said gloomily. "God's blood! Another Hammer war? Just what we all need right now. Interstellar trade's a bit soft at the moment, and one thing's for sure: A war between us and the Hammer will push things right over the edge."

Diallo shook her head. "Well, at least we'll have some help. I got an update from the Frontier desk yesterday. They think it's almost certain that Frontier will support us if we need them. There were a lot of their people on the *Mumtaz*. It was their terraforming package the Hammers stole, and I think it's fair to say they owe us big-time."

Pecora nodded. "I've seen the report. I'm going to send a high-level team to Frontier. We need to start tying things up."

"We do," Diallo said. "It's the Sylvanians I'm worried about. They look soft." Diallo's face turned grim as she continued. "Though you'd have to ask why they wouldn't support us."

"Three words, Marta: tactical nuclear weapons. They remember Vencatia and Jesmond. They're scared shitless the Hammer won't hold back next time. Every survey confirms it, I'm sorry to say, and the appeasers are riding the wave."

"Jeez, Giovanni. Surely they're smarter than that. Can't they see that now's their best chance to put an end to the

Hammer problem once and for all? Lot of economic upside for them and everyone else if the Hammer economy can be freed up and the instability in interstellar trade reduced. I see the insurers are already applying a war premium to traffic inside 100 light-years of the Hammer."

If it were possible, Pecora looked even more depressed. He shook his head.

Diallo cursed under her breath as she got to her feet and started to pace up and down the room. She'd had enough of the Hammer to last her ten lifetimes. "Makes you want to cry, Giovanni. Bloody Polk. If the rebels on Commitment and Faith could have made life difficult for another few months, he might have been forced to make some concessions. But as you say, blaming us made the rebels look unpatriotic, and you can't give a man like Polk that sort of advantage and still hope to win. Poor bastards. The INTSUMs don't paint a pretty picture of what's been going on."

Diallo fell silent.

She'd seen the INTSUMs with their vids of streets lined by lampposts, each with a dead rebel hanging by one leg, the gloating vidnews reports as yet another heretic guerrilla group was hunted down and exterminated, the haunting images as the families of Merrick supporters—men, women, and children, all guilty by association—were dragged away to whatever awful fate awaited them. The images would live in her mind forever.

The surveys showed that it wasn't just Feds who'd begun to ask how much longer humanspace could tolerate such a psychopathic society in its midst. But one thing was sure: All Polk had done was postpone the happy day when the Hammer Worlds would self-destruct or the long-oppressed people of those unhappy worlds would finally overcome the forces ranged against them and throw the Doctrine of Kraa where it belonged: into the rubbish bin of history.

Diallo's arms went up as she tried to stretch the sick tiredness out of her body. "For what it's worth, Giovanni, I think crushing the uprising on Faith has convinced Polk he can do the same to us. I hate to say this, but the more I think about it, the more I think that's what the stupid bastard has in mind. I might rerun some of our sim scenarios to see what that might mean for us. And we need to follow up on those reports from Commitment that the so-called heretic opposition is not as ineffective and fragmented as the Hammer would have us believe. If it comes to a fight with Polk, we'll need to be signing them up on our side." She sounded exhausted.

A dispirited Pecora nodded in tired agreement. "We'll do all of that, Marta. Come on. Let's give Nikolas Kaminski and his people a call. I think a serious chat, a very serious chat, over a few drinks is called for. I'm going to ask him to set up a time for us to talk to the secretary-general. I'm rather afraid we're going to need the Alliance's support. Come on."

Friday, April 23, 2399, UD
The Palisades, Ashakiran Planet

It felt like an age since he'd last stood on the deck of the Palisades. Now that he was back, he realized how much he'd missed it and how much his commitment to a Space Fleet career had cost him. He sighed as he commed his neuronics for the umpteenth time, checking that Anna was still on schedule before turning back to look out at the sunset.

As long as he lived, Michael knew he would never tire of the Palisades, a simple house tucked in under the enormous looming bulk of Mount Izbecki with a huge west-facing deck looking out across the Clearwater Valley.

As another day drew to a close, it was just stunning.

A bottle of Lethbridge pilsner in hand, Michael stood alone, looking out across the valley, happy to comply with strict orders to leave the dinner to his dad, a defective freshwater pump to his mom, and Sam to one of her never-ending calls to Arkady Encevit, her long-standing and sadly absent boyfriend.

Michael smiled.

His dad's enthusiasm for the primitive art of cooking wasn't quite matched by his skill. His mom, in contrast, refused point-blank to cook—why had chefbots been invented? she would always say when challenged—and she had a real way with the long-obsolete AIs embedded in the old and sometimes very recalcitrant systems that provided power and water to the Palisades. As for Sam, Michael wished she'd marry her heart's desire and stop the long-distance mooning that seemingly filled her every waking hour.

Michael had been watching the thick black storm clouds building in the southwest for some time. The oncoming storm was a hard, raw-edged mass driving relentlessly across a horizon painted in lurid slashes of scarlet and gold, and the valley thousands of meters below was now invisible beneath a purple blanket that was rapidly deepening to black. It was going to be a rough night, he thought as he checked the local weather forecast for the umpteenth time. No changes. They were in for a real battering, and his concern about Anna's arrival wasn't wholly unplaced. The Palisades's landing site, a small clearing cut out of the top of the thickly wooded ridge, was an absolute bastard when a southerly bluster was blowing, though it was a matter of family pride that nobody had ever failed to get in safely. As he knew Anna would, even if she'd be the first to admit she wasn't the most naturally gifted flier pilot of all time. Michael told himself to relax. Anna invariably handed control to the flier's AI at the first sign of trouble, and she would tonight if things got tricky.

As darkness began to fall, the wind now gusting fitfully to announce the storm front's arrival, Michael's neuronics pinged softly, reporting that Anna's flier was safely through the Tien Shan Mountains and on final descent.

Finishing his beer, he set off up the hill to the Palisades's landing site. Something told him that time alone with Anna was going to be at a premium, and short though the walk back from the landing site was, he was going to make the most of it.

Dinner had been a cheerful, lively, and at times raucous affair. In part, that was due to the disastrous collapse of Helfort

Senior's pièce de résistance, a hand-crafted vermouth and crab soufflé that sadly had in the end closely resembled a soggy crepe. Michael's father had been devastated. Everyone had stifled an overwhelming urge to say "I told you so" and roared with laughter at Andrew's look of horror as the prize dish, lightly browned, ambitiously bouffant, and as impressive as any soufflé in history, had slowly, inexorably, and tragically deflated in front of them only seconds after it had been placed reverently on the table by the proud cook. Thankfully, the rest of the meal had been much more successful even if, in Michael's humble opinion, the least capable chefbot could have done as good a job with a great deal less stress all around.

He wondered why his dad bothered; he certainly didn't seem to enjoy the process much, judging by the appalling language emanating from the kitchen as the latest disaster struck home.

But in truth the buoyant mood had more to do with an overwhelming sense that the dinner was something special. After what had been the worst year and the best year they'd been through, it was a celebration of survival, of family, of the bonds of love and trust and shared experience and familiarity—and, most important for Michael, a sense that Anna was now an integral part of not just his life but the family's, too.

Well, yes, he thought gloomily, provided that the demands of two Space Fleet careers didn't smash the bond between them.

The passing moment of pessimism didn't last, overwhelmed by the sheer enjoyment that flooded the room. Michael sat back as Sam rattled on about the latest developments in the Arkady Encevit saga, content to listen with half an ear while watching Anna with both eyes. He was transfixed as always by her extraordinary but somehow subtle and understated beauty as the log fire's flickering red-gold light danced across her high cheekbones and flawless skin.

Michael sighed to himself. Anna had done well in *Damishqui* at the Battle of Hell's Moons. Nothing spectacular but a good, solid performance under the intense pressure and stress of combat, well enough for her to know that she'd made the right decision in joining Space Fleet. And that meant that the relationship between them was a castle built on sand. The demands of two Space Fleet careers meant their time together would be fleeting, and that was a poor basis for an enduring relationship.

He sighed again. It was one of the great mysteries of life how his parents had stuck together despite being in exactly the same situation. But they had, so there was at least hope that he and Anna would make it together.

"Come on, Michael! Pay attention," his father said from the end of the table, the soufflé fiasco obviously forgotten, judging by his air of relaxed good humor.

"Yes," Anna chipped in. "I've told you before. You think too much."

"Oh, right," Michael said sheepishly. "What was the question?"

"Your next posting, silly. What do you think, O great hero of the Federated Worlds, holder of the—"

"Anna!" Michael protested. "Stop it. You know that sort of—"

"Yeah, yeah, hero boy!" Anna said in mock umbrage, eyes sparkling as she cut him off. "Answer the damn question."

Michael sighed. He'd fallen for it again. She loved teasing him. You're too serious, she'd always say in her own defense. Not that he didn't have a sense of humor. He did. But he knew he took things too much at face value sometimes, and that of course made him much too soft a target for her to resist. Like now, he thought, as he mouthed a silent "You'll pay for that" across the table at her before continuing. She just stuck her tougue out.

"Ah! My next ship. Yes. Well, that's a good one," Michael said thoughtfully. "I must say I do like the idea of a big ship after the beating the Hammers gave poor old *387*. Don't want that again. And the *Haiyan*'s as big as they get. Well, for ships of the line, that is. So I think it'll be good. Boring program, though. Independent patrols, that sort of thing."

"You won't know what to do with yourself," Anna said

teasingly. "From captain in command to . . . What was the billet again? Do you know, it's so insignificant that I can't even remember what it is you're being posted to do!"

"Pig," Michael said mildly, refusing the bait this time. "Assistant warfare officer in training, as you very well know, Anna Cheung. Responsible for all sorts of important stuff like, er, um, well, warfare training, I suppose, mostly doing op scenarios for sims probably," he finished lamely.

Anna was right; he was going to an insignificant billet.

"Sounds sooooo impressive," Sam said, pulling a face that said just the opposite.

"Yeah, yeah, smart-ass," Michael replied. "The most minor of minor jobs, and well you know it. Mind you," he added, "not that I care. Something well out of the limelight, tucked away in a big fat heavy cruiser, will suit me just fine."

"And me, too," said his mother with considerable feeling.

As Sam hijacked the conversation for the tenth time that evening, Michael glanced sharply across at his mother. Thanks to a very long conversation earlier in the day, he knew exactly what she'd meant by that remark. His new captain, Svetlana Constanza, was the first of her worries. Not the best, was all she'd say when challenged by Michael, whose heart had sunk when she'd let slip the fact that Constanza was a member of the d'Castreaux clan. But her bigger concern, and one Michael shared, was the Hammers. They'd talked long and hard about the prospects for peace before both agreeing that really, there weren't any. And that meant war. Hard to say when, but Michael could see that deep inside his mother, gnawing away at her happiness, was the absolutely unshakable conviction that war between the Federation and the Hammers was inevitable.

That was, of course, why she'd admitted that she'd been happy to see him posted to the relative safety of a heavy cruiser; if things degenerated into a shooting match, it was the best and safest place for him to be. Of course she'd denied furiously Michael's half-spoken charge that she had arranged the posting through her still very active network of Fleet contacts, a denial Michael was still not sure he believed. Not that he cared. After all he'd been through, the relative obscurity of an assistant warfare officer's position in *Haiyan* suited him down to the ground. He'd keep his head down and do what he was told, avoiding whenever possible anything remotely smacking of risk or responsibility.

In the end, Michael had told her that even though she might be a retired Space Fleet commodore, she was fussing too much and he'd be fine. Yes, there might be another fight with the Hammers, but it would end the way all the others had. Only this time, he agreed with her, the Federation would have to pursue the Hammer until it was utterly destroyed, a goal he was entirely happy to pursue.

As Sam went up a gear, Michael sat back again, content to let the conversation wash over him, content to watch Anna, the nanocrystal lights tattooed onto her high cheekbones sparkling white and red-gold against honey-dark skin, her face seemingly flecked with the dust of thousands of tiny jewels shimmering in the light of the log fire. He could only do his best. If Fleet and an uncaring cosmos conspired to break them apart, then so be it. He supposed he'd just have to get over it or die trying.

Anyway, he chided himself, enough of the introspection. Tomorrow he and Anna were off to the Atalantan Mountains. There Space Fleet and all it implied for their futures could be forgotten.

For a few days at least.

Read on for a sneak preview of the second installment in
Graham Sharp Paul's exciting series, HELFORT'S WAR.

Friday, September 3, 2399 UD
Hammer Warship Quebec-One, *Xiang Reef*

Commodore Monroe's mouth tightened into a bloodless
slash. Face grim, he stared at the command holovid. When
his ship's final rail-gun salvo ripped into the FedWorld mer-
chant ship *Betthany Market*, he bared his teeth for a second.
Satisfied, he sat back.

Monroe had to give credit where credit was due.

The captain of the *Betthany Market* had tried his best to escape the trap. With merships exploding all across Xiang
Reef, he pushed his main engines far beyond manufacturer's
limits; Monroe expected the mership's fusion power plants to
lose containment. By some miracle of FedWorld engineering
they hadn't, but nothing was going to help the doomed *Betthany Market* and her ill-fated crew. Fully loaded, sluggish
and unwieldy, the mership had no chance of evading a rail-
gun salvo fired at close quarters, and *Quebec-One* had been
close. Her optronics had picked out every last dent and
scratch on the hard-worked mership's hull.

The *Betthany Market* died like all the rest of the merships
ambushed by Monroe's ships that bloody day. Rail-gun slugs
sliced through her thin plasteel hull. Punched deep into the
ship, three slugs reached the engine room to release the enormous energy bottled up inside her fusion power plants. Microseconds later, the ship exploded into a gigantic ball of
incandescent plasma.

The command team of *Quebec-One* sat silent around
Monroe. They stared in horrified fascination at the command

holovid. The ship had vanished. Only a gas cloud remained; it twisted away into nothing, cooling fast, its dance of death a fading memorial to mership and spacers now dead.

Monroe's ships had executed the operation with brutal efficiency. Most of their victims knew nothing of the attack before death engulfed them. The hellish fires of runaway fusion plants consumed the few lifepods launched. The last witnesses to the latest in a long line of Hammer atrocities survived only a few seconds before they were wiped out.

The operation had been easy. *No*, Monroe thought, *it had been too easy.* Twenty-seven merships destroyed in a matter of hours. Cold-blooded murder was what it was.

Monroe broke the spell only when the last traces of the *Betthany Market* disappeared. He had pushed his luck far enough; they should have been long gone by now. He turned to his chief of staff. "Time we were on our way. To all ships, immediate execute—"

The sensor officer's voice broke in, urgent with alarm. "Sir, we have a positive gravitronics intercept. Designated track 22547. Stand by . . . estimated drop bearing Red 3 Up 1. One ship only. Grav wave pattern suggests pinchspace transition imminent. Vector is nominal for Earth–FedWorld transit. Sir! This one's not on any schedule. Military, sir. Has to be military."

Monroe wasted no time. Everything told him that his sensor officer was right. The new arrival must be a FedWorld warship. The Old Earth Alliance rarely patrolled deepspace this far out; the Xiang Reef gravitation anomaly was too remote. If it turned out to be an Alliance warship, bad luck; he needed to survive before he worried about that possibility.

"Designate track 22547 hostile," Monroe barked. "Immediate to all ships, stand by rail-gun salvo. Targeting data to follow. Kraa's blood! Sensors! Get me the drop data . . . come on sensors, come on! I need a drop time, position, and vector. Now, Kraa-damn it!"

The sensor officer's voice shook under the stress. "Standby . . . okay, sir. Here it comes. She's close. Confirmed Red 3 Up 1 at 85,000 kilometers. Stand by . . . targeting data confirmed and passed to all ships."

"Roger."

Monroe checked the command plot. Impatient, he drummed his fingers on the arm of his chair. The rail-gun crews were taking too long to reload. He forced himself to sit still. Nothing he said or did was going to speed things up.

"Sir! All ships confirm valid firing solutions on the drop datum, full rail-gun salvos loaded, ready to engage." His chief of staff's voice cracked in the heat of the moment.

Monroe wasted no time. "Command approved to fire!"

"All rail-gun salvos away, sir."

"Roger that," Monroe snapped. He forced himself to breathe normally, to ignore the iron bands that crushed his chest with sudden force. If his ships failed to destroy the new arrival the instant it dropped, and it was a FedWorld warship, they were all dead. He buried the thought. Have faith, he chided himself. A six-ship rail-gun attack should overwhelm the unfortunate ship.

Monroe allowed himself to relax a little. *Quebec-One* and her sister ships might be fitted with obsolete Buranan rail guns, but the engagement geometry weighed heavily in favor of his attackers.

Crucial to their chances, the target looked to drop close and broadside three of his ships, the perfect ambush. Provided his ship's firing solutions were accurate, the tightly grouped swarms of iridium/platinum alloy slugs should sweep through the drop datum only seconds after the target dropped into normalspace. True, most of the slugs were destined to disappear into the void. That was the fate of almost all rail-gun slugs, but proximity had allowed his ships to tighten the swarm grouping to put more slugs on target. Monroe checked the command plot again. He liked what he saw. His tactical officer predicted a first strike of more than three hundred slugs. Monroe smiled. The raw numbers looked good. Where the slugs might impact looked even better.

If the attack went as planned, slugs from the first two salvos were to hit where the armor thinned back from the bow. Seconds later, slugs from the third salvo should smash into the target toward its stern, the most vulnerable part of any warship. Hit there and hit hard, its chances of survival were close to zero. All being well, the final salvos were redundant, their contribution limited to finishing off an already dying ship.

The seconds melted away with glacial slowness. Monroe struggled to keep his breath under control. The atmosphere in *Quebec-One*'s combat information center thickened until it threatened to choke him. Monroe cursed under his breath. He had seen action throughout the last war; he should be used to combat by now.

"Sir! Track 22547 is dropping. Confirm drop data nominal." The sensor officer sounded ecstatic. *So he should,* Monroe thought. The man had done well under intense pressure. Targeting data from commercial-grade gravitronics was unreliable at best, but this time the system had worked. Monroe's ships had good firing solutions; the new arrival was condemned to drop directly into the path of the oncoming rail-gun salvos. Absent a miracle—Monroe put no faith in miracles—the hapless ship was trapped, denied any time to react before the massive rail-gun attack fell on her.

Commodore Monroe sat back, and waited for the Fed-World warship to die.